# TWO LIVES FOR OÑATE

PASÓ POR AQUÍ SERIES ON THE
NUEVOMEXICANO LITERARY HERITAGE
EDITED BY GENARO M. PADILLA AND
ERLINDA GONZALES-BERRY

# TWO LIVES FOR OÑATE

Miguel Encinias

PASÓ POR AQUÍ SERIES ON THE NUEVOMEXICANO LITERARY HERITAGE

EDITED BY GENARO M. PADILLA AND ERLINDA GONZALES-BERRY

*University of New Mexico Press*

*Albuquerque*

*To Cristina, a lovely and brave child, and to my family who wondered what I was doing writing and reading day and night without any apparent results. Here is part of the answer.*



FIRST EDITION.

Library of Congress Cataloging-in-Publication Data
Encinias, Miguel.
Two lives for Oñate / Miguel Encinias. — 1st ed.
p. cm. — (Pasó por aquí)
ISBN 0-8263-1777-4. — ISBN 0-8263-1782-0 (pbk.)
1. Oñate, Juan de, 1549?–1624—Fiction.
2. New Mexico—History—To 1848—Fiction.
I. Title.
II. Series.
PS3555.N37T96 1997
813′.54—dc20 96–35687
CIP

## NOTE FROM THE SERIES EDITORS

IT IS NO ACCIDENT that the publication of *Two Lives for Oñate* coincides with the cuatrocentennial of Juan de Oñate's arrival and the establishment of the first permanent Spanish colony in the region. Miguel Encinias self-consciously timed the writing of this text so that it would be ready for release in 1998. His express intent was to educate the people of New Mexico regarding a particular moment in the development of their history. And being the good educator that he is, he has chosen to transmit his lesson through a medium that is at once instructional and engaging. To this end, Encinias has wed meticulous research, intelligent prose and skillful character development.

As is to be expected, Encinias treats his protagonist with a good deal of sympathy, yet, he does not gloss over the atrocities attributed to Oñate's command. He, in fact, succeeds in depicting a complex man, tormented by his own desires, self-interest, obligations, and social codes. In the end the reader cannot help but feel empathy for Oñate, but neither can s/he forget his less noble deeds. And herein lies the value of this book. A catalyst for celebratory remembrance, it is also an invitation to the reader to reflect on the cost of Oñate's venture in terms of human lives, freedom, and repression of native peoples. And for those of us who are here because Oñate and his people came here, this text will give us a greater appreciation of what it took to survive in the land they came to "conquer," a land that conquered their hearts and never let them go.

The primary function of the *Pasó por Aquí Series* is one of recovery and dissemination of Hispanic literature that has been forgotten or ignored by literary historians who, until recent years, exercised narrow criteria in their definition of "American" literature. While *Two Lives for Oñate*, because it is a new work, does not conform to our recovery mission, it does meet our general goal of offering profound recognition of the

Hispanic contribution to arts and letters in the region. As such, we are very pleased to include Miguel Encinias' historical novel in our series.

GENARO M. PADILLA, *University of California-Berkeley*
ERLINDA GONZALES-BERRY, *University of New Mexico*
*Pasó Por Aquí Series,* GENERAL EDITORS

TWO LIVES FOR OÑATE

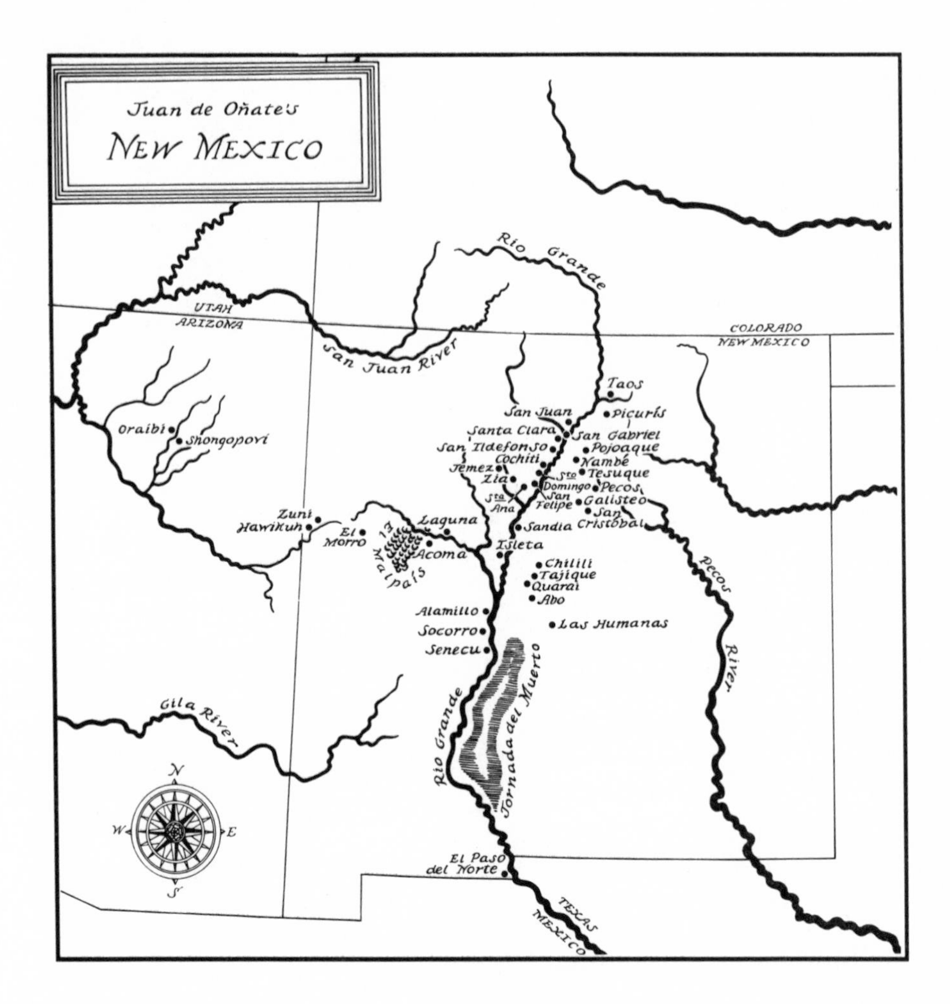
Juan de Oñate's
NEW MEXICO
UTAH
ARIZONA
COLORADO
NEW MEXICO
TEXAS
MEXICO
Rio Grande
San Juan River
Gila River
Pecos River
Taos
Picuris
San Juan
Santa Clara
San Gabriel
San Ildefonso
Pojoaque
Cochiti
Nambé
Jemez
Zia
Sto Domingo
Tesuque
Pecos
Sta Ana
San Felipe
Galisteo
San Cristobal
Sandia
Isleta
Laguna
Acoma
El Morro
El Malpais
Zuni
Hawikuh
Oraibi
Shongopovi
Chilili
Tajique
Quarai
Abo
Las Humanas
Alamillo
Socorro
Senecu
Jornada del Muerto
El Paso del Norte
N
S
E
W

# CHAPTER ONE

THE CHURCH BELLS had started tolling—intermittently, as if reluctant to spoil the cool, resplendent morning. The birds appeared to be competing with the lugubrious tones for the mood of the day.

Don Juan de Oñate sat in the inner balcony of his palatial home and looked eastward at Bufa Peak, his feelings oscillating between enervating sadness and physical well-being as the cool air filled his lungs and the distant hubbub of daily life intruded into his consciousness. Drawn by the tolling bells, yet hardly conscious of what he was doing, he rose from his chair—for the time had come. The church, Nuestra Señora de la Asunción, where his wife's body lay, was nearby, but to don Juan it suddenly seemed as far away as it had appeared to him when he was a child. Time had also taken a new dimension since his wife had fallen ill. Scenes of his courtship and marriage to Isabel flashed into his mind, but they seemed remote, as if from another era.

Their wedding had been a momentous event in Zacatecas and even throughout New Spain. Scion of a family that had amassed one of the greatest fortunes in the New World, son of Cristóbal de Oñate who had campaigned with the great Cortés, and who had been a hero in the Mixtón War, one of the founders of Guadalajara, and discoverer of fabulously rich silver mines, Juan de Oñate had taken for wife Isabel de Tolosa Cortés y Moctezuma. She was equally rich and as aristocratic as one could be, for she was the great granddaughter of the magnificent, but ill-fated, emperor of the Aztecs, Moctezuma II, and the granddaughter of the great Cortés, his conqueror.

After Moctezuma's death, his only legitimate daughter, Tecuichpotzin, who survived *la noche triste* when the Spaniards were expelled from the palace grounds, and the diseases that broke out during the subsequent siege of Tenochtitlán by the Spaniards, was married to her uncle Cuitlahuac, who succeeded his brother as emperor. When he died, she was married to Cuauhtémoc, her first cousin and nephew to Moctezuma. When Cuauhtémoc, the last of the Aztec emperors, was killed by the Spaniards, she was taken by them and christened Isabel. In 1526 she was married to a Spanish captain who died three years later. Cortés then moved her under his roof, and in 1529 she gave birth to a daughter by him. She was named Leonor. Around 1550 a marriage was arranged between Leonor and Juanes de Tolosa, discoverer of the rich Bufa silver mine in Zacatecas, and one of the founders of the city. Circa 1585 Isabel, their daughter was wed to Juan de Oñate.

Now, as he walked to see his wife for the last time, he looked down at his five-year-old son, who was holding his hand in a tight grip as if afraid that he too would go away. His throat became constricted, and his eyes welled at the sight of the bewildered boy. His glance turned to his infant daughter, María, who was being carried by a servant accompanied by Vicente de Zaldívar, don Juan's athletic, twenty-four-year-old nephew. In the background he heard the birds and in the periphery of his sight he caught the magnificence of the day. He felt a surge of unbidden joy at the grand morning around him and at the freshness and beauty of his children.

Despite himself, his thoughts turned away from death and toward life. He thought of the campaigns against the unpacified Indians of the north with don Luis de Velasco, son of one of the greatest viceroys ever to rule New Spain. He thought mainly of the freedom he had felt at leaving the monotonous life of Zacatecas for the open country where the Chichimecas lived, of sleeping under the stars, and of the excitement that each succeeding day promised.

As his wife had lain in her sickbed he had often longed for that kind of freedom. He had been torn between love and compassion born of a life together and the desperate need to escape the stifling world of affluence and privilege into which he felt himself being drawn more and more.

As the terrible mystery of Isabel's death merged with earthly realities, he again thought of the North. During the long hours of vigil it had come to dominate his consciousness. North was the direction he had always taken in his brief forays into freedom, and north was the only direction that offered the possibility of escape from Zacatecas and the opportunity for action—dangerous action that is often the solace of adventurous men. He tried to put those thoughts out of his mind, but they kept coming back, even as his feelings of guilt mounted.

Now looking on his wife, he found it shocking and monstrous that he would never again talk to her, but his son's presence beside him made him think of the future in contrast to what was becoming a distant past—a time that was drawing to a close. And there was María, his delicate daughter whose life was just beginning as her mother's had ended. Tomorrow was theirs, and he felt himself part of it. A twinge of remorse tugged at him at the thought of how little time he had devoted to them—particularly Cristóbal.

It had not been that way between his father and him. Don Cristóbal de Oñate, he remembered, had told him and his older brother, Cristóbal, every detail about the uprising in Nueva Galicia. He knew all about the great army that the fierce Coaticore had formed in 1538 to rid the northern province of the Spaniards. His father had taken over from the governor, Perez de la Torre, when the latter was killed, and Coaticore had been defeated.

Only two years later when don Cristóbal was acting governor in the absence of Vásquez de Coronado, who had gone in quest of Cíbola, another larger rebellion erupted that resulted in the destruction of Guadalajara. Don Cristóbal was able to hold off the united tribes until the viceroy Antonio de Mendoza arrived with the greatest army ever assembled in America up to that time. The Indians were forced to retire to the mountain fortress of Mixtón, which was virtually impregnable. Only the treason of some Caxcán warriors, who showed the Spaniards the way up to the mountain stronghold, permitted a Spanish victory. It was in this war that the impetuous Pedro de Alvarado, who had played a major role in the conquest of the Aztecs and who had triggered the events that led to *la noche triste* in Moctezuma's capital, finally fell.

Young Juan's father had recounted to him details of the earlier siege of Guadalajara by thirty thousand Chichimecas and how he had saved the city by an intrepid counterattack that forced the Indians to lift the encirclement.

Of course, he rationalized to himself, before Isabel's illness Cristobalillo was a very young child who had not yet reached the age of reason. Now that he was five it would be different. He would have more time for him. Now that his son was about to take his first Holy Communion he would understand better. "But what can I tell him?" he thought, "during my father's youth adventure was everywhere."

Don Juan shook his head, and Cristóbal asked, "qué papá?"

"Nada, nada, hijo," he whispered. He felt like taking him in his arms and kissing him and weeping with him. Cristóbal had not cried openly. He looked more like a child whose feelings had been hurt by a confusing event. He had been very close to his mother until she fell ill. Since then, not knowing what to make of his mother's inaccessibility, he had taken most of his cues from his father.

At the cemetery, Cristóbal's cheeks were streaked with tears, but he was not sobbing. Don Juan stood erect with a somber, distant look. He had said his good-byes during the intervals when Isabel was lucid. They had mainly talked about Cristóbal—about his planned studies in the capital. The subject of María had only brought tears. Isabel would ask that she be brought to her. She seemed to know that she was going to die, and she asked through her tears who was going to take care of her baby daughter. Don Juan would answer by saying only "vas a sanar, mi amor [You will get well]."

Now as the priest intoned, don Juan was restless—impatient with the ritual finalizing the mystery that had taken possession of his wife, and that had little to do with their relationship and with his thoughts and feelings. "Take her and keep her for me, Lord," he muttered.

## CHAPTER TWO

During the weeks following the funeral, don Juan became lethargic. He would sit alone in his patio long stretches at a time, thinking of the myriad things he had to do, but feeling too dispirited even to get up from his chair. Thoughts of the North, of Cíbola, would intrude on his desolation but without solace or enthusiasm. His jumbled thoughts would make him weary and sleepy. He took frequent naps, only to awake with a feeling of disarray, but not knowing how to begin restoring order and direction in his life.

One of those afternoons he woke up with a start. He had been dreaming of the time when he was a young man. His dream had turned into a nightmare in which he had been left behind by an expedition on its way to seek out marauding Chichimecas in the northern frontier. Bounding out of bed, he called for a cup of chocolate and went straight to his desk where he sat collecting his thoughts. He slowly drew a sheet of paper from a drawer and started writing. He addressed the letter to his friend and former commander, who since 1590 had been the viceroy of New Spain, don Luis de Velasco II; but, after some reflection, he slipped it into the still-open drawer.

As the days passed, don Juan began to emerge from the incubus that had possessed. He began to seem more like his vigorous self. Because of his slim build, he looked younger than his forty-one years. He also appeared taller than his above-average height. His sandy hair was no doubt a legacy from his Basque father. The dark brown eyes that gave him an austere, intense look until he smiled—which he rarely did—were probably an inheritance from a distant Moorish ancestor through his mother Catalina de Salazar de La Cadena. Her lineage derived from an old Granada family that had distinguished itself during the centuries-long struggle along the ever-changing frontier between the Christians and the Moslems.

He began to visit more frequently with his half-sister, doña Magdalena de Mendoza y Salazar, a plump, rosy-cheeked, vibrant woman with a kindly disposition. She was married to Vicente de Zaldívar of the Oñate-Zaldívar family, also rich and prominent in Zacatecas; Zaldívar was also captain general in charge of the campaign against the Chichimecas. When he went, he took Cristóbal, who enjoyed those visits to his aunt's because his father seemed to regain his vitality as he reminisced with his nephews about happier times and above all when he talked about New Mexico, which in the boy's mind was gradually becoming a wonderland. Vicente, the younger of the two Zaldívar brothers, also was becoming fascinated with the new frontier as described by his uncle. Don Juan's meager knowledge had been gleaned from his father, who had acquired it secondhand from the disgruntled veterans of the 1540 Vásquez de Coronado expedition as they returned to Compostela during the time don Cristóbal was serving as acting governor of Nueva Galicia in the great explorer's absence.

New Mexico was now very much in the minds of official New Spain because the unauthorized, minuscule expedition of Leyva de Bonilla and Gutiérrez de Humaña was at the very moment somewhere in the northern vastness. In 1593 Captain Francisco Leyva de Bonilla went to the northern frontier of New Spain to punish certain hostile Indian tribes. Once there, he recruited a party including Antonio Gutiérrez de Humañna, and penetrated into pueblo country. Since that time they had not been heard from.

Doña Magdalena was not so enthusiastic as her sons about her half-brother's scheme. She did not like the way their eyes lit up as they talked with their half-uncle and cousin. "Why," she asked half in earnest, half sardonically, "do you men get so excited about going to some remote, hostile place to kill or get killed."

"New Mexico could be a great opportunity for Uncle Juan," Juan de Zaldívar answered almost apologetically.

"Opportunity for what," she countered. "He is already forty-three, he is rich, and he has two children to take care of. He should stay here and get married again. Who is going to look after Cristobalillo's education?

"Cristóbal is more excited than anyone, and besides there would be plenty of friars for that," answered Vicente politely but with a tone of finality.

Doña Magdalena shrugged her shoulders and sighed, feeling that perhaps her sons would be drawn into something she did not relish, but about which women never had any say at all.

## CHAPTER THREE

DON JUAN HAD not seen his boyhood friend, Francisco López since Isabel first fell sick. Francisco was the son of Diego López, who had served with don Cristóbal in the Mixtón wars as a sergeant and had come with him to Zacatecas just after the discovery of the Bufa mine by Juanes de Tolosa in 1546. A very enterprising young man, he was soon made mine foreman by don Cristóbal. Their two sons had played together as children and had become fast friends. The difference in their families' stations had not made any difference while they were children, but the boys' relationship became more difficult as they grew older. Juan's mother, doña Catalina, objected gently to her son's relationship with a young man who not only was a foreman's son but who did not seem to have any ambition in life except as she put it, "to chase cattle, hang around the bodegas, and to court girls." Don Cristóbal would not say anything. After all Francisco was the son of a fellow campaigner. Don Cristóbal was a kind and generous man as evinced by the open table he kept at home for anyone needing a meal. He was also very loyal and considerate to his friends, particularly so to those who had fought alongside him.

Don Juan had a good idea where to find Francisco, who was actually just leaving the *pulpería* as his friend walked up. "Juan," exclaimed Francisco as they embraced, "lo siento," he offered his condolence.

"Gracias amigo. I have been wanting to see you."

"Well, here I am. Let's go back in."

They talked and drank until well past nightfall.

Francisco, contrary to his disposition, became expansive if not chatty.

"You know, Juan, I never liked the mines. I often wondered how certain Spaniards could profit so much from the work of people who came and went like phantoms and whom nobody really got to know."

Don Juan felt a bit uncomfortable. "Is that the reason you were so glad that your father gave up mining to raise cattle?"

"No, not really. I just liked the idea of living on a ranch among the cowboys."

Don Juan sighed, "You don't know how I envied you."

"You? The son of Don Cristóbal?"

"Your father and mine were good friends and fellow campaigners."

Francisco looked into his friend's eyes, "You know they said that my father embezzled money from the mines to start his ranch."

Don Juan stared back, "My father never believed it. He was so happy to see your father start his own hacienda."

"Don Cristóbal was a saint. He even helped my old man get a grant of land from the governor."

Zacatecas was growing and the town had a need for beef. The *estancia* was not a large one by northern New Spain standards. It measured only thirty thousand paces in perimeter. Diego filled it with cattle he bought or rounded up with his cowboys from among the many strays that roamed the countryside.

Francisco was twelve years old when this drastic change in his life occurred. His father maintained a residence in Zacatecas, but Francisco preferred to stay at the hacienda, as primitive as it was at first, because there he could listen to the cowboys' stories and follow them as they went through their tasks. He soon became a very skillful horseman, winning the respect of the older men.

Juan, who rode well himself, was at once proud and slightly envious of his friend. They did not see as much of each other as before because Francisco spent as much time as he was allowed at El Azar, as his father's hacienda was called, while Juan was in Zacatecas taking instruction from a tutor his father had hired for his two youngest, Juan and Alfonso, in preparation for further studies in Mexico City.

Francisco had come to the end of his studies the year that his father built the hacienda. At fourteen years of age he had become a working cowboy. He enjoyed the work, but what he liked most was rodeo time, during which there was a good bit of work, but there was also an opportunity to show off his horsemanship, particularly to the other cowboys but also to the townspeople who came out for the festive part of the occasion. At his father's ranch and in the countryside, Francisco had ample opportunity to practice the skills that, at a very young age, made him an accomplished *charro*.

Starting at about the middle of the sixteenth century, there was so much livestock, primarily cattle, in the northern frontier that large herds were roaming the open country, often trampling the crops of Indians in the relatively untamed areas in northern New Spain. There were so many cattle that some cowboys started killing them at the slightest pretext, including entertainment. In the manner of the gaucho of the pampas in early colonial Argentina, who would often kill a cow for a few choice steaks, the Spanish colonial cowboys in New Spain would slaughter them for the hides or even the fat, which they would sell for whatever they could get from miners in the area.

To increase efficiency in thinning out the vast herds, the cowboys developed a weapon called the half-moon because of the scythelike shape of the blade, which was attached to a long handle. The horseman could immobilize a bull or a cow by cutting off its hind legs at full gallop. The coup de grace could then be delivered with relative ease. This became one of the dubious skills of the northern *charros*, who during rodeos could be prevailed upon to give a demonstration of this brutal practice.

By the time he was eighteen Francisco was one of the leading horsemen in the area surrounding Zacatecas. He had matured into a trim, strongly built, and handsome young man. Darkly good looking, he had taken on an air of daring that many took for belligerence.

When Juan came back from Mexico City he would often go riding with his friend, who would teach him some of the fine points. Juan, however, could never get himself to wear the *charro* costume with its silver buttons on the vest, the fringes and tassels on the trousers, and the broad-brimmed conical hat.

As he matured Francisco became his father's foreman. He was fair with the men, considering himself one of them, but he never tolerated insolence. His method of dealing with recalcitrant hands was direct confrontation. Since all of the men wore swords there was always the danger of a lethal fight, but most of the time these encounters led only to hard words or fist fights. Francisco seldom pulled his sword out of its scabbard, resorting instead to his physical strength, either wrestling or knocking down his opponents. He acquired such renown that he seldom had any takers at the ranch. In the *bodegas* he frequented when he was in town, he often faced challenges from brawlers who wanted to test their mettle against the leading *charro* in the region. With his taciturn nature, he never picked a fight, but he never turned one down either, winning many more than he lost.

## CHAPTER FOUR

THE MATURE JUAN de Oñate's face belied his physique. It was delicate and somewhat sallow. His clipped beard accentuated the impression of fragility. Viewed from a distance, however, he projected a strong, agile, and almost athletic image, with moderately broad shoulders and the waistline of a much younger man. His inexpressive brown eyes did not easily reveal his feelings or thoughts.

Throughout his childhood and since his marriage, he had lived an opulent life by New World standards. His very spacious home, built after his father's death, was essentially constructed in Renaissance style. It had often rung with the gaiety of the highest society in the viceroyalty. The viceroy had stayed there on his visits to Zacatecas which, because of its rich mines, had become the most important city in the northern frontier.

It was a two-story building a hundred or so *varas* from the church, down the street that later was to be rebuilt as the cathedral of the regional archdiocese. From a distance the home appeared to be at the foot of the famous Bufa peak that dominated the town. The facade, which came right up to a narrow sidewalk, was very plain, with only its wrought-iron balconies to break the monotony; but, in the manner of most Spanish mansions, which never fail to astonish as one steps into them, the dark hallway suddenly erupted into a profusion of light and flowers in the inner courtyard of what amounted to a fair-sized cloister. The lower and upper arcades were identical, composed of segmental arches supported by square-fluted columns. Broad staircases at each end led to the upper corridor, which was decorated with small pots of flowers hanging along the wrought-iron railings. A small pirul tree growing in the middle of the open patio cast a gentle shadow over three well-worn, leather-backed chairs. On the perimeter several large flower pots graced the edge of the passageways. It was in this cool patio, isolated from the din and bustle of the street and fragrant with the smell of the collection of wild flowers—morning glories, daisies, cincollagas, and others—that the subject of New Mexico had been discussed years before. The incoming viceroy had wanted his friend to undertake the expedition, not only because he could afford it, but because don Juan had served under him and he knew something of his character and background.

Although a member of a very wealthy mining family, Juan was not the heir. Under the ancient Spanish laws of inheritance his oldest brother, Fernando, would inherit his father's fortune. Unfortunately when don Cristóbal died, his debts exceeded his assets, and Fernando accepted an *encomienda* in the vicinity of Puebla and eventually became mayor of that city. The second oldest son, Cristóbal, also received a land grant and left Zacatecas. Juan, who was twenty years old at the time, by consent of the family took over the management of his father's mines.

Zacatecas was a town of some twenty-five hundred inhabitants with a population of fifteen hundred Zacateco Indians who worked at the mines, eight hundred black slaves who also worked extracting the precious silver from the mountain, and two hundred Spaniards who either worked in supervisory positions at the mines or had other business establishments in the growing city.

The Indians worked for a small salary, but in order to induce them to stay at their jobs, the mine owners allowed them to take out a small pouch of ore each day. In the mines, since they were well acquainted with ore processing, they performed such work with the assistance of the black slaves. They followed a process devised by a Spaniard, Bartolomé de Medina, who came to New Spain sometime near the middle of the sixteenth century. Medina's process involved the use of mercury for extracting the silver out of the ore. The ore was first pulverized, brine was then added, and subsequently quicksilver. After a lapse of time, which could be days or weeks, the mercury and silver would fuse. During the washing phase the sand and clay were separated from the fused substance. The last step was the firing, which separated the mercury from the silver. The mercury was salvaged for further use and the silver was sent on its way mostly to Spain in the form of ingots.

Using their own simple techniques, the Indians had been producing small quantities of silver for years. Before the Spaniards came, most of their precious metals were taken from streams where they panned them or from superficial excavations. In either case the soil was simply washed off. Later, as they did in Zacatecas with their own ore, they broke up the rocks by heating them and then pouring cold water on them.

Juan had always been very conscious of his father's achievements. As one of the city's founding fathers and the owner of the most mines, he was the community leader. He was well known not only for what he had accomplished but also highly regarded for his thoughtfulness and acts of charity. Juan revered him, although as a small child with his timid nature he turned more often to his mother for love and comfort. In the manner of most Spanish patriarchs, don Cristóbal lavished most of his attention on the eldest son, but he always found time for all of his children.

Juan grew up an introspective child, but with a penchant for playing out heroic fantasies. Having heard countless times about his father's achievements, he would spend long periods of time wondering if he would ever perform heroic deeds against the Chichimecas and make important discoveries. He admired his friend Francisco for his impetuous nature and his personal bravery, but he knew that he could not emulate him, for such was not his nature. He was, besides, very conscious of his responsibilities as a member of an important family and clan.

While he had kept the vigil as his wife was slowly dying, his eyes would flash for an instant at the thought of what the viceroy had suggested long ago. Now, as he talked to Francisco, who was still a bachelor, he sighed, "How I would like to go out into the wilderness."

His friend, who did not have any inhibitions, answered, "Pues vamos. I would like to go too."

Don Juan, feeling that something as serious as an expedition to claim new lands for the crown and to christianize Indians might not be very appropriate for his impetuous friend, did not pursue the conversation very far. He would no doubt be a good fighter; but then, he might be a source of trouble amongst the settlers with young daughters, or with their wives.

As the days and weeks passed, don Juan thought less of doña Isabel with grief or guilt, and more with the inexorable detachment that the passage of time brings. The period of her illness and death was slowly being replaced in his mind by memories of his youth—of his first campaign with don Luis and of the incredibly starry nights in the desert wilderness. Life was moving on. He no longer felt quite so guilty about the possibility of undertaking the expedition. He had even begun discussing it with relatives and friends other than Francisco. Not many, particularly the relatives (except his nephews), encouraged him. Some wondered out loud why he would leave a comfortable life among his family and influential friends for an unknown land certainly full of unfriendly Chichimecas. "And what about María and Cristóbal," some would ask.

"Oh, I'll take him with me," he would answer, still not knowing what he would do with María. It was after one of those ambiguous conversations that he took the letter he had written several weeks before and sent it off to the viceroy.

Don Juan's forays as a very young man into Chichimeca territory had not been unusual, the only direction into which New Spain could expand was northward. As worthy veterans of the conquest of Mexico were granted *encomiendas,* and as mines were discovered, it became imperative that these interests be protected against frequent uprisings by various Indian tribes that had long since been classified simply as "Chichimecas," which translated roughly into "wild Indians." The territory they dominated ran through most of the province of Nueva Galicia, which extended north from the frontier towns of Guadalajara and Querétaro to a vague border somewhere far beyond the last outposts of Spanish civilization.

Zacatecas, when it was founded in late 1547, was right in the middle of the Gran Chichimeca and great care had to be taken against attack from the Zacateco Indians. Juanes de Tolosa, however, was able to convince the Zacatecos that the Spaniards meant them no harm, and the town was established by Tolosa, Cristóbal de Oñate, another Basque by the name of Diego de Ibarra, and Baltazar de Bañuelos. It was the latter who held fast when the miners wanted to leave in the face of hostilities by the natives of the area. Finally after the danger had passed there was a rush to Zacatecas by Spaniards seeking to get rich either with silver or other business enterprises. The largest operator by far was Cristóbal de Oñate, who had thirteen smelters, over one hundred slaves, many Indian workers, and even a church for all his people.

The new city was modeled after Toledo, which was at the time the capital of Spain. Its name, Nuestra Señora de los Zacatecos, was given in recognition of its the Indian inhabitants of the area. The robust and vital founders lost no time in bringing civilization to the region and Zacatecas became known as the civilizer of the North. Its fathers, with their motto that became the city's, "el trabajo lo vence todo" ("work conquers everything"), also gave it wealth.

During the time of Juan's youth new mines were frequently being opened north of Zacatecas. The Indians reacted by stepping up their attacks on the Spanish settlements. The viceroy, don Luis de Velasco I, established defensive outposts throughout the Gran Chichimeca, as the vast, sparsely settled northern territory was called. The Chichimecas reacted by banding together, and even Zacatecas itself, which by now was considerably to the south of the action, came under danger of attack. The city was armed by Captain Pedro de Ahumada in 1561 and he often sallied forth with a sizeable force to seek the enemy. These were exciting times for young Juan. Oh, how he wished he could go with Ahumada, but he was a bit too young. The captain succeeded in pacifying the Indians to the north, then returned to Zacatecas and once more rode out and defeated rebelling Guachichile Indians to the south.

Although the attacks subsided for a while, they soon started up again and Juan and Francisco got the chance to participate in a campaign under the fourth viceroy, Martin Enriques de Almanza. Luis de Velasco II was on the same campaign. Juan served under don Luis, who was eleven years older. Juan's father had known don Luis's father when the latter was viceroy. Don Cristóbal enjoyed a certain renown from the Mixtón War, as former governor of Nueva Galicia, and later as one of the very wealthy northern mine owners. Don Luis the younger took a liking to the young Juan and they soon became friends. Now don Luis was viceroy, and don Juan a sedentary mine owner, but neither of the men had forgotten that campaign many years ago.

In later years, since expansion to the far north had begun, the intermittent wars had been conducted out of Zacatecas. The traditional policy of "war by blood and fire" encountered strong opposition and was not having success in the task of pacification. The idealistic viceroy, Alonso Manrique de Zuñiga, marquis of Villamanrique, who assumed office in 1585, changed the policy to one of "peace through purchase," which sought to pacify the intransigent northern tribes through conversion to Christianity, diplomacy, and compensation of various kinds. In addition, Indians friendly to the Spaniards would be brought as role models to settle in the Chichimeca regions.

Luis de Velasco II, no less idealistic than his predecessor, but also a practical administrator, succeeded Villamanrique in 1590. He had experienced the Chichimeca War firsthand and knew the frustrations that often resulted from the old policy. Using the funds appropriated for war, he courted the heretofore dreaded enemy with grants of land, presents, and provisions. He also brought the old allies of Cortés, the Tlaxcaltecas, into the area. As a measure of precaution, however, he reinforced the *presidios,* which had been weakened by Villamanrique. He thus succeeded by peaceful initiatives to accomplish what the war of blood and fire had failed to do.

# CHAPTER FIVE

THE QUESTION OF a settlement in New Mexico had never been decided since the failure of Vásquez de Coronado to find anything considered of value in 1540. It remained the only frontier left in New Spain, albeit of very dubious promise. All evidence to the contrary, the idea of another Tenochtitlán, of a faraway Cíbola or Quivira, had not quite died off despite the successive disappointment of all the expeditions, mostly unauthorized, that had been drawn northward by myth, wishful thinking, or merely the taste for adventure.

In certain Zacatecas circles New Mexico was beginning to be the chief topic of conversation. Juan de Zaldívar was not one to get easily enthusiastic, particularly about something he knew little about. Sitting on a bench in front of the church on a balmy late summer afternoon, he and Don Juan talked and watched the people walk by. "There have already been several expeditions to New Mexico; why haven't they succeeded in finding something of value, uncle?"

"I think we know that there will be no Aztec or Inca empires, but there are other kinds of riches to be discovered—mineral deposits, seaports."

Don Juan did not bring it up but there was the opportunity for adventure and the chance of acquiring titles and honors—even if they would be only faint echoes of those earned when there was a Spanish peninsula to be reconquered or empires to be crushed by a few intrepid men.

Pale as the prize might be, there was no dearth of candidates seeking to establish a colony in the north. Among them was Antonio de Espejo, who led one of the few condoned expeditions since Vásquez de Coronado's. Juan Bautista de Tómas y Colmenares's plan had been approved in 1589 by the previous viceroy, Villamanrique, but was rejected by the Council of the Indies because of Colmenare's exorbitant demands.

Oñate's letter had been received with favor by don Luis, but he was obliged to tell his friend that a contract had been awarded to the governor of Nueva Vizcaya, Francisco de Urdiñola. The viceroy held out some hope to don Juan, however, saying that Urdiñola had been accused of murdering his wife and was being held in prison. He added that he felt obliged to go through with the contract, should Urdiñola be exonerated. If Urdiñola were convicted or rejected, don Luis could not think of anybody better suited for the task than his friend Juan.

It was the fall of 1592 when Oñate received the viceroy's reply. The rest of the year passed slowly. Don Juan felt as if the race with time was being lost. He was only forty-two years of age, but he thought of himself as getting old. Now that he had decided to undertake the expedition he was impatient to leave Zacatecas. The Christmas season was glum. Besides the fact that he was observing a period of mourning, he felt himself floundering. He had lost interest in the management of the mines. The New Mexico project was uppermost in his mind, but he had many doubts that it would became a reality. Except for an occasional visit to Francisco, he saw no one but his family. His conversation was mostly about previous expeditions to New Mexico and why they had failed or about the great conquistadores, Cortés and Pizarro. His nephews, Juan and Vicente, were his most frequent visitors. Cristóbal liked to eavesdrop on their conversations, and afterward he would ask, "me vas a llevar papá? [are you taking me father?]."

Don Juan would answer absentmindedly, "Yes, yes, I'll take you my son."

Cristóbal would yell with joy and run out to play at fighting Chichimecas.

The spring of 1593 came with its unpredictable weather—dusty winds one day, cool and sunny the next. Don Juan's moods seemed to change with the weather. There were days when he felt sure that good news was in the offing, others when he felt without hope. His brother, Cristóbal, who was representing him in Mexico City reported that although there was no progress on the case against Urdiñola, it appeared as if he was no longer a serious candidate as the leader of the expedition.

One hot day in early summer as don Juan contemplated the flat, pale blue sky and the countryside bleached by a searing sun that seemed to bake the life out of both man and vegetation, a servant announced that a courier had just arrived from the capital and was waiting in the foyer with a message from the viceroy. Don Juan did not ask for the messenger to be brought to him, instead he rushed to meet him as if he had been the viceroy himself. Don Luis de Velasco was inviting him to come to Mexico City to discuss the expedition to New Mexico! Don Juan could not contain a broad smile as he finished reading the message. Without any hesitation he told the messenger to wait while he quickly penned an answer. Cristóbal, who had overheard, ran to his father shrieking "ya vamos, ya vamos [we are going, we are going]."

His father answered, "claro, hijo."

"Yes, father, to New Mesico."

"We shall see," smiled his father, knowing that he could never leave his son behind, although he had not really decided and felt guilty about taking his young son to an unknown land.

It was mid-September when don Juan was received in the viceregal palace by his old friend. The viceroy, despite the austere, unapproachable look of his long, gray face, which was rendered even more solemn by his pointed black beard and the thin steel-rimmed glasses on his bony nose, was actually quite an affable man.

The subject of the expedition was not brought up until the second day. As the viceroy and don Juan strolled about the palace grounds, don Luis said, "Juan, have you thought seriously about the pacification of New Mexico?"

"Yes, don Luis," don Juan answered. "I have thought of nothing else since I wrote to you . . . you know, since Isabel died . . . I thank you for your confidence in me, your Excellency. I think I am ready."

"Well, we have discussed it before," smiled the viceroy. "Why don't we discuss the details tomorrow?"

The following day don Juan awakened early. It was a cool, bright September morning. He stepped out onto the balcony, took a deep breath and looked northward as if straining to see the land beyond the horizon. Of course Oñate was well acquainted with the reports from previous expeditions, which had discovered nothing of great value. His impression of New Mexico had been formed by the reaction of his youthful imagination to the stories related by his father and to the amazing account given by Cabeza de Vaca of his eight-year odyssey in the wilds of present-day Texas.

Cabeza de Vaca was an officer in the Narváez expedition of 1528, which lost its ship after penetrating into the interior of Florida. He and 241 men drifted westward along the Gulf Coast in crude rafts. Eventually there were only four survivors, including the black Estevan who was the first non-Indian to set foot in New Mexico. During their sojourn they heard stories from the nomadic Indians of the land of "cities" to the north. Spanish imagination was triggered by the vague descriptions provided by people who had probably only heard of them secondhand. This led to thoughts of Tenochtitlán, the fabulous city of the Aztecs. The number "seven" came from the legend dating back to the beginning of the eighth century in Spain when seven bishops were rumored to have escaped from the invading Moors and founded seven fabulous cities in Atlantis, later the Antilles, and finally Cíbola in New

Mexico. The myth persisted until the time of Coronado, who launched an expedition looking for them.

Oñate felt, as did many other would-be discoverers, that the others who had gone into the northern lands had missed the many fruits to be picked there, either through bad luck or lack of resolve. With boldness, determination, and a bit of luck he would meet with success. He was startled out of his reverie by the voice of his son, who had walked up behind him blurting, "Es verdad? Is it true that the viceroy is going to let us go to New Mesico?"

"Parece que sí, si Dios quiere [God willing]," don Juan smiled as he put his arm around his son.

Negotiations with don Luis went well. They were after all going over familiar ground. What Juan de Oñate, rich and influential, wanted out of the expedition was not pecuniary gain so much as adventure, fame, and glory. He would, of course, be governor and captain general, but he wished to be named *adelantado* for four generations, and he dreamed ultimately of being knighted a marquis. Don Luis, despite his friendship for Oñate, as a very able viceroy knew that his office demanded that he show a certain restraint. There was after all the Audiencia, the Council of the Indies, and the king to contend with. "No, Juan," he shook his head, "governor and captain general yes, but four lives as *adelantado*? It is not possible for now. Perhaps after the expedition has demonstrated some success."

Don Juan knew the constraints his friend and protector faced so he extended his hand. Both smiled and don Luis chided good naturedly, "Cuatro vidas, hombre [four lives, come on!]. Let's go have a drink."

## CHAPTER SIX

ALTHOUGH HE DID not yet have the contract, don Juan went about Zacatecas during the year 1594 making preliminary plans for his great odyssey. As he progressed, he drafted a proposal in which he offered to take at least two hundred men, "furnished with everything necessary, provisions sufficient to reach the settlements, and even more, this all at my cost and that of my soldiers, His Majesty not being obligated to pay them wages besides what I may willingly give from my estate."

Juan and Vicente got word that their uncle had spent the night two leagues away from the city and would be arriving probably late in the morning. Anxious to know the results of his visit with the viceroy, they went to his home where lunch was waiting the traveler's arrival. After all the *abrazos* and kisses Vicente, ever the impatient one, smiled, "Well, tío, tell us about it."

Don Juan smiled back at Vicente, then turned his gaze to the older brother, "Juan, do you want to be my maese de campo?"

Juan stammered, "Well . . . I"

"And you, Vicente, will be the sargento mayor?"

The younger nephew answered boldly, "At your orders, your excellency."

Nephews and uncle all laughed, then they embraced, the young men pledging good, loyal service. Vicente, still beaming, said, "Sabes tío, Mother is not at all enthusiastic about this journey of ours."

"I know," replied don Juan. "It's a good thing she is not going. Imagine how that would be." All three laughed.

Vicente picked up Cristóbal in his arms, "And what are you laughing about?"

Cristóbal answered in a shrill voice, "Because Tía is not going, but father says I am."

Juan de Zaldívar was not only two years older than his brother and thus more mature, he was opposite in personality and even physique. Heavier and shorter than Vicente, he had an unruffled disposition, particularly compared to his dynamic, decisive, sometimes stormy and intelligent brother. As children and later as adolescents, Juan, who was often invited on short trips or to visit the mines by his father, had often been the object of his brother's jealousy. Vicente, feeling left out, turned his attention to horsemanship and martial activities in which he soon excelled. At the age of fifteen he insisted on joining an expedition against the Chichimecas because seventeen-year-old Juan was going on his first one. By the time Vicente was seventeen he had participated in three campaigns. Of late the brothers, who long before had reached an amicable relationship, had been working at the mines with their distinguished father, who now held the rank of captain general.

Later in the afternoon don Juan went to look for his friend. He found him where they had met two weeks before—sitting in a *pulpería* with a very young woman who, judging from her attire, was of very simple circumstance but very beautiful. Francisco presented her very casually. "This is my friend Guadalupe; Guadalupe, don Juan de Oñate."

The girl was flustered but she needn't have been for, after don Juan nodded quickly to her, the two men turned their attention to each other as if she had not been there.

Sitting beside his friend, don Juan said with a broad smile, "It looks as if we are going."

"Yes, when do you leave?" Francisco asked unenthusiastically.

"I don't know. We do not have the contract yet, only don Luis's word. Do you want to go?"

Francisco looked down at his cup, "Me with all those captains and ensigns? You know about my problem with discipline. Remember, I was arrested once."

"Yes, but that was long ago when you were a very young man, and that was for brawling. You performed very well in those campaigns with don Luis. He told me so himself."

"Yes, that was also a long time ago. I don't feel so young anymore."

"Well, think it over amigo." Don Juan arose, nodded once more to Guadalupe—this time much slower—then turned and left.

That evening don Juan invited a few friends and relatives to tell them of his good fortune. He felt expansive and talked more than drank. There was no music or dancing, although the period of mourning was considered ended, but there was great animation. Don Juan felt a smug satisfaction at the thought of leaving this soft, easy life for the purity and vigor of the frontier. The evening came to an end with don Juan sitting alone in the great room, imagining himself on horseback, straight and resolute at the head of his army as it penetrated deeper and deeper into the unknown. "That is the life for me, not this salon with its fine furniture and soft carpets," he thought.

## CHAPTER SEVEN

One more year had gone by. Don Juan was becoming more and more impatient but not discouraged. He was, from all indications that came back to him from his brother, the only viable choice for the coveted mission. As the long summer ended, Oñate had completed all the preliminary work he could reasonably accomplish. Now it was up to the king to decide.

In late August 1595 he was once more summoned to the capital by the viceroy, who had received a letter from King Phillip II approving don Juan's appointment. Oñate arrived in Mexico City in early September with the proposal he had been preparing for over a year. For a whole month it was reviewed and discussed by the viceroy and his aides. After one week, Don Juan returned to Zacatecas, leaving his younger brother, Cristóbal, behind with authorization to negotiate for him. Cristóbal managed to get most of what his brother wanted. Juan had asked for six friars; he was given five and two lay brothers. He was named *adelantado* for two lives; he had asked for four. He requested a grant of twenty thousand pesos; he was given six thousand. Of great satisfaction to him was the promise of *hidalguía* for his settlers. They were to be gentlemen of the kingdom.

On 18 September 1595, the semiannual fleet arrived from Spain. Sailing on the captain general's galleon—which was the last one in the convoy—was the new viceroy of New Spain, don Gaspar de Zuñiga y Acevedo, the count of Monterrey. Don Luis had been promoted to the viceroyalty of Peru on June 5, 1595. At Zacatecas the would-be settlers could do nothing but await the outcome of the meeting between the two viceroys.

"What do you think, uncle?" asked the prospective *maese de campo*. "Does the count have to approve the contract?"

"Unfortunately he does, Juan, but don Luis has promised that he will present my case in the most convincing manner. The final decision, in any case, will be King Phillip's, but of course, the count will have much influence on the king's decision. All we can do is hope that don Luis and the count are of one mind."

Viceroy Velasco made plans to meet his successor at the village of Oculma, six leagues east of Mexico City. On 14 October, amid much fanfare, they met. Velasco soon sized up his mild-mannered counterpart as a very cautious and somewhat suspicious man who would not be rushed.

Juan de Oñate's expedition was not the only one being negotiated. Vizcaíno was planning one up the coast of California, and the annual supply fleet was about to leave for the Philippines. Don Luis was not concerned about the latter two, but he was very anxious about the contract he had negotiated with his friend.

With an exaggerated display of courtesy, the two discussed the settlement of New Mexico for several days. Velasco reiterated several times that Oñate was by far the most qualified to undertake the task at hand. "Your excellency has but to ask the members of the Audiencia or any of our leading citizens. You will see for yourself, for I have taken the liberty of inviting him to welcome you."

Several times during the meeting the count appeared to be on the verge of giving his consent, but finally he said, "Your excellency, I have great trust in your judgment, but the press of affairs is such that I cannot in good conscience give my approval until I can study the matter after I arrive at the capital."

Velasco, after failing on several occasions to sway the count finally asked, "Will the illustrious count agree to issue the required patents conditionally? I will take full responsibility for don Juan's performance."

Don Gaspar remained silent for what seemed to don Luis an endless interval. "So be it, but I caution your excellency that I reserve the right to make any change I deem necessary."

On 21 October the patents appointing Juan de Oñate governor and captain general upon establishment of the colony in New Mexico were issued, but the contract was not approved, pending Monterrey's review of it more carefully.

The new viceroy soon thereafter wrote to the king that he did not have enough information about Juan de Oñate to discuss his case properly, but that he would write to his majesty whenever he made up his mind about the modifications he might make in the contract.

Don Juan was satisfied that the delay would be minimal, particularly after receiving an answer to a letter written by him congratulating the count on his appointment. Monterrey expressed regret that Velasco had not concluded the matter. In a second letter he ordered Oñate to gather his provisions and ammunition in the shortest time possible, telling him that he would send him the approved contract after making his modifications.

On 15 December don Juan's brothers, Cristóbal and Luis, who were representing him in the capital, were summoned by the *secretario de gobernación* and presented with articles put in by the count. They consisted of a list of instructions, but they were without final approval because the viceroy was either too busy as he said or stalling as some in the Oñate camp thought.

Don Juan did not waste time in enlisting his family and an even larger circle of friends to the recruiting effort. They scattered to various parts of the kingdom in competition for recruits with a reinforcement fleet to the Philippines and with a maritime expedition to California by Sebastian Vizcaíno. There was, however, no dearth of volunteers for new adventures. Mexico City was always full of hidalgos and would-be hidalgos, as well as simple folk looking for a new life or dreaming of their great opportunity. There were *segundones* from influential families deprived of an inheritance by the laws of primogeniture. There were people who, having nothing in Spain, had made their way across the ocean in the hope of bettering their lives. New Mexico, another Mexico City, sounded intriguing to all. The names of Cortés and Pizarro were still fresh in people's minds and were synonymous with sudden wealth and fame within the reach of those bold enough to face the rigors and dangers of the unknown—why not in la Nueva Mexico.

By early fall 1596, don Juan, as he prepared to leave for Mexico City to welcome the new viceroy, was able to say to his nephew and *maese de campo*, "It won't be long now. We almost have the requisite number of men and Fray Rodrigo Durán has arrived with his friars. I am happy that Fray Diego Márquez is among them. I have known him for a long time."

"Bien, Tío," answered Juan, "I too am ready and Cristóbal is more impatient than anyone. The other day I overhead him making a proclamation of some kind to imaginary Indians. I hope for his sake we can leave soon."

"Yes, I am impatient, too, and you know I am going to Mexico City to greet the new viceroy and get my final instructions," replied don Juan.

The new viceroy, had stated to the king in a letter that he would permit don Luis, the outgoing viceroy who had been named viceroy of Peru, to proceed in his dealings with Oñate; but still he stalled.

Don Juan was not idle during the long period of doubt and waiting. He went about organizing the expedition as if he had a precise date for leaving in mind. But now it was almost a year later and still no decision had been made about launching the expedition, which had gathered on the Nazas River some thirty-three leagues south of the northernmost mining outpost of Santa Bárbara.

Don Luis took it upon himself to write to the king expressing concern about the delay. He pointed out that the rainy season was approaching, and that if the expedition did not depart soon it might have to wait for the next dry season. The newly appointed governor of New Mexico, feeling the frustration of the count's indecision, importuned his friend, Velasco, who was awaiting a fleet to take him to Peru, on the matter. Don Luis once more wrote to the king, although he worded his letters in such a manner as to avoid giving the impression that he was trying to interfere; but he, too, was vexed at the count's suspicion of what had been negotiated with Oñate.

The new viceroy's doubts grew as time passed. To his other concerns he now added the fact that Oñate had too many recruiting parties working in New Spain in competition with Admiral Oganos's less popular and more difficult expedition to the Philippines. He wanted to limit recruitment to one party. Don Juan, however, had already enlisted close to the required number of people. Adding to Oñate's grief, in April 1596 the Council of the Indies received a petition from Pedro Ponce de Leon, count of Bailen, offering to organize an *entrada* to New Mexico. In a letter to the king the council stated that since the contract with Juan de Oñate had not been put into effect, the expedition could be granted to don Pedro.

## CHAPTER EIGHT

During the month of April Juan de Zaldívar accompanied his uncle on a recruiting trip to Nueva Galicia. "Tío," said Juan after a long day of interviewing prospective settlers, "there are many people who would want to enlist, but who do not have the money to buy the equipment they need."

"That is right," answered Oñate, "and our funds are running low. I can't keep going back to my relatives to ask for more money."

"No, and our supplies are being used up. By the way, have you heard from Vicente?" asked Juan.

"Yes, I received a message from him. The staging areas we selected at Santa Bárbara and at the Casco mine are quite satisfactory. The Nazas River appears to be just the place until we can start using them."

"Well, I hope the viceroy makes up his mind," said Juan in a low grumbling tone.

"It is not just the viceroy, now. It seems the Council of the Indies wants to give the contract to some Ponce de León from Bailén," rejoined don Juan.

"But what does he know about this part of the world?" groaned Juan.

"Listen," replied don Juan in an exasperated tone, "since when has that kept anyone from being named to an important post. Queen Isabel was one of the few Spanish monarchs who ever picked people on merit."

One month after the original endorsement of Ponce de León by the council, that august body wrote another letter to the king. It again urged him to appoint the count of Bailén and accused Oñate of mismanaging his estates, owing thirty thousand pesos in bad debts, and of holding off his creditors with deceit. Wagging tongues in the viceregal court were being heard clearly across the ocean.

Oñate, although discouraged, insisted on asking that the predeployment inspection be held. The viceroy appeared to be more reluctant to make a decision than opposed to don Juan's appointment. Finally, since it did not appear that the king was going to decide for him, and since he could no longer put Oñate off, on 6 June he ordered that the inspection begin. For such a task he picked the captain of his guard, don Lope de Ulloa. Don Lope was a gruff, blunt, but efficient man. Such was precisely the man the viceroy needed. The viceroy had not, however, gotten over the many suspicions he had about Juan de Oñate. In his instructions to Ulloa he included the admonition that "it is very important that the people taken by don Juan de Oñate be orderly and disciplined, and cause no harm, and that they be corrected and punished if they cause any trouble."

The first step in the inspection was to name a *contador* who would represent the viceroy. For this task a very reputable man by the name of Gordian Cassano was named. An appraiser was also named by don Juan as leader of the expedition. His choice was Baltasar Rodríguez, whom he knew and trusted. Together they made up a list of goods to be taken, along with the price they had paid for them. The second task was to make an appraisal of the medicines to be taken.

A month and a half after the report on the medical supplies had been filed in Zacatecas, the sword of Damocles, which had been hanging over the settlers' camp, fell. It was the middle of September, and the heat of summer had finally let up a bit. The camp had shaken off the indolence that had beset it since mid-June. A curious optimism had been growing in both camps when suddenly, in the manner of an unexpected summer squall, the news fell that the expedition had been halted.

Late in the afternoon of 9 September 1596, at the Nazas camp, Ulloa himself read don Juan the order suspending the vast enterprise. The order left don Juan stunned, delivered as it was just as he was preparing to cross to the north of the Nazas River and proceed with the inspection at Casco. He felt a weakness in his stomach that shot down to his legs. Don Juan swayed, and the lieutenant governor and royal ensign Francisco Sosa de Peñalosa made a move to help; but, sensing this, don Juan stood straighter and went through the traditional formality of touching the letters to his mouth and putting them over his head as a sign of obedience.

Ponce de León had undoubtedly received information from Oñate's detractors in New Spain. Everything that don Juan proposed, Ponce offered to increase. Oñate committed himself to take two hundred soldiers; the count raised the ante by one hundred. While don Juan offered to take 6,400 head of livestock, Ponce proposed 13,900. Oñate would take twenty ox carts, but the nobleman from Bailén promised thirty. The count on the other hand exacted greater concessions. Once in New Mexico he would be independent of the viceroy's supervision, responsible only to the Council of the Indies—something which had been denied to Oñate. The salary of the *gachupín* (native born) Spaniard would be double that of the creole Oñate.

That evening, feeling a need to unload at least a part of his bitter burden, he went to see the royal ensign on whom don Juan depended for much of his advice. The ensign's family left the tent discreetly. "Muchas gracias, don Francisco, I did feel a little giddy—I don't know what is going to happen," don Juan sighed as he sat down heavily.

"I didn't want to embarrass you, Juan, but I thought you were going to fall," apologized don Francisco.

"If it were not for all these people," don Juan said, waving his arm, "I would go back to Zacatecas, maybe to Spain. I am worried about Cristobalillo. I had hoped we could proceed and get settled in New Mexico so I could attend to his schooling. I don't worry about María because I left her with my sister, but I do miss the little angel. As soon as we establish a capital, I shall send for her."

Don Francisco understood because he had two sons and one daughter with him as well as doña Eufemia, his wife. They were all grown, to be sure, but nonetheless a heavy responsibility. His daughter, Juana, had met Captain Diego de Zubía in the auxiliary camp of La Puana. They were engaged to be married after a swift courtship of only two months. Before he left, don Juan cautioned his lieutenant governor not to let the news of the suspension leak out just yet.

The general spent the following day in his tent, alternately lying down and dozing off into fitful catnaps and writing notes. He declined all meals and asked only for an occasional cup of chocolate. During the following three days he hardly left his tent. On the thirteenth he sealed a thick envelope and gave it to his page. Don Juan poured all the feeling he had suppressed during the long year of uncertainty and frustration into that letter. He regretted that it was not addressed to his friend, don Luis, but to the new viceroy, a person who was little better than an enigma to him. He felt as if he were writing to a statue, but to whom else could he declare his grievances?

> Your Lordship, as I was about to cross the Nazas River, which is the most difficult crossing before reaching the provinces of New Mexico, with most of the people in the expedition and with all the cattle, provisions, and necessary equipment that I am obliged to take, don Lope de Ulloa handed me two letters from your lordship, both of the same tenor, dated the twelfth of last month, and he showed me a *cédula* from his Majesty and the order issued to don Lope by your Lordship instructing him to warn and notify me, which he did. Thus it was that even here we are pursued by the obstacles and hindrances of the devil, as the enemy of all goodness. . . .
>
> The contents of the royal *cédula* and the threats it carries have so touched my feelings that I am filled with grief and have need of the hope of alleviation that your Lordship seems to think will come in the fleet in response to the communications and letters you sent in the second dispatch boat to his Majesty and the Royal Council of the Indies. . . .
>
> While I cannot find words to express my grievances, I was offended even more by the harshness of your Lordship's decree ordering me to obey and carry out what is ordered in his Majesty's *cédula*. The fact that they were orders from my king and lord was enough for me to obey them, and to place them over my head as a loyal subject. Even though some difficulties might have been anticipated, the fact that I was appointed by your Lordship should have been sufficient guarantee to trust me, and half a line in a simple letter would have sufficed to overcome any difficulties arising from the said *cédula*. . . .
>
> I realize, however, that regardless of my efforts I shall not be able to hold the people together. The moment they learn that a change has been made, and that the expedition is being taken away from me and given to another, not more than twenty men shall remain. . . .
>
> Your Lordship should also consider that, however little the people are delayed, it will be a long time if we are to wait the arrival of the count of Bailén who is seeking the contract for the expedition. Even if it were only for the time necessary to go from

Veracruz to Mexico, and from there, after being dispatched by your Lordship, to Sánta Barbara, it would be necessary to take all winter, and the expedition could not move until spring of next year. From this, great harm would follow, especially to the souls of the people there who might be converted and saved quickly if it were not for the delay of the expedition and harm might follow by not stopping properly the damage caused by Captain Leyba and his followers in their penetration of that land. . . .

If God wills that someone should come in the fleet to take charge of the expedition and to supersede me, your Lordship may rest assured that neither I nor any of my men will offer the slightest resistance; on the contrary, I will try to avoid it with all my strength and not only will I relinquish the expedition to the one his Majesty may appoint, but I will also hand over to him the equipment, cattle, provisions and other goods that I have assembled for it. . . .

The humble servant of your Lordship,
Don Juan de Oñate"

The day after dispatching the letter don Juan did not get up at his usual hour. His black servant, Juanillo, was hesitant to wake him up for breakfast, for he had seen a light in his tent until a very late hour. That day again Oñate hardly ventured from his tent. He knew that his soldiers and settlers must be very demoralized, because the rumor was already working its way through the camps, yet he did not know how or what he should tell them.

Afterward Vicente said to his uncle, "No sé, Tío, it looks as if we are doomed never to leave this cursed river."

"Yes, but what can we do?" countered don Juan. "I understand the fleet is coming in this month. Maybe the king will grant us justice."

"What are we going to do?" asked the *maese de campo* that evening at dinner. "Our provisions are running very low."

"What do you suggest, Juan?" Oñate sighed.

"I don't know, but we had better do it quickly. Our people are getting very nervous," warned Juan.

"Yes, some have already left," added Vicente. "Well, at least perhaps we can round up some of the livestock we have lost," he suggested.

"And the people?" snapped Juan. Vicente shook his head.

A week later Captain Gregorio Cessar with a band of horsemen set out to look for the three hundred horses, mules, and oxen that had disappeared. After several days they returned with several oxen. During the search they had passed through a corner of Juan Bautista de Lomas's estate. When the former contender for the leadership of the New Mexico expedition heard of this, he was infuriated, charging Oñate with trespassing on his property and stealing livestock. Lomas took his complaint to a judge in Nieves, a small mining town nearby, who did little more than record it and pass on a copy to the judges in the Audiencia in Guadalajara. They said nothing more than that they were going to send a copy to the viceroy. Nothing more was heard of this. Lomas had, after all, been a serious candidate for the expedition and had lost out. He had previously, for no apparent reason, asked for an injunction against injury from Oñate. He had been granted the injunction, and don Juan had very graciously acknowledged it.

Doña Eufemia, the fifty-six-year-old wife of the royal ensign, Sosa de Peñalosa, had just returned from Guadalajara where she had gone to buy a gown and accessories for her daughter, Juana, whose wedding with Captain Diego de Zubía was waiting for a propitious place and moment. As she was entering her tent, Mercedes, Captain Gregorio Cessar's wife, called to her, "Buenas tardes, doña Eufemia."

"Buenas tardes," answered the distinguished older lady. As Mercedes advanced toward her, she added, "Come in and have a refreshment with me. As you can see I just returned from a trip."

After they had exhausted the amenities over chocolate and sweet biscuits, Mercedes asked, "Is it true what they say about don Juan?"

"I don't know. What is it they are saying?" countered doña Eufemia a bit coldly.

"That he owes money and that he is being replaced by a count from Spain."

"Well, there is talk that the count of Bailén wants to replace don Juan, but I can't tell you whether our leader owes money or not. I don't know of anybody going hungry here."

Don Juan received no answer to his long, plaintive letter. As he reflected on the turn of events, he could not decide on a strategy until Captain Sosa de Peñalosa, to whom he deferred as an older and experienced man, suggested that even though no decision had been made, it would be better to demand that the inspection be made regardless. The inspector Ulloa was still at the Nazas River. The fact that the inspection had been held would add weight to don Juan's position.

As he left don Francisco's tent, the general's pace quickened. As he walked toward his quarters, eyes fixed straight ahead, he failed to acknowledge the deferential greetings of the soldiers who crossed his path. Once in his tent, he went straight to his camp table and started writing furiously to the notary and secretary of the expedition and to don Lope, the inspector. "I call on you to furnish me with an affidavit . . . your Grace is aware that in compliance with the capitulations which I made with his Majesty and with viceroy don Luis de Velasco, I am staying with my army at this place called Casco in Nueva Vizcaya, though a considerable portion of it is at Santa Bárbara. To assemble it I have spent large sums. . . ."

The first letter written on the 28 November was followed by two more, each stronger in tone. On 9 December, Ulloa agreed to resume the inspection, which started the same day at Casco, where expedition headquarters had been established.

On 15 January, Ulloa was recalled to the capital. He had been appointed general of the Philippine fleet. Since the inspection at Santa Bárbara and at some smaller sites had not been held, Ulloa appointed Francisco de Esquibel to finish the task. On 1 February don Juan and the inspector proceeded several leagues farther north to San Bartolomé to continue the inspection. They returned to Casco for the muster that was held on 17 February 1597.

The inspection revealed that Oñate had in all respects met the requirements of the contract, but this did not deter Ulloa before he left from issuing a warning to the general not to start out nor to modify the royal *cédula* from the king pertaining to the expedition. The successful conclusion of the inspection was followed by a mild optimism in the camp.

Cristóbal felt proud that he had passed muster on his own and not as the general's son. "Now that they know we are ready, they will let us go, verdad Papá?" he said as he looked up from playing with toy soldiers he had received as a present several years before on the day of the wise men.

"Ahora sí hijo [now, yes, son]," answered don Luis tenderly.

As the days passed and no word arrived, Oñate embarked on a campaign to reassure his soldiers, settlers, and their families. Although he felt frightened at the prospect of an outright rejection, he never showed it, except at times to his nephews and to don Francisco. When asked when the expedition would leave, he would answer. "Any day now. You see the inspection is over and we are ready."

At times he would stop by a family tent and talk with the young people, asking them what their plans were once they arrived in New

Mexico. The presence of Cristóbal on some of those visits would reassure the mothers who worried about their own children. "Don Juan also has a child and without a mother to look out after him," some women would say to each other.

Captain Cessar had not shaken off the dust from the cattle roundup when Captain Gasco appeared at the entrance to his tent. "Capitan Cessar, se puede."

"Sí, entra Luis," answered the older man, who tried to hide his fatigue, "what can I do for you?"

"Nothing, thank you; I just wanted to talk to you."

"Yes?" Cessar looked at him quizzically.

"All these delays and people deserting. Do you think we shall ever leave?"

"Well, right now it doesn't look too promising," answered the stocky captain from Cádiz with the chestnut-colored hair.

The younger red-headed captain shifted his stance. "Don Juan doesn't appear overly concerned."

"What do you mean?"

"Don't you think he should go before the Audiencia and the viceroy to answer the charges that he mismanaged his affairs and now does not have the funds to carry this expedition off?"

The more experienced captain reflected a while before he answered in a measured tone. "I admit that perhaps don Juan could do more to expedite this undertaking, but if I were you, Captain, I would not question don Juan's behavior too closely."

"No, I don't mean to criticize. I just wanted to hear your opinion."

"My opinion is that we shall soon be moving on," answered Cessar curtly.

## CHAPTER NINE

MEANWHILE, THE WHEEL of fortune was still spinning in Spain. The Council of the Indies still favored Ponce de León, but unbeknownst to them, his fortunes were flagging. First of all he fell sick, and since he was not a young man, it was a matter of concern. Then it was rumored that he had asked the king for a loan. The king issued a brief decree to the council stating: "Since it is understood that don Pedro Ponce is not nearly ready, that he does not have the necessary capital, it will be well to keep him waiting with good hopes, and in the meantime write to the viceroy with the utmost tact and secrecy instructing him that if he believes don Juan de Oñate has in readiness the people and other things needed for the expedition, he shall let him proceed, but that if he does not, he shall notify me without delay, in order that after due consideration I may be able to make the most suitable decision."

The viceroy was beginning to realize that Juan de Oñate had many influential supporters, such as don Santiago del Riego, *oídor* of the Audiencia and Juan Cortés, great grandson of the great *conquistador.* As early as November 1596 the viceroy in a change of heart had recommended to the king that Oñate be allowed to proceed, expressing fear that the whole enterprise would collapse. He cited the fact that the heart of the expedition lay with Oñate and his relatives who had organized and financed it in every respect, and doubted that anyone coming from Spain could generate as much effort and enthusiasm.

In the end the king was moved by practical considerations. Ponce de León did not have the money for the enterprise and he was not in good health. On 2 April the king acknowledged the viceroy's letter and authorized him to let Oñate proceed.

At the various camps, the optimism following the inspection turned to despondence as the settlers reasoned, "If they will not let us go now that we have shown them we are ready, they will never let us go." As people and families began to desert, the main topic of conversation revolved around speculation on who would be next. Some of the settlers would leave at night abandoning their livestock and many of their possessions.

Andrés Palomo had taken part in raids seeking slaves among the Chichimecas in the northernmost provinces. Bartolomé Gonzáles was returning from the corral in San Bartolomé after tending the horses when Palomo called to him, "Bartolomé, a word with you."

Bartolomé wondered what the gruff, husky man with the deep rasping voice wanted. "Sí, senor."

"No, señor no, call me Andrés."

The eighteen-year-old did not answer but stopped and looked at him openmouthed.

Andrés's smile did not do much to alter his vaguely menacing look. "Bring your friend, Marcos, tonight to the corral. I have an interesting proposition for you."

The sky was turning a dark purple as Andrés, accompanied by another man, approached the two young men who had answered the summons of Palomo, one of the camp brawlers.

Palomo got to the point. "Do you two men want to make some money and at the same time get away from this miserable camp?"

The two young men, flattered and overwhelmed, looked at each other and answered simply, "Sí."

Palomo smiled his half-menacing smile. "We are going to take several horses and go up north to look for stray Chichimecas."

"When?" asked Bartolomé timidly.

"Stay close to the camp and be ready to leave at any time. We'll contact you," Palomo answered as he turned to leave.

The two young men looked at each other again, wide-eyed, and shrugged their shoulders.

"Tío," warned Juan, "many of our people are deserting. If this keeps up, we will not have an expedition left."

"I don't blame them for leaving. Their children are running around like loose cattle. I am myself concerned about Cristóbal. His upbringing and education are being badly neglected," sighed don Juan.

"I have heard that the viceroy doubts that Ponce de León can mount an expedition. Is it true?" asked Juan.

"Yes, but he is not the one to decide. If only we had someone to speak for us at the court," observed don Juan wistfully.

Toward the end of the summer, disputes that had been brewing among the six Franciscan friars surfaced once again. Friar Rodrigo Durán, the commissary, or head of the religious contingent on the expedition, resented the inclusion of a representative of the Inquisition, Fray Diego Márquez, among his friars. He had protested to his superiors, but to no avail. The long delays added to their loss of enthusiasm, until one day friar Rodrigo came to don Juan to announce their decision to leave. Only Fray Diego; Fray Francisco de San Miguel, the general's sixty-nine-year-old confessor; and Fray Cristóbal de Salazar remained with the expedition at San Bartolomé.

The defection of the friars apparently encouraged some of the frustrated soldiers to mutiny. Knowing that this would deal a mortal blow to the expedition, don Juan, upon hearing of the mutineers' plans from one of his pages, immediately summoned a council of war. The task of quelling the uprising was given to Juan. "You must put an end to this movement before it spreads. You are authorized to take any action you deem necessary," don Juan instructed the *maese de campo*.

"Why don't you let me take care of it," interrupted Vicente.

Juan looked at his uncle, whose eyes narrowed slightly, but who nodded after a brief hesitation.

"A sus ordenes, mi general [at your orders, general]," snapped Vicente.

After discussing the matter with his brother, Juan, he selected a detachment of soldiers and within an hour left for the northernmost camp to confront the would-be mutineers. Three days later he arrived at San Bartolomé, and as he approached, the rebels, who had not been forewarned but who expected a reaction from the general, started for their horses. The *sargento mayor* and his men, who were mounted and armed, easily overtook them and surrounded them. Without hesitation Zaldívar pointed his sword at the leader, Andrés Palomo, and barked a command, "Off with his head." The terrified soldier was led off to a summary execution. The troop commander turned his horse around and went off in a slow trot, confident that the example would have its effect.

Several evenings later when Vicente got back to Casco, and news of the execution had spread, there was great consternation and much grumbling around the soldiers' campfire. Doña Eufemia, had long been wanting to express her feelings on the unrest that was turning to anarchy in the camp. Her husband had been opposed to such an action, but on this night she felt she could no longer put it off. As she approached the campfire she shouted, "Listen to me, listen to me." As the surprised soldiers quieted down, she declaimed, "Tell me, noble soldiers, where is the courage which you so professed when you enlisted in this noble cause? Why did you give then to understand that nothing could resist the might of your arms if now you turn your back and ignobly desert? What explanation have you for such conduct if you hold yourselves men?

"For shame! Such are not the actions of Spaniards. Even though everything else might be lost, there is yet land on the banks of some mighty river where we may raise a great city and immortalize our names. To such a place we can go and it would be better to do so after halting to rest than to retrace our steps, and incur upon ourselves and our posterity a stigma which could never be erased."

Cristóbal, who had overhead a conversation between don Juan and Vicente about Palomo's beheading, told his friend, Paco Cessar about it. "The bad soldier had his head cut off. I'm afraid it could happen to us or to my father."

His friend stared at him in terrified disbelief.

The following day don Juan called for a consultation with his staff.

"Gentlemen," he began, "the tragic events of the last few days are a call to action if we are to save this expedition. There does not appear to be much hope, but what can we do but persevere? It does appear that Ponce is no longer under consideration. Moreover, the viceroy is now on our side, so that it is probably just a matter of time."

"Yes, but how long can the people hold out," interrupted the treasurer, Captain Gasco.

"That is precisely what I wish to discuss today. This camp has become a nightmare to many and San Bartolomé is without leadership. We have to move in order to consolidate the camp."

"But won't that be construed as disobedience if we start northward again?" asked Captain Sosa de Peñalosa.

"Perhaps," interjected Vicente, "but we shall be again encamped when they find out."

On 1 August 1597 the dispirited army gathered its livestock, loaded its depleted supplies, and headed for San Bartolomé, twenty-eight leagues away on the northern side of the Río Nazas. After the novelty of the move had worn off, once again the camp settled into forlorn dejection.

In the late summer of 1597 Oñate had stopped making the rounds of the camps. It was as if now there was little more he could do. He knew that if they did not receive good news by the onset of winter, what was left of his force would finally disintegrate. The lethargy he was feeling permeated the whole camp, which was quiet and listlessly broiling in the sun. Only the drone of the flies broke the stifling silence. Don Juan, lying on his cot, lapsed into a fitful sleep of troubled dreams. He dreamed the expedition was departing. He was at the rear of the column trying to get his gear together. He had not been ready when it was picked up earlier, and now the host was leaving him behind.

"Don Juan, don Juan," he heard above the din of the creaking wheels and neighing horses. He awakened with a start. It was his page, Jorge de Zumaya, standing at the door to the tent. "Don Juan, a messenger is here with a letter from the viceroy."

Don Juan got up, went to the wash basin, and doused his thinning hair with his hands, then stepped out to receive the message. His face flushed as he read, and he reeled slightly. Holding the letter in his right hand he let his arm drop and he stared straight ahead for a moment. "Por fin, thanks be to God," he muttered.

# CHAPTER TEN

THAT NIGHT AFTER he had announced to the camp that they were finally authorized to make their departure, there was no jubilation among the settlers. Some had already made up their minds to leave the expedition. Others did not know what to think; but to most going to New Mexico no longer held any fascination. Toasts were made and don Juan was congratulated but there were few smiles. The only ones who appeared delighted were Cristóbal and his little friends. To them the trek to New Mexico still promised to be an exciting adventure.

The viceroy, conscious of the ravages the many delays could have caused the expedition, would not consent to let it leave without another inspection. For that task he named Juan Frías de Salazar, assuring the king that he was a man of integrity who would give full satisfaction in this or any matter.

On 17 November 1597, Frías summoned Oñate to break camp and proceed to a location designated by the inspector. Oñate refused to move, saying it would be a terrible inconvenience to collect the whole expedition, move out, and then stop to unload everything. He wanted to have the inspection at the sites where they were already camped, at San Bartolomé where headquarters had been established, Casco, La Puana, and Santa Bárbara.

On the night of 1 December, Jorge came to the commander's tent, saying that a man by the name of Francisco López had just arrived on horseback and had asked to see his grace. The general put on his vest hurriedly and rushed out of the tent. "Francisco, amigo, what are you doing in this hell hole?" he blurted as he gave him an *abrazo*.

"I came to join you, Juan, I mean your excellency," he corrected himself.

"Truly, you want to go to New Mexico with me?"

"Certainly, here you have me with my horse. I am a horseman, a gentleman as you can see, joining you as did those who joined Garci Fernandez centuries ago in Castilla."

"And you shall be named hidalgo, too," laughed don Juan. "This is the first really good news I have had in months, Captain."

"Captain?" Francisco repeated quizzically.

"Yes, one of my captains left yesterday. He did not show up for the review. You shall take his place," answered don Juan as he embraced his friend again.

"But where is Guadalupe?" he continued.

Francisco shrugged his shoulders, "Back in Zacatecas, I guess."

"You guess," smiled don Juan. "I thought you were in love with her."

"I was, and perhaps I still am," he frowned slightly, "but I did not come here to set up a family home."

Don Juan put his arm around him. "Well, you are here my friend and I am glad."

On 8 December 1597, almost a month from the time of the first summons, General Oñate ordered his expedition to move out. On 21 December the notary of the expedition received the order to notify Oñate that the inspection would begin the following day, and the site chosen was at the San Gerónimo River, near the mines of Todos los Santos in the valley of San Gregorio, province of Santa Bárbara.

The expedition was short of livestock from what had been contracted. Some items such as short nails were not listed in the contract. The nails were counted at 13,500. This was done by placing one thousand nails in a dish of a balance scale and filling the other dish with the same weight. They were valued at 135 pesos. Another item not in the contract was four barrels of wine. The inspector wanted the barrels tapped to see if they really contained wine, but the notary took Captain Villagrá's word that they did. There were some supplies for the ladies, too, including Anjou cloth, petticoats, Holland cloth, black taffeta, London cloth, and even black Chinese damask.

Medicines and medical supplies had not been overlooked, from syringes and lancets to green ointment, white ointment, laxatives, sulphur, rose water and alum; neither had the articles for barter, in the form of glass beads, mirrors, combs, and hawk's bells. Food would be mainly on the hoof although such staples as flour, sugar, and chocolate were listed as were other items indispensable to an army, such as lances, halberds, harquebuses, swords, and corselets.

The soldiers were each required to declare what they were taking. This consisted mainly of arms, saddles, and other essential equipment. Captain Marcos Farfán de los Godos listed complete armor of cuisse, beaver, helmet, strong buckskin jacket, one harquebus, a sword, a dagger, and one halberd.

Captain Luis Gasco de Velasco listed the following items: one cart with oxen, ten horses for cavalry, one harquebus, one coat of mail, one sword, one gilded dagger, one helmet and beaver, some cuisses of mail, horse armor, two saddles—one *jineta*, one for bridle—three bridles and three pair of spurs.

Captain Gerónimo Márquez listed his belongings as one cart and oxen, thirty tame cows, thirty-five horses, one coat of mail, beaver and cuisse, horse armor, two harquebuses, two *jineta* saddles and one *estradiota,* one lance, six plowshares, four axes, and some iron hoops and ten iron wheel rims.

In his declaration he complained that when he left Michoacan, he had brought thirty equipped men and eighty horses, but that because of the delays, his people had scattered and that most of his goods were stolen, consumed, or lost. He still had, he declared, most of the tools he needed to work the land, and four boys and a girl to use them.

That evening as a group of men were chatting around a campfire, Captain Gasco came up and sat beside Captain Márquez. "I see you are taking some formidable weapons for the conquest—plowshares."

Márquez turned to him with a smile. "We can always plow under the ones we kill."

Gasco laughed, and then said drily, "I am not going to work the land with my hands."

Márquez continued smiling. "Maybe I can plant enough for both of us."

The expedition was found to be seventy-one soldiers short of the two hundred Oñate had agreed to take. Don Juan appealed for help once again to his cousin, doña Ana de Zaldívar and her husband, Juan Guerra, who were owners of the rich mines at Aviro in the northern frontier. The rich couple agreed without hesitation. In a document issued 27 January 1598, they stated, "We pledge ourselves to make up at our expense any and all requirements imposed upon us by the viceroy, count of Monterrey, to complete the deficiencies that Juan de Frías Salazar, commissary general, may have found in the inspection and may demand to be filled." Their interest in helping don Juan was reinforced by the fact that their sixteen-year-old son Juan had enlisted in the expedition as a soldier.

The main part of the inspection took place at the arroyo of San Gerónimo, which lay a few leagues to the north of San Bartolomé. It lasted from 22 January 1598 to the twenty-sixth of the same month. Since Frías Salazar insisted on continuing the inspection enroute, on the twenty-sixth the expedition set out, stopping at the Todos las Santos mines.

Thirty-six-year-old Captain Diego de Zubía had been raised in the northern frontier of Nueva Galicia. The scar on his forehead attested to many a skirmish with the Chichimecas. Tomorrow he was getting married. The primitive village of Todos las Santos had the last church on the endless desert plain to the north.

Tonight was his last night as a bachelor, and he was having a few drinks with Captains Pablo de Aguilar and Alonso de Sosa. "Señor procurador, by tomorrow at this time you will be enjoying the nuptial bed," laughed Pablo.

"You two have been enjoying it for some time, tell me about it," chuckled Diego.

"Yes, and Pablo here left one of the most beautiful women in New Spain to come on this horrible expedition," said Alonso affecting a grimace.

"What is so horrible about it?" asked the darkly handsome Aguilar.

Sosa's face went from a sham scowl to a genuine sour look. "Well, it might not be so bad if we had a real leader."

Aguilar chided, "Be careful. You are speaking in the presence of the purveyor general."

"Except that the purveyor agrees with Alonso," half smiled Diego.

The sun was just starting to show as the small wedding party, led by the royal ensign who escorted his comely auburn-haired daughter, Juana, entered the front door of the diminutive church. Doña Eufemia followed with her older children. From a side door entered Captain Zubía, escorted by his friend and cousin, Captain Sosa. Don Juan was one of the last to enter; he took a seat at the rear of the church.

The day following the wedding, the mass of wagons, people, and livestock once more spread across the flat countryside like the shadow of a cloud slowly moving on to places that were given names when the stop was recorded. They stopped at Ojo de Agua Honda, Amosso Arroyo, arriving finally at the Río de las Conchas on 20 January.

Since the Spaniards had a practice of crossing a river before making camp, they did so immediately upon arrival. Oñate, sensing a reluctance by his soldiers to cross the rushing waters, mounted a charger and dashed across shouting, "Follow me." He crossed back, the more to impress the timid.

When it came time to cross the sheep, some became waterlogged because of their thick wool. The general ordered a pontoon bridge made of wagon wheels secured by ropes and covered with logs made from felled trees and leveled with earth. After the sheep had crossed safely, Oñate ordered the bridge destroyed as a security measure.

The following morning the inspector departed for Mexico City without as much as a word of encouragement or farewell. When the announcement was made that Frías de Salazar had left, a great cheer went up, which the crabby but dedicated old miner must have heard as he headed back to civilization.

## CHAPTER ELEVEN

On 7 February, the army finally started out for the mythical North with don Juan de Oñate, and only he, in command. Singing broke out as the wagons creaked to a start on that momentous day. Children ran alongside shrieking. One hundred twenty-nine Spanish soldiers and their families, accompanied by more than one hundred Indians who came along as servants and livestock drivers, were breaking their bond with the past and heading out to an uncertain future in an unfathomed land. Women riding in the carts must have shivered at the thought that the stirring but dreaded hour had arrived. Mothers no doubt held their infant children a little closer as the order to start was given.

There was still a feeling of elation when camp was made the first night. It was only three leagues beyond the Conchas River, but the settlers, who had been waiting for almost two years, felt as if a great barrier had been crossed and that they were now out of reach. Juan de Oñate went to several tents and gatherings to thank his people for their steadfastness. He especially thanked doña Eufemia for her encouragement of the disgruntled soldiers back at Casco. Don Francisco got up from his chair as he heard his wife greet the general. "Buenas tardes, don Juan, now we are finally free of the bureaucrats," she greeted the general.

"Yes, thank God," answered don Juan. "Ah, don Francisco," he interrupted himself as he saw the lieutenant governor getting up, "Please don't get up."

Don Francisco stood and gestured to a chair saying, "Por favor."

"Now it is in the hands of our Lord," ventured don Juan.

"And he has placed this great venture in your hands and we shall all help you," don Francisco added gently.

"Gracias, don Francisco. It has been a terrible time for all of us and I am indeed grateful to you, dona Eufemia, and all the loyal people in the expedition. I hope the frustrations and hardships had a purpose. Maybe our trials strengthened us and brought us closer together," sighed don Juan.

From the Sosa de Peñalosa tent, don Juan went to that of his friend, Francisco, who was living in one given to him by the general. "Entre su excelencia," greeted Francisco, as don Juan approached his tent.

"Francisco, when we are alone, please call me Juan," remonstrated the general.

"Either way now seems difficult to me," countered Francisco.

"Well, what do you think?" asked don Juan.

"It is not like the campaigns with don Luis, with all these women and children around," answered Francisco glumly.

"Well, you must remember this is not a military campaign. We are going to New Mexico as settlers and to christianize Indians, not to fight them," admonished don Juan.

"Well, I don't suppose they will just welcome us with open arms," blurted Francisco, eyes flashing.

"That is our hope," replied don Juan softly.

"What does one do here at night," asked Francisco smiling.

"Rest up for the following day," don Juan answered, smiling back.

"Will you have a drink?" asked Francisco as he started to turn toward a camp table with a bottle on it.

"No, gracias," declined don Juan. "I am tired, and my bed calls. Hasta mañana, amigo."

On the way to his tent the general heard laughing and shouting by a big campfire. As he approached, he could hear two servants holding a mock inspection. "Y esto qué es? [and what is this?]" said one in mock seriousness.

"It is a sword," answered the other, holding a stick.

"And what is it for?"

"It is for sticking pigs; and for thrashing you, you scoundrel who won't let us go." The soldiers were roaring. Don Juan laughed and shook his head as he went on.

On 10 February, the army arrived at the San Pedro River, a scant nine leagues north of the Conchas River. Because the expedition had to wait for the friars, the general called for a halt. With the exception of fray Francisco de San Miguel and fray Cristóbal de Salazar, Oñate's cousin, the original friars assigned to the expedition had tired of waiting and had abandoned the enterprise. Captain Farfán had been assigned the task of escorting the inspector back and of bringing fray

Alonzo Martínez, the commissary, or friar in charge, and his five new missionaries and two lay brothers to the expedition.

The day after arriving at the San Pedro River, the general called a council of his officials. Present were the *maese de campo,* the *sargento mayor,* the *tesorero,* and the *alferez real.* "Caballeros," started Oñate, "I do not know how long we shall have to wait here for the friars, but this pause gives us an opportunity to do some planning. You all know that the interminable delay caused most of us to lose livestock and supplies, and this waiting for the friars will not help matters—any suggestions?"

"Well, I don't know what we can do about livestock and supplies, but it seems obvious that we should proceed as fast as we can to our destination," offered Sosa de Peñalosa. "Doña Eufemia and I are frankly worried about having enough to feed our family."

"What can we do?" asked Juan de Zaldívar, the army commander. "We can't travel more than three or four leagues a day more or less."

"Maybe we can find a shortcut," suggested Vicente, the troop commander. "The Espejo expedition traveled along the Conchas to the confluence with the Río del Norte, then northeastward to a point where the northern river turns almost due north. Why can't we go straight to that point?"

"That would be dangerous," suggested Gasco de Velasco, the treasurer. "We would be taking a great risk of running out of water."

"Or even of getting lost," added the *maese de campo.*

"Tío, pardon, your excellency," interrupted Vicente. "One of us could take a small force and find the way."

"I shall go," blurted Juan de Zaldívar.

"No, Juan, I need you here, said don Juan calmly. "And besides I must reflect on this."

The next day the general had lunch with his two nephews. Before they began to eat, Oñate said, "Juan, I have decided to send Vicente up ahead. How long do you think it will take him?"

"Well," answered Juan, "the confluence is about thirty-five leagues from here, and according to San Manuel, who was with Espejo, it is about fifty leagues straight to where the river heads due north. A small party on horseback should make it there and back in three weeks or less."

"That is a long time, but then we don't know how much longer we have to wait for the friars," mused Oñate.

"Well, Tío, asked Vicente, "when do I set out?"

"Tomorrow, if you can. If we are going to do it, we can't wait."

That afternoon Vicente was busy selecting his companions and packing his supplies. The following day broke with high, red clouds streaking across the sky. The sun shone wanly through them as if warning of an impending storm. Vicente, nevertheless, was in high spirits, for he was embarking on his first mission as *sargento mayor*. He was accompanied by seventeen soldiers each, with an extra horse carrying arms and provisions, and three Indian guides. Crossing the San Pedro River, they headed northwest along a great dry plain without many landmarks. The guides who had professed to know the territory soon lost their bearings, and the party became lost.

The *sargento mayor*, determined to accomplish his mission, pushed on without having a precise idea of where they were going. After several days they sighted a campfire. Approaching it cautiously, they came upon a small group of Indians. In their first encounter with the nomadic inhabitants beyond the northern frontier, they captured four of them without a struggle; they promised to set them free if they would guide them to the Río del Norte. The startled desert rovers, once they got over their fright, acquiesced. Enroute they endured three days without water until they discovered a spring. As they neared their destination, their food supply became so depleted that upon arriving at the river they were obliged to kill one of their horses, which provided them with a welcome feast.

On the way back to the army, they did not fare much better. The general, worried about their delay in returning, dispatched his friend, Francisco, along with Captain Villagrá and a small group to look for them. After a journey of ten days the rescue party met up with Zaldívar and his soldiers, who were once again without water and food.

After a month's absence the troop commander and his rescuers returned to the camp at the San Pedro River, having been initiated into the rigors of the great northern desert, but armed with the information that would get the expedition to the big river.

The general meanwhile had word that the replacements for the defecting friars were on their way to join up with him. The presence of fray Diego Márquez, representative of the Inquisition, had been protested to the order of San Francisco; after many complaints by the commissary, Father Durán, he had been recalled from the Río Conchas. As Captain Farfán approached the San Pedro camp with the new friars, the general assembled his entire army to greet them. He dismounted as they approached, and when the new father commissary dismounted also, don Juan knelt on one knee before him. Fray Alonzo de Martínez bowed and offered his hand. As they embraced a great cheer went up. The ceremony was followed by a banquet under some shady trees. The new friars accompanying the father commissary were Fathers Andrés Corchado, Juan Claros, Alonso de Lugo, Juan de Rozas, Francisco de Zamora, two lay brothers, Pedro de Vergara and Juan de San Buenaventura and three Indian *donados*, lay assistant Juan de Dios, Francisco, and Martín.

## CHAPTER TWELVE

Now that the expedition was intact, and a route had been discovered to the great Río del Norte, the time had come for the final push. On the tenth, after a Mass celebrated by the commissary, Oñate's massive army of men and livestock began to spread across the plain. On the twelfth it reached the Nombre de Dios River. A camp was established on the fourteenth at an oak grove farther up the river. The army stayed four days at this camp permitting the *sargento mayor* and his party to rest from the ordeal of the past month.

On the 19 March they reached a site given the name of Agua de San Joseph. Because the following day was the day of the Blessed Sacrament, the general ordered a chapel built in its honor. Throughout the day of the twentieth the people of the expedition came to pray for protection and for help in taking the holy faith to New Mexico. Captain Villagrá was to write later that many of the men, including the general, scourged themselves that day. Be that as it may, they were all able to ride three leagues the following day and another three the day after that, arriving at a grove near a water spout. The place was named Resurrection, for the following day was Easter Sunday. The Lenten season was now over and optimism was rekindled as the day was spent resting and rejoicing.

On Easter Monday the expedition moved out with renewed resolve. Holy Week, the week of penance and reflection was now behind them. The joyful day had come and today was as the beginning of a new cycle. Once again the *sargento mayor* was sent ahead to scout a trail for the host, who remained closely behind.

On 1 April the expedition lumbered for several leagues without encountering a trace of water. Every day the land seemed to get more arid. The wind was blowing unmercifully, contributing to the dehydration that was slowly setting in on man and beast. As don Juan started to drink the last of the water in his canteen, he hesitated. A few minutes later he reined his horse in slightly to slow its pace. As Cristóbal came alongside him he asked him if he had some water. Cristóbal answered, "No, papá, but I am not thirsty."

Don Juan took the boy's canteen and poured his water into it. Cristóbal did not question his father's action, but only smiled as don Juan patted him on the back. As night approached the army came to a halt. The wind had picked up and the skies darkened. Suddenly the ground was dotted with puffs of dust as huge drops of rain began to fall. Soon it was a cloudburst of major proportions. Large pools were formed, and men and beasts drank their fill. Fray Alonso suggested to the general that the place be named Socorro del Cielo to commemorate the miraculous relief that fell from the sky.

Revived and reanimated by the "miraculous rain," the army traveled for two days until it reached the Río de la Mentira. Captain Farfán de los Godos suggested the name because of the mendacious character of the desert river. He said it had everything a river should have except water.

At the beginning of the sand dunes approximately six leagues from the Río del Norte, water once again became scarce and the livestock had to be driven in haste all the way to the river. For the people, a halt was called at the dunes to permit stragglers to catch up. An Indian boy was buried during this seven-day stop ordered by the general in preparation for the final crossing into New Mexico. The burial was attended by the boy's immediate family, the women in the family his mother served, and by doña Eufemia.

The day after leaving the weeklong encampment the expedition struggled through the sand dunes and spent the night without water. The following day was hot for the season, and the wind blew all day. There was no water until the river was reached at sundown on the twentieth. Those who were on horseback drove their horses into the river. The women and children took off their shoes and shouted gleefully as they splashed and drank at the banks of the mighty river.

That night the soldiers lit a bonfire, the women and children caught fish, and everybody feasted. It was getting dark, and the glow of the fire was blending with the light of day when don Juan spoke to his people in kindly, praising tones recounting the hardships they had been through. He had particularly tender words for the women and children who had endured days without drink and sufficient sustenance. He reminded them of the miraculous shower that had succored them when they needed it. Here they remained seven days resting, repairing wagons and equipment, and planning the final *entrada* into the land of the pueblos to the north.

On the twentieth-sixth, for the first time since Easter Sunday, the entire army was together in one place. "When are you going to take possession, Uncle?" asked Juan de Zaldívar that evening as he and Captain Farfán sat around the campfire chatting with the general.

"I was thinking I would delay it until we know a bit more about this country," answered the commander. "We shall soon be going further up the river. Captain Aguilar is leaving tomorrow to reconnoiter," added the general.

"I would like to present a little play on that day," interjected Captain Farfán. "It would commemorate the trials and sacrifices of those who came before us."

"That would be a good idea," smiled don Juan. "Maybe we can have the ceremony on Ascension Day."

The expedition traveled slowly up the river as they awaited trail information from Captain Aguilar. On the twenty-ninth the general decided that he would not wait for him any longer and he would hold the ceremony the next day, for it was Ascension Day. A chapel for the purpose was built in the form of a bower in a shady grove. On 30 April 1598, after solemn Mass, the entire army drew up in formation. First came a fanfare from the trumpets, and then the general began a long speech. "In the name of the most Holy Trinity and of the eternal Unity, Deity, and Majesty, God the Father, and Son, and the Holy Ghost." He finished, "In the name of the most Christian king, don Felipe, our lord, the defender and protector of the Holy Church, and its true son, and in the name of the Crown of Castile, and of the kings that from its glorious progeny may reign therein and for my said government, I take possession once, twice, and thrice, and all the times I can and must, of the actual jurisdiction, civil as well as criminal, of the lands of the said Río del Norte without exception whatsoever, with all its meadows and pasture grounds and passes. And this possession is to include all other lands, pueblos, cities, villas of whatsoever nature now founded in the kingdom and province of New Mexico and all the neighboring and adjoining lands thereto."

When the governor ended his pronouncement, the trumpets blasted another fanfare and the harquebusiers fired a salute as the general set in place the royal standard. The act of possession was signed by the general and his officers and by all the friars present. Thus the immeasurable expanse of land beyond the northern or wild river later to be known as the big river became officially a part of the largest empire the world had ever known.

After the ceremony Francisco asked the governor, "How far does this other Mexican Kingdom extend?"

Don Juan arched his eyebrows, "Who knows? North to the icy Straits of Anian, west to the Southern Sea, and east to the Atlantic Ocean."

Francisco arched his own eyebrows and smiled.

None of the previous inhabitants had ever pretended to exercise sovereignty over such a mighty continent, if indeed they could visualize it as one. Some twenty to twenty-five thousand years before the Castilian navigator of Italian descent had made his first landfall on this new world, nomadic Asiatics had started wandering across the land bridge exposed by the receding frozen waters of the latest ice age. Twelve or fifteen thousand years of peregrination had brought them to the same land the small band of only slightly less bewildered settlers were now starting to penetrate.

Cabeza de Vaca, who roamed the wilds of Teja territory, although he called attention to the land of people who lived in multistoried houses, did not give it a name when he passed just south of it. It was Juan de Ibarra—explorer, founder, and developer of northern New Spain, who ranged over modern Sonora and the southern extremity of the land that had first been called Cíbola—who referred to it as a possible replication of the Aztec empire, another Mexico—*una Nueva Mexico.*

Following the Mass, the drama written by Captain Farfán was enacted. It was with great emotion that some of the soldiers played the part of the friars and others that of Indians coming humbly and kneeling before the priests to be received into the holy faith.

After the ceremony, the army feasted on fish and beef, eating the heartiest meal since departing the Nazas River. The governor, still flushed with the heady events of the day, which had transformed him from a leader of an expedition to a governor and captain general, smiled as he asked his friend Francisco, "What do you think of all this?"

Francisco, who was sitting nonchalantly by the fire staring at the starry sky, started to get up, but don Juan put his hand on his shoulder before sitting down beside his friend. "It isn't the campaigns with don Luis," smiled Francisco. "No hay Chichimecas [There are no Chichimecas]."

"No, Francisco, these Indians are not wild. They are gentle Indians as you will see."

"Then why did you bring an army?"

"Well, one never knows; but we did not come to conquer, only to take possession peacefully and to spread the faith," answered don Juan.

"Do you think you will find anything of value?" asked Francisco in a doubting tone.

"Yes, I think so," retorted don Juan. "If not gold in the streets, perhaps mines such as we found in Zacatecas and other places."

"But you had mines in Zacatecas," countered Francisco.

"Yes, but I was not governor of a kingdom. Here I shall be, and perhaps even marquis," don Juan answered with a hint of haughtiness.

"Well, I hope you find what you are looking for," said Francisco in a falling voice.

"Y tú, Francisco, what do you want out of all this? You can have an encomienda you know," said don Juan solicitously.

"No, I came out of curiosity. Zacatecas was getting me down. I don't know what I want."

## CHAPTER THIRTEEN

THE FOLLOWING MORNING the sun broke on a horizon tinted with thin red clouds. By the time the expedition once more creaked to a start, wisps of wind were beginning to stir up dust devils. Despite the apprehension brought on by the threat of a windstorm, the elation of the previous day was still in the air, particularly among the younger people. By the time the army had traveled half a league up the river, a full-blown duststorm was in progress. The oxen put their heads down against the strong wind as they pulled the wagons as the drivers, who covered their noses and mouths with kerchiefs, urged them on and sometimes even pulled the reluctant beasts. The passengers huddled under blankets and coats. The riders were obliged to tie their hats down with their bandannas. After almost a league, a halt was called, but it was impossible to pitch tents. The wind let up only slightly at sundown. That evening there were very few fires lit and everyone except those on guard duty retired early. The following day the wind came back even stronger. The expedition managed to get started, but after a league and a half it came to a halt as if stopped in its tracks by a wall of dust. At sundown the wind died down but the dust remained. Everything the settlers drank and ate tasted of it. "Dios mío," exclaimed one of doña Eufemia's Indian servants. "It looks like the end of the world."

The following morning everyone was up early after a night of sound sleep. The sun was shining brightly in a perfectly clean and blue sky. Among the trees along the river, the birds were chirping incessantly. Don Juan thought of that other beautiful morning in Zacatecas when he had looked upon Isabel's face for the last time. It seemed as if centuries had passed, yet Cristóbal at his side was still a child. He looked at his son, who had spent the night in his tent. He was sleeping in carefree innocence, his long dark hair, a legacy from Moctezuma, his great, great grandfather, strewn about his face. He had come to see his father the evening before. Don Juan, feeling that Cristóbal was scared, asked him to spend the night. That morning he resolved to keep him close to him for a while rather than making a soldier of him just yet.

The first encounter with the Indians of the territory occurred on 3 May. The expedition had traveled up the river five and a half leagues. The *sargento mayor* had been looking for a ford in the river when he came across a small camp. The Spaniards, who were unarmed, approached the Indians, who showed no sign of fear or hostility. Four of them agreed to go to the Spanish camp to meet the governor. The governor ordered that clothing and gifts be given to them. The Spaniards, true to their nature, gave them a nickname calling them mule drivers because to say, "yes," they made the same clicking noise that Spanish muleteers used in getting their mules to move.

The next day at the ford, forty of the same group of Indians showed up with a large quantity of fish making the sign of the cross and uttering the Spanish words for *tame* and *friends*. They told the Spaniards that the towns of the northern Indians were eight days of travel up the river.

Governor Oñate felt more confident after talking to the Indians from the region. He felt as if now he was about to enter his own jurisdiction, and he had a better idea of what to expect ahead. The river would take them to their destination without any danger of running out of water as they had done crossing the vast arid plain. The Indians would probably prove to be just as friendly as the ones they had already met. After all, they were "gente vestida" (people with clothes on), more civilized and more settled than the Chichimecas to the south.

The day after they left the ford, they came across the ruts left by the wagons of the Castaño de Sosa-Morlete expeditions of 1590 and 1591. Gaspar Castaño de Sosa had been lieutenant governor of the province of Nuevo Leon, east of the modern-day state of Chihuahua and south of Texas, when the governor was arrested by the Inquisition in 1589. Castaño, as acting governor, apparently on impulse and discouraged by the lack of opportunity in Nuevo León, gathered all of the colonists in the vicinity of Almaden (present-day Monclova) and moved them toward the lands to the north without any authorization whatsoever. They left on 27 July 1590, and traveled up the Río Bravo (Grande) to the Río Salado (Pecos) and then northward through eastern New Mexico to Cicuye, later known as Pecos. He explored the land of the pueblos until Captain Juan Morlete arrived to arrest him and take him back to New Spain in chains.

Thus Oñate's multitude would not be penetrating completely unknown territory. The general, however, decided to send Captain Aguilar to search for the first settlement. The captain was warned under penalty of death not to enter any villages, as such action would alert and possibly frighten the Indians.

By 11 May the expedition had reached a place familiar to some of the soldiers who had been in New Mexico before—the spot where Morlete had hanged four Indians for stealing horses. By the fifteenth the intruders were more than halfway to the settlements. This was the day of the Holy Trinity. The seven-year-old son of Gerónimo de Heredia, sergeant in the company of Captain Gerónimo Márquez, had been ill with a fever since the day after the river had been forded. His mother, María, had been caring for him day and night for twelve days. Bringing medicine or some little tidbit for him, doña Eufemia had visited the child every night. On the sixteenth, when the train halted because some of the oxen had strayed, Manuelito was given a respite from the bumpy ride on the wagon. He appeared to get better and had a restful sleep. On the seventeenth once again he awoke with a fever. As the column began to pull out, he was put on the family wagon. After one league of travel, he died in his mother's arms. María started kissing the child, and sobbing, until it appeared she would choke. One of the soldiers on horseback near the wagon galloped to the head of the column, "Don Juan, don Juan, General. Sergeant Heredia's son has just died."

The general raised his arm to signal a halt, reined his horse into a hard turn, and broke into a gallop. When he arrived at the sergeant's wagon, María was still holding her son, rocking him gently. Oblivious to those around her, her delirious sobs had softened to a low moan. Her fourteen-year-old daughter Esperanza sat dry eyed and staring straight ahead beside her.

The expedition made camp for the day. A brief religious ceremony during which Father San Miguel attempted to console the family was held and Manuelito was buried in the wilderness. An entry was made on the expedition log, "Today we buried a child."

The day after the burial of Manuelito, the expedition did not move because the oxen had still not been completely rounded up. Traveling was now getting very difficult because of the uneven terrain near the river. When the army once more got underway on the nineteenth, it could advance only one league. On the twentieth the terrain was so rough that they stopped at noon. Toward evening Captain Aguilar rode into camp. The general sent word that he wanted to see him immediately. Captain Aguilar inclined his head almost imperceptibly, and said, "A sus órdenes."

"What do you have to report?" asked the general stiffly.

"The terrain is impossible near the river. We shall have to go inland if we are going to get the wagons through," answered Aguilar.

"Yes, it seems so; and the Indians?" continued the general.

"Well, the first pueblo is about eighteen leagues away. The natives appear friendly, but we did not see anything of value in the pueblo."

"What, you entered the pueblo against my orders?" Oñate's face turned crimson.

"Yes, I thought it was a good opportunity," countered Aguilar, in a slightly defiant tone.

"Maese, arrest this man," shrieked the general. "We shall see what we are to do with him. Have him taken out immediately."

"We cannot tolerate that kind of insubordination," said the general later after calming down.

"I agree," joined the *sargento mayor.*

With the blood once again rising to his face, the general almost yelled, "We should execute him."

"Execute him?" gasped the *maese de campo.* "Isn't that a bit extreme?"

"No it isn't," broke in Ensign Juan Piñero. "He had his orders."

"Yes, but out in the field one sometimes has to use his own discretion, and . . ."

"No excuse," interrupted Vicente. "He is a troublemaker anyhow."

"Calm down, brother," said Juan in a soft voice.

"Very well, Juan. I won't execute him, but he would do well to watch his step," warned the general.

Early the next day as the expedition was preparing to move out, Alonso Robledo came to the *maese de campo*'s tent to tell him that his father, Ensign Pedro Robledo had died in his sleep. Later in the day Ensign Pedro Robledo of Maqueda, Spain, sixty years old, was buried.

His wife, Catalina, her face gaunt and weather-beaten, stood by impassively with her four sons and one daughter as the dry earth swallowed up the husband who had brought her and her first born from Extremadura an eternity ago.

From the information Captain Aguilar had provided, it became obvious that the expedition could no longer travel along the river. Oñate decided to leave the wagons along with the women and children and a detachment of soldiers for their protection near the site of Ensign Robledo's grave.

He went ahead with his horsemen and just a few carts to the east of the present-day Caballo Mountains. The main body of the expedition under command of the royal ensign was left to follow as best it could. This was the beginning of the Jornada del Muerto, or Way of Death, which was to become a part of the Camino Real from Santa Fe to New Spain. Future travelers would be warned, and thus better prepared.

Oñate and his light troop encountered trouble almost immediately when they ran out of water the first day. Two days later, still without water, which was so close but inaccessible across the barren mountain, one of their dogs appeared in their midst with muddy paws. A frantic search for water holes revealed two of them. But the lack of water continued to be a threat. An attempt to drive the horses to the river proved futile. The eastern bank was described in the expedition journal as "almost like cut rock"; they couldn't get through it to the water below. To make matters worse, the father commissary suffered a severe attack of gout.

Finally after six hellish days, late in the day of the twenty-seventh, they cleared the pesky mountains. In the distance they saw a black mesa by the river. At its foot they knew was Qualacú, the second of the Indian pueblos. The first one about two leagues south on the west side was bypassed.

On the twenty-eighth a Mass was said because the Spaniards, having turned toward the river, were about to make their first contact with the people of New Mexico. They traveled the four leagues to Qualacú, the largest of two villages. The inhabitants abandoned the pueblo at the first sight of the intruders from the south, but some of the Indians were reached and given gifts of trinkets. Oñate ordered his people to retire to the bank of the river where they pitched their tents and stayed for one month. The long stay was to accommodate the father commissary, whose gout had gotten worse. The purveyor general availed himself of the pause to replenish food supplies by collecting maize from the other settlements in the vicinity. Oñate, having received reports of bickering among the people who had stayed back to follow slowly, returned to the wagons to try to quell the disturbances. He had only mild success because by now the camp was divided between the malcontents and those who still had faith in the colonizing project.

On 14 June, with Oñate back, the advance party reached Teypana, which they renamed Socorro in gratitude of the generosity of the inhabitants, who not only did not flee as the others had done, but whose chief, Letoc, furnished them with accurate information of what to expect ahead. The travelers secured a large supply of maize from these kind people.

Four leagues up the river the Spaniards occupied a pueblo for the first time. This one was named Nueva Sevilla because Captain Farfán, who was from Sevilla, thought that in its position in relation to the river it resembled his hometown.

Another four leagues found the expedition occupying a newly built but abandoned pueblo, which received the name of San Juan Bautista in honor of St. John the Baptist, whose feast day it was the day after they arrived. Although the inhabitants had evacuated the town, they came to visit their uninvited guests. They were treated to a sham battle between the Moors and the Christians enacted by the soldiers. The *maese de campo* led one side and the *sargento mayor* the other. Francisco was asked by the *maese* to be on his side, but he excused himself by saying, "I would not know what to do. I'm just a cowboy."

The horsemen dressed in their best armor and attached colored ribbons to their helmets. The battleground was a green meadow by the river. After the two "armies" were assembled, a loud blast of trumpets signaled the beginning of the conflict. Both sides let out a cheer, which was soon accompanied by the sound of thundering hooves and finally by the clashing of steel against steel.

The Indians who witnessed the fray were very impressed. One of them, wishing to ingratiate himself with the general, came up to him and uttered in a loud voice the Spanish words, "jueves, viernes, sabado, domingo."

The general asked, "Did I hear right? Thursday, Friday, Saturday, Sunday?"

"That is what I heard," answered Captain Villagrá. "What did you say?" Villagrá asked the Indian. "What do you mean?" but the Indian would not say another word.

"He is mocking us," said a soldier in the crowd.

"Yes, arrest them," ordered the general.

As the loquacious Indian and his two comrades were apprehended, he uttered two more words, "Tomás, Cristóbal," as he pointed north.

The Spaniards found out that the Indian's name was don Lupe and that he was referring to two Indians from New Spain who had come with Castaño de Sosa and had remained in New Mexico when Castaño was taken back in chains by Morlete. This was a stroke of luck for the expedition. Now they would have effective interpreters.

The general was elated with this development and felt that making contact with Tomás and Cristóbal was now the first order of business. He thought they might be at the large and important pueblo of Puaray in the region of the Tigua speaking Indians. Leaving early the following day, Oñate and his advance party covered sixteen leagues with only two overnight stops; they arrived at Puaray on the twenty-seventh.

Here they were told that the two Spanish-speaking Indians were at the pueblo of Quiqui. Unwilling to wait, the general and his *maese de campo* set out for the pueblo six leagues away, without benefit of overnight rest.

"This is where friars Rodríguez and López were martyred," the general said softly to Juan as they left the confines of the village.

"Yes, so Farfán told me," answered the *maese*. They were referring to the two Franciscan priests who had, in spite of protests from their comrades, decided to stay in San Felipe de Nuevo Mexico, as the province was then known. They were members of the Chamuscado-Rodríguez expedition of 1581, which had reawakened interest in New Mexico, virtually forgotten since Vásquez de Coronado's disappointing expedition.

Arriving at daybreak at the village later to be called Santo Domingo, the general had a short conference in the cool morning air just as the first rays of sunshine were beginning to paint the sky over the eastern mountains a soft pink. After a brief discussion, the general decided to send the purveyor, Captain Zubía, and twelve soldiers to bring the two would-be interpreters and guides to him. They were still in bed when confronted by the Spanish soldiers. They went willingly with them to the edge of the pueblo where the general was waiting.

"We are Christians," said Cristóbal, "but we stayed here of our own free will."

"Yes," added Tomás, "we are married here and we have children. We do not wish to go back."

"We shall not force you to go back," said the general. "All we ask is for you to help us to know this country and its people better."

Tomás and Cristóbal, having no choice in the matter, were taken to Puaray to begin their new careers as interpreters and guides. The governor was impatient to begin the task of taking control of New Mexico. The day after the two Mexicans were conscripted, the *maese de campo* set out for Tzia pueblo. Two days later the general, his staff and guard visited two more pueblos, Katishtya and back to Quiqui, which they now named respectively San Felipe and Santo Domingo. The latter was chosen as the site for the first convent, which was given the name of Nuestra Señora de la Asunción.

The word soon went out from here to every corner of the Pueblo lands about the arrival of the Spaniards. They were no longer a novelty to the natives, however, and no longer inspired the awe of the early days—even though this time they constituted an army and they were accompanied by settlers.

Summoned by the governor on 6 July, chieftains along with their entourages began to converge on Santo Domingo. They made camp outside the pueblo, awaiting the dawn of the next day when a general council was to be held. As the time approached, the chiefs of seven pueblos gathered on a hill overlooking the village to await Governor Oñate. He rode up to them together with his *maese de campo*, the *sargento mayor*, the *alferez real*, and the commissary general. They all dismounted, save for a guard of eight soldiers who remained on their horses. One by one the chiefs approached the governor and dropped to one knee to pledge allegiance to the king. The governor took each one by the shoulders, had them rise, and then embraced them.

After the ceremony, the governor was elated at the ease with which the assumption of power was progressing. Now the principal concern was the establishment of a capital. Speaking to his lieutenant governor, the *alferez real*, Sosa de Peñalosa, he said, "We must find a suitable place for a capital before the wagons come up. As you know, Juan went back to Robledo's grave to fetch them. He should be arriving in a month or so. I have heard that the land of the Teguas is very attractive . . . more fertile . . . cooler," he huffed, wiping the sweat from his forehead. "Besides," he added, "they pledged obedience to the crown during Castaño de Sosa's expedition." The general took his ceremonial helmet off and, blowing air through pursed lips, said, "It would be good if we could escape this cursed heat."

As the advance party progressed northward along the Río del Norte, the vegetation started to get greener, the river deeper, and the air cooler, but the terrain rougher. On 11 August they reached a pueblo called, or so it seemed to Spanish ears, Okhe. It looked more appealing than any they had yet seen. Shade trees were in abundance and the fields near the confluence of the Río del Norte and a smaller river that met just above the village were greener than they had been since leaving San Bartolomé.

"Tío," said Juan de Zaldívar as he and the governor observed the pueblo from a hill, "we are getting into very hilly country. The carts had trouble getting to Bove or San Ildefonso, and it looks much rougher up ahead."

"Well, this is the best-looking location we have seen yet. Let us see how the natives react," smiled don Juan.

As the governor and his retinue entered the pueblo, the people of Okhe came out to greet them. Don Juan, as had become his custom upon meeting a friendly reception, dismounted and embraced the first Indian he came to. It was difficult to tell who was the leader. They were all dressed more or less the same and no one seemed to want to be at the head of the crowd. The village consisted of some fifty houses, and a few ceremonial *estufas*, or kivas. Most of the buildings were two-story houses, but a few had as many as four or five stories, each story recessed from the one under it to form a terrace. They were built around a large common area. The Spaniards were shown into the villagers' homes, where they were most graciously invited to take the noon meal. After the meal the newcomers pitched some of their tents in the open area and some on the outskirts of the pueblo.

That evening as the governor sat under a starry sky with his son, Cristóbal, he asked, "How do you like this place, son?"

Cristóbal looked up at the sky and answered, "How cool it is here at night. Yes, I like it. And the way we were received, it seems like a town of gentle people."

"San Juan de los Caballeros [San Juan of the Gentlemen]," muttered don Juan almost as if talking to himself.

## CHAPTER FOURTEEN

THE GOVERNOR SEEMED to be everywhere at once. He traveled to the Tigua pueblo of Picuries, then to Tayberon, the northernmost of all the settlements. The name of this pueblo was changed, as was the custom of the Spaniards, to Taos. It seems that some of the natives wore an emblem that resembled the Greek letter *tau.*

The whirlwind tour took in San Ildefonso, south of San Juan; San Marcos, a Keres-speaking settlement; and San Cristóbal, one of the Tano-speaking pueblos where doña Ines, who was taken back to New Spain by Castaño in 1590 was born. She was brought to New Mexico by Oñate as an interpreter but she either refused to speak her native tongue or had forgotten it. She apparently was not cast in the same mold as doña Marina, the great Malinche who was indispensable as an interpreter and guide to Cortés in the conquest of Mexico.

By the middle of the month the scouting party had visited Galisteo, another pueblo where the now extinct Tano language was spoken and the great pueblo of Cicuye, which Oñate's party started calling Pecos, the Keres word for this Towa-speaking settlement. At Pecos, Juan de San Buenaventura, a lay brother, acted as interpreter. He had been instructed by don Pedro Oróz, who had been taken to Mexico City by Espejo in 1583, and instructed by a friar by the name of Pedro Oróz, who gave the Pecos native not only his knowledge but also his name. Espejo's idea had been to use the Pecos Indian as interpreter but he died in Mexico City before any expedition could be organized. Before he died, he completed his linguistic task with Brother Juan who was putting his knowledge to good use.

After more than two weeks of state visits to his new dominions the governor went to Santo Domingo with the hope of meeting the *maese de campo,* who was bringing the main body of the army up from the first Indian settlements many leagues to the south. At Santo Domingo he received word that Juan and the settlers were just south of Puaray. On 10 August, the governor was back at San Juan, where there was much to be done, not least of which was the irrigation ditch that needed to be built for the physical survival of the colony and the church that would be just as indispensible to their spiritual well-being.

The day after returning to San Juan, the governor gave the order to impose a levy on the surrounding villages for a work force. The first day fifteen hundred Indians showed up to work on the canal. By now, some of the summer heat had abated, there was plenty to eat, and the era of good feeling continued as natives and Spaniards worked side by side on a project that would be of benefit to all.

On 18 August the long-awaited wagons arrived. The people in the wagons had been through a very disheartening experience. Separated from the vital elements of the expedition, they had suffered great discomfort from intense heat and even from hunger. Having spent the summer in the hottest and most arid part of the province, many experienced disappointment at the obvious poverty of the land. They spoke of the land as dry, hot, and dusty. It did not take long for those who had been in San Juan for some time to exchange ideas and impressions with the new arrivals. Grumbling, which had heretofore been undercover among small groups who muttered criticisms and complaints to each other, began to spread and to surface. "Sterile" and "poor" were added to the growing derogatory vocabulary of the disaffected would-be colonists.

Captain Aguilar had been left behind with the wagons in the shallow river valley near Ensign Robledo's grave to proceed at their own pace. During the hot summer in one of the most forbidding zones in the province he had nursed his grievance against don Juan for having threatened to execute him in front of many witnesses. He had company in the person of Captain Sosa, who simply was disgruntled.

Most of the colonists had been anxious to see their new home and to get settled. Captain Gerónimo Márquez was the most vocal in countering the growing disaffection stoked by Aguilar and Sosa.

"I support don Juan for two reasons," he told Aguilar in a confrontation that might have led to sword play if Márquez had been as quick tempered as Aguilar, "because the king has appointed him our leader, and because the main body of our expedition has not even arrived at our destination."

"And because you are always currying favor with him," snapped Aguilar.

"If loyalty to one's commander seems such to you, you are not much of a soldier."

"I'm not a soldier. I am an officer of the crown."

"Is that why you disdain the idea of working the land?" countered Gerónimo.

"I have my own reasons for coming and they do not include becoming a plowboy."

Captain Márquez shrugged his shoulders. "Some of us saved you once from getting arrested and perhaps executed. I would be very careful if I were you about spreading your discontent among our people."

Captain Aguilar's eyes narrowed and he dropped his hand to the hilt of his sword and stared at Márquez. Gerónimo's face hardened but he didn't make a move. As Aguilar turned without further word and stomped away, Gerónimo shook his head slowly.

Cristóbal had been watching from behind one of the wagons. As Aguilar turned to his friends and the confrontation had abated, the young Oñate looked around for a friendly face. He spotted Juan headed for the corral where the personal mounts were kept.

"May I go with you?" he shouted, catching up with his cousin.

"Of course you can," answered Juan. "Are you going to ride?"

"No, I just want to talk with you."

"Well, I am just going to see if the horses need some water. Why don't we sit under that tree and have a chat?"

"Thank you cousin," Cristóbal answered cheerfully.

As they sat down, Juan put his canteen to his lips, but before drinking offered, "Want some? It's terribly hot today, and tempers were also hot, weren't they?

"Yes," answered Cristóbal, "and that worries me."

"You shouldn't worry. There are always hotheads in every crowd."

"Yes, but some of them seem so unhappy. Why did they come?"

"I don't know," answered Juan.

"But, won't they harm Papá and the rest of us? Why don't we let them go?" asked Cristóbal anxiously.

"Because it will set a bad example. We all came here together. If people start deserting, what will happen to the rest of us?"

Cristóbal was somewhat reassured by Juan's answers, but he had something more on his mind.

"Why," he asked, "don't some of our people like the Indians? I found a friend, and he is very nice."

Juan could not hide a wan smile at Cristóbal's innocent question. "I agree that we should seek out friends among them as you did. After all, one of our reasons for coming is to bring them into the Christian faith. I don't know, Cristobalillo, that has always been a mystery to me. Many people seem to be suspicious of other people they don't know well, and who are a little different from them. That is what has caused most of the wars in this world."

Captain Gasco de Velasco was glad to see his two friends. "What a horrible place this Nuevo Mexico is," said graying Captain Sosa, shaking his head with a pout that made his chin look weaker.

After handshakes Captain Gasco answered, "It is not so bad up here."

Aguilar smiled ironically, "And what has your governor done except parade from pueblo to pueblo."

"Our governor, Pablo."

Captain Aguilar's smile vanished, "Not mine as you will soon see, and I am not the only one who thinks that this expedition is a failure. What has anyone found of value?"

Captain Sosa shuffled his feet slightly. "He is right. If the truth be told, most of the families would go back to New Spain tomorrow if they were given the chance."

Luis Gasco looked at the ground, his hand on his chin. "I don't entirely disagree with you, but I warn you to be careful, not so much of don Juan, but of Vicente. You know the reputation for . . . not exactly ruthlessness . . . in campaigns against the Chichimecas . . . and don't forget Palomo."

Aguilar's face turned red, "Well, I am not in the least afraid of him."

Captain Sosa sniffed in assent.

Two days after the caravan had arrived, a conspiracy to desert came to the attention of the governor. The leader, it was rumored, was the rebellious Captain Aguilar. The camp was divided on the question of punishing the likely deserters. The *sargento mayor* was in favor of making an example of the leaders. "Has not Captain Aguilar shown himself disloyal and disobedient on other occasions?" he argued.

The father commissary and the royal ensign, Sosa de Peñalosa counseled forgiveness and pointed out that one-third of the army was involved in the plot and that to punish even the leaders only might spark a dangerous mutiny. Juan de Zaldívar did not join the discussion, but after the governor had decided to forgive the conspirators, he said laconically, "You did well, uncle."

Cristóbal was confused by all the discussions among Vicente, his father, and Juan. He had not forgotten Palomo's execution, and now he worried that there would be more violence. He was afraid his father would be killed.

The following day was a day of reconciliation; the governor had pardoned all. There was much to celebrate. For the first time since Pedro Robledo's death the entire colony was reunited. The governor declared a holiday with tilting, bull fights, singing, dancing, and a comedy. After two days of fiesta, it was time to start building a church. On the twenty-third every able-bodied Spanish man gathered at the site selected for the house of worship. Some of the Indians were asked to help, but most mainly looked on as the building, large enough to accommodate all of the people of the camp, took shape. It was finished on 7 September.

On the eighth another great celebration was held. The day started with a solemn Mass during which the church was consecrated. The whole camp crowded in. The Indians, curious about the elation among the Spaniards, gathered outside as their uninvited guests concluded dedicating the first Christian church to be built in the new kingdom, the church of Saint John the Baptist. In the afternoon a sham battle between the Christians and Moors was held. Those playing the part of Christians were on foot armed with harquebuses and those who were Moors were on horseback wielding lances. Cristóbal begged his father to let him be one of the horsemen, even though they were the Moors. Don Juan was proud, though apprehensive, to see his son participate for the first time in a sham battle. The Spanish, of course, carried the day. The inhabitants of San Juan, who were still not completely over their awe of horses and Spanish arms, were very much impressed. Late in the afternoon a play was staged under a large cottonwood tree. The Indians were puzzled, wondering why the Spaniards would go through the same motions under the tree that they performed earlier in the day. The Spanish men cheered when the Spaniards scored a triumph and the women gasped when a killing was depicted.

That night the camp slept well. They had feasted and they had played. The entire expedition was at one single location, the Indians were friendly and submissive, and the colony finally had a church.

On the following day a steady procession of chiefs and their relatives from the pueblos that had been visited by the Spaniards began streaming into the village. The governor had summoned them to a general assembly for the purpose of receiving from them acts of obedience and vassalage. The chiefs, the friars, and the Spanish officials crowded into the main kiva to hear don Juan explain the purpose of his coming and to instruct the chiefs on what was expected of them. With Tomás and Cristóbal, the Mexican Indians, and the lay brother, San Buenaventura, serving as interpreters he said, "I have come to this land to bring you the knowledge of God, our Lord, on which depends the salvation of your souls, and to live peaceably and safely in your countries. You are to be governed justly and to be safe in your possessions, and to be protected from your enemies and not caused any harm."

The chiefs replied that they desired to render obedience to God and the king. The governor then told them to rise and approach him and the father commissary. As a sign of vassalage and obedience, the chiefs then fell to their knees and kissed the hands of the two Spaniards. The ceremony over, the governor urged each one of them to take a priest back to his pueblo as teacher of religion and the Spanish language. The chiefs replied that they would be glad to do so. The governor then concluded by admonishing them to take care of the priests and to treat them well, adding a warning that if they failed to obey the priests or caused them any harm, they would be put to the sword and their cities destroyed by fire.

Seven of the eight fathers were each assigned to a province or pueblo. Father Martínez, the commissary, was to stay at San Juan along with fray Cristóbal de Salazar and the lay brother, Juan de San Buenaventura.

The governor did not make an attempt to establish any kind of relationship with the chief of San Juan. Fray Cristóbal, however, who was assigned to the temporary capital, did try to become acquainted with him. Kaa Pin was reticent at first, but when he became convinced of the friar's sincerity, he came to see him every day. It was mainly through this relationship that information was transmitted back and forth. Neither spoke the other's language, but communication nonetheless took place. Cristóbal, feeling more secure now that everyone seemed to be at peace with each other, overcame his timidity and spoke to Co-ha, Kaa Pin's son, for the first time. Co-ha was just as shy, but seemed very happy to break the ice with the Spanish leader's boy, whom he had been watching with fascination ever since the Spaniards arrived.

## CHAPTER FIFTEEN

THREE DAYS AFTER the convocation, don Juan had just finished his breakfast when the *maese de campo* and the *sargento mayor* dashed into his tent. "We have a desertion," said Juan catching his breath.

"A desertion?" asked the governor incredulously.

"Yes, it looks as if Juan Rodríguez, Portugués, and Juan González stole some horses last night and left the camp," answered Juan.

"Let me go after them, tío," said Vicente in a low voice.

"Well, we shall see," replied the governor. "Go see what the soldiers in their company know about the deserters' intentions," he instructed Vicente. After the troop commander had left, don Juan said to his nephew, "I don't want Vicente to go. He had that nasty job back at Casco."

"I agree," nodded Juan.

"Why don't we send Villagrá," asked the governor. "Send Captain Francisco López with him. I want to test him."

"At your orders," said Juan as he turned to leave the tent.

Within the hour a party led by Captain Villagrá and composed of Captain Márquez, Captain López, the soldiers Juan Medel, and Pedro de Ribera set out southward from the pueblo at a gallop. Captain Márquez, by his unruffled disposition and willingness to serve had acquired a reputation as a very reliable officer. They were in hot pursuit of four, not three, deserters. A soldier named Matias Rodríguez had not been included in the initial report. Fourteen days later they caught up with the fugitives, who had almost reached Santa Bárbara. When they saw an armed party approaching from the south, they knew at once what was happening. They scattered into a wooded area in several different directions. Manuel Portugués and Juan Gonzáles were captured but Portugués's older brother, Juan Rodríguez and Matias Rodríguez managed to escape.

"What are we going to do with them?" asked Captain Márquez.

"I have my orders to execute them" answered Villagrá, shrugging his shoulders, "but who will do it?"

There was a long silence as no one answered. Finally, Captain López threw up his hands and said softly, "I will."

After the deserters were beheaded and buried, the patrol continued on to Santa Bárbara to seek supplies for the long journey back.

At San Juan there was a flurry of activity. The friars were all dispersing to their various assignments. Talking with the royal ensign one Sunday afternoon, the governor said, "Well, it looks as if we are getting settled all right."

Sosa de Peñalosa agreed with him, "Yes, we have an irrigation canal, a church, but most importantly we have sent our friars out to do their work."

Don Juan did not answer for some time, then he said, "Yes, the friars should be happy."

"You, too," answered the royal ensign. "You, with the help of our Lord have brought this large group of people all this way."

"You are right. I am very satisfied," he answered absentmindedly. "Good night, Francisco."

The following morning the governor called for his troop commander. As he walked into the command tent, Vicente bumped into Cristóbal, who was just running out. "Qué hay, where are you going in such a hurry?"

"Oh, perdon, primo, I'm going to feed my horse."

Vicente patted him on the head and went into the tent. The governor greeted him with the words, "We must explore this country more thoroughly. There must be something of value somewhere."

"What can I do?" asked Vicente.

"Well, I am thinking of sending you to the east to round up the wild cattle," answered don Juan.

"At your orders."

"I want you to take Cristóbal, but take good care of him, please."

"As if he were my son," answered Vicente with a smile.

The *sargento mayor* set out on 15 September with fifty soldiers but without Cristóbal. At first he was flattered and excited to be going on a mission without his father, but as the time of departure approached, the eleven-year-old said, "I want to stay with you, Papá." The roundup party rode to Pecos by going southward around the Sangre de Cristo Mountains, then taking a northeasterly direction over the foothills. They were well received by the people of that important village, who had already pledged their allegiance. Late that afternoon a chieftain came to see the commander and brought with him a young Indian man who spoke Spanish and who identified himself as Jusepe Gutiérrez, who had been a servant for Antonio Gutiérrez de Humana.

The story that Jusepe told was welcome news to the *sargento mayor*. One of the missions assigned to Oñate was that of arresting the members of the unauthorized expedition that had come to New Mexico in 1593 under the leadership of Captain Francisco Leyva de Bonilla. Jusepe, who was from Culhuacán just north of Mexico City, had been recruited by Gutiérrez to serve as his servant on an expedition to the northern province of Nueva Vizcaya for the purpose of seeking out and punishing the Tabosa and Gavilan Indians who were not submissive to the Spanish government. The small renegade band could not resist the temptation and continued to New Mexico, traveling for almost a year out of San Ildefonso pueblo in northern New Mexico, which Leyva had chosen as headquarters. Inevitably, lured by the siren—mostly of their own imagination—that had called so many into that equivocal land, they wandered further northward. Following an inner voice that seemed to say "just a little farther," they, in the manner of Vásquez de Coronado, stumbled onto Quivira, where the only reward awaiting them was frustration, with which apparently the outlaw band could not cope.

Jusepe told of the falling out between the leader and his lieutenant and of how Gutiérrez, after spending most of the day in his tent alone, ordered a soldier to summon the captain. As Leyva approached Gutiérrez's tent he was surprised by the flashing steel that ended his life and that of the expedition. Jusepe described the panic in the small camp, and his escape with five others who knew full well that disaster was imminent. His comrades all perished one by one, but he made it back to New Mexico where he lived as a slave with Apache and Vaquero Indians. After a year, he managed to escape and settled in the vicinity of the pueblo of Cicuye, which Oñate renamed Pecos.

The night before leaving Pecos, Vicente went to say good-bye to Father San Miguel, who had been assigned there as guardian. The venerable friar received the *sargento mayor* courteously, but not enthusiastically.

"Isn't your reverence feeling well?" inquired the young commander.

"I am feeling all right, but worried about the future of our little kingdom. There is great dissatisfaction among the settlers and even among the friars. I fear for our mission."

The *sargento mayor* bristled but controlled himself. "What do they expect after so short a time? You are here to start your work and soon others will be."

"I know, my son, but maybe we should build our own capital. The work would keep our people busy. I am the first friar to leave for his post, but I have no help nor protection."

Vicente smiled, "Well, father, these people are extremely gentle. It will all turn out well when the governor has had time to explore to see what there is of value here. Goodnight father. I wish you well."

The troop commander lost no time in enlisting the young Mexican Indian as interpreter and guide, and soon he was on his way to help in search of the cattle of the plains. Traveling eastward they reached a small plain in the vicinity of a river later given the name of Gallinas. It was here that they met the first Indians of the endless stretches to the east whom they called the cow Indians because of the bison upon which they depended for their sustenance. Continuing in the same direction, they reached a river that two and a half centuries later was to be given the name Canadian. It was near this river that they saw the first tepees. The *sargento mayor* was so impressed by the tanning quality of their tents that he bartered for one and brought it back to his own camp. He noted in his report that these Indians used dogs as pack animals, putting loads on their backs and a harness on their chests with which they dragged the poles used for raising tents.

After seeing some stray animals, they finally came upon the main herd, but there was no material for building a corral. The following day they arrived at an area abounding in cottonwood trees. In three days a huge corral, which Zaldívar estimated large enough to hold ten thousand cattle, was erected out of logs cut from the trees. The day after the corral was finished, the whole camp went on a mammoth roundup. At first the buffalo moved in the direction of the corral, but after a time they turned around in the direction of their would-be captors. No amount of skill or cunning on the part of these early plains cowboys could get the buffalo to go in the desired direction. All the Spaniards got for their efforts were three horses killed and forty others wounded. The only consolation they got out of the venture was the huge feast they enjoyed that evening, the main course of which was the meat from the animals they had slaughtered. They claimed the meat was more tender than veal. The delicious fragrance from the roaring campfire where the meat was roasting in vast quantities could be smelled a half a league away.

## CHAPTER SIXTEEN

AT SAN JUAN, the royal ensign and Captain Diego de Zubía, the purveyor general, concerned that winter would soon be upon them, tried to persuade the governor to build homes for the settlers so they could move out of their tents into more substantial quarters. "If we are really going to settle here, we should build our own homes," Sosa de Peñalosa suggested. "The Indians are going to tire of our dependence on them."

"Yes, I agree," added Zubía. "Besides, I am told it gets very cold during the winter."

The governor replied, "Well, gentlemen, I can see all that, too; but I think we should keep on looking before we decide on a permanent capital. I find it difficult to believe that we cannot find something more substantial than what we have here. If we do, it would be well to have our capital either at that place or near it."

On 6 October, the general set out once again; this time to look for the famous western salt beds he had heard about, and since he planned to come back to San Juan in a few days, he decided to take Cristóbal with him. The governor's son spent hours preparing his equipment for his first sortie as a soldier. Don Juan left word for the *sargento mayor* to stay at San Juan on his return from the land of the buffalo. The father commissary requested to go with the governor, for he would be visiting pueblos that were without the services of a missionary. He wanted to accompany Father Claros to his mission at Puaray.

Heading southward, they visited several pueblos on the way to the salt beds, which were reported to be in mountains that were later to be given the name Manzano. Traveling on the east side of the Sandia Mountains, the general kept his miner's eye open for signs of ore. The governor was only moderately impressed by the salt beds. The father commissary was very happy to visit people who showed an enthusiastic acceptance of Spanish authority and particularly that of the church. After visiting the southernmost pueblo of the Jumano Indians, they headed in a northwesterly direction to the land of the Tiguas.

Instead of returning to San Juan, the restless governor decided to extend his mission and look for the South Sea. From Isleta he sent a message for the *sargento mayor* and *maese de campo*. The *sargento mayor* was to remain in charge at San Juan and the *maese* was to join up with him at Zuni.

He continued with his small force to Acoma, the pueblo in the sky, which is built on a high mesa, accessible only at one end. The general was impressed by its impregnability, and shuddered to think how dangerous it would be to have to take it by storm, remembering the stories which his father had told him about the Mixtón stronghold. The Acomans were the most independent minded of all the pueblo Indians, confident perhaps that they were immune from attack. They, nevertheless, welcomed the Spaniards with liberal gifts of maize and fowl. They also readily professed obedience to the king of Spain, probably thinking, "the sooner we do it, the sooner they will leave us alone."

From Acoma, the governor continued toward the west in snow so heavy that some horses became lost. After five days of bitterly cold weather, exacerbated by the omnipresent northwest wind, he finally spotted smoke from the houses at Zuni. Spurred by hunger and cold, the Spaniards entered the easternmost of the Zuni pueblos. The Zunians welcomed them into their warm houses where they regaled the near frozen soldiers with a warm feast of maize, tortillas, and rabbit. The village proved to be so inviting that they remained there the following day.

The next stop was the historical Cíbola, or as the Zunians called it, Hawikuh, where fifty-eight years earlier Vásquez de Coronado had had the first major skirmish of his expedition. The sons of two of the Mexican Indians who came with Vásquez were among the inhabitants who not only pledged obedience, but welcomed the intruders with the best food they had to offer. The Spaniards remained there for several days during which the governor sent out an exploratory party to search for a salt lake nearby that purportedly yielded a very high quality salt.

One afternoon three soldiers, who had been dispatched to Agua de la Peña, a huge rock with a spring at its base, to look for the horses that had been lost in the snowstorm, arrived at the pueblo with an extra rider. It was Captain Villagrá who, upon his return from New Spain, had stopped at Puaray, where he was told that the general had left the previous day for Acoma. Villagrá set out alone to join Oñate's party. Not receiving a very good welcome at Acoma, he decided to push on. That night he stumbled on a trap set by the Acomans, falling into a pit during the blinding snowstorm. Since his horse was killed, he had to proceed on foot after divesting himself of all unnecessary equipment. Suffering from extreme hunger, he felt obliged to kill and eat his dog in order to survive. The dog fled from him, but despite his two mortal stab wounds, came back to him when his master called. He could, however, not eat the dog because he had no way of starting a fire in order to cook the meat. In the epic poem he wrote years later in Spain, Villagrá expressed great remorse at having killed his poor dog in vain. The captain was just as thirsty as he was hungry. It was at the stream at the base of the rock that the three soldiers in search of drinking water found the cold, bedraggled captain.

The general was delighted to see Villagrá, who had proven to be one of his most dependable and loyal captains. "Welcome, my friend, how did it go with the deserters?" he said in one breath.

The stocky, prematurely bald young man answered in his usual cheerful manner, "We executed two of them, but the other two got away." The captain then recounted the hostile reception he received at the hands of the Acomans. Don Juan was puzzled, because just a few weeks earlier they had been so cooperative with him. He soon put it out of his mind, telling Villagrá that he had intended trying to discover a route to the South Sea, but that now he was going only as far as the Moqui pueblos.

The following morning the Spaniards resumed their trek westward. The snow continued to plague the small band of Spaniards, which was not fully prepared for the extreme winter weather in the Zuni area and beyond. During the twenty-league trip to the first of the Moqui pueblos, which took four days, they suffered as much from thirst as they did from the cold weather. At all pueblos, now called Hopi, the reception the Spaniards received was courteous and submissive. On the way back from the last of the western pueblos, the general, upon hearing that there were mines in the area, sent Captain Farfán to explore. At Zuni they waited for Farfán's detachment for seventeen long days.

Captain Farfán, after traveling three days, much of the time without water, came upon some Indian "rancherías" or campsites. Their guides told them they were Jumano Indians. Captain Alonso de Quesada agreed to go talk to them. As the Spaniards approached, the Indians, armed with bows and arrows, surrounded them. Captain Quesada reassured them that they came with friendly intentions and persuaded two of their chieftains to accompany him back to the Spanish camp. Captain Farfán embraced them and gave them gifts.

The following morning when Captain Farfán went to the Indian camp, he found it abandoned. The two chieftains and a woman had stayed behind. After offering the captain some dates and venison, they showed him some powdered ore. Farfán asked them to show him where they had found the metal. One of the chieftains readily agreed, and they started on what turned out to be a long complicated trip. The original chieftain, after accompanying them a good distance, wished to return to his people and turned over his job to a chieftain from another Indian camp. After still another change in guides—the Indians being reluctant to stray too far from their own people—the exploring party finally arrived at the mine. It was in the vicinity of the present-day ghost town of Jerome, Arizona. The Indians talked of settlements to the southwest where it never snowed, and the inhabitants grew maize, beans, and calabashes. They also told them that the sea was only thirty days to the west.

After staking numerous claims, the exploring party started the long trip back to report to the governor. They arrived at Zuni on 11 December. The following day, since the *maese de campo* had not arrived, the general decided to head back to San Juan to spend the Christmas season. The day after that, as they approached Agua de la Peña, they were shocked to see Bernabé de las Casas with six other soldiers. Captain Villagrá rode up ahead and shouted, "What are you men doing here?"

"We have news for don Juan," answered Las Casas gravely.

The governor rode up quickly. Dismounting, he asked in an anxious voice, "Qué pasa?"

"Su Senoría," answered Las Casas hanging his head slightly "Juan is dead. He was killed at Acoma as were Captain Escalante, Captain Nuñez, and several others."

The general turned pale, his eyes showing confusion and incredulity. "Qué?" he managed weakly.

"Que ha muerto el maese de campo [the *maese de campo* has died]," muttered Las Casas.

The general looked behind him as his body went limp. He was looking for Cristóbal who was with some soldiers looking for stray horses. Captain Villagrá moved up a stool that Las Casas had vacated, and the general sat down heavily. He remained seated with his head hanging for several moments, then he looked up at Captain Villagrá as if to ask, "What do we do now?"

Every person in the party who was present came up to the general, bowed and said, "I am very sorry, Your Excellency."

After all the condolences had been given, Captain Villagrá said gently to the general, "We must leave as soon as possible. The whole colony might be in mortal danger."

"Yes, Yes, I agree," muttered the general as he got up slowly. "We shall make camp here, but prepare for departure at dawn."

"We must also warn the rest of Farfán's party to avoid Acoma," suggested Villagrá.

"Yes. Send word to them."

Before sunrise there was a flurry of activity as tents were struck and equipment gathered. Tomás, the interpreter, was dispatched to warn the stragglers from Farfán's party who had remained back at Moqui, when their horses, exhausted from malnutrition, could go no further. The sun was just starting to show wanly from behind the mountains when the general emerged from his tent. His eyes were swollen from lack of sleep and from weeping. He had the men assembled and in a choking voice delivered a eulogy of those who had perished. He ended his discourse by saying, "And now let us lay aside our grief and sorrow, and lifting our thoughts to God, place our trust in Him. If we but follow His footsteps, without fail, He will extend His helping hand in time of need."

## CHAPTER SEVENTEEN

UPON RECEIVING ORDERS from the governor to leave Vicente in charge, the *maese de campo* had set out on 18 November from San Juan to Zuni to join the expedition in search of the South Sea. Juan de Zaldívar's troops arrived at Acoma on 1 December, at about four o'clock in the afternoon. From the foot of the rock he sent Captain Gerónimo Márquez to the top to get provisions from the pueblo. When Márquez returned he reported to the lieutenant general, "They gave us only this small quantity of wood and water, and they did it very unwillingly." He had brought two chieftains with him, and suggested that they be held until the Acomans came to terms.

"No, Captain," answered Zaldívar gently. "I want to assure them that we do not want to abuse them or hurt them in any way. I think they will relent and give us what we want." He then ordered the chieftains released and sent them back to their people with some gifts.

The Spanish leader thought it would be prudent to establish his camp a good distance from the rock. "I want to avoid the possibility of a hostile action by either side," he told Captain Márquez.

The following day he left early in the morning with twelve men to go to the top of the mesa. He warned all of his men to avoid any sign of hostility. Once again he asked for provisions. "I want more flour for a long journey we are taking," he explained patiently. "I have already given you, and you have accepted, many articles in trade." The Acomans gave him a few tortillas and a small quantity of flour.

"Why don't we take the flour by force?" suggested Las Casas.

"I told you once and for all, we do not want to harm or even alarm these people. Let us withdraw in an orderly fashion and return to our camp. I need time to think this over."

Back at the camp Juan discussed the best course of action with his officers. Captain Márquez suggested attacking the fortress city immediately.

Captain Tabora agreed, adding, "We cannot continue to the west empty handed."

Zaldívar objected, "They are too numerous for the number of men we have, and an attack would only inflame the rest of the Indians in the kingdom."

The following day, 4 December, acting as if nothing had happened, but prepared for trouble, the Spanish leader once more went up to the rock with eighteen men. Once again in a patient voice he asked for the flour.

Tya-Ni, who was now doing the talking for the Acomans, shrugged his shoulders and said, "Why don't you go among the houses and look for some."

Zaldívar, a bit apprehensive, sent Captain Nuñez with six men. They were accompanied by a crowd of about sixty Indians, some carrying clubs. Meanwhile the Acomans had maneuvered Zaldívar and his men to a place between the houses and the edge of the cliff. The *maese,* anxious about Nuñez and his men, sent Captain Tabora to see what was happening. He reported back that the villagers were not giving anything. The commander gave him six men to assist in the collection, remaining near the edge of the cliff with four men.

One of the soldiers with Captain Nuñez, Martín de Viveros, frustrated by the Acomans' refusal to give flour, grabbed two turkeys at one of the houses. An Indian watching from the terrace of a neighboring house shot and killed him with an arrow. Other Acomans began shouting and advanced, brandishing their clubs.

Hearing the commotion, Captain Tabora quickly rejoined Zaldívar. "They are attacking Nuñez," he shouted. The many Indians who had remained with the *maese* also started advancing. "Fire!" cried Captain Tabora.

"Fire over their heads," shouted Zaldívar. Hernando de Segura fell close to the commander's feet. The Spaniards, unable to reload their harquebuses, drew their swords and started slashing frantically.

Some of the Nuñez men, after seeing their captain fall, clambered up a terrace to defend themselves. When they were driven down, they managed to join the *maese* and his men. So many Indians were attacking that the Spaniards were all soon on their own: Juan de León and Juan de Cabanillas jumped, fell, and rolled down the cliff to safety as did Alonso González.

When Antonio de Sarinara saw the *maese,* who had already been wounded by an arrow in the right thigh, fall from a blow by a stone, he realized that there was no other way to survive than to go down the cliff.

By now the *maese* and two of his three officers, Escalante and Nuñez, were dead. Captain Tabora, when he saw Juan de Olague and Pedro Robledo jump off the cliff, realized that he was the only one left alive. He broke toward the spot where Sarinara had gone and began the perilous descent to the desert floor.

Thus the skirmish ended. Bernabé de las Casas, who had been ordered to stay with the horses, watched helplessly from below as the *maese de campo* and his few men defended themselves at the edge of the cliff. After they had been killed, he saw Juan de Olague and Pedro Robledo jump down. He watched with horror as Robledo was torn to pieces as he hit the jutting stones. The Robledo family had now given up two lives to the expedition—the father who was buried shortly after entering New Mexico and now Pedro, his son.

The survivors made their way back to camp. The first to arrive was Bernabé de las Casas, who had been guarding the horses when hostilities broke out. He and some of the unwounded survivors, including Captain Tabora, *alguacil real*, put the wounded on horseback, and took them back to camp. After caring for them, the camp was lifted immediately and all headed back for San Juan except Tabora, who went westward to warn the general lest he stumble into an ambush on the way back.

At the capital, the *sargento mayor* was beside himself with grief at the news of his older brother's death. He managed to compose himself long enough to seek out the widows and orphans to console them. His grief soon turned to anger. He could barely contain himself from marching to Acoma at that very moment to exact revenge. He, nevertheless, made arrangements for religious services, which were held amid the wails of the women, who grieved not only for their dead husbands, but also for their children, left behind to an uncertain future.

On 6 December, two days after the tragic incident, Tabora came into San Juan, saying that he had lost his way. The *sargento mayor,* now chomping at the bit, immediately ordered Bernabé de las Casas, who had distinguished himself at Acoma, to go in search of the general. Las Casas left immediately, with six soldiers, skirting Acoma by a wide margin. On the tenth, he met up with the general.

Not knowing what the reaction had been among the Indians, the small force proceeded back to San Juan with great care. From La Bajada, some nine leagues from San Juan, the general, acceding to Cristóbal's request, who was most anxious to see Vicente, sent him ahead in the company of Captains Villagrá and Quesada to announce his imminent arrival to the troop commander.

When Oñate arrived at the provisional capital on 21 December, the shadows were getting long. The bleak sun shone intermittently through the streaked clouds. As he rode into the village with his retinue, the *sargento mayor* ran out to greet him. The general dismounted and stood immobile for a moment as Vicente rushed to him and wrapped his arms around him. As if afraid their voices would break in front of the whole camp, neither of them spoke for a long interval. Finally, don Juan spoke in a hoarse voice, "Where is Cristóbal?"

Vicente swallowed hard and answered, "Visiting with his friends. I will get him."

"No, wait until I get to my quarters," don Juan said, as he turned to walk to his house.

The *sargento mayor* turned to a soldier and ordered, "Put up the general's horse."

That evening the governor dined with Vicente and Cristóbal. He was more relaxed than he had been since receiving the news of his nephew's death. He appeared to be enjoying the relative luxury of the house, which had been requisitioned and refurbished as his residence. The only reference to Juan made during the evening was when the governor asked Vicente if he had sent word to his mother. Vicente nodded. Cristóbal, still confused by the family tragedy, tried to restrain his happiness at being back in the company of his favorite cousin.

The following day broke with snow flurries. The governor slept late, as did Cristóbal. The *sargento mayor* awakened early and came twice to the governor's residence before he found him up. Over a cup of chocolate and some bread he asked bluntly, "What are we going to do?"

The general did not answer immediately, and when he did it was with another question, "What do you think we should do?"

"We should punish them as severely as we can," said the new *maese de campo,* with eyes flashing.

"I agree with you," said the general in a weak voice.

"I want to lead the army," blurted Vicente.

"We shall discuss that later," said the general, gently, but firmly. He did not want to risk his other nephew, particularly in view of the unrest that was developing in the colony. "By the way," the general said. "I would like to reward Bernabé de las Casas for his skill in finding me to inform me about Juan." Vicente nodded in agreement.

The governor spent the Christmas season in a mood of apprehension over an unpleasant and difficult task that had to be accomplished, but which the governor knew could not be undertaken until after the greatest of holy feasts. Wanting to put it out of his mind and concentrate on having a happy Christmas for Cristóbal's sake, he did not act on the matter for two days.

Cristóbal was reluctant to go see Co-ha, but his friend came to see him. He acted as if nothing had happened, calling Cristóbal out of his father's house. Cristóbal approached the Tegua boy, his head slightly down.

"Tell me about your trip to the Moqui," Co-ha greeted Cristóbal cheerfully in Tegua and with gestures.

"It was fine, but a lot of snow," Cristóbal smiled, picking up some snow from the ground and stretching his arms.

Saying something in Tegua and wrapping his arms around his body, Co-ha smiled back at him.

Pointing westward and making a motion of eating and of warming his hands, Cristóbal answered, "Yes it was cold, but the Zuni were good to us."

They then fell silent until Cristóbal spoke. "Much fighting with Acoma. My uncle killed," he said making a striking motion.

Co-ha understood because he already knew. He came up to Cristóbal and put his hand on this shoulder, then turned around and left.

The *sargento mayor* brought up the subject of punishment at every occasion. Although this rankled the governor, he would answer patiently. "There is no great hurry. The Acomans are not going to leave their fortress," he added. Then he changed the subject, "I am going to appoint las Casas to the rank of ensign."

"Good, Uncle, I think he is a good man," Vicente answered perfunctorily before he realized that the governor was indeed serious about avoiding the unpleasant topic. But he persisted: "If we don't act quickly, there will be no lesson learned and others might get the idea to resist us and maybe worse. Don't forget, Uncle, they killed Juan."

Don Juan answered with a trace of irritation, "We have been through all this. Wait until after the holidays."

Vicente buried his hands. "We can't be hesitant or lenient about this. If Juan had not been so trusting and so reluctant to use force, he would be here with us today."

After Vicente left, the governor went to see Francisco, knowing that his friend seldom brought up official matters. They talked mainly of their youth. On one of these visits, Francisco, noticing that his friend was restless, asked bluntly, "Do you want to meet a woman?" Oñate did not answer. Francisco continued, "My friend, Juana, has a friend who would like to meet you."

After a pause don Juan said without looking up, "y quién es esa mujer? [and who is that woman?]"

"She is the widow of Juan Gonzalez. He deserted as much because of her as for any other reason," explained Francisco rather enigmatically. Again don Juan did not answer as his friend continued, "I have a hut in a grove on the other side of the river."

The next day was Christmas Eve. It had snowed during the night. On this crisp morning the whole countryside was a resplendent white. A soft, orange sun was shining through the thin, high clouds. It highlighted the green pines in the nearby mountains. In the stillness, sound carried far. The voices of people about their daily tasks could be heard from the high ground near the pueblo. Don Juan took a deep breath as he surveyed the bucolic winter scene. Cristóbal's eyes were wide with appreciation, "Oh, Papá, I wish I had a sleigh."

"You shall have one, son," he answered, smiling. A frame from a small cart was quickly converted into one by the carpenters, who substituted some planks for the wheels. The boards were smoothed out and smeared with buffalo fat. An old mare was hitched to it, and Cristóbal had his sleigh. As don Juan watched his son ride back and forth, a dull pang shot through his stomach as he thought of the unpleasant task that lay before him. He shook his head almost imperceptibly and shouted to Cristóbal, "Wait, let me ride with you."

As María, the *alcalde's* ten-year-old daughter, watched her neighbor and sometime playmate have such a wonderful time, she cried out, "Cristóbal, Cristóbal, please let me ride with you."

Cristóbal shouted back, "No, María, this is too dangerous for girls."

That evening don Juan went to Francisco's quarters. After the greetings he asked in a subdued voice, "And what is this woman's name?"

"Magdalena, Magdalena González," answered Francisco.

"I would like to talk to her," said don Juan, raising his head and looking at his friend in the eyes.

"When?" asked Francisco.

"Tomorrow afternoon."

"Done."

On 2 January 1599 the governor called a council of war with the *sargento mayor,* Captain Sosa de Peñalosa, Captain Gasco, the treasurer, Captain Villagrá, the quartermaster, and Captain Zubía. The meeting was short. The governor announced that Vicente Zaldívar would be the *maese de campo.* It was decided that stern action be taken against the Acomans lest other pueblos follow their example. It was also decided to consult the friars on the moral aspects of the situation. Two questions were posed to them: What conditions are necessary to wage a just war? And what may be done with the persons and property of those against whom a just war is waged?

The friars themselves had a council in order to answer the two momentous questions. A day later they delivered their opinion to the governor. For a war to be just, they wrote, there must be proper authority. The representative of the king has such authority. The cause must be just, such as in the punishment of wrongdoers or to establish peace. War must moreover be waged without malice. As to what could be done with the defeated, they declared, if the cause of the war is to punish the wrongdoers, they and their possessions are at the mercy of the conquerors according to the laws of the land.

After the governor received the opinion, signed by all the friars, he declared war on the Acomans by blood and fire. He announced that he would lead the attack in person, but the friars and many settlers dissuaded him. Reluctantly, he assigned the mission to his nephew, the new *maese de campo.*

Vicente was gratified that he was selected for this mission. He picked seventy of the best men in the colony. Among them was Captain Francisco López, who, although not reacting outwardly, was pleased that something was finally about to happen. That evening, while talking to don Juan, he said, "Well, here you have me almost an old man but I am going to test my mettle once again. Too bad you are not going, Juan."

"Yes, they won't let me. Besides, Vicente views this as his war. I have never seen anybody as avid about combat as he."

"Yes, he is a young wolf," confirmed Francisco.

Early the following morning, as the skies were beginning to turn a silver gray, a Mass was said for the intention of those going to Acoma. Every man confessed and received communion except Francisco. His comrades in arms could not understand how he could contemplate going into combat without receiving the sacraments. He did not say anything but simply refused to confess and take communion.

# CHAPTER EIGHTEEN

On 12 January 1599, Zaldívar set out for Acoma with seventy soldiers and instructions to demand the delivery of those guilty for the attack on the Spaniards and, failing to achieve that, to wage relentless war and to take all of the inhabitants prisoner, regardless of sex or age. Cristóbal had begged his father to let him go with his beloved cousin. Don Juan did not for a moment entertain the idea of sending his son on such a dangerous mission, but that did not keep the young soldier from playing out his fantasies.

At Acoma there was great consternation, after the incident in which several lives were lost on both sides. Kho-Ka-Cha-Ni, the chief, regretted the lives lost by the Acomans and by the Spaniards because it had broken the peace that had reigned since the coming of the intruders. He had learned that the best way to deal with them was to give them what they asked for and to wait for them to leave. None of them had ever stayed. Shu-Wi-Mi, a chieftain of one of the wards, agreed with him. "It is folly to let pride alone dictate what we shall do. Because of their superior weapons and their horses, we have never been able to defeat them."

"I am afraid that now it is too late; Tya-Ni has inflamed the rest of the chieftains," sighed Kho-Ka-Cha-Ni.

"They actually think they can defeat the Castilians, and the Castilians must now seek revenge for the death of one of the leaders. Even as we talk, I am told, the brother of the slain general is on his way to seek satisfaction for his family's honor."

"We should at least evacuate the women and children," suggested Shu-Wi-Mi. "They are blameless and besides they would only get in the way."

"I will try to convince Tya-Ni and the others," answered the chief weakly.

At a council that evening the old chief did not argue the merits of resisting the Spaniards or not. He merely tried to get agreement on the evacuation of the noncombatants. "The Castilians will be here tomorrow. We must act immediately."

Tya-Ni answered, "You talk as if we were already defeated. The intruders are men like us. There is only a small number of them on their way here. We will outnumber them greatly. If you do not want to fight because of your age, we will understand; but I believe we should make a stand, all of us together. The presence of their children and wives will make our men fight better." Most of the war captains agreed.

Then it was once more Kho-Ka-Cha-Ni's turn to talk. "I predict a great catastrophe for our people, but let no one suggest that I do not want to fight. This old arm can still wield a club and will do so until there is no more life in it. If we are going to fight, let us prepare."

Vicente Zaldívar arrived at the foot of the boulder at four o'clock in the afternoon of 21 January. The Spanish leader had cautioned all his soldiers not to shoot or use any offensive language until the Acomans had a chance to agree to his terms, which were to surrender and to give up all of those implicated in the death of his brother and the other soldiers.

As the Spaniards circled the mesa, the Acomans could easily see that it was a small force that had been sent against them. Tya-Ni and his cohorts danced with glee at the prospect of defeating this group of arrogant foreigners who thought they could win over three thousand people with only seventy men. Kho-Ka-Cha-Ni watched silently.

As Zaldívar spoke through his interpreter, don Tomás, asking the Acomans to come down, they began to hoot and holler, calling the Spaniards "whoremongers" and pelting them with arrows, rocks, and even chunks of ice. Since it was getting late, the commander ordered that camp be pitched. The Spaniards remained on a high state of alert all night lest the Acomans overwhelm them in their sleep.

On the mesa there was dancing and reveling until dawn. The drums and chanting could be clearly heard by the soldiers who, between fitful snatches of sleep in the bitter cold night, pondered what the morning would bring. The entire camp was up before dawn as if eager to get a difficult job done, or simply because they could not sleep. It was one of those perfectly clear, raw, cutting days of a high desert winter. The men gathered around the campfire with swollen eyes, rubbing their hands to get them warm. Francisco was up earlier than the rest, but he looked rested. He went to see the members of his squad to make sure that everything was in readiness, then waited for orders. As the soldiers were finishing their scanty breakfast, some of the horses wandered to a large frozen puddle at the base of the rock. The Acomans who were on that side of the high mesa rushed over and started shooting arrows at them. Two of the horses were killed. Zaldívar ordered two soldiers with harquebuses to open fire. As they did so, one of the Acomans came tumbling down dead from a shot. The others scattered. Thus began the Battle of Acoma.

At a quickly assembled council, the commander spoke, "It is useless to discuss with such savage beasts. With a well-conceived plan this task will not be so difficult. We shall feign an open attack against the northern rock, and as the enemy is distracted, we will climb the southern one and gain a secure foothold." There was no dearth of volunteers. Francisco was one of the first, but the *maese de campo* selected twelve others, mostly younger men. He knew that Francisco was his uncle's friend, but he didn't like him nor trust him, although they had never exchanged more than a simple greeting. Captain Pablo de Aguilar, the rebellious one, was one of those chosen, as was Captain Villagrá, the poet.

The commander and his men on the southeast side made for the crag between the two big rocks as soon as the Acomans, believing that the Spaniards were about to storm them, rushed to defend the main access on the opposite side of the other rock. The thirteen remained hidden until it was safe to climb to the top. Shu-Wi-Mi and Tyami, discovering the ruse, rushed over with four hundred warriors.

The Acomans had to cross a makeshift bridge between the two rocks. This gave the Spaniards time to fire at the massed men, who, although they inflicted some damage on the Spaniards, soon retreated with some of their dead and wounded. This respite gave the Spaniards time to reload and prepare for the next onslaught. The Acomans, led by Shu-Wi-Mi, who had earlier counseled moderation, once more resumed their fierce attack.

The young Spanish commander directed the firing, which quickly scattered the mass of warriors enough for him to see a young Acoman wearing his brother's bloody clothing. Fighting his way to where the young man stood waving his club, he began hacking away furiously with his sword. The astonished warrior tried to defend himself but soon dropped dead at the enraged Zaldívar's feet. Breathing heavily, the Spanish leader looked around him defiantly, but there was no one to fight since the fire from the harquebuses had dispersed the Indians momentarily. He returned to his men where he caught his breath before the next wave attacked.

It was not long in coming. Shu-Wi-Mi rallied his men who despite their mounting losses came back to face the blistering fire from the Spanish firearms. The Acomans, Shu-Wi-Mi leading them, were making progress until the Spanish leader shattered the chieftain's arm with a shot from his weapon.

Meanwhile at the rock staircase at the western side, several Spanish horsemen dismounted and pretended to be climbing to the top where the main force of Acomans sent down a shower of rocks and arrows. In the background behind the dismounted horsemen Captain Márquez along with captains López, Quesada, and Zubía started firing at the Acomans above, who were led by the impetuous Tya-Ni. There were so many Acomans that it was difficult to miss, and many came tumbling down head over heels from the top of the mountain fortress.

At sunset, because of sheer fatigue on both sides, the battle slowly came to a halt. The commander, leaving Pablo de Aguilar—his and don Juan's nemesis—in charge, descended from the occupied rock and rejoined those who were conducting the diversionary attack below to make plans for the coming day.

Not many in either camp slept that night. The Spaniards had the task of finding a way across the chasm they had to cross in order to reach the main part of the northern rock where the village stood. The Indians spent the night mourning their many dead and tending to the wounded. The beautiful Ku-Wai-Dii was distraught at her husband Shu-Wi-Mi's injury. The wound was so severe that it seemed beyond healing.

Zaldívar ordered a great beam prepared and taken to the occupied rock for use in crossing from one rock to another.

Sometime during the night as the Acoma war council was making plans for the morning, someone in the rear murmured, "We want Shu-Wi-Mi."

Someone else followed a bit louder with, "We need Shu-Wi-Mi."

Then another person shouted, "He has been doing all the fighting." Soon there was a clamor.

Tyami, a friend of Shu-Wi-Mi, was asked by several of the council members to go get him. He answered, "Hasn't he done enough? He is badly wounded. He is resting with his wife."

"We need him, we need him," cried several of the warriors.

When Tyami went to get Shu-Wi-Mi, Ku-Wai-Dii begged him not to go, but sick as he was, he went. At the meeting he was appointed commander by acclamation. Before accepting he stated three conditions: first, that should he and Tya-Ni both perish, "I ask that we, along with our lieutenants, be buried together so we can settle our scores. Second, all of you here and your followers must promise to fight to the last man. And third, if we should be victorious in this vain and destructive war, I shall be the sole ruler of Acoma."

The plans made for the following morning were to hide five hundred men in a cave just on the south side of the fissure where the

Spaniards were sure to cross. From there the men under Tyami's command were to surprise them just after they crossed over from the rock they occupied.

The die was cast, and the only choice was to resist and either triumph or perish. Shu-Wi-Mi still expressed concern for the children, the women, and the aged. Tya-Ni, though deposed, was still the firebrand and declaimed, "What good can it be for the women and children to survive if we don't? They will be at the mercy of the Castilians. As for the aged, they have lived long enough. What difference will a few months, a few years make? I say fight to the death of all of us if necessary." Kho-Ka-Cha-Ni remained silent. It was as if the turbulent events of the past few weeks had been too confusing and too powerful for him to cope with, and now he and his gentle people had no choice but to weather the storm and the cataclysm that appeared inevitable.

At sunrise Shu-Wi-Mi said a tender good-bye to Ku-Wai-Dii, who begged him not to leave her. He answered that Acoma depended on him. "It is impossible that I abandon the fight against the Spaniards. I must leave you now, but my heart and soul remain with you that you may know the tender love I bear for you."

As the sky grew pink in the direction of San Juan, the Spaniards, with the exception of Francisco, who, disgusted at having spent the previous day shooting from the base of the rock, talked to nobody, gathered around Fray Alonso to hear Mass. The friar spoke to them, "Knights of Christ, strong in battle, defenders of the Holy Faith . . . I beseech you, through Christ our savior, to restrain your bloody arms as much as you can lest needless blood may flow. The true valor of Catholic arms is to conquer without death or bloodshed. Go in Christ's name. In His Holy Name, I bless you one and all."

In the bright sun that bathed the countryside with its stark, raw light but failed to warm the bitterly cold air, the Spaniards once more reached the top. As they looked across the chasm, they found the village apparently deserted. Using the beam that had been brought up during the night, the first wave of Spaniards rushed across to the other side. In their excitement two of the soldiers picked up the beam for possible use in crossing other gaps, leaving the rest of the Spanish force stranded.

Lying in hiding according to plan, Shu-Wi-Mi, his arm wrapped in bandages, with a mighty war whoop gave the signal to attack. He could not use the captured sword he was carrying very effectively but he was everywhere exhorting his men to action.

The Spaniards who had been temporarily left behind fired from their position, helping to scatter the Acomans, but the principal action was joined by the thirteen who got across, and among them was Francisco. They fired once, bringing down some Acomans, and thinned out their ranks sufficiently but not enough to gain time for reloading—only to unsheathe their swords. Francisco seemed to be everywhere slashing and sticking with a recklessness bordering on frenzy. As Tyami brought up reinforcements, the thirteen withdrew to a cave nearby, despite Francisco's exhortations to stay and finish the job. Juan Piñero pulled him aside hollering, "Vamos hombre, there are too many of them." Francisco, his eyes glazed, followed, breathing deeply and soaked in sweat. From the cave they now could hold the Acomans at bay with their harquebuses until help came.

Those who had remained on the rock occupied by the Spaniards needed desperately to cross the chasm that separated the two rocks. Since the beam was on the other side, someone had somehow to get across to set it in place. Villagrá, in the manner of a long jumper, took a running start and bounded through the air to the other side. Once the beam was in place, the Spaniards streamed across as the trumpeter blasted the call to charge. The Acomans were at a disadvantage in that they had to close in to attack. The Spaniards with their firearms could fight from a safe distance. The ones in the cave soon joined the action.

As the fighting continued some of the Spaniards stayed back and continued to fire, but as the Acomans broke ranks some of the others closed in with their swords. Captain Quesada, Ensign Carabajal, and the soldiers Francisco García, Antonio Hernandez, and another named Licama were wounded seriously. What saved their lives and prevented others from being wounded were the metal helmets and the heavy leather jackets they were wearing. Another soldier by the name of Lorenzo Salado from Valladolid, Spain, who was fighting hand-to-hand was accidentally shot by his best friend Asensio de Arechuleta, who was aiming at an Acoman coming up behind his friend. Knowing he was dying, he asked to be taken down to the base of the mountain to the confessor. Arechuleta, crying out his friend's name and asking his forgiveness, left the battle. Down at the base, although he was in excruciating pain, he confessed his sins and managed a sad smile for his friend before he died.

Although the Acomans were being decimated by the Spanish firearms, they kept coming on wave after wave. The Spanish commander ordered two small culverins brought forward. The Acomans in turn charged with some three hundred warriors. The two culverins, which had been loaded with two hundred nails each, erupted with a dull burp, and as the poet Villagrá was to write later, "It was like watching a flock of magpies suddenly stop their chirping and croaking—some escaping, some with broken legs, some dead, and others sweeping the ground with their wings, their black beaks open and their intestines dragging."

And so were the Acomans as the two small cannon took their terrible toll. The Spaniards, taking advantage of the weapon's effect, charged into the pueblo and began to set the houses on fire.

At this point the Spanish commander called upon the Acomans to surrender. Shu-Wi-Mi accompanied by Tya-Ni and a group of women carrying the offerings of blankets and corn, offered to surrender, but when Zaldívar gave them his terms, which required the Acomans to turn over the instigators and ringleaders of the original attack on the Spaniards, they refused and went back to resume the hopeless struggle.

The Acomans were now in desperate straits. Many started taking their own lives, some leaping to death from the top of the rock. Captain Villagrá, seeing this, remarked to Captain Farfán, "They are acting like the numantinos," a reference to the inhabitants of the Celtiberian city of Numancia which, in 133 B.C., when besieged by the Romans, chose to perish down to the last child rather than surrender. Among the suicides, it was believed, were Shu-Wi-Mi and Tya-Ni, but their remains were never identified.

Villagrá heard later that Shu-Wi-Mi had made it through the carnage and the smoke to his burning house where he found Ku-Wai-Dii weeping with other Acoma women and awaiting a fiery death. He took her out to the rear of the house, where he held her in his bloody arms trying to console her. They were found, the poet was told, her head bashed in and he lying beside her with his uninjured arm around her, the sword he had taken from a fallen Spaniard in his stomach.

Late on the twenty-third, the old and bent Kho-Ka-Cha-Ni came to Zaldívar offering to surrender. With tears running down his wrinkled face, he knelt before the Spanish commander. Zaldívar lifted him by the shoulders and embraced him, and then asked him to lead him to the spot where his brother had met his death. Vicente wept for his brother, Juan; the rest of the Spaniards bowed their heads. When a cross was raised on the spot, they all sank to their knees and prayed. Kho-Ka-Cha-Ni continued weeping quietly.

The next day, the Spaniards occupied the ruined pueblo, establishing their camp in the main plaza. They then began trying to apprehend the Acomans. Many of them hid in their kivas and underground passages, refusing to come out. Some of those hiding out were killed by their own leaders who would rather they all die than surrender. The new recalcitrance enraged the already unnerved Zaldívar. He ordered that they be smoked out, and that if there was any resistance, to kill them. As the terrified Acomans were forced out by the smoke, most were put to death by the swords of a black servant and some of the soldiers. Zaldívar, who was distraught at having seen the place where his brother was killed, could not contain his fury. He ordered that what was left of the pueblo be laid waste and burned to the ground. On that day, Acoma, the invincible sky city, ceased to exist. It was not to be rebuilt for many years.

After the battle it was estimated that six to eight hundred Acomans had perished. Out of the six hundred survivors, only seventy-eight were warriors. All the rest were women and children. A very small number escaped from the rock. Two of these were captured by Captain Zubía, who had been dispatched by Zaldívar to take the news of his victory to the governor. They were taken to San Juan and locked up in a kiva. They later requested rope and hanged themselves.

## CHAPTER NINETEEN

THE GOVERNOR RECEIVED the news of the victory from Captain Zubía somewhat coldly because he knew that Zubía had been criticizing him of late. He was nevertheless elated about Vicente's success with but one Spaniard killed accidentally, but a bit dismayed at the violence that had taken place. He feared that the tragic event would have an adverse affect on the rest of the Indian population. The peace that had reigned from the beginning had been broken and relations would never be the same. He felt confident in his army, however. They had been tested and had met the test most successfully. Several of his men were wounded, but none seriously. Iron age weapons and armor and military organization had once more proven too much for the Stone Age First Americans.

Francisco had just finished dinner when the governor came into his quarters. "Buenas noches, Francisco, how did you fare at Acoma?"

"It was a good campaign up to a point," he answered curtly.

"What do you mean?" queried the governor.

"Well, I mean the Indians had to be punished, and the fighting was worthy, although you know it is really always the same. With our superior weapons it is not much of a contest."

"And what was wrong?" the governor asked.

"You have received your report, I'm sure," answered Francisco evasively.

"Yes, but I want to hear it from you," insisted don Juan.

"Well, all that killing and burning afterward," answered Francisco.

"They continued resisting even after surrendering, didn't they?" countered don Juan.

"I would not call trying to get away or showing terror, resistance," argued Francisco.

"Well, this isn't over yet. We still have to make an example of those rebellious savages," continued don Juan.

"Yes, I suppose so," answered Francisco in a tired voice.

When Fray Miguel, who was in Pecos, heard of the tragic happenings at Acoma, he hurried to San Juan to see the governor. As an older man and confessor to the governor, he could allow himself some frank observations. Don Juan did not particularly want to discuss Acoma with him. He knew that he would have to be the one to decide on the punishment to be meted out. Except in official discussions nobody talked about the trial; only the nature of the punishment. That was precisely what Fray Miguel wanted to discuss with his old friend.

"Juan, hijo, what are you going to do with those poor wretches," he said, embracing don Juan.

"Father, doesn't it depend on how the trial turns out?"

"Juan, listen to me. What do you intend to do? Was it not enough to destroy the village where they have lived for centuries?" pleaded Fray Miguel.

"Padre, you know the burden of responsibility which I bear. I am responsible for the safety of all of you," replied don Juan.

"Granted," continued Fray Miguel, "but don't you think that destruction of a society is example enough to the others?"

"Well, father, we shall see, but we still have not punished the guilty ones."

"They are probably all dead," sighed Fray Miguel.

Several councils were held in preparation for the trial. It was decided to hold the trial at the ecclesiastical capital of Santo Domingo. Captain

Alonso Gómez Montesinos was appointed defense counsel. When informed, he listened with a sagging face. "I shall do my best," he said unsmilingly.

Captain Farfán was given the task of transporting the vanquished Acomans to trial site. It was like a vast cattle drive with hundreds of people, mostly women and children, strewn across the desert countryside. Spanish colonies, despite abuses and cruelties that result every time a people conquers another, were not without a conscience or at least legal procedures for dealing with discordant situations. This had been established by Ferdinand and Isabel from the very outset when they declared the people from the New World to be Spanish subjects under the protection of the crown. The Laws of the Indies first appeared in 1512. So many of them were written and rewritten that in 1563 the supreme judge of the tribunal in New Spain was obliged to make a compendium. In 1680 another more comprehensive one ordered many years before by Phillip II was published.

As Spanish subjects, the Indians were entitled to a trial. With the friars looking over the governor's shoulder and with the reports that had to be made, there was no way to avoid one.

When Vicente arrived from Santo Domingo to wait for the prisoners, the governor reproached him for not accepting the Acomans' first offer of surrender.

"What are we going to do with all those people now that their village is completely destroyed? It is not just a matter of punishment, of making an example of them—and you know we must have a trial—and all this has to be reported to the authorities and eventually to the king."

"Tío," began Vicente. "We still have to make an example of those savages from Acoma if we are to survive in this forsaken land."

"There are only some seventy warriors among the captured," countered Oñate.

"We can deal with those as we wish."

"I am not so much concerned with them as I am with the women and children. We can't hang them."

"Maybe not," retorted Vicente. "But we can send them into servitude somewhere."

"Well, we shall see," said don Juan in an exasperated tone.

The captives were held in a hastily constructed compound on the outskirts of the pueblo. The only shelter the Acomans had was what they could carry on their backs. It had been a very harsh walk from Acoma to Santo Domingo. The severe weather that had started on the eve of the assault upon Acoma still persisted. The Santo Domingans and those from adjoining pueblos were given the responsibility of feeding the prisoners.

The trial convened on 9 February, with the governor presiding as judge. The testimony by the Spanish officers and soldiers was monotonously consistent. It centered on the events immediately preceding the assault on the *maese de campo* and his soldiers, who in their search for flour had separated into two groups. The testimony of the Acomans also was quite uniform. Ca-O-Ma and Cat-Ti-Ca-Ti stated that they were not at Acoma at the time of the incident. Ta-Xyo gave very frank testimony, stating that the Acomans did not want peace with the Spaniards. Zu-Nu-Sta stated that the Spaniards had been the first to kill an Acoman. He also stated that the people of Acoma had been divided on the subject of surrendering or resisting. Ca-U-Ca-Chi testified that the Spaniards had wounded an Acoman and that it was that act that had incited the Acomans to retaliate. The governor introduced the opinion of the friars on whether or not the war against the Acomans was just. The opinion of the Spanish community, and the instructions given to Vicente de Zaldívar on the conduct of the campaign against Acoma were also presented. The Acomans stated through their defense attorney that they did not have anything further to say. Thus, on 12 February the governor declared the trial closed and prepared to give his sentence. He had discussed the question of punishment only with Sosa de Peñalosa, and with Vicente. Fray Miguel had made an appeal for clemency.

Lieutenant Governor Sosa de Peñalosa argued for some kind of mild punishment. He advised the governor not to let his grief over Juan's death influence his decision. Don Juan listened attentively to the older man.

The next day he summoned his nephew to ask his opinion. "Vicente, the royal ensign thinks it would be much better to make the punishment a mild one."

"Tío," retorted Vicente in a mildly exasperated tone, "they killed Juan. If we do not teach them a lesson, the others might attack us here at San Juan."

"Well, I don't know what to do. There is already much criticism of the way the campaign was conducted."

"Yes, by the people who were not there," glowered the young army commander.

Two days later the governor pronounced sentence. All males over twenty-four were sentenced to have one foot cut off. Twenty-four individuals were subjected to this punishment. The males between twelve and twenty-four were sentenced to twenty years of servitude. The women over twelve years of age were given the same sentence. The two Moqui Indians who happened to be at the pueblo and who participated in the battle were sentenced to have their right hands cut off and then set free to carry the terrible story to their land. The girls under twelve were put under the care of the father commissary and the boys under the tutelage of Vicente Zaldívar. The old men and women were sent to live with the Querecho Indians. Kho-Ka-Cha-Ni never made it to the land of the Querechos. He died at the Santo Domingo camp just as the trial was ending. Those condemned to servitude were distributed among the captains and soldiers.

Co-ha avoided Cristóbal for several days. He wasn't angry with him nor particularly distressed, considering that he had overheard discussions in his family about the disaster at Acoma. His father and his chieftains knew the Spaniards were divided in their opinions about the conduct of the battle and the punishments that followed. Nonetheless he did not know what he would say to his Spanish friend.

Two days after the trial as Cristóbal ran around the corner of one of the houses he almost bumped into Co-ha. The two boys stood facing each other smiling awkwardly. Finally Cristóbal spoke up, "I'm sorry for what happened."

Co-ha looked at Cristóbal with sadness in his eyes. He did not speak, but simply nodded.

## CHAPTER TWENTY

After the trial and punishment of the Acomans, the discontent that had started growing almost from the beginning after reaching San Juan once again surfaced. The friars, particularly Fray Miguel, who had been critical of the treatment accorded the Indians, were shocked at the severity of the punishment of the Acomans. They and most of the settlers advocated moving out of San Juan, where friction between the hosts and uninvited guests grew with each passing day. Sosa de Peñalosa, who had the confidence of the disaffected faction, was increasingly worried that the grumbling would swell to an outright mutiny or desertion.

On one of his daily discussions with the governor he said, "Senor Gobernador, why don't we construct a capital and remove ourselves from this situation which is so uncomfortable to us and to the people of San Juan."

"Yes, Yes. I intend to do it just as soon as we know more about the whole province," Oñate answered in an evasive tone.

"Even the friars are beginning to complain. They don't see any plan being developed that will permit them to do their work with a clear conscience," continued don Francisco.

"Don't you think I know that?" snapped the governor. "We shall do something about all this when the time comes, and all those faint-hearted people need is a little patience."

Don Francisco inclined his head slightly and said, "Buenas dias, General, con su permiso," then turned on his heel and walked out briskly.

Don Juan called for a cup of chocolate and sat down at his camp table for several minutes thinking, "I have to find something of consequence." After finishing his chocolate, he got up and walked to his nephew's tent. As he entered Vicente's quarters he uttered a curt, "Buenas dias," then after a long pause said, "They are continuing to press me to build our own capital."

Vicente answered, "Well, it is a bad situation here at San Juan."

Don Juan continued, "But I don't want to settle down to farming yet. What if Cortés had written back saying, 'I planted some crops today.'"

Vicente reflected for a while then offered, "What if we build a capital and then continue looking."

"It would take up too much of my time," protested don Juan.

"Well, what if we take over a pueblo from the Indians," proposed Vicente.

"Can you imagine the howls from the friars?" answered don Juan.

"We can relocate them in some other pueblo. How about Yoongeh Oweengeh, it's just down the trail," pursued Vicente.

"It would be large enough," mused don Juan.

"Yes, and it would be only a short move," added Vicente.

"I shall discuss it with Sosa de Peñalosa," concluded don Juan with a relieved look, "but I still need something important to report back to New Spain. Many of the people are discontented, as you know, and I expect all that will get to the viceroy."

"We should keep on looking," suggested Vicente.

"Precisely," shot back don Juan, "and I have been thinking of trying to find the South Sea."

"Do you think it would be wise to leave the bulk of the army and settlers here to stew while you go on a prolonged expedition?" asked Vicente.

"Maybe not, but what can I do?"

"You can send me."

That night don Juan thought about the situation in the village as he lay in bed unable to sleep. He felt uneasy about the criticism that buzzed all around him, but he did not know exactly how to handle it. "If only I could find a rich mine or a site for a good port," he reflected as he tried to relax.

The next morning he called Vicente to his quarters to inform him that he was sending him in search of the South Sea. Vicente appeared pleased that his uncle and commander had accepted his advice, and entrusted such an important mission to him. He was just as pleased at the prospect of leaving the bickering and the friction between the factions, which were becoming more polarized with each passing day.

Don Juan continued seeing Magdalena despite the gossip that came back to him. He liked sharing his aspirations with someone who would not criticize him or give him advice. Relaxed after their passionate embraces, they would lie in bed and chitchat about San Juan life. He gathered a good bit of information about what people were saying about him and New Mexico. Most of it was negative and superficial, having to do with the severe winter weather and the discomfort it was causing. Words such as "sterile," "poor," and "unproductive," had begun creeping into the vocabulary of the settlers. Don Juan told Magdalena about his plans to move the colony to Yoongeh Oweengeh. "Maybe when they start living more comfortably in their own homes they will stop complaining," he told her. She did not venture an opinion.

During the next few days he discussed the move with the royal ensign. The lieutenant governor agreed that a move would be desirable, but he questioned the wisdom of rooting the people of Yoongeh Oweengeh out of their homes. "Why don't we build a capital of our own?" he asked.

Don Juan answered that eventually they would build one, but reiterated his objection to doing so until the province had been better explored. He stated that two months or so ago he had spoken to Jusepe, the Mexican Indian who had been the sole survivor of the Leyva de Bonilla expedition of 1593 that had perished after Antonio Gutiérrez de Humana had murdered Captain Leyva de Bonilla with a butcher knife at Quivira. The young Indian had told him that although he had not seen any, he had heard stories from the inhabitants of the area that farther north there were a number of great cities. Sosa de Peñalosa reminded the governor that Vásquez de Coronado had been through the entire Quivira area without finding any riches, and that besides such stories only served to inflame those with ideas of finding quick, easy treasure.

The governor put the Quivira expedition in the back of his mind, concentrating on the more immediate problem of discontent among his people. One day in the middle of April he announced at a public meeting in the church that the following day he was going to start evacuating the Indians from Yoongeh Oweengeh and moving them to San Juan. All colonists and soldiers who had been living in San Juan homes would also have to move out. He, Vicente, Captain Villagrá, and Captain Sosa de Peñalosa had been surveying Yoongeh Oweengeh, counting the houses and making notes concerning assignment of them to soldiers and families. The people of the village had been notified as had those of San Juan. Both protested the move, but once the Spaniards had decided, the people of the pueblo had no recourse, and resignedly moved to San Juan or away to other places where they might find a welcome.

The chief at San Juan complained bitterly to his counterpart at Yoongeh Oweengeh. "First they come here and pitch their camp in our midst, then move in to many of our homes, and now they ask that we take you in."

"Yes," added So-Ekhuwa, "they take our blankets, they take our food, and now they take our homes."

Kaa Pin also complained to his friend Fray Cristóbal, who sympathized with him, but who was powerless to help, "We, the friars, have suggested time and again to the governor that he build a capital. Maybe he will relent one of these days."

Cristóbal, who knew everything that was going on from overhearing conversations between his father and his uncle, went to tell his friend Paco Cessar of the move.

"Have you told Co-ha?" Paco asked.

"No," answered Cristóbal with a troubled look. "I don't know how to tell him that we are taking homes away from his people so we can move in."

"Well," countered Paco, "we need the homes."

Cristóbal did not answer, but simply looked at his friend as if asking for an explanation.

There was much confusion during the move to Yoongeh Oweengeh. Fortunately the worst of the cold weather was behind them because some people—Spaniards and Indians—were left without shelter for several days.

About a month after they were settled in their new capital, which was given the name of San Gabriel, the *maese de campo* set out to discover the South Sea.

Sergeant Heredia was one of the soldiers going on the western expedition. Doña Eufemia, who had maintained a close relation with his wife María, told the sergeant that she would look after her. María had not yet recovered from her son's death. She seldom ventured outside of her home. The sergeant was glad to be going with Zaldívar, if only to get away from the gloomy atmosphere of the camp and of his home.

Esperanza, his daughter, was now seventeen years old. For almost a year now she had been seeing Jorge de Zumaya, the governor's page, who called often. María hardly noticed. He would call for Esperanza and she would come out. They would sit on a crude bench by the door until the sergeant called for her to come in. Now as her father waved goodbye, she thought, "I hope you will be safe, father," but despite herself she thought, "now I shall be able to spend more time with Jorge."

The long winter was now over. The rivers had thawed out and were running strong and full as the snow melted in the mountains. The settlers were in better spirits. Those going west with Zaldívar were elated at the thought of a change in scenery, and those staying felt mildly optimistic as the earth renewed itself once again. Cristóbal had asked his father if he could go with Vicente, but don Juan, thinking of the many things that had happened since he last traveled to the west, said, "No, hijo, I shall take you to Quivira later on." The boy frowned but quickly forgot—he was just as glad to be staying with his father, whom he dearly loved and looked to for comfort and protection.

Everyone was up early on that sunny, mild morning in early June to see the *maese de campo* and his twenty-five men set out to the west. Those staying behind felt a certain nostalgia—a certain longing—as one does when a ship leaves port. The departing soldiers appeared glad to be shaking off the winter gloom as they started westward. It felt good to sit in the saddle again.

In view of the still-seething discontent, Vicente felt uneasy about leaving his uncle. Reports had come to him from officers loyal to him and the governor that captains Aguilar and Sosa were still talking mutiny. Captain Sosa wanted mainly to take his wife and five children back to New Spain, but Aguilar was more desperate because he had left his beautiful, aristocratic wife in Mexico City and now saw no reason to stay. Because of the bitter disagreements he had had with them, he felt increasing hatred for the governor and to a lesser degree for the *maese de campo*. He had twice been forgiven by the governor and this rankled the proud, handsome captain.

Vicente embraced don Juan and Cristóbal and then mounted his horse and gave the signal to start. As the crowd started to disperse, the governor and his son stood side by side watching as the small troop disappeared behind a hill.

The governor thought that this period while the colony awaited the *maese de campo's* return was a good time to sum up everything that had happened to date. He did so in a letter to the viceroy dated 2 March 1599, which, despite his effort to sound optimistic, was plaintive in tone. He cited few assets but many problems, asking for additional aid in the form of supplies and men. Stating that "with God's help I am going to give more pacified worlds, new and conquered to his majesty, greater than the good Marqués (Cortés) gave him." He added that "although on occasions like this, one's means often multiply, and in a situation like mine others usually complain, I prefer to bear my difficulties, to being burdensome to his majesty or your lordship, confident in the hope of meeting the needs of many poor people who may wish to join me. If your lordship will grant me the favor of sending me the best qualified persons to my camp, as is proper, it being such an important matter for the service of God and his majesty."

He did not forget his little daughter, María, asking the viceroy to grant him permission to bring her and any of his relatives who might wish to come. He also told the viceroy that he was sending captains Villagrá, Farfán, and Piñero as his personal representatives to plead his case for reinforcements in the capital.

Two weeks later Captain Villagrá, as commander, accompanied by Captain Márquez, Captain Farfán, Captain Piñero, Ensign Las Casas, Brother Pedro de Vergara, commissary Fray Alonso Martínez, and Fray Cristóbal, the governor's cousin, left for Mexico City in the hope of receiving the much-needed help, but also of convincing the viceroy that the colony had promise. With them were sixty half-excited, half-scared young girls captured at Acoma. They were bound for convents in the capital of New Spain.

Fray Cristóbal de Salazar was returning because he was starting to feel the ravages of age.

The evening before his departure he paid a visit to Kaa Pin at San Juan. "So you are leaving our land, my friend?"

Fray Cristóbal sighed, "Yes, I feel that my days are not long. I need to get home."

"I understand," answered Kaa Pin through Jusepe, who had been asked by Fray Cristóbal to translate where it was necessary. "I hope you reach your loved ones."

That same evening Captain Márquez came home to find his wife, Ana, sobbing. "What is bothering you?" he asked impassively.

Ana shrugged her shoulders continuing to sob.

"I didn't ask to go," he continued apologetically.

"You went after the deserters. You went to Acoma and now you are going again. You are going to miss Diego's baptism, which has been delayed once already."

He answered in a more tender tone. "I know but I am a soldier and don Juan doesn't have many people he can trust."

"Why doesn't he want to build a town, so that we can start to have real homes with fields?"

"Whom have you been talking to?" frowned Gerónimo.

"They are all saying the same thing. Ines Sosa; Captain Gasco's wife, Ana; Vaca's wife; and others."

"Well, they had better watch their tongues. Do they think it is easy for don Juan? That is why we are going—to get reinforcements."

Don Juan hoped that now that he had sent Vicente in search of a port and captains Villagrá and Márquez in search of support, material and moral, he would have more time for Cristóbal. He was concerned about his son's lack of formal education. He never seemed to have time to arrange for it. He realized that he did not have enough of an intellectual bent to do much for Cristóbal himself, but he always meant to talk to the father commissary about it. Perhaps one of the lay brothers could tutor the boy. The problem was that Cristóbal never wanted to stay home. It was obvious that he preferred the saddle to the school desk.

Fray Juan was glad to help out with the young lieutenant's education. He discovered that the twelve-year-old future *adelantado* was practically illiterate. What was worse, he did not show much of an interest in his studies. The classes nevertheless continued throughout the summer, often under a cottonwood tree by the red waters of the Chama River. Cristóbal came to like the lay brother. He confided his dreams to that gentle monk, but also his fears. The greatest one he had was that his father would die and he would be left alone. He told him how his life had changed when María, his little sister, was born. After that his mother was always either in bed or sitting on a large stuffed chair. All she could do was smile at him. He would sit long hours by her side, mostly watching her as she dozed. He talked to her from time to time to make sure that she was still alive. All she could do was smile and reassure him in a weak voice. "Estoy bien, hijito, y tú? Why don't you go out to play?" He would get up and go out to play but he would never fully put her out of his mind.

When she died, he was more confused and scared than grief stricken. He would constantly seek comfort from his father, who was himself wrapped in his thoughts. He would sit for long stretches of time near his father watching him, to see if he showed any sign of debility. Another of his fears when he first heard of the expedition was that he would be left behind—that his father would go off without him and perhaps never come back.

The good brother had by now become a fast friend of Jusepe. They were the only ones in San Gabriel who spoke Towa, the language of Pecos. With their frequent contact with the people of San Juan and San Ildefonso they were starting to learn Tegua, and to make many friends among the Indians who regarded them as different from the other Spaniards. Among them was a friendly young man from San Juan named Awa Tside.

There was otherwise not much contact between the Spaniards and the Indians, except for some liaisons that developed between the young soldiers and some San Juan girls.

Miguel Martín, a twenty-two-year-old with light hair and blue eyes, was seen frequently with Oyi. It was obvious that their relationship was more than a flirtation. His friend, Alvaro García, brown-eyed and dark, would accompany him to San Juan on Sunday afternoons. Awa Povi, a sixteen-year-old friend, came along as chaperon. Together the four would stroll by the banks of the river.

## CHAPTER TWENTY-ONE

DON JUAN FELT relatively at peace. His visits with Magdalena became more frequent. He had started taking walks with her in the late afternoons after the heat of the day had subsided. He began to confide in her, telling her of his dreams and aspirations. She would listen and sympathize with him, knowing full well that she could never be a part of them. They never discussed her life except superficially. Her destiny did not seem to go beyond the day-to-day occurrences that defined her precarious existence.

Underneath the relative calm that had settled over the colony, the ever-present threat of discontent lay like an unsteady fault line. Only a few of the settlers were repairing their houses and planting crops. The rest sat as if waiting for something momentous, good or bad, to happen. They appeared reluctant to waste their energy on an enterprise they knew in their heart of hearts would not endure. They watched the governor, and they listened to the mutterings and whisperings of those who no longer thought just of desertion, but of the total destruction of the governor's reputation.

The treasurer and the purveyor general of the province were not particularly friendly to each other, but they were frequently brought together by common, official business. "We are having a meeting tonight at Sosa's house," Captain Gasco said nonchalantly to Captain de Zubía.

"You and your meetings, Luis. I don't want anything to do with them."

"You agree that Oñate is not going to accomplish anything here."

"What if I do? I don't want to be part of any mutiny, Luis."

Gasco held his palms upward, "We are not going to talk mutiny, just discuss possibilities."

"Who's going to be there?"

"I can't tell you that, besides you have a good idea, I am sure."

"Yes, I do, but I still don't want to go. Don't forget that my father-in-law is lieutenant governor."

Luis persisted, "I am sure he is not happy with the situation either."

An exasperated look crossed Diego's light complexioned, regularly handsome face. "Do you know the punishment for mutiny?"

"I told you we are not talking mutiny. Why don't you come and find out?" He paused a moment. "Half of the colony feels the same way we do. Don't you realize that there is strength in numbers?"

"Some other time, Luis," Diego said with finality. "I have to get home. The royal ensign is coming to dinner," he smiled as he turned and left Luis trying to return the smile.

One day in early September as the serious colonists were going about their work of irrigating and hoeing, and the others were simply living out the day, the *maese de campo* rode in with his bedraggled troops. They were dusty and tired. Some of their horses were being led because they were lame. Don Juan could tell by the look on their faces that they had not accomplished their mission.

Only part of the camp turned out to greet the returning soldiers. Some absented themselves from the town; others merely looked up from what they were doing and went back to their task. The governor and his faithful captains and soldiers scurried out to welcome the tired travelers after they heard Cristóbal running through the town square hollering, "Llega Vicente, llega Vicente [Vicente has arrived]."

That evening at dinner Cristóbal was full of questions for his cousin. After he had been sent to bed, don Juan said calmly, "I suppose you did not find anything."

"No," answered Vicente. "We had a hard time even finding people from whom to ask directions. We saw a few rancherías but no established settlements."

"Did they speak of the South Sea?" queried the governor.

"Some did, but most of them did not seem to have any idea. They are very poor people, tío. Besides, the terrain was terrible. We had to leave our mounts at a sierra called Topia and proceed on foot. According to the last people we talked to, the ocean was just a few days away but we could not continue without our horses, particularly since we were told that some Indians in the area planned to attack us. So we returned to where we had left the horses and came back."

"Well," snapped don Juan with a set jaw. "We shall try again, because we do need a port." He checked himself, smiled, and patted Vicente on the back.

Vicente told his uncle later that the Jumano Indians to the south of the Manzano Mountains had refused to give them provisions when they had passed through on their way west. "I would like to go back there and show them how to respect the soldiers of the king."

"I shall go myself," replied the governor. "I have been tied down here long enough. I am getting tired of seeing the long faces of the malcontents. Some of the younger people are beginning to avoid Cristóbal."

"I told you, Uncle, that you should have taken care of Aguilar and some of the others a long time ago. Eventually you are going to be obliged to do it."

"Well, you are right, of course, but they have a large following."

"All the more reason to act quickly," warned Vicente.

The governor started organizing the punitive expedition against the Jumanos the following day. He was motivated as much by the desire to leave the tense atmosphere of San Gabriel as by a desire to exact retribution from rebellious natives. Knowing the nature of his mission and the fact that he was not to be gone for very long, he left Cristóbal in the care of Vicente at San Gabriel. It was the latter part of June when the governor assembled his force of fifty soldiers and set out. The loyalists assembled under an already hot morning sun to see the general off. Having found out the nature of the mission, Cristóbal was clearly troubled He did not say anything except, "Adios, papá," but his worried look was far more eloquent than his words.

The governor was not particularly enthusiastic as he rode southward. He had a sinking feeling as he thought of how badly his enterprise was faring. He knew he had some unpleasant decisions to make concerning the rebellious captains, but he tried to shake the thought out of his mind. Once on the trail he started to feel better. He thought, "With the reinforcements from New Spain, I shall have more people to support me." As he rode through the valley east of the Sandia Mountains he thought of the last time he had ridden there. Cristóbal had been with him because there was no danger from the Indians. But since Acoma, things had changed. Now he was on his way to fight.

As he entered the first pueblo, he saw that there was going to be trouble. The people parted very reluctantly with the tribute that was asked of them. The governor withdrew from the town to think the situation over. On the following day he returned with an interpreter. The general told the Indians who met with him that he was going to punish them for their insolence to him and to the *maese de campo* three months before. He then ordered his men to set fire to some of the houses. The villagers retreated immediately to their homes. As they did so, the general ordered his men to fire on them. Six of the townspeople were killed and several wounded. Later, two of the apparent leaders among the Indians were hanged. Oñate acted throughout the incident with an uncharacteristic rage as if he were lashing out at all his enemies. When one of his soldiers told him that the native interpreter had altered the meaning of what he had said, he ordered him hanged on the spot.

# CHAPTER TWENTY-TWO

WHEN THE GOVERNOR returned to San Gabriel several of his loyalists came to report to him that a plot was hatching among the rebellious settlers to desert. Captain Aguilar and Captain Sosa's names were prominent in most reports. The governor consulted with his nephew who urged a quick resolution to what he considered a dangerous threat to the welfare of the colony. "You should have them tried," he counseled.

"For what specifically?" asked don Juan.

"For fomenting desertion," answered Vicente.

"The problem," countered don Juan, "is that those whom he is enticing to desert are malcontents and would not testify against him."

At dinner that evening Cristóbal was very relieved to have his father safely at home. He had overhead conversations about don Juan's expedition to the Jumano pueblos. While don Juan tried to make conversation he thought pleasant to his son, he noticed that Cristóbal was a bit fidgety. Finally he asked, "What is it, son?"

Cristóbal cleared his throat. "Papá, what did the Jumanos do for you to punish them?"

Don Juan was surprised to hear such a question from his mostly passive son. "They were insolent to Vicente when he asked them to barter for provisions, and later to me when I went to investigate."

Cristóbal looked at his father in acceptance, but also in expectation of further explanation, but don Juan said no more.

That night don Juan sought out his friend, Francisco. They talked a bit about the trip to the land of the Jumanos, but then the conversation turned to what was becoming an obsession with the governor—the plot against his authority. "Why don't you kill the leaders?" Francisco asked bluntly.

"What? Just walk up to them and run them through?" protested don Juan.

"No, catch them in the act of deserting and give them a summary trial, then execute them."

Don Juan did not answer. He changed the subject to ask Francisco if he had seen Magdalena during his absence. Francisco answered laconically, "Once or twice on the square."

The hot, dry weather lasted until mid August. A lethargy took over the capital; the only activity was that of the children who were oblivious to the heat as they played on the banks of the river. "Que infierno," became almost a greeting. Some afternoons the clouds would gather over the mountains and threaten to drench the countryside. The wind would blow, thunder would roll down the canyons, and lightning would flash in the sky, but there was no rain.

After sunset it was as if the whole colony breathed a deep sigh of relief. They came out to the square or went to the riverbank to fill their lungs and immerse their bodies in the cool air. Two hours later those who had not brought a wrap scurried back to their homes.

Esperanza and Jorge, who were now taking walks by the river, were oblivious to the heat. Esperanza's best friend, Isabel, would accompany them. María, Esperanza's mother, did not seem to notice the breach of custom and propriety, and Sergeant Heredia, who was fully aware, apparently influenced by the lax conditions in the colony where signs abounded that age-old customs were not being strictly observed, pretended not to know.

At the Sosa de Peñalosa home there was some discussion of the matter. The royal ensign brought the subject up one evening while he and doña Eufemia were watching the brilliant sunset in the distant horizon. "Have you seen Sergeant Heredia's daughter walking unchaperoned with the governor's page?"

"Unchaperoned perhaps, but not unaccompanied," retorted his wife. "That very sensible daughter of Gerónimo Márquez goes with them everywhere they go." After a moment of reflection don Francisco added with a hint of disapproval in his voice, "Yes, and she is a captain's daughter, too."

"Francisco," answered doña Eufemia. "What possible difference does that make out here in this wilderness?"

The royal ensign looked agitated. "It is precisely in this wilderness where we need to be more vigilant. If we are careless about our moral values we will be in danger of moral and cultural collapse."

Doña Eufemia smiled broadly and shook her head. "Poor little Esperanza, bringing down an empire."

"Laugh if you will, but some of our boys are courting Indian girls, something they would not do if they were back in New Spain."

Doña Eufemia gave her husband a scarcely forbearing look. "Cortés, our great conquistador, did a few things because he was in a strange land and not home. Among other things he fathered Tolosa's wife, a grandchild of the emperor Moctezuma and Isabel de Oñate's mother."

"Yes, I know, but mestizaje is going to do us great harm."

"Do you think Cristobalillo is not as good as some of the rest of us?" pursued doña Eufemia.

Don Francisco, looking distraught, did not answer.

Doña Eufemia tried not to look triumphant, "Think of our history. Everybody came to the peninsula from somewhere—even the Celts and the Visigoths."

They both sat in silence until the sun disappeared behind the distant mountains, then ambled into their house.

In early September the first crop of corn and wheat planted by the Spaniards was harvested. Since many of the colonists did not participate in this agricultural endeavor, the harvest was still not enough to meet the colony's needs. The governor himself was apathetic about such an enterprise, although his own garden tended by his servants produced a respectable harvest of vegetables.

Life was improving, but only very slightly. The homes of San Gabriel, which had formerly been occupied by Indians, were very uncomfortable for the Spaniards who had moved into them along with their servants, who were plentiful since the conquest of Acoma. Bedbugs and lice were such a problem that some of the colonists slept outside in their gardens when the weather permitted. At night the only light was that from the fireplace that produced so much smoke and so little heat that everyone's eyes watered and smarted, even though they gathered around it when the weather got colder.

Don Juan had never been satisfied with the treatment he had gotten at the hands of the viceroy, the count of Monterrey, who modified his contract in so many ways. The governor continued to press for restitution of the original contract. His relative, Juan Guerra de Resa, the rich miner, became the chief financial supporter of the expedition and was in charge of recruiting reinforcements and purchasing supplies. The governor's brothers, Alonso and Cristóbal, became his principal agents, with authorization to speak for him at the viceregal court. Although Cristóbal had accepted the modifications made by the viceroy in October 1599, his other brother, Alonso, went to Spain to plead to the Council of the Indies for reinstatement of the original contract made with Viceroy Velasco.

From the time that don Juan had left for New Mexico with the original settlers, Juan Guerra had started organizing the second phase of the expedition so that by the time captains Villagrá and Márquez arrived in the middle of the summer of 1599 in New Spain to lead the new group to New Mexico, the expedition had been largely assembled. All that was needed now was the indispensable inspection. The count of Monterrey's choice for this task was Captain Juan de Gordejuela Ybarguen.

The point of departure was the same one that had been used in 1598, San Bartolomé in the province of Santa Bárbara. Among the usual supplies of nails, powder, and medicine was a box marked for Juan Guerra the younger containing shirts made of woven linen, a silver plated dagger and sword, cordovan shoes, fine satin-faced hats, another sword, this one gilded and with a belt trimmed with gold, and many other luxury items. Another box marked "don Cristóbal" contained much the same, including six pairs of cordovan shoes, three pairs of ordinary boots, two pairs of cordovan boots, two pairs of calfskin boots, and a gilded sword and dagger along with a bag of soap containing eight hundred cakes. There were also several large boxes marked for don Juan de Oñate with many luxury articles and a large quantity of fine clothing.

Bernabé de las Casas, who had been promoted to ensign by Oñate after he succeeded in finding the governor to notify him of the death of Juan de Zaldívar at Acoma, was unexpectedly named commander of the reinforcement expedition. The viceroy, the count of Monterrey, who was not pleased with Oñate's persistence in trying to get the modifications he had made to the governor's contract revoked, took command of the expedition away from Captain Gaspar de Villagrá and gave it to Las Casas, whom he promoted to captain. Captain Márquez, an Oñate loyalist, was named *maese de campo*. The *sargento mayor* was Captain Conde de Herrera, a newcomer to the expedition, but whose son was already in New Mexico. Captain Villagrá was given the same position as with the original expedition. He was named procurator general or legal officer. He had expected that he would retain his command with Márquez as his *maese de campo*. Captain Farfán, who was to have been the expedition's *sargento mayor* did not return from a visit to his parents. His father, who had been ill for some time, died during his son's visit. Being the oldest son, the extensive family holdings would now be his responsibility.

On 5 September 1600 the expedition began to move. Captain Villagrá was not present. He had left a few days before and had taken refuge in a convent, resentful that command of the expedition had been given to Bernabé de las Casas by the viceroy. Villagrá was threatened by Juan

Guerra with arrest, but to no avail, thus New Mexico lost its poet historian, and Oñate lost an invaluable ally.

Seventy-three soldiers, many married and taking their families, began the trip full of apprehension about the future; among them was a fifty-four-year-old soldier by the name of Gonzalo Fernández Benhumea and his wife, eighteen-year-old Guadalupe. They had heard rumors of the discontent in New Mexico, but it was too late to turn back. The commander himself, Captain las Casas, was not very enthusiastic about returning to an unpromising strife-ridden colony. When asked by the newcomers about conditions at their destination, he was evasive. Captain Márquez, the *maese de campo* of the expedition, sought to paint a good picture, explaining the possibilities of the new territory now that reinforcements would permit a more thorough exploration of it.

The journey was much easier than it had been for the main body two years before. The leaders were all veterans of the first expedition and not only knew the way but also what to expect at each step.

## CHAPTER TWENTY-THREE

CHRISTMAS EVE MORNING at San Gabriel had begun under a perfectly cloudless sky. The whole day was sunny and warm and even those who were clamoring to leave the colony were at peace, partly because they were enjoying a surcease from the severely cold weather that had started two weeks before, and partly because it was the day before Christmas.

Toward midafternoon the sound of creaking wagon wheels became audible in the town. The townspeople knew that the reinforcements would be arriving at any time. The advance party of eight soldiers led by Fray Alonso de la Oliva had alerted them some weeks before. They knew moreover that the travelers, if there was any chance at all, would try to reach San Gabriel by Christmas.

As the riders rode in ahead of the wagons, the governor looked for Captain Villagrá; then he spotted Bernabé de las Casas on the lead horse. As the rider reined in don Juan asked, "Dónde está Villagrá?"

Las Casas dismounted, took off his hat and said, "I'm sorry, general, but Villagrá stayed back at Santa Bárbara."

"What?" exclaimed the governor obviously shaken. "What is all this? Captain Márquez you are the only one who seems to be in place. You tell me what is going on."

Captain Márquez in a matter-of-fact tone said, "Your Excellency, command of the expedition was given to Captain Las Casas upon orders from the viceroy."

"Where is the father commissary?" blurted the governor.

A tall distinguished friar of about forty-five years of age dismounted and said politely, "Padre Escalona at your orders my governor."

Captain López was talking to Captain Tabora and not really looking at the wagons as they pulled up at the plaza. Out of the corner of his eye he caught a glimpse of a familiar person—a very pretty young woman. He said to himself, "It can't be," but as she got off, assisted by a soldier he did not know, he muttered, "My God it is. It's Guadalupe." He pulled his hat lower and turned to leave. Captain Tabora looked at him quizzically but did not say anything.

Despite the tension in the town, when the reinforcements and supplies became a reality, the townspeople forgot their animosities, and for a few brief days harmony reigned. Cristóbal was particularly pleased at the dozens of gifts he received. He could not believe his eyes when he saw all the delightful things inside the crates marked in his name.

The night of the caravan's arrival Francisco went to don Juan's house, where both father and son were still admiring all of the finery they had received. "Come in Francisco. Look at what Juan Guerra sent us."

Francisco felt some of the shirts with his fingers, then said, "May I have a word with you."

Don Juan dropped what he had in his hands and looked at him with curiosity. "Of course. Let's go into my office."

After don Juan had closed the door, Francisco said, "Do you know who is here?"

Don Juan shrugged his shoulders, signifying "tell me more."

"It is Guadalupe. Márquez tells me she is married to a soldier Fernandez . . . much older than she."

Don Juan broke out into a smile. "Aha, she has followed you."

Francisco smiled back weakly and shook his head. "That is all I needed in this forsaken place—besides this Fernandez brought two grown sons with him."

Both don Juan and his friend broke out into laughter.

Christmas day Cristóbal and his father wore the Rouen shirts and the fine hats they had received. After Mass, he and don Juan spent a long time talking not only to the newcomers but even to some of their detractors. The good weather that had arrived the day before held throughout Christmas week. The unseasonably warm days brought the people out to the square. The new arrivals, after many weeks on the trail, welcomed a roof over their heads and the privacy of a home, rudimentary as it might be.

Cristóbal, who had been worried about the changes in attitude toward him that he had started to feel more than to perceive, began to worry less. "Now that the new people have arrived we shall be stronger, and people won't be so unfriendly toward us," he said to his father.

Don Juan took a good interval to answer, then he said casually, "Has someone been unfriendly to you?"

"Not exactly," replied Cristóbal, "but it is not the same as it was when we first arrived."

"Well, I'm glad that the reinforcements are here," concluded don Juan.

By the time the new year arrived the weather had turned not only cold but windy as well. The houses were drafty and were leaking. Since there was little work to do, the new settlers had plenty of time to dwell on their physical discomforts and to talk about it among themselves and with the discontented faction among the original settlers.

The governor had not gotten over the resentment he felt at the appointments the viceroy had made. He issued a proclamation ordering everyone to present his commission. One of the captains, Alonso Donis, having fallen sick, sent his appointment with another captain, Pedro Alonso. When Alonso presented the commission, the governor asked, "Is he being sent by the viceroy or my brother?"

When Alonso answered, "By the viceroy, your excellency," the governor replied in a sharp tone, "Then tell him to wipe his rear with his patents."

Francisco was in a good position to know the machinations that were occurring in the capital. He drank and hobnobbed with the single men and he had two lady friends, one a widow and one married. He warned don Juan every time he saw him that the camp was on the verge of open mutiny. "Sí, yo sé," blurted the governor. "It is Aguilar and Sosa who are behind this."

"But they are not the only ones," responded Francisco. "The friars are complaining—even Fray Juan de Escalona, the new father commissary, is listening to the complaints."

"They are all upset because it has not been easy and the weather is cold. How can I help that?" added don Juan plaintively.

"Well, I'm just telling you what is going on," answered Francisco, shrugging his shoulders.

There was serious discontent even among the friars. The optimistic plan for the establishment of missions in several pueblos had not materialized. Most of the friars had returned to San Gabriel seeking reinforcement in their frustration from their fellow friars. Wary as they were of expressing their true feelings except in the strictest privacy, the governor was oblivious of their disaffection. Father Escalona who had just arrived, found his fellow Franciscans almost totally inactive and with plenty of time to brood. He sought out Father San Miguel, who told him that the governor seemed to be paralyzed by indecision, and that he listened too much to his nephew.

A few days later Escalona crossed paths with Vicente as he walked past the church. He addressed the army commander in his usual dignified manner, "Buenas días, Senor Maese."

"Buenas días, Padre," replied Vicente in a deferential tone.

The father joined the young man, who instinctively slowed his pace. They were chatting about the weather when Father Escalona, seeing a young Indian man hopping on one foot aided by a roughhewn cane, remarked, "This is the third such young man I have seen this week."

"Yes, they are Acomans," replied Vicente nonchalantly.

"I see," said the priest gravely.

"Yes, we had to punish them," volunteered the *maese*.

"And yet our kings have said that we must treat them the way we would Spanish subjects which they are—and, of course, children of God."

"We treat them better, Father. We just beheaded some Spanish soldiers for deserting."

The father remonstrated gently, "Yes, but desertion and treason, offenses against one's duties and responsibilities to God and King are much more serious than defending one's self."

"It was more than self-defense, Father."

"But perhaps not in their minds. These are simple, gentle people."

"But, didn't we come here to teach them, Father?"

"Yes, yes, we did," the aristocratic priest said slowly as he slackened his pace and began to take a different direction. "Good day, Senor Maese."

Vicente doffed his hat politely and continued toward his uncle's house.

As he entered he remarked to don Juan, "The father commissary thinks we were too harsh with the Acomans."

The governor replied, "He, too? It seems everybody is turning against me."

"Not everybody," snapped Vicente. "But it is time we did something about it."

Vicente was adamantly in favor of drastic action against the two whom he regarded as the ringleaders. Exasperated, don Juan asked, "But what can we do?"

"Eliminate them," exploded Vicente. "Either let them go back to New Spain or execute them."

Don Juan frowned, paused a moment, then said haltingly, "If I let them go back, they will spread derogatory stories around the capital."

"Then there is only one other thing you can do," answered Vicente, his jaw tightening.

"One can't suddenly execute someone, just like that," protested don Juan.

"We have done it before," said Vicente, staring at his uncle.

## CHAPTER TWENTY-FOUR

ONE MORNING IN late February there was a great deal of agitation in the square. People gathered in small groups, engaged in hurried conversations, then moved on to another group. Captain Aguilar's body had been brought to the church in a sealed coffin.

"He is being buried this afternoon," someone in the crowd volunteered.

"What happened to him?" others would ask as the muffled conversations continued.

The funeral services were very brief and Captain Pablo de Aguilar of Ecija, Spain, was no more—consigned to the cold, bare New Mexico earth. Those attending stood dry-eyed as they stared at the ground, wondering what would happen next, now that the bubble of equivocation had burst.

The governor called a council of his trusted captains the next day to explain what had happened. "All of you know that Captain Aguilar had been wanting to desert or mutiny for some time now. He was saved from execution twice because the people interceded. Last night he fled with five soldiers. I was apprised in time and he was captured, tried, and executed. The others got away."

His officers remained silent for a moment, then began making comments such as, "He deserved it," and, "I knew it could come to that."

Despite the official explanation, rumors were soon circulating that the governor had had him murdered by inviting him to his residence where his servants were waiting with butcher knives. It was even rumored that don Juan himself had run him through with his sword.

Cristóbal didn't know what to think. When he went to see his friend Paco, he was told that he was out with his father. That night at dinner he asked his father, "Will someone try to kill us?"

Don Juan was surprised and hesitated before he answered gently, "No, son, nobody wants to hurt us."

The answer did not satisfy Cristóbal but he remained silent.

Two days after that mysterious, if not sinister, incident, Governor Oñate issued a proclamation that, due to the loss of a large number of horses, a general roundup was to be held. The governor, against the advice of some of his officers, had followed the policy of letting the horses loose, thus obviating the necessity of feeding them. Now with the trip to Quivira planned, the horses were needed. The roundup required the services of every able-bodied male, except those of the religious community.

After the roundup, the horsemen started drifting back to town in small groups and individually. By early evening Captain Sosa's wife was desperate, asking if anyone had seen her husband. She went to the father commissary to see if he could help. Since he had not been in the roundup, he knew nothing of what might have happened, but he referred Señora de Sosa to Captain Gasco, the treasurer, who would surely know or be able to find out. Captain Gasco told the señora that he did not know for sure, but that he suspected that her husband had been killed. He said that he, too, was very concerned. A soldier told him, he related, that he had seen the captain enter a ravine, and that shortly thereafter the *maese de campo* and some other riders had entered the same ravine. Captain Sosa was not seen after that. Señora de Sosa had for some time feared the worst would happen. She knew that her husband was involved in the dispute with the governor and his nephew, and had asked him on several occasions not to get entangled, but to try simply to get her and his family out of the province, which she detested. When she left Captain Gasco's house, she was sobbing almost uncontrollably. "What is to happen to us now—my poor children? Who will look after us?"

The official explanation given to his officers and the father commissary by the governor was that, inasmuch as Captain Sosa had tried to desert before, and since he had confessed to a new attempt, the governor had him executed according to the practices of war, and buried in an unmarked grave.

Cristóbal did not ask any more questions of his father, but for several days followed him everywhere he went.

Although the colony was still divided, those opposed to the governor and his policies became very circumspect, knowing that the majority of the officers and soldiers were still loyal to him. His enemies, however, continued their campaign to undermine him, talking in very cautious tones to those who were not known supporters of the governor. Among the more outspoken leaders were Captain Zubía, the purveyor general, and Captain Gasco, the treasurer. A chill settled over the colony. The people barely greeted each other, unsure on whose side their neighbors might be.

Father San Miguel, who had been frustrated at Pecos by the lack of response by the Indians and the reports he had heard of what was going on in San Gabriel, decided to abandon his post and return to the capital. Juan de Oñate knew that his confessor was unhappy with his policies, but he also thought that perhaps his age was taking its toll.

The day of his arrival the governor invited him to his house for a *merienda*. The friar was more circumspect than Oñate ever remembered him. Finally don Juan asked him outright, "Is there something you would like to tell me, Father?" Fray Francisco waved his hand as if to dismiss the subject but the younger man insisted. "I hear that you have said you wish to return to New Spain."

Fray Francisco answered, "To that I must say yes, Juan."

"Are you not feeling well?" asked don Juan.

"I am not sick, if that is what you mean, but I must tell you, my son, I am not feeling very well about this enterprise."

Waiting for Father San Miguel to proceed, the governor did not answer. "I cannot be happy when we keep taking corn and other provisions from the Indians without making an effort to sustain ourselves by planting crops."

Here Oñate broke silence, "I have always said that I intend to do just that and more whenever I decide on our permanent settlement. I have not completed the explorations I had planned."

"I can sympathize with that, but why do we have to mistreat the Indians and take so much from them? We have been here long enough to be producing our own provisions and maybe even helping the natives increase their yields. We do have an evangelistic mission here. Don't you believe in it?"

Oñate reflected for a long interval then answered. "I can do more to ensure the success of our mission, Father, if I find something of value for the crown."

"Another Tenochtitlán, another Cuzco perhaps?" interrupted the venerable friar.

"No, I am no Cortés. The time is past for such discoveries, but I mean something like a port or rich mines. I believe in your work, Father, but I did not come here just to found missions. We could have done that in Nueva Vizcaya without coming all this great distance."

"I detect some false pride in what you are saying, Juan. Are you looking for honors?" asked Fray Francisco.

"If I am, it is not just for me, but for my country, and my family. What man does not aspire to recognition? The great civilizing mission which God entrusted to Queen Isabel and to Spain depends on the efforts and will of the adelantados, of the men who dared to dream."

Father San Miguel shook his head, "This is no longer the age for that, Juan. We already have a New Spain and other vice-royalties to the south. This is no longer the age of conquest."

"Maybe you are right, Father, but I must be true to my beliefs as you are to yours, and there is still an unfathomable land to the north of us."

"Yes, there is," answer the old friar, "and it will swallow you as it swallowed up Humana and Leyva, that is, if your pride does not consume you first."

With that, a silence ensued until it was broken by Father San Miguel. "I must go Juan. God bless you."

That was the last time Juan de Oñate and his confessor spoke to each other.

The royal ensign, who had been a good friend and supporter of the governor, was mortified at the recent developments. He was caught between the two factions. At a dinner held for his entire family one Sunday in April, the state of the expedition came up, as always. Captain Zubía criticized the governor and his nephew bitterly. The royal ensign said in a calm voice, "Cuidado, hijo—you know the walls have ears."

"Well, I don't care," Zubía almost hollered. "They had Aguilar and Sosa killed. Aguilar might have deserved it, but Alonso certainly didn't."

"We don't know for sure how it happened," answered don Francisco softly.

"Because you do not want to know," hissed Diego.

"Don't be rude," interrupted doña Eufemia.

"I'm sorry, mother, but nobody wants to see what is going on," continued Zubía.

"Diego," pleaded his wife, Juana, "why don't you leave this to another time?"

After the mysterious deaths of captains Aguilar and Sosa, the governor felt less threatened, and began to think seriously of the expedition to Quivira. The first person he consulted was Vicente, who was not enthusiastic about the idea.

"We already know there is not much in that country and with all the rumors about a desertion, do you think this is the best time to go there?"

Don Juan looked annoyed. "Yes, we know that Vásquez de Coronado did not encounter much, but he did not go far enough, and as to those who are disloyal, I don't want them to affect my decisions in any way. I don't even want to take them with me."

Vicente shot an incredulous look at his uncle. "What, leave them here to plot against you. There is no telling what they might do."

Oñate looked off to one side as if the subject did not merit his attention. "I am not sure I wouldn't like them to desert."

Vicente looked puzzled. "I don't understand."

Don Juan fixed his gaze on Vicente's eyes. "I don't want them here, but I can't order them back to New Spain. If they desert, I not only will be rid of them, but I can charge them with a most serious crime."

Vicente raised his eyebrows then shook his head slowly. "That, uncle, would be a great risk. If they get away, they will spread stories about you."

"I guess they would, but how in the world could anybody condone desertion?"

"Do you want me to stay behind uncle?" asked Vicente.

"No," don Juan answered emphatically. "I need a good field commander; we might have trouble with the Indians, who are very numerous."

"Well, then, whom will you leave in charge," pursued Vicente.

"I don't know, but there is Márquez or Montesinos and staying behind will be a number of good friars and the royal ensign. Besides, I don't think they will have the courage to desert."

"I think we should take at least most of the malcontents so we can keep an eye on them," proposed Vicente.

"To tell you the truth, Vicente, I would like to get away from them and to conduct this expedition in peace," sighed Don Juan.

"I hope we won't have to pay for that peace with worse trouble when we get back," said Vicente in a resigned tone.

On 3 May, just as the governor was finishing his breakfast, the royal ensign came into his tent to ask him what he was going to do about the missing five men who had apparently deserted. The governor shook his head slowly, then said in a tired voice, "Please ask Vicente to come see me." At the conference between the governor and his *maese de campo* it was decided to send Captain Márquez after them.

The royal ensign stayed on until the others left. Don Juan asked him, "Do you have something else, don Francisco?"

The older man looked him straight in the eyes. "Shouldn't we build a capital, and give our people a feeling of stability and a chance for a normal life? Most of them are idle not knowing what your intentions are."

Don Juan answered with unaccustomed informality, "Amigo, my father came to the New World as a young man. He didn't have to leave his home in the Pyrenees. His family was not rich, but had a comfortable life. However, he had a dream, and it was part of Spain's dream. As our country's destiny started to materialize, his did also. He became a founder of great cities and governor of a province. This is my only opportunity to follow in his footsteps. If I stay here and just plant crops, it will mean abandonment of his dream and mine."

The loyal captain with eight men was underway before noon. Two days later as they approached the east side of the Manzano Mountains they heard several voices shouting in Spanish. After a while three riders came into view. They were three of the deserters who appeared anxious to be captured. One of them, Pedro de Rivas addressed Captain Márquez, "Captain, we are on our way back to San Gabriel. The Jumanos killed Castañeda and Santillán."

Captain Márquez did not answer him, but looked back at his men and shouted, "Arrest them." The three did not resist. After they were put in chains, Márquez interrogated them. They told him that Indians at Abo had not only killed the two Spaniards, but apparently invited other pueblos into open rebellion. They were heading back to San Gabriel, they said, to warn the governor.

When they arrived at the capital the governor was alarmed, but he was well into preparation for the expedition to Quivira in present-day southeastern Kansas. He consequently did not react as he had after the Acoma incident that precipitated the war. It took a petition by the whole population, feeling that the colony was in great peril, particularly if the governor left for Quivira, to move the governor to consider a punitive expedition. At a meeting of the officers and soldiers all agreed that the governor should dispose of this pressing matter before proceeding to Quivira.

Vicente once more was charged with the perilous mission. He chose a force of fifty men, including Captain Cristóbal Vaca, and set out on 8 May for Abo. He declined Francisco's offer, made indirectly to don Juan, to participate. He told his uncle that he did not feel comfortable with his friend.

The Jumano Indians knew that when the companions of the two soldiers they had killed reported the incident, the Spaniards would retaliate. A week later their scouts confirmed this assumption when they reported a large force of horsemen headed toward their territory. They assembled in the pueblo of Acoloco north of Abo to await their arrival.

Because they were still several leagues from Abo, Zaldívar's small army was traveling in a relaxed mode and not fully ready for action. Suddenly shots were heard. They came from the vanguard of three soldiers who had been attacked by a large force of warriors shooting arrows, even though they well out of range.

The main Spanish force came alive as Vicente shouted, "Put on your armor and prepare for battle." Within moments they were galloping toward the skirmish that was taking place near the pueblo. When the Indians saw the dust kicked up by the horses, they retired behind the houses. The Spaniards did not pursue, instead withdrawing a safe distance to prepare their assault.

Zaldívar, perhaps remembering Acoma, offered peace if they would turn over those responsible for killing Santillán and Castañeda, but the Indians answered with a shower of rocks and arrows.

Shouting, "Santiago," the *maese* led an attack to the outskirts of the village. Several Indians were killed and two Spaniards wounded. Zaldívar, not wishing to risk any more wounded, signaled a withdrawal. Setting camp on high ground with a good view of the pueblo, they spent the night making plans and resting. "I don't want to storm the village," he told Captain Juan de Montoya, "we can lay siege and attack and withdraw until they surrender."

For six days the *maese* in his usual tireless fashion led attack after attack. Wounded himself, he was very mindful of the others who suffered the same fate.

On the third day Ensign Alvaro García suggested, "Why don't you rest today. Captain Cristóbal Vaca can lead us."

"I'm all right," he answered in a low voice as he prepared his equipment for the day's lethal work.

"Why don't we mount an attack and put an end to this," ventured García.

The commander looked up at Alvaro. "I don't want any more people killed than is necessary—particularly women and children."

Alvaro raised his eyebrows, then smiled nervously, "Bien, maese."

The punishing raids were beginning to break down the Indians' resolve. The *maese* estimated the Jumanos had lost four hundred men. "They can't hold out much longer—not with such losses and their water supply cut off," he said hopefully.

The fifth day the fighting was particularly ferocious. Spurred on by their desperate situation the Indians took cover behind their houses, shot their arrows, and retreated behind another house. As the *maese* chased down two warriors he failed to notice another one who remained hidden behind one of the forward huts. As Zaldívar galloped past, the warrior shot an arrow that missed the commander, but felled his horse. The *maese* fell to the ground with a thud. One of his soldiers who was following close behind spotted the young Indian. He wheeled around and chased the warrior down, running him through with his sword. The commander got up slowly, his left arm limp. He ordered the soldier to deliver a coup-de-grace to his horse, mounted behind him and galloped with him out of the village and safe from the fray.

The losses among the Indians, estimated now at nine hundred, spurred the Indians to try to escape from the doomed pueblo. The commander, despite his wounds, did not let up in his efforts, not only in the fighting but in looking after his troops. In the end Spanish arms and organization once more proved too much for the doomed city. On the sixth day fighting stopped. The women and children were set free but the men over twenty-five were given to the Spanish soldiers as slaves.

When the *maese de campo* arrived back at San Gabriel, he was greeted as a hero by the loyalists, and with mixed emotions by the others. Captain Las Casas and Captain Zubía watched from a distance as Zaldívar was met by don Juan just outside the confines of San Gabriel. "Well, you must admit that Vicente accomplished what he set out to do," mused Las Casas. "We must be very careful with him."

"He doesn't scare me," grumbled Zubía.

## CHAPTER TWENTY-FIVE

THE GOVERNOR ONCE more turned his attention to the Quivira venture. He selected seventy-three men, including Francisco, on whose loyalty he could count, with Vicente as *maese de campo* and *sargento mayor*. He took with him two religious representatives, Fray Francisco de Velasco, a priest, and Pedro de Vergara, a lay brother. The governor, as he had promised, took his son as a full-fledged soldier.

The night before their departure Francisco had a rendezvous with Guadalupe. She had sent him a note that she would be walking by the confluence of the two rivers with a friend.

Francisco was not too keen about going, mainly because he already had a girlfriend. As he told Gerónimo, "This place is too small. I have enough trouble seeing Rosa."

He went anyhow. They went behind the bullrushes where they could have privacy. He embraced her but with a certain coolness.

"Well, I guess you are married," he said awkwardly.

She blushed. "I married that old man so I could come to you."

"This is a very small place, Guadalupe. It will be difficult," he stammered apologetically.

"You don't like me anymore?"

He looked at her for a moment then began smothering her with kisses. After what seemed like an eternity to her friend, Francisco and Guadalupe emerged from behind the underbrush hand in hand, smiling and chattering.

Considering the group too large to assemble at San Gabriel, the advance echelon under Zaldívar left on 23 June 1601 for Galisteo, a few leagues to the south. Five days later the main body, led by the governor, joined up with them. The entire expedition, consisting of the seventy-three soldiers and the two friars, along with many servants, set out for Quivira. They skirted the Sangre de Cristo Mountains to the east and crossed the southern edge of the Glorieta Mesa, headed in a northeasterly direction. They crossed the Pecos River just north of present-day Antón Chico, then the Gallinas River a few miles north of its junction with the Pecos, and on to the Canadian River, which they admired very much not only for the water it offered but for its beauty. They did not suffer any shortages of water, which was abundant not only in the river, but from the springs nearby. Fruit trees were everywhere, and the further east they went the taller the grass grew. They encountered very few Indians, but as they first reached the plain they met up with some nomadic Apaches who were very friendly to them. As they progressed eastward, they came across huge herds of buffalo, which provided them with the most delicious meat they remembered tasting.

After following the river for many days, they were forced to turn northward by some sand dunes, which made traveling very difficult. This point was just beyond the modern Texas Panhandle. By turning northward they came upon broad plains with even more buffalo than before, as well as a great variety of game, including quail, turkeys, deer, and jack rabbits.

It was on this plain that they encountered the first large group of Indians, who turned out to be hostile at first, but after a brief discussion became friendly. They visited the Spanish camp the first night, and the Spaniards returned the courtesy the following day. The Indians allowed the Spaniards to visit their huts, which were made from tree branches placed in a circle approximately ten feet high. Most of the huts were covered with tanned skins. Some were as large as ninety feet across, which made them look like round circus tents. These were the Kansas Indians, who considered themselves enemies of those who lived further on—the ones who would later be called the Wichitas. Here, as elsewhere, it was difficult to tell who were the chiefs, since most of the people appeared quite independent.

When they found out that the Spaniards were going to investigate the disappearance of the Leyva-Humana expedition several years before in this region, they were quick to blame the Wichitas, who they were at war with. They volunteered to go with Oñate's men, guiding them as far as the Arkansas River. The Spaniards then went on their own.

When the Spaniards made contact with a new group of Indians, they, too, seemed ready to fight, but the Spaniards placated them with palms-up signs, indicating peaceful intentions. The Wichitas proved to be very friendly, bringing the first corn they had seen in this country, and even huge loaves of corn bread which were as much as two feet in diameter.

The Kansas Indians, meanwhile, came up behind the Spaniards and started shouting insults and challenges to their enemies. They told the Spaniards that it was here where the Wichitas had killed the members of the Leyva de Bonilla expedition, of which Jusepe, who was now the interpreter and guide for the Spaniards, had been the only survivor.

The governor decided to capture the chief of the Wichitas, whose name was Catarax, and hold him until something definite could be ascertained about the Spaniards who had perished, but as they advanced, they found the Wichita villages completely abandoned. The Spaniards had never seen so much stored corn. In addition, they found beans, calabashes, and plums. They were very impressed by the fertility of the land, which produced amazingly tall stalks of corn and yielded so many other crops. The Indians from this area told the Spaniards that farther on there was another great river with a network of smaller rivers, and that alongside these tributaries lived people much more numerous than anywhere else in the region. They also said that they were the ones who had killed the Leyva de Bonilla party and were to be considered hostile.

The governor wanted to press on, but the soldiers of the expedition held a council during which they decided to present a petition to the governor asking him not to go on in view of the large number of hostile Indians. They pointed out to the commander that their mission had already been accomplished.

Feeling that what they had discovered was not substantial enough, Oñate wanted to proceed. He had, however, become more amenable to suggestions now that he was surrounded by loyal troops. He listened carefully, presented his arguments for continuing, but finally acceded to his soldiers' wishes.

Preparations to return to San Gabriel were quickly made. Vicente went ahead to assess the situation among the Kansas Indians, whom he did not trust. He found that they had retreated to their houses, which they had fortified. He reported what he had learned to the governor, who ordered all of his soldiers to put armor on their horses, and prepare for battle.

Cristóbal became elated at the thought of his first combat. As he nervously put the armor on his horse, he dropped several articles. His father, who felt that a fight was imminent, came to reassure him. As he handed Cristóbal one of the plates he had dropped, he smiled at him.

Cristóbal's face turned pink as he returned his father's smile with a weak one of his own. Don Juan put his arm around Cristóbal's shoulder and gave him a reassuring squeeze.

After he left Cristóbal he went to where Francisco and his men were preparing their mounts. "Francisco," he said as he reined in, "may I speak to you privately?" Once they were out of earshot from the others he continued, "Would you ride near Cristóbal and keep an eye on him. I don't want him to think that I am unduly concerned."

"Certainly Juan," replied Francisco.

As they advanced southward, the Spanish soldiers turned their palms upward as a sign of peace, but these Kansas Indians, who were resentful that the Spaniards had not helped them against their enemies, were determined to punish them. The first formation the Spaniards encountered consisted of more than fifteen hundred warriors in a semicircle. Cristóbal was riding to the right and slightly behind his father. Francisco and his men were right next to him. He felt a weakness in his stomach, which radiated to his arms and legs. He saw the enemy only as a blur of people. He was oblivious of the shower of arrows falling around him. Somehow he managed to raise his harquebus and he fired into the enemy crowd. It became very difficult for him to put away his firearm in order to unsheathe his sword because he needed both hands to control his horse. Suddenly he saw his father and those next to him wheel around to the left. He followed, not knowing what was happening, as the Spanish troop retired to a safe distance beyond arrow range. Here the Spaniards dismounted, assumed a formation, and started a fusillade with their firearms. As the enemy attack subsided, Vicente called for a cease-fire. It was not until then that Cristóbal felt a slight, stinging itch on his left shoulder. As he brought down his hand after scratching the offending area, there was blood on his fingers. His father, who had forgotten about his son during the heat of the encounter, rushed over to him. Quickly checking the wound, which turned out to be no more than a superficial skin break, he said, "Ya eres soldado, hijo [You are now a soldier]." After this, Cristóbal shook off his nervousness and confusion, and started to feel the elation bordering on joy that most soldiers feel after their baptism of fire.

The battle lasted another two hours. The Kansas would advance within arrow range and the Spaniards would fire volley after volley until the Indians retreated. Cristóbal now could see the enemy more distinctly, and he fired with steadier aim and a good bit of relish. There was no need for any particular attention to Cristóbal either by his father or his father's friend.

Seeing that just about all of his soldiers were wounded, although none seriously, and that numerous Indians were getting killed, the governor ordered his men to fall further back, releasing most of the prisoners they had taken during the first part of the battle. This gesture had the effect of stopping the battle. Oñate's small army returned to its camp and made preparations for the return to San Gabriel.

On 25 September the Quivira expedition started back to the capital. Don Juan had rather enjoyed the outing, even though it had produced nothing, but now as he headed back to New Mexico, he began to worry about the situation there, and about the future of the colony. As he rode along, a variety of thoughts came to him. Gazing at the endless plain, a feeling of unreality would possess him for an instant. The whole scene seemed dreamlike to him as if he were on a treadmill—walking, but not making any progress. His back hurt most of the time. Sometimes the pain would shoot through to his stomach, causing nausea. He would occasionally call a halt, get off his horse, and sit on the ground for several minutes until his mind cleared and the pain subsided.

Vicente was impatient to get back. He had nagging apprehensions that something drastic was happening back at the capital. He had opposed leaving the dissident ringleaders at San Gabriel. He had mentioned this concern several times to the governor during the Quivira trip, but don Juan invariably changed the subject as if the possibility of a mutiny or desertion was too monstrous to contemplate.

The expedition, nevertheless, did make a very quick trip home, due mostly to the efforts of the *maese de campo*, who kept the soldiers moving without deviations or unusual rest stops. Don Juan mounted when all the rest did, and dismounted at the end of the day without conversing much with anyone. The feeling of unreality and depression persisted. He did not complain of the pain he was suffering, although his ashen face revealed it.

When the Sangre do Cristo Mountains came into view, most of the small army cheered. Don Juan looked at them and blinked as if he did not comprehend that the mountains meant they were nearing home.

At Pecos they received the news from the natives that most of the Spaniards at San Gabriel had left. The news jolted the governor out of his trance, but he felt too tired to continue. Vicente at once said, "I will go on to San Gabriel immediately."

# CHAPTER TWENTY-SIX

AT SAN GABRIEL, talk of desertion had surfaced the moment the governor and his troops disappeared behind the first hill. Captain Bernabé de las Casas had not gotten over the stinging rebuke he had received from the governor for having "conspired," as the governor put it, to take over command from Captain Márquez of the reinforcements on their way back to New Mexico. He was by no means the leader, however, that distinction going to Captain Luis Gasco de Velasco and Captain Diego de Zubía, who were much bolder. In one of their numerous discussions, Zubía told Captain Gasco, "We must act now that the governor and the *maese de campo* are gone."

"I know," answered Gasco. "But what about Márquez and Gómez? They will never agree to let us leave without trying to stop us."

"Luis," countered the younger man, "we outnumber them, and they know it."

"Well, I think that we should approach them anyhow to get an idea of what they will do," replied Gasco.

"Yes, perhaps, and we should contact all the friars, also," added Zubía.

At a meeting called at Captain Gasco's home by him and Captain Zubía, the abandonment of New Mexico was discussed with Captain Bernabé de las Casas; Captain Cessar; Captain Alonso Quesada; Captain Alonso Sánchez, the *contador*; Captain Antonio Conde; and Captain Pedro Valle. Captain Zubía brought up the necessity for at least near unanimity in the venture. "It could after all, be construed as desertion by the authorities in New Spain."

"We must have the royal ensign's accord in this," said Captain Quesada.

"What do you think, Diego?" he asked of Captain Zubía.

"Well, he won't stop us, but he won't join us, either," answered Zubía.

"Can we get him to call a meeting where we can all go on record with our grievances?" asked Captain Cessar.

"I don't know," replied Zubía. "I had a misunderstanding with him. Maybe if Captain Cessar and Luis approach him."

"We also need to get the friars behind us," said Captain Sánchez.

"Well, most of them are very discouraged," joined Captain Gasco.

"Yes, the ones we need to convince are the father commissary and Fray Miguel," added Zubía.

"Why don't we all meet with them as soon as possible?"

The friars did not need much convincing. They, themselves, were making plans for discussing desertion with the officers and soldiers. Both groups agreed to meet at San Ildefonso, which presented the advantage of offering a place for a more or less secret meeting nearby without conducting it in the capital itself, where it might provoke the loyalists. All of the leading conspirators among the officers attended except Captain Zubía. He stayed away in deference to his wife, who appealed to him not to cause her father, the lieutenant governor, any more problems. Zubía knew what the outcome of the meeting would be anyhow, but he asked Captain Gasco to assure the friars that he was very much in favor of abandoning what he considered a doomed colonial enterprise.

The outcome of the meeting was indeed a foregone conclusion. Fray Miguel had already been swayed by the argument that missionary work was all but impossible under the governor's policy of dependence on Indian tribute. Father Escalona agreed in principle, but said that he could not leave the province for fear that the Franciscans would be looked upon as deserting their flocks. He felt that they must not jeopardize their ecclesiastical jurisdiction in New Mexico, where he knew there was much work to be done if conditions were to change. They all agreed to ask the lieutenant governor for a meeting.

Fray Francisco and Fray Miguel, along with Captain Cessar and Captain Gasco, presented the petition to the royal ensign for a meeting of the disaffected friars and colonists where their reasons for departing New Mexico could be stated and recorded.

Captain Sosa de Peñalosa, as lieutenant governor, was very reluctant at having anything to do with the plot. He felt that he was caught between two irreconcilable forces. He received the emissaries from the rebel group coldly. "I cannot in any way condone your contemplated action," he told them. "I sympathize with your grievances, but desertion is not the way to resolve any problem."

"We appreciate your position, and we do not ask you to join us," replied Captain Cessar somewhat timidly.

"Yes," concurred Captain Gasco. "All we want is a hearing. We do not want to leave without having publicly stated our reasons."

"But certainly you must see that even that will be construed as at least tacit approval," answered the lieutenant governor.

"Why don't you listen to both sides," suggested Father Miguel.

"You don't have the power to stop us, and you must show that you did something," added Captain Alonso de Quesada.

The lieutenant governor reluctantly agreed to hold the meeting. On 7 September 1601, he called all of the friars and all of the officers who were planning to abandon the province to a meeting at the Church of San Miguel. The friars responded to the summons to a man except the father commissary, fathers Lugo and Oliva, and Lay Brother San Buenaventura, who were out working in their missions. The lieutenant governor asked each person present to state his views in turn. The first one to testify was Father Francisco de San Miguel, the governor's own venerable confessor. He stated that from the time he arrived his conscience had been bothered by the mistreatment of the natives. He said, "Instead of coming to preach the word of God, we Spaniards have blasphemed it." He further stated that "our people do not leave them anything in their houses, nor any living thing, food, or anything of value. For this reason, the Indians run away. This witness has seen many pueblos abandoned, the people having fled for fear of ill treatment. When this witness was prelate, he asked the governor many times to have pity on the suffering of the natives, and not to tolerate robberies and injustices. But since this country is so wretched and poor, the governor has not been able to effect any remedy, nor can he do so. For this, and many other matters that trouble his conscience, and on account of the poverty of the land, this witness is of the opinion that now, while there is an opportunity, we should return to New Spain and report to the king, our lord, the viceroy, the Audiencia, and their prelates about all these matters and any others that would be brought out in the courts."

Fray Francisco de Zamora followed. He reiterated many of the grievances of the first witness, asking the question that, in view of such treatment, why should the natives want to become Christians? He added that he knew for sure that the soldiers often violated Indian women. He mentioned the great sterility of the land. He did not necessarily advocate returning to New Spain, but simply moving away from the area of San Gabriel and building their own capital.

Fray Lope Izquierdo was the next witness. He, being among the reinforcements, gave credit to the original settlers who "with the loyalty, enthusiasm, and courage of true subjects, have endured more than three years of numerous and diverse labors such as had never been borne in the service of their king and natural lord. This situation was due," he said, "to the fact that the land was so poor and lacking in everything necessary to support life." He concluded that "the only decent way to overcome the harm done the natives is to depart from their lands and leave them free, or to let our people perish when their provisions give out." The other friars present confirmed what the witnesses had said.

The first of the officers to testify was Captain Alonso Sánchez, the expedition *contador* or accountant. He did not cast any aspersions, but simply stated that because of the extreme sterility of the land, his numerous family had suffered much privation and he wished to leave.

Captain Zubía stated that supplies were exhausted and whatever the Indians had to offer had been consumed. All he asked was that he be allowed to seek his own remedy.

Captain Bernabé de las Casas cited the extreme sterility of the land, saying that nonetheless he married in New Mexico and had settled down to do his best. He felt, however, that he could no longer stay because of the governor's hostility since he had been appointed by the viceroy to lead the reinforcement expedition in 1600. He asked permission to leave with his wife and child.

Captain Gregorio Cessar testified that, having been among the original settlers, he had accompanied the governor to the pueblos, which he had explored, and had always found the land sterile, lacking in everything essential to support human life. He requested that he be allowed to go back to New Spain lest his wife and seven children risk the danger of perishing.

On 1 October, the lieutenant governor wrote a letter to the viceroy apprising him of the desperate situation. He started the letter by writing, "I do not know how I should explain to your excellency the events and changes that have taken place in these provinces of New Mexico. I am at a loss to know who is responsible for the situation. If I blame the governor, it would be unjust, since he is away with most of the army in search of new provinces, enduring many hardships in the service of your majesty. If I blame the friars, they quote so many texts from the Holy Scriptures to prove that we cannot take food and blankets from the Indians. If I blame the captains, they answer that they were acting to overcome their own privations in order to survive. Who, then, are we to blame if not our sins? All will be lost if our Lord does not remedy this situation by allowing the governor to discover something so important that the men may overcome their indifference and lack of confidence in finding anything worthwhile in these lands." The lieutenant governor entrusted the letter to Captain Gasco de Velasco, one of the leaders in the movement to abandon the province.

Father Escalona, in his letter of the same date to the viceroy was openly critical of the governor, saying, "The first and foremost difficulty, from which have sprung all the evils and ruin of this land, is the fact that this conquest was entrusted to a man of such limited resources as don Juan de Oñate. The result was that after he entered the land, his people began to perpetrate many offenses against the natives and to plunder their pueblos of the corn they had gathered for their own sustenance." He went on to say that if the king wanted to maintain the land, he should distribute the pueblos among the married men. They should receive help from the king for a time, otherwise it would be impossible to live because the land is so sterile and cold. He went on to say that of the three parts of the army at San Gabriel, two were leaving. He and the lieutenant governor were staying to await the return of the governor.

## INTERLUDE: THE WOMEN OF SAN GABRIEL

While the meeting was in progress in the church, women wrapped in shawls, almost as if to disguise their identities, began to head for María de Heredia's home, one by one, as if they had made appointments. They were principally widows or wives of soldiers who had gone to Quivira with the governor. María was nursing the wife of one of her husband's soldiers. The woman had fallen sick a week before with a very high fever, which would abate one day and rage the next. She was lying in a small bed at one corner of the large room that served as kitchen, bedroom, and sitting room. Mercedes, the patient, had been married only one year when her infant child had died of an illness that took him in a matter of days.

The house was dark, illuminated only by the light of one small window that had been cut out by Sergeant Heredia at the time the house was requisitioned from its Indian owners, and from the light of the small fire in the fireplace.

Esperanza, María's seventeen-year-old daughter, bustled around the room in a late effort to tidy up as the first woman approached the house. The bells in the church began tolling. Mercedes observed the scene through glistening eyes and heard the conversations as if coming from inside a well.

(Habitación sencillisima, casi sin muebles, mesa y sillas muy rústicas. Suenan las campanas de la iglesia.)

CORO: O Tierra triste, / Tierra fría, / Tierra abrasada.

MARIA: ¿Por qué suenan las campanas, hija?

ESPERANZA: Se están reuniendo en la iglesia para ver si nos quedamos o nos vamos.

MARIA: Las iglesias son para las cosas de Dios y no para las de este mundo.

ESPERANZA: Dicen que nos vamos a morir de frío o de hambre si nos quedamos.

MARIA: Que nos vayamos o nos quedemos, quién va a resucitar a mi hijo?

ESPERANZA: El ya ha muerto, madre, pero nosotras vivimos.

MARIA: Tú vives, you no, yo me quedé en aquel triste desierto con my hijito que apenas comenzaba a vivir.

ESPERANZA: Ya la iglesia se está llenando. Voy a mirar por la puerta abierta.

MARIA: Ve, hija, tú tienes vida. Yo me quedo. (La hija se va.)

CORO: Tierra de vientos cálidos, / de tormentas sin lluvia, / Tierra de vientos helados, / Que congelan el alma.

(JUANA entra.)

JUANA: Hola, María. Has oído lo que dicen los frailes?

MARIA: Ya los frailes no me dicen nada desde que me dijeron que mi niño se iba al cielo y yo me quedaba sola en este páramo.

JUANA: Vamos, María! y Esperanza no cuenta?

MARIA: Yo hablo de niños. Ella ya tiene diecisiete años y me dicen que tiene novio.

JUANA: Hablas como si ya se te hubiera acabado la vida.

MARIA: ¿Hay vida aquí en esta tierra?

JUANA: Tu marido vive.

MARIA: Sí, pero no para mí. El está contento mientras anda con don Juan en sus Quiviras, o sus Cíbolas, buscando riquezas—ilusiones, ensueños.

JUANA: Claro, así son los hombres, María.

MARIA: Si, así son, pero ellos se divierten aún en las circumstancias más penosas y peligrosas, con sus guerras y fantasías infantiles.

JUANA: Pues, el mío no fue esta vez, pero se le ve en los ojos que quisiera.

MARIA: Y vosotros ¿os váis o os quedáis?

JUANA: Claro que nos quedamos. Paco cree que don Juan va a tropezar sobre algo importante.
MARIA: No encontrarán nada más que llanos sobre llanos, sin fin, sin horizonte.
JUANA: Espero que traigan buenas noticias.
MARIA: Que vengan a trabajar. Por qué no sembramos? Porque a don Juan y mi marido no les importa si morimos o vivimos.
JUANA: Bueno, María, quédate con Dios. Voy a ver si encuentro un poco de maíz para la cena.
CORO: O tierra vasta, / Tierra árida, / Tierra yerma.
(Crepusculo. MAGDALENA entra.)
MAGDALENA: Buenas. ¿Qué haces sola, mujer?
MARIA: Sola, más que sola estoy, y solos estamos todos.
MAGDALENA: Pues yo no, aunque haya muerto mi marido huyendo—no sé si de mí o de esta tierra.
MARIA: Que Dios lo tenga en paz!
MAGDALENA: El en paz. Y yo en vida.
MARIA: ¿No te importa lo que dicen de ti y de don Juan?
MAGDALENA: ¿Y que más da? El gobernador es viudo y yo también. El es hombre y yo mujer.
MARIA: Según dicen, se le quiere ir la gente.
MAGDALENA: Que se vayan los cobardes, los débiles. Yo me quedo porque vivo y porque sé que la vida es igual en todas partes.
MARIA: Sí, es igual cuando hay vida. Pero aquí no hay más que hambre, frío, calor y muerte . . . muerte de los nuestros y muerte de los pobres indios de los cuales tenemos que robar para sobrevivir. Morir para vivir.
MAGDALENA: Tú hablas como los frailes. ¿Para qué hemos venido sinó para quitarles a los indios lo que tienen?
MARIA: (irónicamente) Concepto muy cristiano, ese.
MAGDALENA: Para bautizar a los indios tenemos que vivir.
MARIA: Matar y robar para bautizar, qué bonito.
MAGDALENA: ¿Por qué no te vas con los demás? Los frailes quieren irse porque tienen los mismos escrúpulos.
MARIA: Yo no me voy porque ya no tengo vida, ni aquí, ni allá, pero aún moribunda como estoy, no me gusta robar y matar.
(Se va MAGDALENA.)
CORO: Tierra de llanos sin horizonte, / de sierras coronadas, / Tierra de cielos infinitos, / sin tiempo ni dimensiones.
(Anochece. Entra ANA.)

ANA: Buenas tardes, María. ¿No has oído que se van todos los frailes con la excepción del padre Escalona? Se van los Céssar y los Sánchez.
MARIA: ¿Y quiénes se quedan?
ANA: Casi nadie. el Alférez Penalosa, Alonso Gómez, Gerónimo Márquez y otros pocos.
MARIA: ¿Y tú, te vas?
ANA: ¿Cómo? Aunque quisiera, ya sabes que a Cristóbal le gusta este país.
MARIA: A mi marido no le importa mientras anda errando como vagabundo.
ANA: Y supongo que te quedas.
MARIA: Yo ya me fui. Que más da si me quedo o me voy?
ANA: ¿Cómo? Y tu hija, y tu marido?
MARIA: Mi marido tiene sus Cíbolas y sus Quiviras, y mi hija tiene su novio.
ANA: Los hombres fueron a Quivira bajo órdenes.
MARIA: El mío se fue porque le gusta más que estar en casa.
ANA: Nosotros hemos venido porque en España no teníamos nada.
MARIA: (con ironía) Y aquí tenéis mucho?
ANA: No, pero tendremos. Cristóbal dice que hay riquezas aquí, si las buscamos con paciencia.
MARIA: No encontraremos más de lo que ya hemos encontrado. Nunca han podido olvidar sus Tenochtitlanes y sus Cuzcos. Son niños avarientos.
ANA: Cristóbal no habla de esas riquezas. (Se va.)
CORO: Tierra humilde, / Tierra pasible, / Tierra sufrida.
(Mañana resplandeciente. Tres semanas después.)
(Sale la hija.)
ESPERANZA: O, Madre, dicen que la expedición está a veinte leguas.
MARIA: Quién lo dice?
ESPERANZA: No sé—lo dicen.
MARIA: Y a nosotras qué?—Estamos más muertas que vivas—Qué nos puede importar?
ESPERANZA: A mi sí. Viene Jorge y me padre también!
MARIA: Y crees que te va a querer aún, tan flaca como estás.
ESPERANZA: O, sí, porque yo lo quiero tanto.
MARIA: También dicen que no han encontrado nada. Chozas y llanos—llanos y chozas.
ESPERANZA: Qué importa, madre, vienen ellos. Nos traen vida.
MARIA: ¿Qué vida? Tal vez vienen mas harapientos que nosotras. Ya

hace dos semanas que se fueron los demás y cada día hay menos vida en San Gabriel.

ESPERANZA: Pero nosotras vivimos y nos viene más vida, toda la vida a veinte leguas de aquí.

MARIA: (pensativa, distante) Vida a veinte leguas, y mi hijo tan lejos.

CORO: O Tierra encumbrada, / Ara del continente, / Tierra donde se reza a gritos, / Que retumban por los cañones.

SCENE

(A simple dwelling, almost devoid of furniture—a table and some very rustic chairs. The church bells are sounding.)

CHORUS: O, sorrowful land, / Land hard and cold, / Parching land.

MARIA: Why are the church bells ringing, daughter?

ESPERANZA: They are calling everybody to meet in the church to decide if we are staying here or going away.

MARIA: Churches are for the things of God and not for those of this world.

ESPERANZA: They say that we are going to die of cold and hunger if we stay here.

MARIA: Whether we go or stay, who is going to bring my baby son back to life?

ESPERANZA: He is dead, mother, but we are still alive.

MARIA: You are alive, not I. I stayed in that terrible desert with my little boy who had scarcely begun to live.

ESPERANZA: The church is already filling up. I'm going to peek through the open door.

MARIA: Go, child. You still have life. I shall stay.

(The daughter leaves.)

CHORUS: Land of hot winds, / Of rainless storms, / Land of chill gales, / That turn souls to ice.

(JUANA enters.)

JUANA: Good afternoon, María. Have you heard what the friars are saying?

MARIA: The friars have nothing to say to me since they told me that my baby was going to heaven and I must stay alone in this empty desert.

JUANA: Come now, María. Esperanza doesn't count with you?

MARIA: I'm speaking of children. Esperanza is already seventeen years old and they tell me she has a sweetheart.

JUANA: You talk as if your life were over.
MARIA: Is there life in this country?
JUANA: Your husband is alive.
MARIA: Oh, yes, but not for me. He is happy going with don Juan to his Quiviras, his Cíbolas, looking for riches—running after dreams, illusions.
JUANA: But that's the way men are, María.
MARIA: Yes, that's the way they are. They find amusement in danger, misery, wars—all childish fantasies.
JUANA: Well, mine didn't go this time. But I could see he wanted to go.
MARIA: And you—Are you staying or leaving?
JUANA: It seems that we are staying. Paco thinks that don Juan is going to stumble across something important.
MARIA: They won't find anything but barren land and more land, with no end, never a fixed horizon.
JUANA: Well, I hope they bring good news.
MARIA: Let them get down to work. Why don't we plant? Because to don Juan and my husband it's not important if we live or die.
JUANA: Ah, well, María. God keep you. I have to see if I can find a little corn for dinner. (She exits.)
CHORUS: O vast land, / Barren land, / Empty land.
(Twilight. MAGDELENA enters.)
MAGDALENA: Good evening, María. Woman, what are you doing all alone?
MARIA: I am more than alone. And aren't we all alone?
MAGDALENA: Not I. I am not alone. Even though my husband died running away—and I don't even know if he was running from me or from this country.
MARIA: God give him peace.
MAGDALENA: Yes. Peace for him. Life for me.
MARIA: Don't you care what they say about you and don Juan?
MAGDALENA: Why should I? The governor is a widower and I have no husband. He is a man and I am a woman.
MARIA: Well, the people are saying they want to leave.
MAGDALENA: Let the cowards go, the weak ones. I am staying because I feel alive, and I know life is the same no matter where you go.
MARIA: Yes, it's the same when there is really life, but here there is nothing but hunger and cold, or heat and death—death for us—death for the poor Indians that we have to rob in order to survive. Death to support life.

MAGDALENA: You are talking like the friars. Why did we come if not to take from the Indians what they have?
MARIA: (Ironically) A very Christian idea that.
MAGDALENA: In order to baptize and save Indian souls, we have to stay alive.
MARIA: To kill and rob in order to baptize—very pretty.
MAGDALENA: Then why don't you go with the rest? The friars want to leave because they have the same scruples.
MARIA: I am not going because I have no life left—neither here nor there. But dead as I feel, I don't like robbing and killing.
(MAGDALENA leaves.)
CHORUS: Land of plains with endless horizons, / Eminent peaks crowned by snow, / Land of skies, blue and unbounded, / Dimension and time without measure.
(NIGHTFALL. ANA enters.)
ANA: Good evening, María. Have you heard that all the friars are leaving except Father Escalona? The Céssars and Sánchezes are leaving.
MARIA: Who is staying?
ANA: Almost nobody. Alférez Peñalosa, Alonso Gómez, Gerónimo Márquez, and just a few others.
MARIA: And you—Are you leaving?
ANA: How can I? Even if I wanted to, you know that Cristóbal likes this country.
MARIA: Nothing matters to my husband so long as he is roaming like a vagabond.
ANA: And I suppose that you are staying.
MARIA: My life has already gone, so what difference does it make if I stay or go?
ANA: What difference? What about your daughter and your husband?
MARIA: My husband has his Cíbolas and his Quiviras, and my daughter has her sweetheart.
ANA: The men went to Quivira because they were ordered to go.
MARIA: Mine went because he likes it more than being at home.
ANA: We came here because in Spain we had nothing.
MARIA: (Ironically) And here we have a lot?
ANA: No, but we shall have. Cristóbal says there are riches here if we have the patience to look for them.
MARIA: We won't find more than what we have already found. They can never forget their Tenochtitláns and their Cuzcos. They are greedy children.

ANA: Cristóbal is not talking about those riches. (She leaves.)
CHORUS: Humble land, / Languid land, / Stoic land.
(A glorious morning. THREE WEEKS LATER. ESPERANZA enters.)
ESPERANZA: Oh, mother, they say the expedition is only twenty leagues away.
MARIA: Who says it?
ESPERANZA: I don't know. They say.
MARIA: And what can it mean to us? We are more dead than alive. How can we possibly care?
ESPERANZA: Well, I care. Jorge is coming home, and my father too.
MARIA: And you think he is still going to want you—as skinny as you are?
ESPERANZA: Oh, yes! Because I want him so much.
MARIA: They also say that they have found nothing. Huts and prairies, plains and tents.
ESPERANZA: What does it matter, mother? They are coming—and bringing life back to us.
MARIA: What life? They may be coming back more ragged that we are. It's already been two weeks since the others went away, and each day there is less life in San Gabriel.
ESPERANZA: But we are alive, and more life is coming toward us—all of life only twenty leagues from here.
MARIA: (Pensively, distant) Life at twenty leagues, and my son so far away.
CHORUS: Oh, lofty land, / Altar of a continent, / Land where prayers become screams, / Resounding down the canyons.

## CHAPTER TWENTY-SEVEN

THE DIE WAS now cast. Everybody knew where everybody else stood. The night after the meeting, Captain Zubía and his wife came to see the lieutenant governor. Relations had been strained ever since the outburst by the captain during dinner at his father-in-law's residence. Doña Eufemia had been at her daughter's house several times, but only when she knew that her son-in-law was not there. The distinguished lady, while criticizing don Juan, was very much opposed to desertion. She wanted to go back to New Spain, but not as a renegade. "We are still subjects of his majesty, and as such we must act within the law," she repeated several times to her daughter and to her husband.

Don Francisco received Diego and Juana coolly, not out of resentment, but simply out of indecisiveness and confusion. He felt equally ill at ease whenever he met one of the loyal colonists. Captain Zubía, who was not in the least timid, started the conversation. "Well, now that everything is out, will you be coming with us?"

Doña Eufemia did not speak, but she shook her head slowly.

Diego's face hardened perceptibly, but he took some time to speak again. His wife looked at her mother as if pleading for understanding. "Well, we are leaving," replied Diego, slowly and emphatically, "and we are going to charge your don Juan with all the crimes he has committed. Vamos, Juana."

As they turned to leave, Juana cast another pleading glance at her mother, who made a gesture of understanding with her eyes.

That same day Juan met Awa Tside as he was crossing the village square. The two friends greeted each other in the usual manner, but Brother Juan noticed a certain reticence in his friend. He asked if anything were wrong.

Awa Tside answered by asking, "Are you leaving, too?"

"I don't know," answered the brother. "I don't believe we are doing much for your people."

The young man bowed his head slightly, perhaps not willing to engage in a fruitless conversation.

"Go with God," smiled Brother Juan.

Awa Tside nodded and continued across the square.

Several days later, as Captain Alonso Gómez, who was ostensibly in command of the colony, was walking across the square, Captain Zubía called to him. Captain Gómez stopped, and Zubía came up to him and greeted him. "Buenas tardes," answered Gómez.

"Why do your followers refuse to leave with us?" asked Zubía.

"Mr. Purveyor," Captain Gómez snapped. "Even if we were not in the service of our king, our master, could we show greater cruelty than to abandon the governor and his forces in the interior and leave them without refuge or shelter on their return? Even if I am left alone, I am going to wait for him."

Captain Zubía's eyes flashed and his face reddened as he replied. "Mr. Captain, what we are doing is not cruelty, but the work of men as honorable as your grace." His voice grew husky and lower as he continued. "And I swear to God that your grace and your companions deserve to be beheaded for issuing the order not to abandon the land, contrary to common desire. By refusing to leave, you and my father-in-law are rendering the king a poor service."

Captain Gómez's jaw tightened as he answered, "Well, I swear to God and your grace that if I were on an equal footing I would settle this question; but your grace has sixty men and I have only eight. But some day we will meet before the royal Audiencia, where the one who deserves it will be punished."

Recovering somewhat from their anger, they inclined their heads almost simultaneously and backed up a step as they turned and parted.

Captain Gómez was at a loss as to what to do. He knew where the power lay, at least temporarily, until the governor returned from Quivira. By then he feared the deserters would be gone and out of reach. Feeling that something should be done, he consulted with Captain Márquez. They agreed that since they did not have the power to stop those who had decided to abandon New Mexico they should at least go on record, one by one, as opposing desertion of the colony. In a meeting of the loyalists, called by Captain Gómez, Márquez was appointed to handle the matter, which would be conducted in the form of an interrogatory. Both captains, Gómez and Márquez, approached the lieutenant governor who, as an ostensible loyalist, could not very well refuse. Captain Márquez drew up the questions with help from Asensio Arechuleta, the colony's secretary. Together, they made up the list, which included everybody who was staying.

When Cristóbal Vaca's wife, doña Ana, heard that her husband had been summoned, she asked Cristóbal, "Why do you have to get involved?"

He answered, "I have no choice in the matter. I have been ordered to, but even if I had not, I would still want to do it."

"Why, isn't it enough that we are staying in this harsh land?"

"I don't think it is so harsh," replied Cristóbal, "but even if it is, what did we have in Mexico City? Here we can have all the land we can use."

"Bien, bien, but don't say anything bad about the ones who are leaving—doña Juana is my friend," pleaded dona Ana.

"I shall say only what is required of me. Besides, I don't care if they leave—they would not be anything but a nuisance if they stayed."

On 2 October, the interrogatory, presided over by the lieutenant governor, Francisco Sosa de Peñalosa, was held. The first witness was Cristóbal Vaca who, true to the promise made to his wife, told only what he knew without embellishments or exaggeration. Ten witnesses were presented. They each rose and gave essentially the same testimony, saying that conditions were not as bad as depicted by those who had decided to leave. They also gave the names of ringleaders among the deserters, and stated that the friars had suddenly changed their minds from their previous stance when they had urged the colonists to stay in the province to help in the conversion of the natives.

On 9 October, Captain Márquez made a formal presentation of the interrogatory to the lieutenant governor and asked for a copy. The document was signed by the lieutenant governor and the secretary, and a copy was later given to Márquez.

After the loyalists' interrogatory, the line between them and the disaffected ones became perfectly clear. Efforts to convince each other ceased. There was little or no communication between the two groups. The wives and children with friends in the opposing camp were obliged by the circumstances to stop seeing them. Ana de Vaca had become very close to Juana de Zubía, who had befriended her when she and Cristóbal had arrived with the reinforcements on Christmas Eve 1600. Knowing that Juana was leaving, Ana went to visit her. "Well, so you are going back," she said as Juana opened the door.

"Yes, and you are staying," replied Juana gently.

"I would like to go back, but Cristóbal says we must have faith because this is our only chance to be somebody."

"I understand, and would be happy to stay, but Diego is so angry with don Juan."

"I can't stay long," Ana apologized uneasily. Trying to hold back their tears, the two ladies embraced

"Maybe we shall meet again," whispered Juana.

"Maybe. Good-bye, my friend," sobbed Ana as she turned to go.

The two young soldiers, Miguel and Alvaro, were not involved in the controversy, which they scarcely appeared to notice. One night as they were returning from San Juan, Miguel suddenly stopped his horse and faced Alvaro. "I am leaving," he said abruptly.

Alvaro looked stunned. "You told me only last week that you were going to marry Oyi and stay."

"Well, I've thought about it, and I could not live among the Indians."

"Well, good luck, my friend. I am going to marry and if it means living among them, so be it." The two young men rode back to San Gabriel in silence.

On 25 October the expedition, which had started forming after the meeting of the defectors, began to move out. It had been a mild fall, but that day the first signs of winter began to show. High streaked clouds had gathered during the night, and at dawn the wind started to blow. As the wagons started to line up, those who were staying peeked out of their rustic windows, making sure not to light candles or fires so as not to be seen.

Awa Tside knowing that Brother Juan San Buenaventura was leaving that day, made the trip from nearby San Juan to say good-bye. Two days before Brother Juan had gone to see him, "My friend, I want you to know that I am not deserting. All my friar friends are leaving, and I feel I must go with them, but I intend, God willing, to come back."

"I understand, brother," he answered gently using the term *brother* for the first time.

"My respects to your elder, Kaa Pin, whom I did not get a chance to see."

As they embraced both men said, "Good-bye, brother."

Alvaro García also watched through his window, but spotting his friend Miguel he bolted out calling, "Miguel, Miguel."

Miguel, who was already mounted, turned his horse in the direction of his friend. "I am glad you came out, Alvaro," he said as he dismounted.

There was a moment of silence between them until Miguel said, "Please say goodbye to Oyi for me. It wasn't that I was afraid to. I just couldn't think of a way to explain my decision."

"I will," answered Alvaro, looking down at the ground.

"Well, I must go my friend. I am truly sorry to leave you and to leave this land. Please remember me to your bride-to-be. I hope you and Awa Povi will be happy."

"Good-bye my friend," Alvaro called out as Miguel rode away to catch up with the departing horsemen and wagons.

Gerónimo Márquez's wife, Ines, was watching while her husband, feigning indifference, was puttering with his breakfast. "Look," she said suddenly, "they are taking the servants."

"I know," answered Gerónimo. "They are setting them free; taking them as far as Tiguex."

"That is good of them," sighed Ana.

"I understand that some of the servants did not want to leave," added Márquez.

"I wonder why," his wife said softly turning away from the window.

Those who were leaving were, with the exception of the little children, in a somber mood. At seven o'clock, just after daybreak, the creaking of the wagons filled the air as they began to move. As they left the village, the others came out, some feeling that they should be going with them. After a few minutes, as the sun began to shed its dull light, all that could be seen was the dust of the discontented colonists leaving the intolerable land. Doña Eufemia, whose daughter and grandchildren were in the caravan, wrapped her shawl tighter around her shoulders, then touched her fingers to her eyes as she turned and walked slowly toward her house.

During the ensuing weeks, a doleful lethargy descended on the village. Most left their homes only to get firewood or to tend to their animals. Everyone had been affected by the departure of either a friend or a relative, and some of those remaining were not necessarily close to each other. A feeling of isolation and vulnerability pervaded the minuscule colony. The Indians were fully aware of the situation, and had they been hostile, could have annihilated the handful remaining with ease. The Spaniards' anxiety increased as each day passed without word from the Quivira expedition. The colony was further depleted when Captain Márquez left for Mexico City on 5 November to deliver the loyalist version of the desertion to the viceroy.

## CHAPTER TWENTY-EIGHT

On 19 November, toward sunset, Captain Juan Martínez de Montoya, a tall, sandy-haired, and handsome man with a pleasant demeanor arrived with two soldiers. Since the colonists were at dinner, nobody saw them as they entered the village square. They went straight to the lieutenant governor's residence who, upon hearing the sound of hooves, stepped outside. After the usual greetings, the lieutenant governor said bluntly, "Most of the people have left."

Captain Martínez answered, "Yes, I know. We were told at Pecos." After a brief conversation, during which the captain informed don Francisco that don Juan would be arriving on the twenty-fourth, they each retired to their homes. Captain Martínez was anxious to be with his family, whom he had not seen in almost five months.

The following day, don Francisco went to see Captain Martínez immediately after breakfast. "What did don Juan say when he found out about the departure?"

"Well, I must tell you, Mr. Royal Ensign, that he was not at all happy about it. He is determined to pursue them. My instructions are to prepare some men with fresh mounts to leave for New Spain just as soon as the maese de campo arrives, which should be the day after tomorrow."

Don Francisco suggested that the pursuit might be too late. "They left almost a month ago," he added.

When don Juan arrived around noon on 24 November, he went straight to his quarters. Esperanza, who was out on the square waiting, rushed in to tell her mother. "They are here, they are here," she screeched. María did not react and Esperanza did not wait for her. She ran back out and craned her neck as she tried to spot Jorge. When she finally located him, he saw her also and reined his horse in her direction.

He dismounted, walked toward her smiling. "How are you, Esperanza," he said.

She lowered her head, then looked up at him radiantly. "Very well, Jorge, and you?"

He then took her hand, squeezed it as he said, "I'll be over to your house in a few minutes. I have something to tell you."

That afternoon Francisco sent word to Guadalupe to meet him at the church where a rosary was being said after dinner in thanksgiving for the safe arrival of the Quivira expedition. He was counting on her to come without her husband since few men attended such functions unless prodded by their wives.

As Guadalupe approached with a friend who knew about the trysts with Francisco, he stepped out of the shadows and hustled her to the rear of the church. She put her arms around his neck and kissed him. "I'm so happy you called me."

Francisco smiled weakly, "I'm glad to see you too, Guadalupe, but I am leaving tomorrow for New Spain."

"Oh, you are going after the deserters?"

"Yes, but I am not coming back."

Guadalupe looked stunned for a moment, then started sobbing.

"Francisco, how can you leave me after I came all this way to see you, to be with you?"

Francisco shook his head. "This is no way to be together. You have a husband and this is a very small village."

"But you told me you loved me."

"Yes I did, and I do, but I also told you I could never marry—and now you are married."

She pleaded, "Please take me with you; Gonzalo would not really care. He knows I came to be near you."

Francisco put his finger to her lips, "Mi amor, please don't hope for what cannot be. I am too old to change."

He held her in his arms a moment, then turned around and left Guadalupe sobbing in the darkness.

Cristóbal went to see how many of his friends were left. That evening, in spite of his pain, and throwing caution to the winds, don Juan paid Magdalena a visit at her house.

"¿Qué tal? don Juan." she greeted him. "Are you surprised to see me still here?"

"To tell you the truth, I didn't know. You had a much better reason to leave than some of those pigs who deserted."

"Perhaps," she replied. "But I had no real reason to leave."

"And you had a good reason to stay?" he smiled weakly.

"I'll let you judge that, Juan," she answered with a shrug. He stayed late into the night. The camp was still as he stole back to his quarters under a cold clear sky.

When he got home, Francisco was waiting for him. "Juan, I need to talk to you. As you know, I would do anything to help you, but I frankly think that it isn't fighters you need."

"What are you trying to say, my friend?"

"That I want to leave, but not behind your back."

Don Juan smiled. "I don't blame you, Francisco. I'm fed up with all this, but I am the governor and I must stay."

"I understand that, and I sympathize with you my dear, dear friend." They embraced without further words. As Francisco walked out under the flickering stars, don Juan stood for a long while with a look of despair, thinking that Francisco was right to leave.

The next morning, Vicente came to see him right after breakfast. Over a cup of chocolate he told don Juan, "I hate to press you, but if we are going after the deserters, shouldn't we leave as soon as possible?"

The governor did not look up from his cup, and said in a tired voice, "Go when you are ready."

"I am leaving today," replied Vicente.

"I thank God every day that you are with me, dear nephew. If everyone had your loyalty and courage, there would be little to worry about," he said as he looked up at Vicente who stood up as if ready to leave.

The governor and Cristóbal rode with the *maese de campo* as far as San Ildefonso. When it came time to part, don Juan first went over and gave his old friend, Francisco, an *abrazo*. He then waved to the rest, and finally embraced his nephew. His voice faltered a bit when he said, "Que vaya Dios contigo, hijo [May God go with you]."

Cristóbal's eyes brimmed with tears, but he smiled as he embraced Vicente. He was saying good-bye not only to his favorite cousin, but to a fellow soldier who had witnessed his baptism of fire. As he trotted away, Vicente looked back at his uncle, who was more like a father. Don Juan looked old and bent. Father and son stood watching until all they could see was the dust of the departing horsemen.

Father Escalona waited until Vicente had left before he came to see don Juan. "Your excellency, you have undoubtedly been told, but I want you to hear it from me. I favored the departure of those you call deserters."

Don Juan looked uncomfortable. "Your reverence did me a great wrong."

"Perhaps, but I acted in response to my conscience."

"Did your conscience tell you to leave the province devoid of friars, halting the work of conversion?"

"Yes, your excellency, because the existing situation did not permit us to do that work."

Don Juan's face reddened. He took a deep breath then said in a low, metered tone, "And what does your reverence intend to do now?"

"To ask your excellency to accept my resignation."

Don Juan regained his composure. "Why didn't you tell me before? You could have left with the caravan."

"Because I did not, and don't intend to leave."

The following day the governor asked Fray Francisco de Velasco to serve as interim commissary, "until the commissary general can send us a prelate of his choice."

He also asked him if he would be his confessor. Father Velasco looked at him with perplexity, but he quickly assented.

That evening much to the new commissary's surprise the commander paid him a visit. "Father, I want you to hear my confession."

Father Velasco nodded and with a sweep of his hand showed him through a door leading to the church and a confessional.

Juan de Oñate came quickly to the point. "Bless me, Father, for I have sinned. I have committed the sin of weakness."

Fray Francisco interrupted. "I don't know if weakness itself is a sin, but it can lead to sin."

The governor continued, "My sin was one of weakness."

The friar answered, "Please tell me what your weakness was."

"I handed down someone else's punishment against the Acomas. I did not follow my conscience."

"And what would have been your punishment?" asked the prelate.

"I don't know," answered the penitent, "but it would have been mine—my conscience speaking."

Father Velasco was silent for a long interval, then spoke slowly and softly. "It was your sentence, don Juan."

Don Juan in turn was silent, then asked, "And what is my penance, Father?"

"Your penance is to remember Acoma."

Father Escalona asked Fray Francisco if he would permit him to work alone at Santo Domingo. Father Velasco asked don Juan what he thought of the odd request.

"It is perfectly all right with me. Maybe he wants to atone for his sins." Fray Francisco smiled at don Juan.

Cristóbal experienced the first really unhappy Christmas of his young life. His father was still sick, although recovering, and most of his friends had left. He longed for Zacatecas and his mother, whom he remembered only as a soft-spoken person with whom he had felt warm and secure.

The arrival of spring was labored, as it usually is in the high desert—windy one day, threatening to snow another, with a truly magnificent day interspersed here and there as if to keep the inhabitants from despairing. The arrival of warmer weather brought relief to the tiny band of colonists, but no joy. The whole camp was in a state of suspended animation. They seemed to be waiting for something—anything—to happen. A few had started plowing for the spring planting, but most, although they knew they must eventually get on with it, kept putting it off from day to day.

Don Juan was feeling better, but the lethargy that had descended on the village afflicted him as well. The message he received in late April that Vicente had arrived too late to apprehend the deserters only heightened his feeling of helplessness, but he sent a message back for Vicente to go on to Spain as he had suggested, to carry the appeal to the king if he did not get satisfaction from the Audiencia.

The news that he had been appointed *adelantado* brought a sardonic smile to don Juan's lips. He muttered to himself, "Por sólo dos vidas, dos vidas."

In Mexico City Vicente appeared before the Audiencia, where, after reviewing the history of the New Mexico colony, he presented don Juan's proposal for the conquest and pacification of Quivira. Don Juan proposed to furnish one hundred additional soldiers if the king would contribute three hundred.

The Audiencia listened to the *maese de campo*, but after getting other reports about the situation in New Mexico, recommended against any further exploration. It did, however, recommend the maintenance of the colony, primarily because of the "good qualities and peaceful disposition of the natives." The *fiscal* who advised in financial matters took much the same position, saying that the expectations for wealth were no greater than they had been in 1598. He concurred with the Audiencia that, for the benefit of those already baptized, the colony should be maintained.

The viceroy, in a summary of the situation sent to the king, stated that the land in the province of New Mexico was not as sterile as described by the people who came back, but also not as prosperous as others painted it. He further stated that although the friars had been in New Mexico five years, not many people had been baptized. He recommended that only a total of one hundred soldiers be sent as reinforcements.

Meanwhile the theologians who had been consulted by the viceroy expressed the opinion that the people who had defected were not exactly soldiers because a state of war did not exist and, moreover, many had their families with them. For these reasons they stated that the deserters must be heard according to judicial procedure, not by the governor of New Mexico, but by the viceroy. This decision precluded that they be forced to return to the colony.

At San Gabriel, as spring progressed, the planting was done. The small group of people who had remained while the governor and his troops were at Quivira led the efforts to put the colony on a firm footing. Cristóbal Vaca complained to his wife, "If only the rest would make up their minds to become New Mexicans, we could do something here. This is not the most fertile soil in the world, but the Indians grow corn and calabashes. Why can't we?"

Ana answered, "But if almost everybody else does not like it here, how can we ever establish a real colony?"

"Well, if those people want to leave, let them. I intend to stay, and there will be a New Mexico," he blurted out as he put on his hat and headed for his fields. On the way he thought, "If only I had three sons and one daughter, instead of the opposite."

What Jorge wanted to tell Esperanza was that during the expedition to Quivira he had asked Sergeant Heredia for his daughter's hand in marriage. The sergeant, who had been expecting the proposal, was not surprised but he did have some questions for Jorge. "What do you intend to do, stay or go?"

Jorge answered very quickly, "Stay, Sergeant, stay. I am not looking for riches. I think Esperanza and I can have a good life."

"I think so, too," replied the sergeant. "You have my blessing and I think also my wife's, although I don't know because she has not been right since our son died."

The wedding was quickly arranged. It was not elaborate because neither family involved was well off. At the church, as the wedding vows were being spoken, María came out of her depression. She sobbed, but now more out of a realization that she had neglected Esperanza all these years because of her grief for her lost son. She experienced a brief moment of lucidity. Her daughter was entering a new phase of her life and staying in New Mexico. She herself, through Esperanza, saw a future in the land she had blamed for her son's death. Drying her tears she took her husband's hand for the first time since Manuelito's death and looked him in the eyes as if to say, "It's all right now, Gerónimo."

Another wedding took place a few days later in San Ildefonso. Alvaro García took for a bride Awa Povi. The ceremony was first performed according to the Indian ritual, then two days later in San Gabriel. This, the first between a Spaniard and an Indian girl, raised some eyebrows but no real concern. Alvaro had obtained permission from the governor, who assented after a few perfunctory questions about where the young soldier intended to live.

Without Vicente, don Juan was strangely disinterested in the affairs of the province. He often thought of giving Cristóbal more responsibility, but Cristóbal did not show any inclination to take charge. Now that Vicente was gone, the young man looked more and more to his father for strength and guidance, but don Juan, absorbed in his deteriorating position, did not respond very well.

"¿Qué vamos a hacer, papá?" Cristóbal asked one evening at dinner.

"Wait for reinforcements," he answered casually. Cristóbal lowered his head and continued eating in silence.

Now that most of his friends were gone, and because Co-ha lived in San Juan and he in San Gabriel, Cristóbal started going more frequently to the *alcalde's* home on one pretext or another to see his daughter, María. She was always glad to see him, although their visits were limited mostly to halting, awkward conversation.

Don Juan's visits to Magdalena became more frequent. He now confided to her even his innermost thoughts. One night as they were lying in bed, she asked him, "What do you expect from all this, Juan?"

He paused so long that she was about to fall asleep when he answered almost inaudibly, "No sé, Magdalena."

## CHAPTER TWENTY-NINE

IF DON JUAN was becoming more and more detached about the fate of the colony, his brother, don Alonso, was not. He had gone to Spain to intercede in the court on don Juan's behalf. In a letter to the king he once again sought redress from the modifications the count of Monterrey had made to Oñate's original contract. The king, in a *cédula* dated 8 July 1602, ruled in favor of don Juan as far as observance of the original contract with Viceroy Velasco went, but rejected or referred to the viceroy all requests that went beyond the provisions of the contract. Thus he lost his appeal to have his titles remain in effect for more than two generations.

In New Spain, conflicting reports abounded, causing myriad opinions concerning the guilt or innocence of the deserters, and Oñate. Some opinions would have had all the Franciscans removed from New Mexico in favor of another order. In a letter to the viceroy dated 13 November 1602, authorities of the Order of Saint Francis wrote that the task of conversion in New Mexico should not be withdrawn from them just because some friars had defected. Had not many Franciscans made the ultimate sacrifice from the very beginning? Were the countless contributions to be wiped out by the actions, not entirely unjustified, of a few of them? The blame lay principally with the governor, they argued. He had always made the work of the religious body difficult, particularly after they had admonished him for his cruelty to the Indians.

Don Juan, wanting to rid himself of a thorn in his side, asked the viceroy to send in some Jesuits, but the viceroy declined, knowing full well what the reaction among the politically powerful Franciscans would be.

Vicente de Zaldívar, meanwhile, was not making any progress in Mexico City. The defecting group had gotten there before him with their version of the situation in New Mexico. On 22 and 23 April 1602, Zaldívar made another presentation to the Audiencia in which he reviewed the accomplishments of the New Mexico colony. He had with him six soldiers and officers from the troubled province who answered a series of questions prepared by the tribunal. That influential body once more recommended against any new settlements, but did go on record favoring "maintaining what has been pacified." Since he had planned to go to Spain if he could not get satisfaction in Mexico City, Vicente turned his attention to that alternative.

A fleet left twice a year from the West Indies colonies. April and August were considered the best months from the standpoint of weather. Some individual ships also made the crossing, but it was considered unsafe and too expensive. English and other buccaneers still prowled the Spanish routes in search of opulent Spanish ships to plunder.

Although Vicente had never been to Spain, and he had never before made a long ocean trip, this adventure, after more than four years in New Mexico, seemed rather bland to him. He was, nonetheless, curious about seeing the motherland and about going to the court as he hoped to do.

Veracruz was a bustling, busy port. There were fortunes, large and small, to be made at this, the crossroads to the largest and most productive viceroyalty in the New World. The numerous *bodegas* were bursting with customers, mostly sailors away from home, looking to spend their wages on whatever pleasures they could find. Women were still rather scarce, and competition for them sometimes led to drunken brawls, some ending in stabbings—often fatal. Vicente made the rounds, but mainly in a spirit of curiosity. He was, after all, on a serious mission—a fact which seldom escaped his mind.

When he boarded the ship on 20 April 1602, he was astounded at the large number of other ships that filled the harbor. They were all loaded with riches of some kind, making their way to the wealthiest, most powerful country in the world. He felt a certain pride and comfort to be a part of the affluence, power, and splendor that surrounded him. He also was conscious of the very considerable contribution his family and that of the Oñates had made throughout the years to the prosperity of Spain.

The arrival of the fleet from the Indies was always an occasion. If Veracruz was the busiest port in the New World, Seville was the most important one in Spain. Ships from all over the Spanish empire were anchored downstream on the great Guadalquivir, awaiting their turn to a dock where they could unload their cargoes of chocolate, sugar, hides, dyes, and of course, precious metals. Important passengers from the various ships debarked onto rowboats, which took them to the docks not far from the cathedral. Vicente spent a few days looking at the sights of the great city before he left for Madrid. Seville, a city of ninety-five thousand souls, was the richest and largest by far of any city in Spain. The next largest one was Valladolid, with a population of thirty-six thousand inhabitants. Madrid was the fastest growing city and if a census had been taken when Vicente was there, it might have surpassed Valladolid.

Seville was the nerve center of trade with the New World. The Casa de Contratación, through which all transactions with the New World had to pass, was still there. In the eighteenth century, however, as the increased traffic and tonnage became more difficult for the Guadalquivir River to handle, the Casa was transferred to Cádiz.

The city on the Guadalquivir was a sight to behold. As the Torre de Oro came into sight, Vicente felt proud of being a Spaniard. Little did he know that at the very moment when he was marveling at the first really big city he had ever seen, Miguel de Cervantes was languishing in one of its jails, formulating in his mind the thoughts and ideas that would result in his stupendous novel, *Don Quijote*. The thought came to Vicente that all this splendor was possible because of the courage, hard work, and sacrifice of men like him and his maligned uncle. He itched to tell the king so.

With that purpose in mind he made his way by coach to Madrid. Ever since Phillip II had moved his court from Toledo to the Alcazar, Madrid had been increasing, not only in importance, but in population as well, having gone from four thousand souls in 1530 to perhaps thirty-eight thousand in 1594. As he approached the city he marveled at how much the landscape resembled that between Tiguex and the Tewa pueblos along the Rio del Norte. He remained in the city for several weeks, during which time he consulted with his uncle, Alonso Oñate, who had been in Spain for over a year promoting his brother's fortunes at the court in Valladolid, but living in Madrid because housing was next to impossible in the new capital.

When King Phillip II died in 1598, his son Phillip III ascended to the throne. He was a rather passive young man about whom his father had said, "God, who has given me so many kingdoms, has denied me a son capable of managing them." The new king fell under the influence of the duke of Denia, later Lerma, who was bribed to persuade the king to transfer the court to Valladolid. This he did in 1601. Many of the hangers-on, including Oñate's brother, who had built or bought homes in Madrid were still living there until their new homes could be completed in the new capital, but a great exodus was in the making. One person who remained in Madrid was the renowned Golden Age dramatist and poet, Lope de Vega.

Don Alonso de Oñate had not seen Vicente since late 1597. "How is Juan taking all these setbacks?" he asked as they retired to the drawing room.

"There are times when he regrets having gone to New Mexico. He worries about Cristóbal, who is growing up without any schooling, and he longs to see María."

"Poor Juan. He had such hopes for the new kingdom. He planned to take all of us there. I guess he envisioned a kind of dynasty. What do you think of the place?"

Vicente got a faraway look in his eyes. "There is nothing there, but I agree with uncle that there has to be something of value in that huge expanse if only we get the right kind of support."

Don Alonso put down his glass. "But you have been to the southern sea and to Quivira and have found nothing."

Vicente frowned slightly. "Well, not exactly nothing. We know of a port that could serve a vast land larger than Spain, and we just touched the fringes of Quivira. We just don't have enough men, particularly since the desertion."

Don Alonso looked pensive. "I agree. Pizarro had to travel hundreds of leagues before he stumbled on the Inca empire."

"And don't you suppose that in all that immense land there are mineral deposits to equal those in New Spain?" added Vicente.

"Yes, nephew and that is why we are here. Hearing all this from someone who has been there should help convince the council and the king."

Getting to see the king was no easy task. Don Alonso had made some preliminary contacts that facilitated Vicente's appointment considerably, but he still had to wait. It would be months before the king would have an open date. Vicente whiled away his time seeing the sights such as the Escorial, which until just the last year had housed the court, and Toledo, one day's journey to the south, which had been the capital until Phillip II transferred it to the ancient Arab alcazar in Madrid in 1561 at the behest of his most beloved and ailing wife, Isabelle de Valois, who detested Toledo. He decided he would try to get an appointment with the Council of the Indies. The council could not see him until mid-January, so he had more free time in Madrid.

The thought occurred to him as he was strolling about town, and as he thought of San Gabriel, that he would like to stay in Spain. Life was so settled, and there were so many things to see. He had gone to some bullfights which were, judging from the number of *toreros* killed, much more dangerous in those days than they are today. He had been to the theater a few times in Mexico City and had seen some traveling companies in Zacatecas, but there was so much more offered in Madrid. Vicente had heard of Lope de Vega, and was curious to see the work of this contemporary playwright, if only to find out why people were so enthusiastic about him. The *corrales* were once again beginning to thrive in Madrid after they had been shut down during one of the periods in which theater had been prohibited in the city. He went to see Lope's *Las doncellas de Simancas* at the Corral de la Cruz.

A *corral* was a rectangular patio formed by the three sides of buildings at the end of a street or small plaza. The balconies of the building served as boxes for distinguished patrons, while the patio was for the general audience. Performances were held in the afternoon, weather permitting. Many people came armed with whistles and other noisemakers, with which they expressed their pleasure or displeasure very noisily.

He was impressed with the courage of the female protagonist in the play, who shamed the king of León into resisting the demand of the Moors for tribute consisting of one hundred women annually, by undressing as she was being delivered along with the ninety-nine others. She explained her behavior by saying that since there were no men in León there was no embarrassment involved in exposing her nude body.

He did not return to the theater. He was too preoccupied with his mission and with the thought that don Juan and the few loyal colonists were depending on him.

The meeting with the Council of the Indies took place during the third week of January. The trip across the Guadarrama Mountains had been difficult in the opinion of the other passengers in Vicente's coach. He smiled, thinking of the many times he had slogged through snow as deep as that covering the road to Valladolid without even knowing what awaited him at the end of his journey. He sat back, comforted by the fact that it was up to someone else to worry about getting the coach through. Valladolid was very crowded. He was fortunate to get a small back room at an inn on the outskirts, on the road to Peñafiel. Most of the guests had to sleep in a dormitory with several beds.

The meeting with the council was not as formal as he had imagined it would be. There was some curiosity among the members about New Mexico. It was, after all, one of the last frontiers left in the New World. Vicente, who had felt nervous with anticipation, soon relaxed and made his case for help quite convincingly, telling the council that don Juan had too few people and supplies to continue his exploration and colonization, and asking for three hundred men to accompany the one hundred his uncle would provide.

Vicente returned to Madrid to await his audience with the king. He was fairly satisfied with his meeting with the council, and when he returned to Valladolid in early April, he finally realized the goal of his mission to Spain. He was surprised at how callow the king seemed. He had expected to see a more mature, dignified person. He was also surprised at how quickly the king appeared to agree with his request.

On 17 May 1603, the Council of the Indies made a written recommendation to the king advising him to grant Zaldívar forty men with the skills he had said he needed, that is, pilots, shipwrights. On 23 June, the king sent a letter to the Casa de Contratación in Seville advising them that he had agreed to pay for forty musketeers and ships carpenters and that he had authorized the recruitment of two pilots who would join Oñate at his own expense.

Unfortunately, Vicente had already left for America in early May. Don Alonso notified the council of this, and they referred it to the Junta de Guerra, which recommended to the king that the expense for the reinforcements be passed on to don Juan, who would be lent the money by the viceroy.

Vicente left Spain with a certain regret, but he was glad to be going home and he was satisfied with the way his mission had gone. The trip back seemed much longer than the trip over. He had plenty of time to reflect on his life and on New Mexico. He would catch himself wishing that he would not have to go back to the northern province. He would shake his head as if to banish such thoughts from his mind. The possibility of not completing his mission was unthinkable, so why entertain such ideas, he reprimanded himself.

He was glad to spend several weeks in his mother's home in Zacatecas. His cousin, María, don Juan's daughter, was now eleven years old. He tried to talk to her about her father and her brother, but she had only a hazy recollection of them. He thought to himself that she was getting to be a very lively and pretty girl.

During the summer days he would spend long hours sitting in the patio thinking of what had happened in his life during the past year. He had visited the fabulous Seville, he had seen a play by Lope de Vega, and he had met the king. Then he would think of San Gabriel and his brow would wrinkle. He felt, however, that the time had come for him to return to duty, but he could not go without the men and support he came for.

While Juan de Oñate waited for decisions to be made, one factor remained constant and that was the resolve by everybody concerned to salvage the evangelical work that had been started. Because of delays in communication, the Council of the Indies, and the king on the one part, and the viceroy and the Audiencia on the other, were issuing divergent instructions.

Although the king had acceded to the bulk of the governor's requests, including the one asking for independence from the viceroy of New Spain, the count of Monterrey acted as if he had no knowledge of the developments and continued to issue instructions of his own.

Oñate's request that the Franciscans be replaced by the Jesuits was ignored, probably because of the strength of the Order of St. Francis, and partly because of the derogatory information, true or false, imparted by the deserters of 1601 about the governor's administration.

In early 1603, a caravan of friars was dispatched by the viceroy to augment the three who were left after all the others joined the disaffected settlers. Led by Fray Francisco de Escobar, who later was named commissary replacing Fray Francisco de Velasco, six friars made their way to New Mexico in May 1603. Among them was Brother Juan de San Buenaventura, who true to his promise had come back to New Mexico. Fray Alonso de San Juan, lay brother with the Escobar group, asked him bluntly just before they arrived why, if he was coming back, did he desert in 1601. "I didn't desert. I left because my brother friars were leaving. I always intended to come back."

As the months passed, word got back to New Spain that the king had approved the forty men and two pilots, but nothing else happened.

In the spring of 1604 Vicente, still at Zacatecas, heard that the king had authorized don Alonso to bring the musketeers and shipwrights, but don Alonso could not pay for a ship to take just the men and arms he was transporting. The council agreed on 19 July 1604 to let him take some merchandise that would pay for the trip but the order was lost somewhere in the bureaucratic morass. Vicente became increasingly frustrated and helpless in the face of indecisions by higher authorities and the bureaucratic delays. He began to turn his attention from expedition business to that of the family mines. After a few months he began to feel less and less like the *maese de campo* of the New Mexico colony.

This outpost, in the manner of other New World enterprises, suffered from the absolutist nature of the Spanish government, where even a matter as small as permission to reinforce a faltering colony by a handful of men needed the approval of the king, who in turn depended upon the advice of the Council of the Indies, the viceroy, and even individuals like the provincial treasurer, or a bishop, depending on the case. The procedure was complicated, moreover, by the fact that all these bodies and officials were available to anyone who wanted to provide input, particularly if it was negative in nature.

## CHAPTER THIRTY

IN NEW MEXICO, where he was acting *maese de campo*, Cristóbal had taken certain initiatives—with his father's consent to be sure. Jorge de Zumaya, who had been commissioned captain by the governor in the spring of 1604, became a friend and mentor of the young Oñate. Cristóbal was entrusted with the leadership of several visits to outlying pueblos.

One evening in April after dinner, as don Juan and his son were sitting under a starry sky enjoying the unseasonably warm weather, Cristóbal remarked almost casually, "I wonder how the people of Acoma are faring."

Don Juan was taken slightly aback because he had not given them much thought since the desertion, when many of the Acoma servants had left with the departing expedition along with those who were set free. "I don't know, son," he answered softly. "I suppose they have rebuilt their town by now."

Cristóbal seized the opportunity to ask his father and commander, "May I take a small force to pay them a visit? Brother Buenaventura can accompany me. Maybe we can bring them back into the fold."

Don Juan was hesitant about his answer. "A very worthy mission, my son, but wouldn't it be a bit dangerous."

"I don't think so, sir. They, nor any of the others, have shown any hostility toward us."

"Well, I shall think about it."

The following day don Juan was actually enthusiastic at the thought of effecting a reconciliation with the people of Acoma. He had after all not been fully in agreement with the harsh punishment they had received. Besides if he was being accused of mistreating them, it might help his reputation if he went on a peace mission to the Sky City.

That evening he brought up the subject to Cristóbal. "I have reflected some on the visit to Acoma. We shall do it and you will be my second-in-command.

Cristóbal became exhilarated at the thought of visiting the mysterious place where the great battle had taken place, never mind that his uncle had been killed there. "Can we take Alvaro and Jorge?" he asked almost breathlessly.

"Of course we can, they can look after you," he teased.

"I don't need anybody to take care of me, but I would feel good if they were with us."

Don Juan laughed as he patted his sixteen-year-old son on the back.

A week later the small force of twenty men left San Gabriel on the first expedition organized for the purpose of seeking reconciliation with a former enemy. Not only were Alvaro and Jorge among the soldiers, the father commissary and Brother Buenaventura also answered the roll call. Unlike the other expeditions, this one captured the imagination of the colonists.

With a fanfare and smiles all around, it was on its way. Even the weather seemed to cooperate. It was a day worthy of a wedding. The spring showers of the night before gave way to a cool, bright morning with only a few white fluffy clouds clinging to the mountains.

Cristóbal had not seen Co-ha since after the Battle of Acoma and the move to San Gabriel. He asked his father to go by San Juan on the way west. Co-ha was reticent with Cristóbal at first, but when the young Oñate told him the purpose of the trip, he smiled. "Please come back and tell me about it," he said as Cristóbal embraced him.

Since there was no hurry, the Spanish contingent stopped at virtually every pueblo along the river. The inhabitants, sensing the purpose of the mission, came to meet them with offerings of friendship.

Leaving the river the party headed almost due west directly to the bluff, which could be seen from a long distance. The Spaniards were proceeding with confidence, almost with a festive air. An envoy had been sent ahead to apprise the Acomans of Oñate's mission.

The Acomans did not wait for the Spaniards to come to the top but descended to the desert floor to greet them. The spokesman said in a loud, resonant voice, "Welcome to Acoma. I was only a child during the great battle. I am happy to see you come in peace."

Don Juan with Cristóbal dismounted and walked toward the man who spoke and who apparently was the chief. The two leaders bowed almost simultaneously, then don Juan embraced Tyami (Eagle), son of Tyami, hero of Acoma.

That night at the village at the top of the mesa the feast lasted all night. The Spaniards anticipating the festivities had brought some wine to share with their guests. The Acomans sang and danced; the Spaniards offered their music.

Oñate and his men descended to their camp just a few hours before daybreak. The Acomans, as soon as they saw the Spanish camp stirring, once more descended from their huge boulder to send the Spaniards off.

## CHAPTER THIRTY-ONE

SHORTLY AFTER THEY arrived back at San Gabriel, preparations were started for the long deferred trip to the South Sea. The *maese de campo* had been to the area of the Gulf of California three years before, but had not done any real exploration nor charted any of the region. Since the colony had been depleted so much by the desertion of 1601, Oñate had to settle for only thirty soldiers for this venture. He was also accompanied by Father Francisco de Escobar and the longtime New Mexican, Juan de Buenaventura. Among the soldiers was Alvaro García, who had acquired a reputation as a good soldier and an industrious colonist. This left San Gabriel with a minimal garrison, and virtually indefensible should trouble arise. However, don Juan did not feel he was placing his people in jeopardy. Relations with the Indians, while not close, had since the early days and the catastrophe at Acoma been cordial and pacific.

On the eve of his departure, Brother Juan went to see his friend, Awa Tside, at San Juan. He told him about the uneasiness of a few of the people of San Gabriel. Awa Tside only shook his head slowly and smiled. Brother Juan knew that at least as far as the people of the neighboring village were concerned, the Spaniards would be safe. There was always the danger of attack from the Athabascans, but the Teguas of the immediate vicinity faced the same danger. Nothing was ever certain in a frontier.

Cristóbal went with Fray Juan, but he went to see Co-ha to tell him about the Acoma visit. Co-ha was very happy to see Cristóbal. After chatting with him about the Acomans for several minutes, he looked at Cristóbal directly and said softly, "You are a true friend of our people."

The governor was not embarking on this trip with any enthusiasm or sense of adventure. By now, the only hope that he had was that Vicente would show up with a substantial number of reinforcements. He did not have a clear idea of what he would do with them other than launch further explorations or intensify his search for precious metals.

Cristóbal had lost his boyish enthusiasm, but he, too, was glad for the opportunity to shake off the apathy and despair of the decrepit capital for a fresh vista. He was now sixteen years old and had scarcely known any other life than the one he was leading now.

On 7 October 1604 the governor assembled his small troop in the plaza for a brief ceremony before departing. Some of the women sobbed, remembering other ceremonies in better times. This one seemed perfunctory and rather sad. The soldiers' uniforms were frayed, and the formation lacked military crispness and precision. Cristóbal, acting as *maese de campo*, craned his neck looking for María. She was there in the background with Esperanza, whose husband was also in the expedition. Cristóbal waved timidly, and she answered his gesture enthusiastically.

The expedition got underway, heading west on the north side of the Río del Norte. The Spaniards did not make any contact with the Indians along the way until they got to Zuni. When they passed near Acoma, they saw smoke coming out of the chimneys. They, of course, already knew that Acoma was once more functioning as a village. Most of the women who had been taken as servants in Spanish homes had long since left to rejoin their people, who were wandering back from all directions.

As tragic as the Acoma incident was, it had still been a time of hope for the Spaniards. The colony was just getting started. Now don Juan ordered a halt, dismounted, and fell on one knee in silent prayer in remembrance of his beloved nephew, Juan. As he remounted his horse he wondered how different the fortunes of the colony might have been if he had continued toward the South Sea at the end of 1598. He still commanded credibility and respect then, and any discoveries he might have made would have been taken seriously. Now he had a feeling that, short of discovering a fabulous gold or silver mine, nothing that he could do would make much difference.

As he had done several years before, Oñate stopped at Zuni, where he and his troops were received courteously. The cuisine had not changed from the last time he was there, as it probably had not changed in hundreds of years. Once more they were treated to grilled rabbit, well salted from the nearby flats; calabashes, which had been cooked in the native *horno*; and tortillas made of corn meal. Don Juan was grateful, but not effusive, giving the impression of indifference to Zuni graciousness and generosity.

The next stop in the dispirited odyssey was Moqui, which lay some twenty leagues to the northwest. As at Hawikuh, here they were also well received. Father Escobar was impressed with the heavy cotton blankets he saw, commenting that they were not only the best in the land, but the best colored as well.

Ten leagues from Moqui they came across a river, which they named St. Joseph because the day they spent on its bank was the saint's day. It was the Little Colorado River, so named later because of the red color of its water. Next, they came upon a river they named San Antonio, which was probably the western branch of the Rio Verde. They noted that from this point on, the climate became more temperate.

Along the river they called the Sacramento, which was later to be known as the Santa María River, they came upon some Indians in the area west of modern Prescott, who had evidently had encountered some Spaniards even before Espejo's time in 1553, because the early explorer had related the fact that they wore crosses over their foreheads, tied to their hair, thus inspiring the name Cruzados.

They wore the crosses mainly in the presence of Spaniards, which the latter interpreted as a sign that Indians meant to please. These were most likely the modern Yavapai Indians, who now live in the area of the Grand Canyon. These people did not grow corn or beans, subsisting mainly on venison. It was December, but the climate kept getting warmer and warmer, which pleased the Spaniards, who had come to hate the cold winter weather of San Gabriel.

As Brother Juan and Cristóbal gazed from a prominence upon the light brown desert floor below, Cristóbal remarked, "One can see fifty leagues away."

"Yes," Brother Juan said with wonder in his voice, "it looks as if we are descending into a perpetual summerland."

By the time they reached the bottom, the travelers had shed their jackets and their hats. Birds were chirping in the cottonwood trees along the foothills. Cactus was visible in the distance. A dusty haze clung to the distant barren mountains. "I could stay and live here," shouted Cristóbal, remembering the cold, biting north wind of San Gabriel.

"Maybe we can move the capital here," laughed Brother Juan, squinting in the bright sunlight.

The next large river they encountered was the Colorado River, which was given the name Buena Esperanza (Good Hope). It was bordered by meadows that were densely populated.

Cristóbal looked away and wondered what lay beyond the towering mountains in the far western distance. "Perhaps the South Sea," ventured Alvaro.

The young Oñate half shut his eyes as he gazed at the forbidding landscape beyond the green strip along the river banks. "This land is endless. We have been traveling for months and the end is not in sight."

Alvaro strained his eyes and said to himself, "All this belongs to Spain, but it won't satisfy the authorities; their view is dim sighted."

Don Juan, who was now generally referred to as the *adelantado,* sent Captain Márquez with four soldiers to talk to the natives of the region. He came back with two men who were regaled and sent back to bring more people. The next day forty people led by a man called Curraca came, bearing corn, beans, and calabashes. The chieftain delivered a long speech expressing friendship for the Spaniards. These were the Amacava people.

They met other people of the region, who were equally friendly. They were, according to Father Escobar, tall, good-looking people who went around completely nude, but not the women, who covered their private parts with grass or fiber.

These people told the Spaniards that further on were people living around a lake, who wore bracelets made of a yellow metal. When one of the Spaniards showed them a toothpick made of gold, one of the Indians nodded and put the toothpick to his wrist. Further on, another group told them that farther west were people who ate out of bowls made of the same material as some of the silver utensils the Spaniards had with them. They lived on an island one day's boat trip from shore.

Along the Gila River, called by the Spaniards Nombre de Jesus, the Osera people were found not to be as tractable as others in the region. It was here that the Spaniards left twenty horses because the grazing was good. When they returned for them, thirteen had been killed and eaten. The Spaniards did not take any action, reasoning that the Indians had never behaved improperly in their presence and that, besides, the Spaniards had tempted the Indians too much by leaving a source of food on the hoof unguarded.

Before the expedition reached the gulf, the Spaniards went through several settlements each with thousands of inhabitants until they reached one called Cocapa, which extended to the coast. It was on the day of St. Paul's conversion (25 January) that the Spaniards finally reached the bay formed by the mouth of the Colorado River and the Gulf of California. It was given the name Port of Conversion in honor of the converted apostle.

Thus, during the first month of 1605 Oñate had almost accomplished what he set out to do—discover the South Sea. He did not reach the Pacific Ocean, although he learned from the natives where it lay in relation to the gulf. The local people evidently did not venture westward much beyond that point because of the fantastic stories that were told of the people who lived near the sea. Don Juan was suspicious that they might be joshing him, but the Indians seemed serious enough. Their stories, while fantastic, were consistent with what Vicente de Zaldívar had been told several years earlier. The whimsical stories of people with huge ears, of others who slept underwater, those who sustained themselves purely on the odor of food, and of those whose sexual members were so long that they could wind them four times around their waists, were all repeated exactly as they had been told to Vicente.

The governor did not push his expedition farther because supplies were getting very low. Although the Indians of the area were generous enough, they did not have much to give. On the way back, the Spaniards had to slaughter and eat some of their emaciated horses. They did not get adequately supplied until they reached the land of the Moqui.

On 25 April 1605, the exhausted expedition reached San Gabriel. Those who had stayed behind were relieved that the expedition was back after a six months' absence, which seemed interminable. They had all been hoping that something of value would be discovered to break the wearying stalemate, but for the moment they were mainly glad that their husbands and sons were safe and that they themselves were more secure. María had been counting the days when Cristóbal would return. Before he left, he had spoken to Jorge about asking for her hand. Jorge had told his wife, who in turn had told María. Now, as a seasoned frontiersman seventeen years old, he felt entitled to take that crucial step.

The day after their arrival, Cristóbal broached the subject with his father. Don Juan was not surprised, but he did feel that Cristóbal was a bit young for marriage. Feeling that his son had been denied a tranquil and secure childhood, he relented quickly. When Cristóbal approached Captain Gutiérrez to ask for his daughter's hand, the captain said, "Both of you are so young, but these are not normal times—God bless you."

## CHAPTER THIRTY-TWO

DON JUAN HAD resolved to send his father commissary to Mexico City to report on his recent accomplishment. After a few days' rest, on 29 June, the governor wrote a letter to the viceroy advising him that he was sending Father Escobar to inform him of the state of affairs in New Mexico. The more he thought about it, the more he became convinced that this was a propitious time for him to report in person. Besides, he thought to himself, it would be a good opportunity finally to bring María to New Mexico. Since preparations had already been made for Father Escobar, the small party led by Oñate left for New Spain without delay.

Cristóbal did not go with his father this time, staying back at San Gabriel to maintain the Oñate presence in case anybody became restless and started thinking of deserting. His fiancée had expressed hope that he would not leave her again so soon. With the governor were the lieutenant governor, don Francisco, and his wife, Eufemia. The governor had long since given permission to the elderly couple to return, but the occasion had not presented itself. Seven years of harsh New Mexico life had not dampened doña Eufemia's spirit very much, but she longed to see her son and grandchildren. She made the rounds saying good-bye to all the families.

"I am leaving," she said, "because I am getting too old for this kind of life. I want to live my last years among my grandchildren. But you younger ones, don't think of giving up your new homeland. It has everything for a good life if you work at it. Make the most of it. May God keep you."

By 7 August the party was in San Bartolomé. From there don Juan wrote the viceroy, the marquis of Montesclaros, asking permission to continue to Mexico City. On 1 September the viceroy answered, granting permission reluctantly. But by the time the letter reached San Bartolomé, don Juan was having second thoughts about meeting a hostile viceroy and was thinking of returning to New Mexico.

Don Juan had been planning to spend some time in Zacatecas on the way to Mexico City. When the viceroy's reply was delayed, and he had made up his mind to return, he had his daughter, María, brought to him with the intention of taking her with him. María was now a refined fourteen-year-old young lady. The more he saw her throughout their short visit, the more he felt disinclined to take her to his crude home in San Gabriel and to a failing venture. As he heard her speak, the contrast between her and his son Cristóbal alarmed and disheartened him. It was obvious that she was becoming well educated, and in New Mexico there were no schools.

María had come prepared to join her father and brother in New Mexico; Vicente, who had escorted her, knew just what to bring. Don Juan felt a flush of optimism when he saw his beloved daughter standing by his trusted and equally beloved nephew. He thought to himself, "With him and her, New Mexico might be agreeable."

María was shy at first, but soon was chattering about everything that came to her mind, but mainly at the great life she and her brother would have in the new kingdom.

The day after arriving with his cousin, Vicente waited until don Juan was alone before coming to see him. "Tío, I have something to tell you."

"What is it, Vicente," don Juan answered, alarmed about his nephew's serious demeanor.

"Our enemies have apparently talked to the new viceroy. I do not think he would give you a good reception and he might try to keep you from going back."

"I had thought of that, Vicente. That is why I had you bring María. Now that I have seen her, I don't know."

"We could take care of her," encouraged Vicente.

"Yes," answered don Juan with a grimace, "but in view of what you tell me you should go back and see what you can do to counter the wagging tongues."

Vicente did not insist. "As you wish, uncle."

"No," continued the governor, "with the depressed state of the colony and its uncertain future, I cannot take her there."

He resolved to get back where he belonged before his hold on New Mexico became weaker than it was. He felt an urgency to get back to Cristóbal, who, for better or worse, was already a New Mexican. Toward the end of September he recalled all those who were to return with him and made preparations for the trip back to New Mexico. As he said good-bye to María, he thought of the seven-year-old girl he had left in 1598. His dream of reuniting his family vanished in the harsh light of conditions in New Mexico and of court politics. As the last days of a beautiful September came to an end, the tired, dispirited governor began the long trek to his sad, little colony.

The viceroy meanwhile received the report of the recent discovery from Father Escobar. The fantastic stories contained in it did not help Oñate's cause. They gave Montesclaros an opportunity to ridicule and minimize Oñate's accomplishment. In a derogatory report to King Phillip III, the viceroy proclaimed Oñate's conquest "a fairy tale."

It was this letter that sealed Oñate's and his colony's fate. The king gave instructions to his secretary to answer the viceroy "to observe what has been ordered relating to the discovery of New Mexico and the affairs of Juan de Oñate. With this understanding he may stop further discoveries, taking measures for the preservation of the converted Indians at the least possible cost to his majesty. And if the conquest should continue, let it be with friars only, as has been instructed."

When the governor got back to San Gabriel, he was a defeated man. Watching were an elder in San Juan and the younger Awa Tside. They saw a tired and bent man dismount from his horse to embrace Cristóbal and greet Captain Márquez and the others who had turned out to welcome him.

Awa Tside remarked, "He is a very different man from what he was when he first came."

"Fray Juan tells me the leaders of his nation have lost confidence in him," the elder answered.

"Yes, maybe they will have to leave this land," observed Awa Tside dryly.

Don Juan told Captain Márquez that night that he wanted to resign, but that he was afraid one of his enemies would be named governor. "How I miss Vicente," he confided. Captain Márquez remained silent.

Oñate sought solace with Magdalena, but more infrequently now. When he did see her, he did not talk very much. His spent most of his time staring out the window as if thinking that somewhere out there lay the answer to his problems and aspirations.

Across the ocean in Spain the curtain was slowly being drawn over the *adelantado*'s fateful venture. On 16 January 1606, the Council of the Indies recommended to the king that he order the viceroy to bring Oñate back to New Spain and to replace him as governor. In one of his brief notes at the end of the council's report, the king agreed to that plan. A week later the council transmitted the decision to the viceroy. By now Phillip III was back at the Escorial. It was from there that he sent out an order to the viceroy.

## CHAPTER THIRTY-THREE

One afternoon in the middle of June as San Gabriel baked slowly in the sun and most of its inhabitants were inside either sleeping or at least seeking respite from the stifling heat, one hardy soul who apparently did not have a taste for the siesta was riding back to the village when he spotted a small party of horsemen approaching. He knew that the *maese de campo*'s arrival was imminent, so instead of going up to greet them, he went into the square at full gallop, hollering, "el *maese de campo*, el *maese de campo*!" Little by little the village came to life as the drowsy inhabitants came out blinking and rubbing their eyes. By the time Vicente rode up to the square everybody was out.

It was a bittersweet reunion between uncle and nephew, leader and loyal second-in-command. Don Juan was happy to see Vicente, but he was not relieved as he had been so many other times when he had returned from an assignment. He already knew that Vicente's mission had been a failure. Vicente dismounted quickly and embraced his uncle. They did not say anything beyond a cursory greeting, but only looked at each other with a sadness verging on tears. Cristóbal stood by looking at the ground until his cousin noticed him and gave him a big *abrazo*. Cristóbal was now eighteen years old. He was fourteen and still a boy when they had last seen each other. That evening for the first time in several years, the village was alive. Don Juan invited those close to him to dinner, and the wine continued to flow till a very late hour.

The following morning don Juan had a headache. He had awakened early with a heavy feeling that carried over from the dreams induced by the emptiness of Vicente's return. Instead of the three-hundred-some soldiers he had hoped for at the time of his nephew's departure, he welcomed two friars and a handful of men. He remained in bed, as if reluctant to face the world. At nine o'clock Vicente stood at the entrance to his uncle's quarters. In the past he would have walked straight in. Don Juan, who was picking at his breakfast, looked up and smiled weakly, "Why don't you come in?"

Vicente took off his hat and sat at the table with him, thinking of the many times they had made plans over breakfast. Now he simply sat down.

Don Juan asked in a low voice, "¿Qué vamos a hacer? [What are we to do?]"

Vicente, who came back only because it was his duty, and out of a sense of devotion to his uncle, answered also in a low voice, "No sé, tío."

The summer of 1606 was particularly dry and particularly hot. The colony was at a virtual standstill, with San Gabriel simmering and the colonists, with the exception of the young people, inside their houses most of the time. When they did venture out, the men hardly bothered to dress properly, some going into the square shirtless. Greetings, other than perfunctory ones, were becoming rare. It was as if they did not want to remind one another of their existence, because to acknowledge that would be to acknowledge their desperate plight. It was not the absence of comforts that caused their depression. It was sheer boredom and hopelessness.

Don Juan had long ago given up on San Gabriel and its environs. He had been pinning his hopes on another expedition, which depended on reinforcements.

"What would you have done with the three hundred soldiers?" asked Vicente.

After a pause, don Juan answered, "I don't know exactly, but we would have moved from here."

"I see," muttered Vicente, then fell silent. They sat there for several minutes without uttering a word. Vicente rose to leave.

"Oh, by the way, " don Juan called to Vicente, who stopped and turned around, "Father Escalona passed away last week." Vicente remained silent looking at the ground. Don Juan continued haltingly,

"He had been serving at Santo Domingo since he was replaced by Father Escobar."

"I'm sorry," muttered Vicente as he turned and left.

Vicente, ever the man of action, soon became restless in the languid atmosphere of San Gabriel. He started taking long rides on horseback with Cristóbal. On one of those they had been riding in silence when Cristóbal spotted some Indians in the distance.

"I wonder who they are," Cristóbal thought aloud.

Vicente broke into a gallop, "Let's go see."

Upon closer examination they saw two horses being led by a halter in their midst. As the Indians noticed the two Spanish horsemen, they started running and soon let the two horses loose. Cristóbal and his cousin did not give chase, simply catching the horses.

As they trotted back to San Gabriel Vicente said, "They looked like Apaches to me."

Cristóbal concurred, "Yes, why didn't we chase them?"

"Because," answered Vicente, "they were probably part of a larger group. This is very serious—Apaches this close to San Gabriel and stealing our horses."

The two rode back swiftly, Vicente thinking out a plan of action; Cristóbal excited about the prospect of a campaign against the marauding mountain Indians.

Don Juan was surprised to hear the *maese's* report and agreed that a troop should be sent without delay to clear the area of raiders.

Cristóbal, as *sargento mayor,* insisted that he be included.

The early autumn sky was still pink when the force of twenty soldiers accompanied by veteran Captain Gerónimo Márquez, Ensign Alvaro García, and Ensign Escarramad, who accompanied Oñate in 1598 as a simple soldier, left San Gabriel.

They rode west on the northside of the river following what they knew was the route the Apaches took to their mountain homes. On the third day at the foot of the western Jemez Mountains they spotted the smoke of an early evening campfire.

By the time they got within earshot they could see clearly several silhouettes, including those of several horses. Intending to form a semicircle around the camp, the Spaniards spread out but one of the Apache lookouts heard the soft clinking of swords or harquebuses. He ran quietly toward the center of the camp and gave the alarm. As the Spaniards sprang forward to attack, the camp rose as one. The Indians who could mount did so and rode off trying to drive the loose horses in front of them.

By the time the Spaniards reached the scattered embers of the campfire, all of the people had scrambled into the darkness. The Spanish soldiers gave chase, but to no avail. The following morning a few of the horses were rounded up.

Don Juan could not conceal the look of relief in his eyes as he saw Cristóbal riding in front of the column with Vicente. Later in the privacy of the governor's quarters, the *maese* brought up the subject of the horses that were being lost to the nomadic raiders.

"We discussed this on the way back," Vicente spoke earnestly with the governor. "Not only have they been stealing horses, but we saw some of them riding them. Do you realize what this portends for the future?"

"Yes, Vicente, I do. Thank you for your report. This gives us one more argument why we should have more reinforcements; but it is a bit late." He shifted his eyes from Vicente and stared blankly ahead. He stammered slightly, "Where is Cristóbal?"

The young Oñate was with his friend Alvaro. The two young men had struck up a friendship during the reconciliation expedition to Acoma in early 1604. Later they traveled together to Taos and finally to the South Sea. It was after the latter expedition that the governor commissioned Alvaro an ensign.

Cristóbal also became very close to the Zumaya's—Jorge and Esperanza, who had two children and every intention of staying in New Mexico.

His wedding had been postponed because don Juan was waiting for a more propitious moment. Now with the arrival of the *maese de campo* without reinforcements he began thinking seriously of resigning, an act that would once again delay the promised nuptials.

In a conversation with Vicente and Captain Márquez he first revealed his thoughts. Márquez was the first one to react. "Don Juan, in God's name, don't leave us alone here."

"What choice do I have?" don Juan answered weakly.

"Tío, you are right," interjected Vicente. "As long as you are here and your enemies are there at the viceregal court you will never receive any help."

With a resigned look don Juan nodded. "I have been putting my son's wedding off; now I think we can have a decent one in Zacatecas."

"And you deserve much better your excellency," interposed Captain

Márquez, "but what will happen to those of us who have decided to stay come what may?"

"I honestly don't know, Gerónimo, but perhaps a man without enemies in the capital might be better able to govern."

Gerónimo did not answer but Vicente did. "With due respect to Gerónimo's ambitions or taste, it is not just the people who speak against you, uncle, it is also this land. There was some truth in what the deserters said. We have found exactly nothing here."

"Please don't mention those cowardly ingrates to me," frowned don Juan.

"We have done quite well since they left," joined Gerónimo.

"Perhaps as a simple colony, but what have we earned for the crown, or for ourselves other than a hand-to-mouth existence?"

Gerónimo persisted, "Isn't Christianization one of our purposes?"

"Yes, and look how many friars we have—nine with the two we brought here. That is not the problem, but nine friars are hardly a basis for a thriving colony."

Don Juan raised his hand as if asking for silence, "There is no sense in arguing. If I leave, someone will take over and the colony will go on for better or worse."

Vicente and Cristóbal made one more attempt to catch the Apaches with strayed or stolen horses in 1606, going as far as the mountains north of Taos, but were forced back by severe winter weather.

"We must come back in the springtime. This country must be beautiful when the weather gets warmer," remarked Vicente.

"It is beautiful now," corrected Cristóbal, adding, "I love this country."

"Yes, I suppose it is," smiled the *maese de campo.*

The moment the rivers started running full and the first geese were spotted flying north, Vicente, ever restless, told Cristóbal. "Cristobalillo, when do we leave for Apacheland?"

"Tomorrow if you wish."

Within a week a force of twenty-five soldiers was saddled up and ready to go. The small army stopped at Santo Domingo, where a mission had been established and maintained by Father Escalona until his death during the past year. They also stopped at Cia, where a mission was being installed.

Two days after leaving Cia, Cristóbal was riding side by side with Jorge, "That is the place where we surprised the Apaches last fall," Cristóbal pointed out to his friend.

"What a strange land," observed Jorge, "barren jagged hills to the west and towering mountains to the east."

Cristóbal squinted as he gazed at the high peaks in the distance, "That, according to Vicente, is where the Apaches live."

Camp was made that night near the site pointed out by Cristóbal. The festive air by the campfire appeared to belie the purpose of the mission. Food and even drink were plentiful. Cristóbal felt an unaccustomed warmth surrounded by his favorite relative besides his father, and by his best friends. He felt that this would probably he his last outing with Vicente, for don Juan was planning to send him home to New Spain with a message to the viceroy that would probably contain his resignation.

The following morning was very cool, but bright and sunny, promising warmer air in the afternoon. The leaves on the cottonwoods and aspens were beginning to appear.

"This is so pure, so peaceful," sighed Cristóbal. "I do love this magical country." The older members of the troop who had not been brought up in New Mexico just looked at each other. Some shrugged and smiled.

On the fourth day as Alvaro García, who was scouting for the main party, rode over a rise, a magnificent little valley splashed with wildflowers spread out before him. When he got a better look, he spotted some tepees by a small river. Not wanting to take a chance of being spotted by a lookout, he wheeled his horse around.

"Señor Maese," he called to Zaldívar, "There is a camp just over that rise."

A consultation followed and preparations were made for attack. "Did you see any horses?" asked Cristóbal.

"I am sorry, but I didn't take time to look that well."

Vicente mounted his horse, "Well, let us go see."

Suddenly the pleasant excursion turned serious. The *maese* began giving crisp, pointed commands, "Captain Zumaya, take five men about two hundred steps to the left. Ensign García, go with your men another hundred to the right. Report back to me what you see. Cristóbal, you stay with me."

As he was second-in-command, Cristóbal felt a bit slighted, but he went willingly and comfortably with Vicente.

The *maese* and his young *sargento mayor* observed the peaceful, pastoral encampment for several minutes.

"I see some horses," whispered Vicente.

"Where?"

"Over to the right of the creek by the clump of trees."

"Oh yes, I see two, but there are only five tepees and some women and children."

Vicente had meanwhile received the same information from Captain Zumaya who had a more direct view of the camp.

"Tell Captain Zumaya to await my signal to attack. Keep us in sight," he instructed the messenger. He told García's messenger to tell the ensign to rejoin the main force.

A shadow crossed Cristóbal's face. He looked agitated. "What is the matter?" asked Vicente.

"There are only about fifteen people down there and they are all women and children. The men must be away hunting."

"Or stealing horses," interrupted Vicente.

"Maybe," he answered in a weak voice.

Vicente looked into Cristóbal's troubled eyes, "What in God's name is the matter?"

Cristóbal dropped his head half ashamed.

Taking a few steps, Vicente turned away from him. He gazed at the camp for a good interval, then turned to his aide, "Recall Captain Zumaya's and Garcia's men." When they had all gathered he said. "It is not worth it, let's head back."

Cristóbal stayed at the rear as the troop started down the slope. Vicente slowed his horse to allow his cousin to catch up. As he rode up, Cristóbal avoided Vicente's gaze. Vicente searched his eyes, then put his arm around him.

During the trip back nobody said a word about what had happened. The soldiers did not see or hear. The officers could guess but did not.

When they arrived at San Gabriel don Juan was relieved to see everybody arrive safely. "What did you find?" he asked Vicente.

"Nothing of any value, uncle," he answered nonchalantly.

Co-ha had heard that the expedition into Apache territory was in Santa Domingo on its way back and would arrive in San Gabriel the following day. He had not seen his friend in over a year. During that time Cristóbal had become acting *maese,* and upon Vicente's return sargento mayor and had not made any of his customary visits to San Juan. Feeling that perhaps Cristóbal was too busy, Co-ha hadn't gone to San Gabriel. Now, he felt compelled to go; after all, it was an appropriate occasion, and there would be others from the neighboring pueblos welcoming the young governor home.

At San Gabriel Co-ha stood in the back of the small crowd. After a warm greeting from don Juan and the other Spaniards, Cristóbal walked over to the Indian gathering to acknowledge their gracious gesture. While exchanging courtesies with the elders, he noticed Co-ha in the back. He made his way to him and gave him a big *abrazo*.

"Thank you for coming, my friend. How have you been?" Cristóbal said with a big smile.

Co-ha smiled back. "Very well, and how was your trip? Did you recover any of the horses?"

Cristóbal grinned sheepishly. "No, we didn't; but the scenery in the mountains was beautiful."

Cristóbal invited him to his home for refreshments. The two friends chatted for a while, but Co-ha did not feel comfortable surrounded by so many Spaniards who wanted to talk to the governor. He excused himself and as he was leaving Cristóbal said, "Ill go see you soon."

As the summer droned on, don Juan became more and more settled in his resolve to give up the governorship. On 20 August he called a meeting of the *cabildo*, in which he reviewed the situation for them, then stated his intentions of resigning, saying, "Señores, in view of the fact that the authorities have ignored our plea for help, I can no longer go on as your governor. I can no longer ask you and your noble families to make the sacrifices which have been commonplace in your lives since even before we came to this land. If by the end of June of the coming year you have not received the help which you need, I will grant you permission to leave. Once more I am sending my beloved nephew to Mexico City to intercede for us. I have consulted with the friars in all the deliberations which led to my decisions." The *cabildo* murmured as don Juan finished his statement, but nobody ventured a comment.

On 24 August 1607, don Juan wrote a letter to the viceroy restating what he had told the *cabildo*, but in addition resigning his office:

> Your excellency, the arrival of the friars and the *maese de campo* with so few people caused such discouragement among those who were at this camp that it required no little ingenuity and effort to maintain them this year, but it has served no good purpose, considering the many good men and abundant succor you promised, and therefore I am awaiting the answer from Spain which your excellency promised in your first letter to me. Although I do not tire of waiting or of enduring the hardships that one encounters here, the soldiers are so worn out by seeing themselves put off for so long

with mere hopes that they do not wish nor are they able to wait any longer. Nor do I find myself able to restrain them, for they are exhausted, hard pressed, and in need of help as I am helpless to furnish it. Furthermore, the friars do not care to proceed with the baptizing of the natives until they know that the affairs of this land are settled, nor am I sure that they are inclined to remain here, as one may judge from a petition of the father commissary, which I beg your excellency to read. Finding myself helpless in every respect, because I have used up on this expedition my estate and the resources of my relatives and friends, amounting to more than six hundred thousand pesos, and anxious that the fruits of so many expenditures and of more than eleven years of labor should not be lost, and especially because I am eager that our Holy Catholic faith should be spread in these lands and that the king our lord should increase his dominions by the addition of great and rich provinces, which according to our information, are at our threshold, I find no other means to attain all of this than to renounce my office, which resignation I am sending your excellency. I am doing this in order that his majesty, since he has failed to support this undertaking as its importance demands, may appoint for this post a person who may be able to carry on the service I have started. To effect this change it is necessary to reach an agreement with the soldiers in the name of his majesty, whereby they will await an answer from your excellency until the end of June of next year. From that date on, I granted them permission to leave at will. Therefore, I beg your excellency to send word within this short period, since I had to promise them that failure to obtain an answer would permit them to leave, and they will not want to remain a moment beyond that date, nor could I force them to stay. This is in accordance with the opinion of the friars who put this matter upon my conscience. They have fulfilled their obligations for so many years, always with great fidelity and perseverance, without ever receiving any support from his majesty or his ministers. Nor have they ever been encouraged by good words, faring equally in this respect with the soldiers and the governor.

As far as I am concerned, matters have moved in such a way that my feelings have been greatly hurt, in view of the fact that those who fled from this camp have gone entirely unpunished. Through extensive testimonies and falsehoods they tried to justify their treason, and they have remained free and my honor has been placed in doubt by those who do not want to see that my perseverance in this land rests solely on my desire to work for the cause of God and the service of his majesty and not for selfish interests, for what we have thus far discovered is nothing but poverty. Nor have I been moved either by rewards received, for my compensation, or lack of it thus far, has been the occasion for my present feeling. Of course, as the devil is so interested in this matter, he will try by all ways and means to hinder this enterprise, and he has brought things to such a state that, unable to overcome my zeal and good purpose, he has exhausted my resources and I find myself unable to explore any further at a moment when the reports are most promising and encouraging, for last year the reports of riches and greatness in the interior of the land were verified, as your excellency may see by a report which I am enclosing.

Therefore, in order that my limited means should not be a hindrance to the work of baptism and the extension of the royal crown, I decided, for the unburdening of my conscience, to resign my office, which I cannot maintain without more help, assured in doing this I am rendering a most important service to his majesty. Even if I had not incurred so many expenses and endured so many hardships by my many past services, I trust your majesty will honor and reward me, even if he should not wish to use me in the prosecution of this undertaking.

I wish to point out that if what has been built here should be destroyed, as will be the case unless your excellency sends succor by the time I have stated, many grave inconveniences will result. This must be given serious consideration, for should his majesty wish to make this expedition later, more than six hundred thousand pesos will not suffice to bring matters to the state in which they now are. If we should all leave the land, it will be necessary to take along more than six hundred Christian Indians. The result of this will be not only that holy baptism will be refused in these lands at all times, but the natives will not even dare to welcome the Spaniards in future years if their children, brothers, and relatives are taken away. They are incapable of understanding the reason for our leaving, no matter how much it is explained to them. This will no doubt give rise to many difficulties and dangers, for at the time of their removal the land will rise and take up arms to prevent it. This can be taken for granted, considering the nature of these Indians, for even though they may not be naturally warlike, they would become bold on seeing how few of us are left for this task. Were they not to be taken away but to be left here to re-

> vert to idolatry, no lesser difficulty would ensue. It would be less harmful to cease making more Christians than to allow those who have already been converted to be lost.
>
> May your excellency be pleased to weigh prudently the gravity of this affair, keeping in mind the Christian zeal that his majesty feels for the preservation of souls, which is the main object that he urges in these discoveries.
>
> The *maese de campo* is going back to intercede for this cause. He leaves me comforted and even encouraged to hope for an entirely successful arrangement since it will come from the hands of your excellency, to whom his majesty so wisely entrusted the government of New Spain. In this good fortune, I hope that a solution will be found for a province as important as this one, and I believe that I am providing the necessary remedy by withdrawing and placing this government in the hands of your excellency.

The *cabildo* wrote the viceroy a letter the same day stating their position, which was that they could not maintain the colony without help from the viceroy or the king. They praised Oñate who, they said, "treated us as if we were his children, and we looked upon him as a father."

During the year, don Luis de Velasco had once more become viceroy of New Spain. The burden of deciding the fate of the New Mexico colony and its leader was now in the hands of the sympathetic viceroy who had chosen don Juan for the task, and who had helped him so much in the early days, but the situation had deteriorated to such an extent that even the good will of a friendly viceroy might not suffice.

During the first week of September the *maese de campo,* accompanied by Captain Márquez, in his tireless fashion, once more took to the saddle to go plead for what appeared to be a lost cause. With him to present the spiritual side of the argument went Fray Lázaro Ximénez and Father Francisco de Velasco. Vicente, who by now had despaired of getting any assistance from the authorities, was mainly going home to Zacatecas. He was never again to see New Mexico.

## CHAPTER THIRTY-FOUR

DON JUAN HAD not seen Magdalena in two weeks. The night after finishing his long letter to the viceroy, he paid her a visit. Magdalena let him in without a word. He was the first to speak. "How have you been, my friend?

She replied without a trace of resentment, "Well, as you can see."

He muttered as he started to explain why he had not been to see her.

"Don't concern yourself with this, Juan, I know why," she said quietly.

"I don't think you do completely," he answered softly, looking out the window.

"I know enough, Juan. I am not a girl."

He took a long pause before he cleared his throat and said with a hint of a waver in his voice, "Magdalena, mi amiguita, I think you should leave with Vicente."

She also took a long while to answer, and then in an unnaturally composed voice replied, "Como tú quieras, Juan [As you wish, Juan]."

Don Juan turned around to face her. They looked at each other for an interval, then embraced. Don Juan's eyes glistened; tears rolled down her cheeks.

After sending off the letter and once more sending off his trusted nephew, his thoughts turned to his son's wedding. As discouraged as he felt, he wanted to make the occasion a happy one for Cristóbal and María. The date had been set. It was to be on Saint Gabriel, the archangel's, day, 29 September 1608. Little by little the colony started to come back to life. The happiness and optimism of the young couple was starting to spread. Even the most depressed took comfort from this expression of faith in each other and in the future by the young man and his bride to be. Cristóbal had grown to be rather diffident and polite. María had somehow managed to reach her young age a refined young woman despite the crude environment that surrounded her.

Don Juan ordered the most sumptuous feast ever seen in New Mexico. On his return from New Spain, he had brought back a new uniform for Cristóbal and a magnificent gown for María. Vicente had brought the ingredients for several delicacies and a good supply of wine.

The day of the wedding the sun came up from behind the Sangre de Cristo Mountains to an impeccable sky washed clean by a shower during the night. Don Juan felt confident that he was not losing a son. The strong family tradition started by the patriarch Cristóbal remained intact. Although he was sure that the New Mexico adventure was drawing to a close, he thought to himself, "There are always the mines in Zacatecas." His father had provided opportunities for him; now he would provide them for his son.

His principal regret was that he could not favor them with happier circumstances. The bride and groom, however, having lived in New Mexico most of their conscious lives, were not only oblivious to their primitive surroundings, they were also quite detached from the events that caused don Juan such distress. Absorbed with each other, young love was uppermost in their minds. How could external circumstances, which had never been good to begin with, affect the euphoria of the day? If the curtain was beginning to drop for most of the settlers, for them it was about to rise.

Cristóbal, still a submissive young boy at heart, had confidence that whatever the trouble, his father could take care of it. María, in the manner of the Spanish women of the time, did not question nor concern herself outwardly with political matters, which were clearly the domain of the men. She knew that she loved Cristóbal and that Cristóbal loved her, but she was conscious of the fact that, had they lived in Zacatecas, Cristóbal would most certainly have entered into a more socially and economically advantageous marriage, as was the practice among the rich and powerful.

The ceremony was lavish by New Mexico standards. All the friars in the colony were in attendance and attired for High Mass. As don Juan watched the ritual, he remembered his own wedding in another world—a thought that rendered this one a touch unreal. The bride and groom entered the church followed by Esperanza's little daughter, María, and by Cristóbal Vaca's young son, Antonio. They knelt before the altar, and the priest covered María's head and Cristóbal's shoulders with a fine lace cloth as a symbol of feminine submission. María, he thought, was strikingly beautiful in the gown and veil that his own wife, the princess Isabel, had worn at their wedding. Cristóbal looked almost stately but for his discomfort in his high official's uniform, as he cast uneasy glances at his father.

Don Juan felt a pang as he thought of the excited but timid ten-year-old whom he had brought to the chaotic camps north of Zacatecas on his halting way north. He tugged at his collar and looked for the door, but kept his seat. As the ceremony progressed, he regained control of his wandering thoughts, but the depression engendered by the recurring frustrations of the years in New Mexico could not be expelled entirely.

The outdoor feast that followed was extravagant, but except for the young people, a bit hollow. Don Juan was compelled to show cheerfulness. "If only Magdalena were here," he muttered to himself as he reached for the wine. He drank a bit too much, and he did feel better. He danced with the bride and one or two of the other ladies. As the fiesta came to a close, and Cristóbal and María retired, don Juan remained seated at his table sipping wine. As the people left, they came by his table to say goodnight. He felt relatively good in the cool air of the magically starry mountain night. He thought of other fiestas in Zacatecas and this cheered him. "If they don't want me here," he thought, "I shall go back to my family, my daughter. Cristóbal and I can revitalize the mines. I am foolish to brood about a place as miserable as this."

The following day, reality prevailed again as the governor entered into yet another period of waiting—this time for permission not to try to accomplish something, but to give it up. In Mexico City it would be don Juan's friend, Luis de Velasco, who would be making the decision, but don Juan no longer had any illusions, and he was mentally prepared to go back.

It was shortly before the sunset of a mild, mellow autumn day when Cristóbal Vaca came in from repairing a sluice gate with his son Antonio. His wife looked up from setting the table.

"What were you doing out so late?"

"Fixing the irrigation gate," he answered as he took off his sweat-stained hat and sat down heavily on a wooden bench.

"I don't know why you bother when hardly anybody else does," she muttered without looking up.

"We have been through this before," he managed in a weary voice.

"But surely you know as well as I do that this colony is dying."

"Yes, perhaps, but we are not," he answered in a rising voice, "and as long as we are alive, we must do our work."

Isabel and María, who had been helping their mother along with Antonio, had left the kitchen.

"Just because don Juan does not want to make his home here . . ."

Ana interrupted him in a pleading tone. "But what if the colony is disbanded and we are ordered to return?"

"What if the sky falls in?" he almost shouted. "What if this, what if that? I am not going to put my fate, our fate, in someone else's hands.

We are New Mexicans, Ana," he said in a falling voice. "This, for better or worse, is our destiny before God. Yes, this miserable place is our home and as the Lord is my witness, I intend to make it worthy of my family, of our progeny."

"Bien, bien, Cristóbal," she sighed as she set down the last plate.

A few days later Cristóbal met Captain Márquez as the two headed for their fields. "Buenas días," Vaca greeted Márquez. "There aren't too many of us doing agricultural work."

Gerónimo smiled. "I guess not. I myself have not done as much as I would like, because the governor is always sending me off to New Spain or somewhere else."

"Well at least you have three sons who can help you. I have only one," smiled back Cristóbal.

"Well, this time I am not going with Fray Lázaro, who is leaving tomorrow to deliver the bad news to the viceroy."

## CHAPTER THIRTY-FIVE

IN MEXICO CITY Fray Lázaro and Fray Francisco, who had been sent by the governor to clarify the evangelical situation and Vicente, who was to deliver Oñate's resignation and ultimatum threatening to abandon the colony, met with the viceroy. They reviewed conditions in the colony and concluded that the settlers would like to abandon San Gabriel and relocate the capital, taking with them the natives who had been baptized. The viceroy asked them how his friend the governor was taking all this. They replied that he was very tired and anxious to bring his son home. He thanked them, saying that he concurred with their request, but could not give them a definite answer until he consulted with the king.

On 27 February 1608, the same day that he wrote to the king about the transfer of the colony to another location, he also wrote to Oñate, accepting his resignation and appointing Captain Juan Martínez de Montoya, whom he did not know, as interim governor. Don Juan was enjoined from leaving New Mexico until specifically authorized. He dispatched the letter with Father Ximénes, who was returning without Fray Francisco, who had been reassigned to duty in Spain.

When the news arrived at San Gabriel in early 1608, there was great surprise and consternation among the colonists. Captain Martínez was as surprised as anyone. As the people gathered in the square, they asked each other, "What good will this do? Martínez does not have any resources." Others would say, "He was appointed captain, but he does not have much experience as a soldier." Still others would complain, "He is one of us. How in the world is he going to exert any authority? How is he going to deal with his Excellency or even Cristóbal?"

Captain Martínez presented his patent at a meeting of the *cabildo* the day after it arrived. The members of the town council had already made up their minds and refused him outright, citing as a reason that he was inexperienced as a soldier. They had a list of other objections that had to do with his personal behavior, but they, out of consideration for one of their comrades, did not include it in their report to the viceroy. The basic reason for his rejection was that he was simply not a man of means or stature. The captain accepted the *cabildo's* decision without protest—even with relief. He confided to Captain Márquez that he did not want to inherit such a difficult situation because he did not have any idea how he would be able to handle it.

Juan de Oñate's name immediately surfaced as the only possibility. In a show of affection and confidence he was reelected governor by acclamation. Visibly touched, he thanked those present and the colony as a whole for their kindness, but told them that he could not agree since his resignation had already been accepted by the viceroy and probably the king.

"If we can't have don Juan, let us elect Cristóbal," someone shouted in the back of the council hall.

"Yes, Cristóbal," others joined in.

The commissary, Father Escobar, then made a formal nomination, and the council proceeded to elect don Juan's twenty-year-old son as the second governor of New Mexico. The father commissary approved of the election, but Cristóbal asked for a brief postponement until he could consult with his father. When the meeting resumed, he donned the sash of office.

The viceroy reported these happenings to the king in a letter dated 13 February 1609. He accepted the *fait accompli* as a temporary solution, telling the king, however, that he considered Cristóbal too young, inexperienced, and of little wealth, and that he would begin looking for an appropriate person. Two months later he appointed don Pedro Peralta, who was not a wealthy man. The viceroy was careful to point out to the king that he could not find any wealthy person to take the post and that, therefore, Peralta and his assistants would have to be paid from the funds appropriated for the wars against the Chichimecas.

Meanwhile at San Gabriel, Cristóbal, with the aid and counsel of his father, took the fragile reins of office in his hands. Nothing much was happening, and word had gotten back that Cristóbal was not considered an acceptable choice by the authorities in New Spain. Don Luis de Velasco, knowing that Oñate was there and not distrusting him as much as others might, did nothing to invalidate Cristóbal's appointment for the time being.

Three days after he had been appointed governor one of the settlers came into his office with a complaint that one of his neighbors had stolen some rabbit pelts he had left hanging to dry from a viga protruding from his home. Cristóbal tried to look solemn but after the soldier, Juan Rodríguez, who had recently returned from New Spain with Captain Zaldívar, finished his complaint, he coughed once then told the soldier, "I cannot consider this complaint today. Come back day after tomorrow, please."

That afternoon he found don Juan sitting on a chair outside his office staring at the Sangre de Cristo Mountains. "Father, soldier Rodríguez came to me with a complaint that his neighbor stole some pelts from him. I went to his neighbor's house and he denies it. What should I do?"

Don Juan asked absentmindedly, "Does Rodríguez have any evidence or witnesses who saw the alleged theft?"

"No. He says he knows his neighbor stole them because he is the only one who had seen Rodríguez hanging them."

"Well, son, you will have to get them both in, question them and then decide, but you have to do these things without coming to me."

A few days later as Alvaro was visiting with Cristóbal in his office, Francisco de Ledesma, a soldier, brought in an Indian boy about fourteen years old whom he said he had caught stealing.

"What did he steal from you, Francisco?" asked the young governor.

"Food," answered Ledesma, "some jerky I had hanging in the line."

Cristóbal turned to the boy and asked him, "What is your name?" When the boy answered that his name was Chai, Cristóbal asked, "Did you steal the jerky?"

The boy shook his head and shrugged his shoulders.

"Call in the interpreter," Cristóbal asked a soldier standing by the doorway.

When the interpreter came in, Cristóbal said to him, "Ask him if he stole the jerky."

The interpreter, after talking to Chai in Tegua, said, "He says that he did."

"Ask him why."

"He says that his mother is sick and that his father is dead," answered the interpreter.

Cristóbal then asked the Indian interpreter if he knew the boy's family and if what he said was true.

"Yes, he is an orphan, and his mother has been sick for a long time."

Cristóbal reflected for a moment then said to Chai, "Go home to your mother and never steal again."

As the boy left Ledesma asked, "And what about my jerky?"

Cristóbal answered, "Well, if you do not want to donate it to the boy's family, we will replace it out of the military supplies."

Ledesma answered, "It's not worth the trouble, your excellency," and walked out.

When they were alone, Alvaro smiled at Cristóbal, "I would not have done the same."

Cristóbal smiled back and asked, "What if he had been your son, and had done as much for you?"

Alvaro continued smiling and just shook his head.

That evening after dinner as Juan and his son sat outside watching the sunset, Cristóbal broke the silence, "Father, I don't feel comfortable being governor. You will still be the one people will look to for guidance."

Don Juan sympathized with his son. He felt guilty that he had put such a burden on him. "Yes, I'll be here to advise you. Besides aren't we of one mind about most things?"

Cristóbal answered respectfully as usual. "Yes, most things, father."

"What do you mean?" asked don Juan. "Is there something in particular about which you don't agree with me?"

"I think you know, father."

"Well, tell me so that I will know," answered don Juan with a trace of impatience.

"Pardon me, papá, but I have always wondered why we are not satisfied with what we have and with what we can accomplish instead of yearning for greater things, maybe impossible things."

"Son, listen to me. We had things, as you say, in Zacatecas, many things, but you must know why we were sent here. It wasn't just to establish a miserable little village. Our mission was to expand the empire."

"Yes, papá and we are starting to do it. Perhaps not in a grand way, but in a modest way that is good for our settlers. Look at Captain Vaca and Captain Hernandez. They cultivate their fields, which will produce enough riches to satisfy them and keep their families together. Isn't that enough? Why do some people always want so much?"

Don Juan did not answer his son's question right away. He looked at him with great tenderness. Although Cristóbal was the son of a rich man, he had never known luxury, and he never seemed to mind his humble, spartan life. "You will do fine as governor," he said with a cheerless smile.

Having heard from Father Ximénes that the Apache Indians had recently been mounting attacks against both the Spaniards and the pueblo Indians, the viceroy sent a letter on 16 March 1608 to the governor of New Mexico to organize a punitive expedition. It fell, therefore, upon Cristóbal's shoulders to carry out the viceroy's orders. He was now twenty years old and fairly experienced in skirmishes against marauding Indians. He picked the most experienced of the colonists, which meant effectively just about all the adult males who could be spared. Among them were Cristóbal Vaca and Captain Juan Martínez along with Alvaro and Jorge. Don Juan, ever the protective father, felt apprehensive about his son, but he knew that some very reliable and experienced men were going with him.

They headed west in mid-June toward the mountains where the Apaches and their Athabascan cousins, the Navajos, preferred to live for the safety provided by the rugged terrain. The Athabascans had come to New Mexico only a relatively short while before the Spaniards. As is the case with most latecomers, they were left with the dregs. Moreover, the Anasazis, the ancestors of the pueblo Indians, had started settling along the Rio Grande and cultivating the land mainly for corn, the magic vegetable that had played such an important role in the development of the great Mesoamerican civilizations.

The Athabascans, in the manner of the Aztecs some two or three hundred years before in the central valley of Mexico, became raiders. But while the Aztecs or Meshicas went on to dominate and imitate and improve on the pre-Aztecan civilizations, the Athabascans, thanks in part to the coming of the Spaniards who kept the mountain Indians at bay, never until modern times got beyond their newcomer, have-not stage.

For the most part the young governor and his army of twenty-five made only a few tentative contacts. Captain Montoya reigned up beside Captain Oñate, "I am beginning to wonder if the Apache actually exist."

Cristóbal looked up at the peaks, "Even if there are thousands of them, it would not be too hard to hide in this country of a hundred canyons."

"If they do not want to fight and keep retreating into the mountains, isn't that more or less what we wanted," reasoned Montoya.

"Except that Viceroy Velasco, my father's friend, asked us to go on a punitive expedition," answered Cristóbal, stressing the word *punitive*.

Alvaro García rode up to join the discussion. "One of our guides just told me that there is a lake just beyond that peak about two leagues from here."

"Yes?" smiled Cristóbal, "and you think they might be there?"

Alvaro smiled back, "They might, but if they are not, it will be a good place for us to rest."

Cristóbal, who was hot and tired, looked longingly at the cool blue peak and shrugged his shoulders, "Let's go."

The heat of the day had begun to abate as the little army reached the top of the foothills in front of the peak that had served as their landmark. In the green, grassy valley before them was the lake about a thousand paces wide. On the east side, basking in the lowering sun, were the largest number of tepees any of the Spaniards had ever seen.

Captain Vaca suggested they make camp for the night without putting up tents. "This will give us time to scout and plan, and will give us the whole day tomorrow to carry out the attack."

Cristóbal agreed, "Yes. We can have a cold meal and retire early." The young captain did not sleep very soundly. He had depended to a great extent on Alvaro and Jorge in planning the assault, but the pressure of responsibility of his first major battle as leader weighed on him.

After a hasty, cold breakfast well before sunrise, the soldiers began to deploy according to plan. Captain Montoya with five men was charged with starting a fusillade on the south side of the camp to draw the Apache soldiers out. The young commander with the main force would cover a group of five soldiers with torches who would set fire to the tepees. Ensign García with two men would stay back to fire the culverin as needed.

As soon as everyone was in place, Captain Oñate gave the signal by firing his wheel-lock gun. The sun was just beginning to glimmer above the peaks when pandemonium broke loose. As the armed Apaches started to pour out of their tents some were cut down by the gunfire but most faced the attack. Cristóbal grimaced as the tepees were emptied and the Spanish soldiers with the torches began flinging them on the fragile nomadic homes.

The women and children herded by a few warriors began heading for the hills opposite the attack. Some of the women carried little brown bundles of children. Cristóbal thought of his little three-year-old godson Juanito, Alvaro's mestizo son, and shook his head as if shaking off the thought. As they began to run, the firing subsided since most of the warriors took to flight as well, followed by three horsemen from Captain Montoya's group. They succeeded in capturing two of the Apache warriors. As soon as the *maese* saw this, he gave the signal to stop firing altogether. The burning continued until every tepee was completely in ashes. Five Indian men lay dead on the bloodstained grass—one of whom was given a *coup de grace.* There were no Spanish losses and only two superficial arrow wounds. On the way back to the Spanish camp, Ensign Alvaro García caught up with the young commander and without a word lay his hand momentarily on his back.

Cristóbal and his men returned to San Gabriel a month after they had departed. Don Juan was much relieved and proud to see his sunburnt son returning at the head of a column of men. Cristóbal held his head perhaps a bit higher for the experience. After embracing his father, he saw María in the forefront of the women who had remained slightly in the background. He excused himself from his father and walked over to her. When he held her shoulders in his hands and she blushed, he knew at once what it meant—she was with child.

## CHAPTER THIRTY-SIX

NOW THAT OÑATE'S resignation had been accepted, the debate about continuing the colony intensified. As early as 1606 the king had already instructed the marquis of Montesclaros to "halt the discovery and not permit it to continue." Viceroy Velasco on 7 March 1608 recommended that due to the "small harvest of souls" and the fact that the Indians did not seem inclined to accept the gospel, further efforts in New Mexico should be discontinued and the few Indians who were baptized should be brought to New Spain. He added that "if the land should be preserved for the good of the souls and the spread of the gospel, your majesty has here in New Spain a number of other places which need help, and they are only forty leagues from this city."

In September 1608, Oñate sent Father Ximénes back to Mexico City to clarify the situation in the dying colony. He was escorted by Gerónimo Márquez and accompanied by Fray Isidro Ordónez. Captain Martínez de Montoya, who was also part of the escort, never did return to the province which, because of its loyalty to Juan de Oñate, would not have him as governor.

By late October, Fray Lázaro was in the viceregal capital telling the viceroy that a more careful assessment had shown that there were many more Indians who had received the sacrament of baptism—up to seven thousand—than he had reported on his previous visit. In addition he brought proof that New Mexico was not as poor as had been thought. Viceroy Velasco was not very much impressed with the ores the friar presented to him, and he later stated to the king that conversion of the Indians was "the only fruits we can hope for."

Don Juan had sent a message to the viceroy with Father Ximénes asking that Cristóbal be confirmed as governor, and once again had requested enough soldiers to explore and pacify the buffalo plains. The *fiscal* who was assigned the task of looking into the request, and the situation in New Mexico in general, recommended strongly against confirming Cristóbal because he lacked experience and hardly knew how to read, explaining that he "cannot have the intelligence, capacity, or authority necessary to give stability to and guide matters where personality must make up for the lack of forces and power."

He recommended that fifty married soldiers be maintained in the colony for the protection of the friars who were to continue their task of instructing the Indians in the faith. He closed by suggesting that since Oñate, in view of the poverty of the land, could not recover his expenses, he be appointed as governor elsewhere in keeping with the merits of his services.

The king, upon receipt of the viceroy's letter, put out the order of 13 September 1608 commanding "the suspension of the discovery and exploration of New Mexico" until the council could receive the reports of the new assessment of conditions in New Mexico. Velasco was instructed not to make any *entradas* with soldiers or by way of conquest.

Oñate meanwhile had received indications that his request was going to be denied, and asked for permission to return to New Spain. On 29 January 1609, Viceroy Velasco issued an order permitting him to do so. On the same date he signed a decree implementing the *fiscal*'s recommendations. Only twelve additional soldiers were to be sent. This would leave the colony terribly weakened, as out of the sixty males in the shrinking province only thirty were capable of combat duty, and only the ten best of these were to be equipped with arms. In addition, six friars and two lay brothers were to be sent to work among the Indians.

At San Gabriel, the colony went into yet another period of suspension. Most, including Cristóbal Vaca and Jorge de Zumaya, were relieved that the colony was to be maintained, although at a very reduced level. Captain Márquez and Jorge had been granted *encomiendas*, which meant that according to Spanish law, they had economic control of large tracks of land along with the people living in them. Because of the unsettled conditions, they had not yet exercised such control, but still had hopes of seeing greater profits in the future.

Captain Vaca, feeling that there was enough land available without having to take it from the Indians, had not seen fit to seek an *encomienda*. He had enough sons and daughters to help him, and he knew that he could always hire local people who were willing to work for just compensation.

Don Juan was disappointed at the decisions taken by the authorities, but not for himself. He knew that Cristóbal was somewhat inclined to stay, particularly because his brother-in-law had decided to seek his future in New Mexico. María's good friend, Esperanza, and her husband were also staying. When the news arrived, Don Juan went to Cristóbal's hut to tell him, "It looks as if they do not want us to stay in New Mexico, Cristobalillo." Cristóbal did not look particularly downcast. He did not say anything, looking at his father as if expecting a decision from him. Don Juan, after a pause, said gently, "You can't stay here as a soldier." Cristóbal still did not answer. He lowered his head, then turned to look out the window. A tender, sad look crossed his father's eyes as he watched his son. He suspected that Cristóbal had tears in his eyes so he turned quietly and left the house.

In January 1609, the much anticipated arrival of the Oñate heir took place. The Oñate family, which began in the Basque country of Spain, had now extended it lineage to the upper reaches of the North American portion of the Spanish Empire.

Cristóbal, who was very proud at having contributed to the continuity of the family with a male heir, looked at his father for approval. Don Juan embraced him with great affection. He found it hard to believe that the ten-year-old boy he had brought to this primal land was now a father himself.

The people of San Gabriel greeted the man whom they still considered their leader and governor with a warm *enhorabuena* as if he were the father.

The baptism a few days later in which the infant child received the name, Juan, was the occasion for the last great fiesta in San Gabriel. Everyone knew that don Pedro de Peralta was on his way to New Mexico to found a new capital and it was just a matter of time when all of them would either be going back to New Spain or moving to the new township.

Now that there was no hope of a future in the colony either for him or his son, Oñate wanted to return to New Spain as soon as possible, but he had been ordered by the viceroy not to leave New Mexico until the fate of the colony had been decided. He had since received an authorization from the viceroy, but knowing that Peralta was enroute, he deemed it better to await the arrival of the new governor.

On 15 March, Viceroy Velasco formalized don Pedro de Peralta's appointment as governor and named the officers and soldiers who were to accompany him. There were sixteen in all. Among them was Captain Márquez, who was returning home as *maese de campo*.

Among the instructions received by Peralta was an order to establish a new villa in the shortest time possible so that the settlers could begin to live in an orderly manner and cease their dependence on the Indians. In the typical bureaucratic procedure that King Phillip II—who had died during the first year of the expedition—had established during his reign, the new governor was given detailed plans for the construction of the city. He was to mark out six districts, or as the Spaniards termed it, "neighborhoods," and a square block for government buildings. He was to apportion to each individual two lots for a house and a garden, two others for vineyards and olive groves, and an additional five *caballerías* of land, which were to be used for the maintenance of livestock.

The viceroy must have known from the many reports that described the land as infertile, dry, cold, and poor that vineyards and olive trees were out of the question. These plans underscored the inflexibility and inadequacy of government by long distance decree where even the most minor matters such as the appointment of a mayor of a small town had to be approved by the king.

Trips for the purpose of exploration were prohibited until all matters pertaining to living conditions and the evangelization of the Indians had been taken care of, because, as the viceroy put it, "experience has shown that greed for what is out of reach had always led them to neglect what they already have, when they should devote their efforts primarily to maintaining and making secure what has been discovered. Until the villa has been founded and settled, nothing else should be undertaken."

Don Pedro departed for his new post in late March 1609. With him he carried a formal order for don Juan to leave New Mexico. The small force of seventeen followed essentially the same route of the original Oñate expedition, which by now was well known. Moreover, Captain Márquez, a veteran of numerous trips over the route, was with them as was Ensign Alvaro García. Also in the small force were the new officers and men who would be the driving force in the revitalization of a colony that had come perilously close to disintegrating.

## CHAPTER THIRTY-SEVEN

When Peralta arrived in early May, the entire colony came out to greet him. Don Pedro halted his horse a few meters from where don Juan was standing with Cristóbal and dismounted. He walked up to them and bowed. Cristóbal hesitated, but don Juan took a firm step forward and embraced Peralta. New Mexico had a new governor!

Don Juan and Cristóbal accompanied by the commissary, Father Francisco de Escobar, took a few steps to the left and forward to where Fray Alonso de Peinado, the new commissary, was standing. They knelt on one knee. The father took them by the hand, helped them up, and embraced them in turn. Don Juan reserved his most affectionate *abrazo* for his friends, Fray Lázaro, Fray Isidro, and Gerónimo Márquez, who had worked so hard on his behalf and on behalf of the colony during the past two years.

Not since the early years had New Mexico enjoyed the presence of so many friars—fifteen in all with the twelve who accompanied Peinado. Evangelization was indeed about to enter a new phase.

The Oñate family had been making preparations to leave for some time. The old governor's spirits were markedly higher that afternoon as he made the rounds saying good-bye to his friends. The weather had been warm without being oppressively hot during the past few days, and he was anxious to leave before it got hotter.

Now that his future had been decided, Cristóbal, the father of a fourteen-month-old baby, was anxious to leave, mainly for the sake of his wife and child. He also made the rounds. María and he spent nearly an hour with Esperanza and Jorge, who by now had three children, and talked of happier times. "I am sure that we shall see each other again. Surely Jorge at least will come to New Spain to escort friars or to bring back supplies," smiled Cristóbal. "I might escort a caravan myself," he added.

Don Juan was particularly grateful to Gerónimo Márquez, who from the very beginning had been ever ready to take on any mission requested by the governor. He embraced Captain Márquez, "I'm sure I will see you again, my friend. There are still a few more trips to New Spain in your future."

Márquez's entire family surrounded the governor. After he embraced Ana and her daughters, he shook hands with the young Antonio. "This young man will be a great help to you," he said as he turned to Gerónimo.

"Yes, my beloved governor. You know that I always meant to make this land my home. For me and my family there is no turning back."

"Que les vaya bien, amigos. I know that with you to take care of them, your family will be safe and do well." They embraced, then don Juan left hurriedly as Gerónimo stood in his doorway watching the man he had served so long and so well, wondering what the future had in store for the anemic little colony.

Cristóbal Vaca and his family were just finishing dinner as don Juan approached. Cristóbal arose from the table and went to the door. "Buenas tardes, Señor Gobernador. I hear you are leaving shortly for Zacatecas."

"Yes, my friend, tomorrow," answered don Juan.

"Well, I know you will do well and that God will protect you and your dear family," said Cristóbal as his own family stood up and approached the ex-governor with respect.

Don Juan looked at all of them and said with feeling, "And He will be here with you and your family, for you are a good Christian and a hard, honest worker." He extended his hand to Cristóbal as he said,

"You stay here in your New Mexico. I wish I could have made it mine, too, but it was not meant to be. "Adios, amigos," he added as he turned and walked out into a twilight dotted with stars.

Cristóbal had spent the whole morning the day before with Co-ha, who was now twenty-two years old and being primed to succeed his ailing father Kaa Pin as *cacique*. They talked about everything: the early days before Acoma, their feelings about the battle and the visit to the Sky City later, and of course, the difficulties that led to don Juan's resignation and now their departure. Fray Juan was with them most of the time and translated for them when Co-ha's Spanish and Cristóbal's Tegua failed.

"You must be glad to be going home to your sister and your aunt and cousins," remarked Co-ha toward the end of their visit.

"Yes," answered Cristóbal, "but this is my home. I love this land."

Co-ha looked sad. "I will miss you. I know that these were difficult times between our peoples, but you have always been kind. You were not obliged to pardon Chai for taking the jerky, and I heard about your reluctance to attack the Apache women and children."

Cristóbal smiled at his friend. "When we first came here we named your village San Juan of the Gentle People, and you have been truly gentle. I am sorry that we had battles with some of the other villages."

Co-ha raised his hands as if to stop him for saying anymore. "There are good and bad persons among all peoples. Some are even pin-e-he [crazy]."

Cristóbal, who felt he had to return to San Gabriel, finally said, "Well, my dear friend. I don't know when we shall see each other again but, please, don't forget me as I will never forget you."

Co-ha tried to look stoic, but his sadness shone through. "You are my ke-ma [friend]. I will remember."

Early the next day, Cristóbal Vaca and Ana watched from a rise at the edge of their field until the small party disappeared around the hills to the south. The young Cristóbal riding alongside María's cart sighed almost inaudibly as he reached for María's hand. She brushed her eyes before taking his. The returning party proceeded along the west side of the river at a fast pace. They were small in number, had an abundance of carts, and were traveling over very familiar ground.

The second evening they camped just below La Bajada opposite Santo Domingo after they had crossed to the east side of the river. After dinner Cristóbal came up to his father, who was sitting on a camp stool facing the incredibly luminous sunset. It looked as if the entire western horizon was engulfed in huge flames that reached high into the sky. "I shall miss these marvelous sunsets," he thought. They did not speak for a while as they both stared ahead beyond the Sandia Mountains. Finally don Juan turned to Cristóbal, "Qué piensas, hijo?"

A vague frown crossed the young man's face as he spontaneously looked back over his right shoulder. In a muffled voice he said, "Ahora sí."

"Yes, son, and we are headed back to a new life which you have never known. I won't always be around and since our family is prominent you will be given appointments of extreme responsibility such as that of your uncle Vicente de Zaldívar, our Vicente's father, who is captain general in charge of keeping peace with the Chichimecas.

Cristóbal listened quietly, wondering what his father was getting to.

"I didn't want to mention it at the time, but I thought that you were a bit too lenient with that young Indian boy who admitted stealing the jerky."

Cristóbal's face flushed as he interrupted his father. "But Chai's mother was sick and he was the only one caring after her."

"Yes, I know," answered don Juan patiently, "but stealing is stealing. You could have punished the Indian boy and still done something for his mother."

"His name is Chai, Father and he was just a boy."

"That does not matter. We sentence thieves as much to set an example as to punish them," don Juan answered in the same gentle tone.

"I am sorry, Father, but I felt sorry for him, and a bit guilty. They are poor, gentle people."

Don Juan did not pursue the subject, but continued gazing at the sunset.

Sergeant Gerónimo de Heredia had volunteered to go back as don Juan's *sargento mayor*. His wife, María, did not fully understand where they were going. She asked her husband repeatedly, "Are we going back for our son?" She appeared happy, feeling perhaps that by going back they were somehow going to undo what had happened on the way to New Mexico.

At the start of the eighth day as don Juan was finishing his breakfast, Cristóbal came to his tent to wish him good morning. "Buenas dias, papá," he said in an almost childish tone.

"What is the matter, son?" don Juan asked intuitively.

"Nothing, papá, I just have a headache."

"Well, let's go, son, it's getting late."

A few hours after the contingent started rolling, as they approached the northern end of a ridge of mountains later named Fra Cristóbal Mountains, Cristóbal reined his horse and turned back to María's cart. "I can't stand this headache," he complained in a weak voice.

Maria asked the driver to stop. She handed Juanillo to her young servant and got off. "Qué tienes?" she asked in a frightened tone as she saw his ashen face.

Cristóbal did not answer, but fell to the ground as he started to dismount. María gasped, but Cristóbal got up quickly and reassured her, "It is nothing. I just lost my balance." He was shivering and María insisted that he get in the cart, where she covered him with a blanket.

When they stopped for the night, María sent for don Juan, who was riding ahead of the main party with Sergeant Heredia. As the elder Oñate dismounted María rushed toward him, "I don't know what is wrong with Cristóbal. He has a high fever, and he appears confused."

Don Juan ran to the cart where his son was lying. "Qué tienes, hijo?" he said in a tender, but frightened voice. Cristóbal, looking at his father with glazed, pleading eyes, did not answer.

Don Juan remembered that his son had been complaining of headaches the last three days. He had thought it might be the change in weather, which had turned considerably warmer the fourth day out. Now he knew that Cristóbal was seriously ill. He cradled his son's head in his arms and looked into his eyes. "Don't worry, son, I'm here. Everything will be fine." Cristóbal's eyes softened, and he managed a weak smile.

That night the young man's fever got worse. Bandages soaked in vinegar were put around his head, and toward midnight the lancets were brought out, but Cristóbal only became more delirious after blood was drawn, alternately calling for his father and shouting with the excitement of a long remembered skirmish.

Don Juan stayed with him until Sergeant Heredia and Fray Joseph Tavera, his confessor, gently suggested that he get some rest. As day broke, he awakened with a start. His servant who had been watching him for some time, asked him if he wanted some breakfast. The general shook his head absentmindedly as he arose fully dressed. He sat on the edge of his bed, then rose slowly and walked outside where he stared at the sky, pink with thin cirrus clouds, for a moment; then, as if anticipating bad news, he dropped his eyes and turned slowly toward his son's tent.

All morning don Juan stood by helplessly as Cristóbal lost consciousness and went into a coma. Shortly after noon Fray Joseph was called to administer extreme unction. Don Juan, María, Sergeant Heredia, and the servants stared at the ground in disbelief as Fray Joseph anointed Cristóbal and intoned repeatedly, "By this Holy Unction and His most loving mercy, may the Lord forgive thee all thy sins." By nightfall Cristóbal, who had spent the greater part of his young life in New Mexico, had died.

María, who had passed the whole day by turns holding her infant child, Juan, and praying, finally broke into a fit of sobbing. Her servant had closed her husband's eyes and covered his face with a veil. She also lit two candles, placing one on each side of the young man's cot. Don Juan sat a short distance from the bed, his head bowed till close to midnight when his servant entered with Sergeant Heredia, who must have remembered how it felt to lose a child. The sergeant whispered into his ear. Don Juan looked up at him as in assent. The two helped him up, and one at each arm led him to his own tent and to his bed. He soon fell into a fitful sleep.

The following day he had to be awakened in time for the funeral, which had been arranged by the sergeant and Fray Joseph. Don Juan's servant had laid out his captain general's uniform, which he put on slowly with the help of Juanillo.

At graveside, the aging general lifted the veil from his son's face, and stared at it for a while, then bent down to kiss his forehead. When he straightened up, his face was streaked with tears. As Fray Joseph intoned, don Juan began to shake as if trying to suppress his sobbing. As the first shovelful of earth fell on the makeshift coffin, he regained his composure. As the shoveling continued, he looked eastward to the mountains in the distance. His face broke into a vague, sad smile as he thought to himself, "One would think that Cristobalillo did not want to leave his New Mexico."

Sergeant Heredia watched the proceedings with a distant, pained look. His own boy, Manuelito was buried just a few leagues to the south. His wife, María, was sitting in her tent virtually mute. She had not reacted in any manner to don Juan's tragedy.

As if paralyzed by grief, the small party did not move the following day. On the third day at daybreak a Mass was said at the graveside. Don Juan, looking very old and bent, stared at the mound of earth, which was now the principal sign that Cristóbal had ever existed. He remembered another funeral in what seemed a different age. Then his sadness had been invaded by optimism and by the wonder of his children's youth and beauty. He thought for the first time since his son had become ill of his daughter, María, whom he had seen but once in twelve years. A tremor, almost a pang went through his body as he tried to visualize her, but those thoughts were once more obliterated by the stark reality of the mound.

As soon as Mass was over, the packed and ready train got underway, ironically proceeding into the most difficult part of the journey—the Dead Man's Trail. Don Juan did not dare look back. In eight more days they were out of New Mexico and into Nueva Vizcaya south of the Rio Bravo. The old general now took one last look at the land that had been so inhospitable to him. He knew that, despite Cristóbal's being buried there, he would never come back. He tried to place in his mind Cristóbal's grave in the vast expanse that lay to the north.

He muttered, "Adios, my Cristobalillo, hijito de me vida. We could have learned so much from you." He then turned slowly, his eyes brimming with tears and fixed his gaze southward.

During the six weeks it took to complete the long trek home—after a few days rest at Santa Bárbara—don Juan did not speak much, except when asked for instructions. Sergeant Heredia kept the small caravan moving at a fast and steady pace. Occasionally the tired, aging commander would go to his grandson's cart and look intently into his face. After those visits it seemed to those watching that his body straightened and his gait quickened.

## CHAPTER THIRTY-EIGHT

ON 21 JUNE at midmorning, la Bufa came into view. By now don Juan was feeling much better. During the last few days he had been thinking almost constantly of his daughter. He had once again taken the lead position in the caravan, urging it to travel faster. Now he knew he would be home by sundown. The pain he felt for Cristóbal had been softened by the glow he felt as he thought of his inviting home and the people who would be there—Maria, Vicente, and his beloved half-sister.

At sunset the travelers were met at the outskirts of the town by Vicente and a group of horsemen. As he approached, don Juan looked at the city, which had grown considerably, and felt a mild thrill at the changes that had taken place. The returning conquistador was beside himself with joy, but when he embraced Vicente, his voice broke and with difficulty he said, "Cristóbal is not with us."

Vicente answered softly, "Yes, I know, tío."

Tears soon turned to joy again as they reached la Calle Real and came near the Oñate home, just a hundred or so meters away from the Church of the Assumption, soon to be demolished to make way for the baroque cathedral that now guards over the city. The street was lined with curious onlookers, many of whom had only heard of "the conquistador." María and her aunt, doña Magdalena, now very old, came out to the street to meet them. As they embraced and kissed they all cried more from joy than grief. "You are home, papá, home," cried María, who was now a very pretty and ladylike seventeen-year-old. Don Juan called for his daughter-in-law, "María, come, come and bring little Juan. Here is your nephew, my daughter—oh, pardon me, you two have not met. This is your brother's wife, María. The younger María had seen her brother only once that she could remember at the camp in Gasco when she was six years old. She had been very anxious to know him better, but her hopes had been dashed by the courier who brought the sad news from Santa Bárbara.

María, under the tutelage of her aunt, Magdalena, had grown into a very gracious young lady. Her complexion revealed the Aztec side of her heritage, and her carriage perhaps her royal lineage. Her long black hair, a gift that could have come to her from a distant Moorish ancestry or from New World ancestors, accentuated her light brown eyes, which were undoubtedly a legacy from her father. They reflected a kind disposition that reminded the older relatives and friends of the family of don Cristóbal, her paternal grandfather.

Two days after his arrival don Juan asked Vicente about Francisco.

"He died four or five years ago," answered the favorite nephew somewhat evasively.

"I had heard," replied don Juan, "but do you know how?"

"Not exactly," answered Vicente a bit uncomfortably. After a pause he added, "He was found stabbed in the street one Sunday morning." Vicente was relieved that his uncle did not pursue the matter further.

When Vicente had come back in 1607, María was still a child to him whom he treated as a little sister. She looked upon him as a half-brother, half-father. When he married the beautiful and haughty doña

Ana de Bañuelos, María was secretly very disappointed. Ana was the daughter of Baltasar de Bañuelos, one of don Cristóbal's colleagues and cofounder with him of Zacatecas. María at first became cold and distant with her new cousin. As time went by she felt less hostile to Ana, but she never warmed to her.

Vicente, in addition to doing what he could from Zacatecas to help his uncle alleviate the situation in New Mexico, had dedicated himself to his silver mines, stamping 240,000 pesos since coming back. He had also taken charge of don Juan's mining interests, both in Zacatecas and in Pánuco two or three leagues away, which had been virtually undeveloped since don Juan had inherited the potentially rich mines from his mother.

It was at Pánuco that the old miner began concentrating his efforts a few weeks after his return. He had the help of a loyal comrade and subordinate, Sergeant Heredia. Grateful for the long service, and particularly for the help the sergeant had given him during Cristóbal's illness and death, don Juan had made him one of his principal mine foremen.

Before settling down to the task of reviving the mines, a visit to Mexico City was very much in order. Don Luis de Velasco II, who had awarded him the contract to settle New Mexico fifteen years before, had been back as viceroy for about two years. This time don Juan was accompanied by his daughter, María. He thought with tenderness, and with diminished pain, of his last trip to the capital city when he had been accompanied by his son.

Don Luis received them with all the warmth of earlier and better days. Although don Juan did not bring up the subject of his removal, the viceroy explained his actions.

"Juan, New Mexico was a failure from the beginning. I heard about it in Lima. I would have brought you home much sooner."

Don Juan, staring out a window, did not answer. Don Luis did not pursue his point. After an awkward silence, don Juan said in a low, hoarse voice, "You know that I left a great part of my life there."

"I know," answered don Luis after a long pause.

"And Cristobalillo," muttered don Juan almost inaudibly.

"I'm so sorry," commiserated don Luis, no doubt remembering the excited seven-year-old who could talk of nothing but New Mexico long years ago.

That evening at dinner, the erstwhile governor brought up the subject of the charges that had been filed against him by the deserters of 1601. The viceroy answered that he was very much aware of them.

"Those things are always happening, and there will always be willing ears."

"They were, after all, deserters," shot back don Juan in an exasperated voice.

"I know," sighed don Luis, "but nothing excites some people more than intrigue and calumny."

"Well, what do you think will happen?" asked Oñate anxiously.

"Well, all I can tell you," said don Luis shrugging his shoulders, "is that I do not take the charges seriously."

"And how about the deserters, will they go unpunished?" countered don Juan in a rising voice.

"Juan," replied the viceroy slowly in a pleading tone, "leave well enough alone. You know the politics of the capital."

While he was in the capital, don Juan inquired discreetly about Magdalena. He was relieved to hear that she had married a merchant and was living in Puebla. He had thought about her often and had worried that she might be in need.

A week later he was back in Zacatecas, immersed in his work at Pánuco. Although he spent most of the day at the site a scant two leagues away, he maintained his home in the city. After years of emptiness except for a caretaker couple, the spacious house was coming to life. Now not only was María, his daughter, living in it, Juanito and his mother were, too.

Vicente, who had his own mining operation to supervise, helped to acquaint his uncle with the Pánuco mine. Don Juan had a small cottage built, which became his headquarters. It was in that cottage that, with Vicente and Heredia, he designed machinery to improve the efficiency of extracting the ore, transporting and smelting it. Time, which had passed so slowly in New Mexico, now passed incredibly fast. The two years since his return seemed like months to him. He often found it difficult to believe the progress he was making. The mine was producing silver at an unbelievable rate.

The euphoria, which was shared by Vicente, because his financial situation was also thriving, was shattered by his wife's sudden death. She had started complaining about a dull pain in her stomach shortly after the return of the New Mexicans. One year later she was dead, leaving Vicente with a very young son.

Uncle and nephew seemed to draw strength from adversity as they redoubled their efforts. They saw each other frequently consulting on methods for improving their mining operations.

Vicente became even closer to his uncle and his family. As for don Juan, if he was not particularly cheerful, he appeared at least to be contented. María had become a very attractive young woman and Juanito a toddler who was well taken care of and who every day looked more and more like his father.

## CHAPTER THIRTY-NINE

ONE YEAR TO the day after the death of his wife, Vicente ended his period of mourning, and started coming to the Oñate home almost every day. María was delighted, because Vicente's visits always put her father in good spirits. She enjoyed listening to their conversations, which often took them back to their great adventure into what remained to her a mysterious, forbidding land far to the boundless north.

When don Juan was not at home, having stayed at Pánuco or traveled to his other mines, María would pester Vicente with questions about the episode in her father's and brother's lives that had been almost a fairy tale to her. At first he had answered the questions as one would a child, but as time passed, he began conversing with her as an adult, talking not only about events but about how he had felt about them. During one of those tête-à-têtes Vicente took her hand as he had done many times before. This time he felt a tremor of excitement that caused him to remove his hand quickly. María looked at him puzzled, then as her face flushed, he stammered, "Buenas noches, Mariquita, ya es tarde."

In the days that followed, Vicente stayed away when the head of the house was not there. Although María sensed the reason, with a feigned naiveté, she told her father about it wondering if Vicente was vexed with her. Don Juan immediately guessed the reason, but to María he simply said, "He has been very busy lately."

A week later over lunch at Pánuco, don Juan asked his nephew bluntly, "Why are you avoiding María?" A panicky look crossed Vicente's eyes, and knowing he might stammer, he remained silent, lowering his head slightly. Don Juan understood, so he did not pursue the subject.

During the next few days, he ruminated over the situation, until it occurred to him that Vicente would be the ideal husband for María. He told him so the next time he saw him. "Do you love María?" he asked outright. Vicente's face once more revealed his flustered state, but don Juan raised his hand and looked at him as if to say, "let's stop this comedy." Once again the impatient uncle asked, "La quieres [Do you love her]?"

"Vicente answered a bit sheepishly, "Si, tío." The older man's smile reassured Vicente more than words could have done.

The mine at Pánuco was yielding more silver than ever, and don Juan was almost totally engrossed in his work. The money he was making did not seem to matter as much as the success he was enjoying. His only relaxation came on Sundays. He would spend the morning sitting in the spacious courtyard from which the top of the historic Bufa could be seen, writing letters, checking his accounts, or just sitting with his eyes half closed. In the afternoon he would play with Juanito or take him for walks in the nearby park or along the streets of the town. His daughter remarked to her aunt that Juanito's presence seemed to be the only source of genuine joy to her father. On Sunday nights he would often brood restlessly as if he had left something undone. The next morning he was up at dawn and off to his mine.

The wealth he was amassing did not change his manner of living. He lived simply, giving the impression of frugality. He had after all lived under spartan conditions for a very long time. Some, nonetheless, thought that he was saving his money for a purpose. He spoke casually if not cryptically of doing something "worthwhile," something of "true value" in the future. He also spoke occasionally of a monument in Cristóbal's memory, but since he never elaborated, it remained a source of speculation what he intended to do with the huge fortune he was amassing.

Three full years had passed since the New Mexicans had returned. María's wedding to Vicente had been set for the middle of May. She was now eighteen and nearing her nineteenth birthday.

Vicente and María had decided on a private family wedding. It wasn't so much that Vicente had been married and had a six-year-old boy, Vicente, but more out of deference to don Juan, who although he was no longer in formal mourning, was still not up to a festive wedding. María was happy for herself, but also for her father, knowing the esteem and affection don Juan had for his nephew, whom he had long regarded as a son.

The bride looked regal in her wedding gown, as the descendant of the Aztec princess, Tecuichpotzin, might have been expected to look. Her dark skin and hair contrasted sharply with the whiteness that enveloped her. She also looked content and secure, perhaps remembering those twelve long years of hearing about her father and brother and wondering if she would ever see them.

The father of the bride looked on with decided approval. He thought of the wedding of his little Mariquita, about whom he had worried so much while he was away, as a haven for her. She would be secure and would undoubtedly give him several grandchildren. During the ceremony he looked down several times at Juanito, who was standing with his mother off to one side. His eyes glistened as he no doubt thought of Cristóbal and another wedding, but a sweet smile from Juanito kept the tears from forming, and he smiled back.

At the wedding feast don Juan danced for the first time since the New Mexico wedding, first with his daughter and then with his daughter-in-law. Throughout the night he drank and talked expansively with relatives and the few family friends who had been invited. The wedding marked the end of his mourning. He still thought frequently of the northern tragedy, but now it was without despair and with a certain optimism. He began formulating vague plans for what he would do to honor his New Mexican son and for his New Mexican grandson who, if he regained his titles, would be the one to inherit them.

Not very long after the wedding, his daughter-in-law fell ill. Ever since Juanito's birth she had been in delicate health. During her pregnancy she had retained a slight cough after a bad cold. Although it persisted after she came south to Zacatecas, it did not appear to affect her health, except that she became susceptible to chills. One night in early April 1613 while returning to Zacatecas from a visit to Pánuco, she, Maria, Vicente, and Juanito were caught in a sudden downpour. Because of the relatively mild weather, they had been riding in an open carriage. Late that night the slight chill turned into a violent one. The following day the physician who attended her diagnosed her illness as pneumonia.

Don Juan rushed to Zacatecas as soon as he was notified. For two whole days he and the family waited for the crisis to pass, but at the beginning of the third day María died while her father-in-law stood by incredulous and helpless. When told that María had passed away, his face became contorted for a moment as if in anger or utter despair, then his head dropped to his chest as he muttered, "Por qué?"

During the day following the funeral don Juan stayed home with his four-year-old grandson, who was oblivious to the tragedy that enveloped the family. As a religious man, the old campaigner resisted the feeling that was invading his confused mind—that he was cursed. A scene involuntarily flashed through his consciousness—that of the Acoma Indians being killed as they emerged from their smoking hideouts. He shook his head and muttered to himself, "I did not order that." A moment later he arose from his chair and walked quickly to Juanito's room. The child was sleeping peacefully.

As time began to insulate him from his latest misfortune, his thoughts turned once again from grief to practicality—to how he could best honor the memory of his son and assure the future of his grandson.

María wondered out loud why she and Vicente were seeing less and less of her father. Vicente heard her and offered a tentative explanation. "Whenever I see him he talks almost of nothing but Cristóbal. I think I'll go see him to see what he really intends to do."

Vicente did pay his father-in-law a visit on the pretext of asking him for advice on a minor business venture. Soon the conversation turned personal as Vicente ventured, "Tío, we have not seen much of you lately."

Don Juan answered, "Yes, and I am sorry, but now that I have found someone reliable to stay with Juanito, I have been staying overnight at Pánuco or at least getting home late."

Vicente looked at his father-in-law with concerned exasperation. "Tío, why don't you relax a bit more? You have some very competent foremen and the mines are producing better than ever."

Don Juan answered in a tone of kindly appreciation. "It is not the mines, my dear Vicente. You know that my real battle still lies ahead. I have been trying to decide what to do."

Vicente understood, so he simply asked, "What do you intend to do?"

"I don't know yet. I have been in contact with Villagrá through some people from Sombrerete. You know that his epic poem about New Mexico was published shortly after I came back, and now it is giving me some ideas."

"What do you mean?" asked Vicente.

"Well, Gaspar's poem tells quite a bit about me in the first part and later when he writes about Acoma, a good bit about you, but nothing about Cristóbal."

Vicente looked a bit puzzled and shot an inquisitive glance at his uncle, but don Juan said no more.

Don Juan had recently received a copy of Captain Villagrá's *La Historia de la Nueva Mexico,* which he had written upon his return to Spain in 1602 and published in Alcala in 1610. Villagrá was now living in Madrid. Although his epic poem about the settling of New Mexico and the Battle of Acoma was not considered significant as literature, the subject matter did stir up considerable interest in Spain and New Spain. Gaspar had been consequently received in literary circles as a minor colleague. Don Juan was glad to hear from an old and loyal comrade.

As he read Villagrá's letter, he thought of his comrade's poem. In the days that followed he continued to think of the people and events mentioned in the minor epic, and he felt proud. One Sunday as he sat half dozing in his courtyard, he sat up with a start. "That's it," he muttered to himself, "that's it, an epic poem honoring Cristóbal."

That evening Vicente told María about his somewhat cryptic conversation with don Juan.

"He talked about Villagrá's poem and how there is nothing about Cristóbal in it," but then he stopped short as if he were revealing something inadvertently.

"Villagrá's poem?" asked María, half smiling and eyes widening with understanding. "Did you know that Father did a favor at Villagrá's request for the son of a highly placed literary man in Spain?"

Vicente's eyes widened too and he chuckled with glee, "Now, I understand. He wants a poem written about Cristobalillo."

After rejoicing about their deduction, Vicente said soberly. "I don't know how anyone can write an epic about him. He was so young most of the time he was in New Mexico, and he was so gentle."

Maria shook her head slowly. "Poor Father. He wants so much to find significance or great purpose in Cristóbal's death."

# CHAPTER FORTY

DURING THE TIME he had been home and even before, the deserters of 1601 had been pressing for a trial of Oñate. In 1607 an official had been appointed to conduct an investigation of the charges filed against him, but no trial ensued. Don Juan had powerful friends, and chief among them was the viceroy himself. But his enemies were implacable. Diego de Zubía, one of the leaders in the desertion and the former Captain Gasco were still at the vanguard of those who had not forgiven nor forgotten. They too had powerful friends, but as long as Velasco was present, they could get no satisfaction in this matter.

Velasco had now served six years in his second term as viceroy of New Spain. He, as before from 1590 to 1596, had done a superior job. His reputation, which was enhanced by the four years as viceroy of Peru, was so good that nobody thought of trying to force his hand. It was this same excellent reputation, however, that worked to have him transferred again just when don Juan needed his continued support and protection. He was named president of the very prestigious Council of the Indies in Spain.

As in 1596, when the incoming viceroy almost destroyed Oñate's expedition, partly because he felt a need to exercise his authority and partly because he listened to court gossip, the new viceroy apparently came with the same disposition. Juan de Oñate's fortunes were about to take a dip. The marquis de Guadalcázar was only too glad to hear dirt about one of his predecessor's favorites. More and more of the deserters began to surface with complaints, no doubt encouraged by the two men who had never forgiven Oñate for having had Captain Aguilar and Captain Sosa killed.

Don Juan had always felt uneasy about the charges. Remembering what happened when Viceroy Velasco left in 1596, he knew that he would have to fight them eventually. He complained bitterly to Vicente, "I have spent twelve horrible years in that miserable place where my poor son is buried, but that is not enough for them. What those cowardly deserters want is blood."

"Zubía is one we should have gotten rid of," answered Vicente with a harshness he had seldom shown since leaving New Mexico.

"Perhaps," countered don Juan, "but he was Sosa de Peñalosa's son-in-law."

"What difference would that make now? Sosa is long dead." answered Vicente in an impatient tone reminiscent of the many times the nephew had had to lead the uncle through a difficult decision.

"Well," sighed don Juan, "all that is water under the bridge."

In the year that followed, he started staying more at home, sitting in the same place in the patio he had sat while waiting for the New Mexico contract. This time there was irritation where before there had been impatience in expectation of a great event about to unfold. Now it was anger causing his inertia. He was too angry to work, so he mainly relived the past. In more lucid moments he wondered about some of the more serious charges. Had he been too harsh on the Acomans? He thought perhaps he had allowed his grief for his nephew, Juan, to justify the punishment. But even so, it was not his idea to cut off the young men's legs at the ankle. But he did sign the order.

"I honestly liked the Indians of New Mexico," he mused. "How could anyone ask for gentler and more patient people?" Suddenly he felt a nostalgia for San Gabriel where his son had spent his late childhood and early youth—where he had spent many a night with his good friend, Magdalena, under the cool, starry sky. Oh, how he wished he had a faithful, unquestioning friend like her, but she now lived in a different world.

The execution, as he had termed it, of Captain Aguilar flashed into his drowsy consciousness, making him sit up with a start.

"But he was a mutineer who was planning to desert," he rationalized. "Hadn't I forgiven him twice before? Thank God, I had Vicente to advise and support me, otherwise I would have lost the whole colony."

He went to Pánuco two or three times a week, but he did not have his mind on his work. Fortunately, by now the mine was working at peak output and his wealth was increasing by the hour.

Several investigations of the charges had been launched during Velasco's term. King Phillip III himself as early as 1607 had ordered his inspector of the Audiencia in New Spain, Diego de Landeras, to investigate the "excesses, crimes, and offenses attributed to Juan de Oñate." A few months later he had a change of heart and ordered the investigation suspended. The king then appointed another person, Juan de Villera, to the task, but Villera stated that he could not accomplish it until the accused returned from New Mexico. He then turned the matter over to Archbishop Fray García Guerra, who was acting viceroy until the arrival of the marquis de Guadalcázar. The archbishop appointed don Francisco de Leoz who, after starting the investigation, begged off, stating that it would be very difficult to sentence the accused because he would have to live among the very powerful and influential people who favored don Juan. The king then, in a *cédula* dated 1 June 1613, put the whole matter in the hands of the newly arrived viceroy.

The marquis de Guadalcázar had no reason not to prosecute since he did not know Oñate. The royal patent was reason enough for him. He consequently appointed don Antonio de Morga, a dour-looking member of the Audiencia of New Spain, as "legal advisor." The marquis, himself, would be the one to decide if Oñate was guilty or not, and it was he who, according to the *cédula*, was to pronounce sentence.

Don Juan was summoned to Mexico City at the beginning of May for the trial, which was more a review of the case by the "legal advisor" who acted much as the judge of instruction acts today in France. He arrived in Mexico City a few days before the verdict was announced. In the meantime he was confined to the residence of his brother, Alonso. On 13 May, the viceroy gave the verdict and pronounced the sentence. The following day the clerk of the court read it to don Juan.

The clerk first read the sixteen charges of which Oñate was absolved. They were by and large frivolous accusations such as permitting the royal standard to be lowered before him at the time that he took possession of New Mexico and another that accused him of letting his nephew, Vicente, address him as "your majesty," and yet another that claimed he had sent soldiers out at night to pick wild fruits for him. There were also a few serious charges of which he was absolved, such as the execution of mutineers at San Bartolomé and at Casco before the expedition was launched. The clerk then read twelve charges of which he was found guilty. Most were very serious, such as the killing of Captains Sosa and Aguilar, execution of the early deserters who were caught by Captains Villagrá, Márquez, and his friend, Francisco, before they reached Santa Bárbara. There were some frivolous charges among these also, such as the charge that "he lived dishonorably and scandalously with women of the army, married and unmarried."

After all the charges had been read to him, the sentence was pronounced. While don Juan stood with his three witnesses, one of which was his brother, Alonso, the clerk intoned the sentence:

> Based on the aforementioned charges which have been adjudged proved against don Juan de Oñate, I should condemn him and do condemn him to perpetual exile from the provinces of New Mex-

> ico, and from this court and five leagues around it for exactly four years. Moreover, I condemn him to pay six thousand ducats, half of which I allot to the court of the king, our lord, and the other half for war expenses and pacification of the aforementioned provinces, and to pay the cost of this trial. This is my judgment, which I pronounce and order as my final sentence, with the approval and advice of Doctor Antonio de Morga, my legal advisor. Signed marquis of Guadalcázar and Doctor Antonio de Morga.

Don Juan's face flushed with anger; his witnesses lowered their heads. By now the old campaigner was too inured by adversity emanating from official sources to be really shaken. But he knew that the deserters, the ones who he felt should be punished, had won. Despite his anger, he declared in a loud voice, "I understand the sentence," turned on his heel and walked out quickly.

Vicente was tried also, as were a number of persons who remained loyal to the expedition. He was found guilty of a total of six charges including the severe punishment administered to the Acomans who survived the battle, and of the murder of Captain Alonso de Sosa and of Andrés Palomo. He was absolved of seven other charges. His punishment was similar to don Juan's in that he too was banned from New Mexico for eight years and from the court for two.

Captain Márquez received perhaps the most severe of the sentences given to an officer. He was banned in perpetuity from New Mexico, stripped of his rank and fined. Captain Márquez was in New Mexico at the time of the sentence. The judgment against him was never carried out, probably because of his excellent reputation among New Mexicans and the fact that he settled with his family in a remote area of the province.

Two captains, Domingo de Lizama and Juan de Salas, were sentenced in absentia for involvement in the killing of captains Aguilar and Sosa, and captains Alonso Gómez and Dionisio de Bañuelas for the killing of Sosa. They were all assessed fines and banished from New Mexico and from Mexico City for a period of time.

The sentences imposed on the enlisted men were radically different from those pronounced on the officers. Francisco de Vido, a mestizo, and Juan, a mulatto, who were found guilty of participating in the killing of Captain Sosa, were sentenced to two hundred lashes to be given in public, and perpetual banishment from the capital.

## CHAPTER FORTY-ONE

THE CONCERNS AND afflictions uppermost in his mind remained the humiliation of returning to Zacatecas empty handed, the trial, and Cristóbal's death.

The trial had opened all the old wounds from the New Mexico debacle. He felt it as one would the lash of a whip. His bitterness was assuaged only by the memory of his son. He still felt a deep sadness and a nagging guilt that he could not face up to.

One evening as he sat looking at the Bufa he suddenly reconciled the two feelings. "Why am I bitter?" he asked himself. "There was an injustice done to me, but injustice is all around us. It is my pride, my overweening pride which makes me bitter."

He hung his head in deep reflection for such a long interval that one would have thought he was asleep. Suddenly his head bobbed up. "Yes," he thought, "my pride, and I sacrificed my son, my dear Cristobalillo, in order to become an adelantado."

His head still down, his body began rocking with sobs until a numbing drowsiness took him as if by the hand into a merciful sleep.

Now that the trial was over, don Juan settled down to work with a vengeance. He instructed his brother, Alonso, to file an appeal. Meanwhile, he stepped up his correspondence with Villagrá and others in Spain, who urged him to go there to seek restitution of the titles and honors that had been taken away from him as a consequence of the trial. Don Juan was more interested, however, in securing recognition for his son, Cristóbal. Villagrá, whose epic poem about the early days in New Mexico had caused a mild stir in Spain, encouraged don Juan to have one written about Cristóbal's deeds. From that time, conscious of all the things that required his presence, don Juan began to consider seriously a trip to Spain.

María, his daughter, was opposed to the idea. "I'm afraid, father, that if you go to Spain we shall probably never see you again." María held back her tears. "Papá, why don't you have everything done from here or send an emissary. It is such a long and perilous trip."

Don Juan's face softened as he remembered the little orphan girl he had left behind in 1598, but his resolve was unshaken. "My sweet little Mariquita, what needs to be done in Spain, only I can do and it will take only a year or so. In any case, I can't wait until my sentence is reviewed."

Maria controlled her emotions until she was safely ensconced in her carriage on her way home, then she let loose a torrent of tears. Dim memories of staying behind in Zacatecas when her father and her brother—her entire family—had gone bewilderingly away to some strange and remote land crept back into her consciousness. And now, her father was leaving her again, and for the same basic reason.

The heavy feeling lasted well into the evening. Vicente found her in the patio staring as into the distance. "What did your father have to say, Cariño?"

Maria stood up to face him. "Nothing much except that he is going. He has made up his mind."

Vicente put his arms around his young wife. "You know María, everything he has done since he came back has in some way been in preparation for that."

María could not hold back. Between sobs she vented her frustration in a mixture of pity for her father and the resentment she had never expressed. "He might get back his titles and he might build a monument to Cristóbal, but *we* will never get him back."

Vicente answered in a soothing voice, "He knows that, querida, but he wants to get the recognition he himself never got which would have passed on to Cristóbal. So it is really a vindication, a validation of both their lives."

"I can understand that, but why must he blame himself for what happened to Cristóbal? Why must he continually atone for it?"

Don Juan took her concern to heart. He really did not want to leave his beloved family and the only life he had known—that in the New World. He felt particularly distressed at the thought of not watching his grandson grow to manhood. He was, besides, constrained to stay until the review of his case was accomplished.

Don Juan was now sixty-seven years old. His attention shifted slowly from managing his mines to planning his projects in Spain. He felt somewhat satisfied by the fact that he had paid the enormous fine of six thousand Castilian ducats very promptly and easily. During the early part of the seventeenth century the monthly salary of a carpenter was a little under one *ducado*. The cost of construction of a galleon stood at approximately 700 ducats; while the cost of one slave was calculated at approximately 125 ducats. Don Juan was able to pay this small fortune because he had become one of the richest men in New Spain and indeed in the New World.

His projects were not entirely personal. With some thoughts of vindication, he had begun to consider some philanthropic ventures. He had cultivated a friendship with the *rector* of the Colegio Real de San Luis de Gonzaga who recommended "good works" as a way to allay his grievances.

Despite his enthusiasm for his plans and his excitement at the thought of seeing his father's homeland for the first time, the days went by slowly. Former sergeant Heredia had taken over the operation of the mines, and except for an occasional visit, don Juan seldom went to Pánuco. His days were spent writing letters, mainly to Spain, and walking around Zacatecas sometimes with his grandson.

Although there was a kinship in sorrow between the former governor and *adelantado* and Sergeant Heredia, they never talked about their personal losses. It had now been seventeen years since Heredia's boy had been buried in the barren New Mexican desert not very far from where Cristóbal lay. The sergeant and his wife had not had any more children, and Esperanza had stayed in New Mexico. María, his wife, since her return had ceased talking about her son. She had long since regained her mental composure, but she appeared to have forgotten the New Mexico experience altogether. No one ever questioned her, and when asked about Esperanza, she would answer that she was living with her husband in Puebla where she had been born and that some day she would come to visit her.

During the ensuing years don Juan divided his time between preparing his appeal and building up his financial status in Spain. Through his nephew, Fernando de Oñate, son of his oldest brother who had been mayor of Puebla until his death shortly before don Juan had returned, he began acquiring mining interests in Cartagena. Fernando had been sent to Granada to care for his grandmother's considerable property. Catalina de Salazar y de la Cadena, who was a native of Granada, had left for the New World with her daughter, Magdalena, some said abandoning her husband. Others said after he had died. She had inherited the Belicena hacienda a few leagues from Granada after her brother, the male heir, had passed away.

He also started sending more and more of his profits to Spain. His family surmised that failing to get just recognition in New Spain, he was counting on doing it in the mother country. In fact, although he did not tell his family, he had resolved to go Spain as soon as his appeal was decided.

With characteristic patience he bided his time. The mines were still producing at a very profitable rate, and it was mainly the finality of the move in view of his age that occasioned what was only a temporary procrastination. Although he planned to return, he was afraid he might not be able to do so.

His daughter María's oldest son was now three years old, but don Juan, although he was loving to him and to María's and Vicente's one-year-old, spent most of his time with Juanito, now over six. He lived at home with him and the caretaker family who took up residence with them after Juanito's mother died.

The couple had been selected carefully. The husband, Jose de Barrios, was a middle-aged clerk who helped don Juan with his accounts and correspondence. His wife was, for women of the time, a well-educated, thirty-year-old daughter of a Zacatecas merchant. Juanito soon came to think of her, if not as a mother, at least as a doting aunt. The couple was childless and were delighted to share in the upbringing of the Oñate family heir.

## CHAPTER FORTY-TWO

IN LATE 1616, Juan de Oñate was finally granted a review of his case. It was to be in the form of a *residencia,* which was the inspection usually held at the end of an official's term. Don Juan had, because of the chaos that accompanied his departure from New Mexico, not been subjected to one.

In this case an inspection could hardly be held. The *residencia* was therefore reduced to a *consulta,* a discussion of the ten charges of which the former governor had been found guilty.

The format used consisted of a statement of the charges followed by an exposition of the proof and concluded by a rebuttal. The rebuttal portion of the proceedings consisted mainly of an attempt to discredit the witnesses as acknowledged and bitter enemies of the governor, because he had condemned them as traitors who had deserted the army.

The rebuttal of the most serious crime of which the governor had been accused—the unduly severe punishment of the Indians after the Battle of Acoma—was worded in the following manner:

> No blame can be held against him [don Juan] from this charge, for on learning that the Indians of the pueblo of Acoma had killed don Juan de Zaldívar, it became necessary for the Spaniards, after consulting among themselves, to send someone to punish

> them, and the commission was given to Vicente de Zaldívar. He took along six captains, but was not authorized to inflict any punishment without agreement of the majority. Consequently, although he was a brother of don Juan de Zaldívar, his appointment was not improper, because any prejudice from this relationship would be balanced by the presence of the soldiers, and what is stated in the chapter did not take place. The fact that he was given a commission to proceed against the Indians and punish them was due to the urging of the entire army and had the approval of the friars, all of whom remonstrated that unless the said punishment was meted out, they would not be safe in the land and would have to abandon it.
>
> The punishment inflicted on the Indians was very moderate. The pueblo now has as many people as on the day of the battle. As for his taking one-fifth of the booty, he was entitled to it; this has been the custom everywhere in New Spain. He did not appropriate it for himself, but distributed his share among the neighboring pueblos, though he allotted some Indian women to serve the poor settlers.

The report, dated 10 October 1617, was turned over to the Audiencia, who in turn gave it to the *fiscal.* After examining the report, he stated that it did not seem to him that any charge or complaint should be made against don Juan. The Audiencia issued a statement that declared that the former governor had satisfied the *residencia* and that no guilt or charge whatever had been made against him.

No further action was taken in this matter, probably because only the king could either pardon or modify the sentence of the trial held earlier. Further, the *residencia,* which found him innocent of wrongdoing, was an action separate from the trial.

Don Juan's only hope was to appeal to the king. The report, he thought, would certainly improve his chances to be exonerated by King Phillip III. He was now more convinced than ever that he should make the trip, but he kept putting it off.

## CHAPTER FORTY-THREE

THE YEARS PASSED almost imperceptibly except for the fact that Juanito was getting to be a young man with whom his grandfather could have serious conversations. During the many long hours they spent together in Zacatecas and in Pánuco, don Juan, at Juanito's insistence, recounted the more pleasant highlights of the New Mexico episode. He dwelled particularly on Cristóbal's deeds, telling him that of the tender age of fourteen he had participated in his first battle. He also answered Juanito's many questions about the land where he was born, and about his mother whom he remembered only vaguely.

One night after having had dinner with Vicente, Juanito, María, and the children, he announced, "I am going to Spain as soon as the trip can be arranged."

Vicente frowned slightly. He did not believe that his uncle could really accomplish anything by going. Now in 1620, he worried about him. He was after all seventy years old. How would he get along in a country that was virtually foreign to him without his family to sustain him? Vicente had discussed this problem with María. She agreed that he should stay at home, but she observed that her father had a compulsion to accomplish certain things before he died.

Vicente corrected her, saying, "You mean he has to finish what he started in 1598."

"Yes, I suppose so," sighed María. "He has appeared anxious, even haunted, ever since he came back. I guess he won't feel at peace until he has done everything he can about all that is bothering him. It almost looks as if he is doing penance."

"Yes," agreed Vicente, "it is that damned, miserable New Mexico. He cannot accept the crushing defeat it handed him and the terrible price it exacted."

"You mean Cristóbal," confirmed María.

"Yes," sighed Vicente.

The year 1620 went by in a flurry of activity—shipping silver, writing letters, and putting his affairs in New Spain in order. Although he did not talk about it because he knew that it would trigger an unpleasant discussion, he had some doubts about whether he would be able to come back. In quieter moments he dreaded the time when he would have to say good-bye to all the people he loved and who depended on him. He knew he would be drawing farther away from Cristóbal and leaving the land where his father and mother were buried and where he himself had spent his entire life.

Juanito at eleven years of age was only slightly shorter than his grandfather, who despite his seventy years maintained—when he was feeling good—an erect, almost military posture. The young man had inherited his mother's light chestnut hair rather than his father's, which was black. He was the product of very gentle upbringing by older people who treated him as a young prince.

"Why must you go away from us, Abuelito?" Juanito asked suddenly one Sunday afternoon as they strolled in the sun.

"Juanito, you might find it hard to understand, but it is for your father—and for you—that I am doing it."

Juanito stopped and faced his grandfather, "How so?"

Don Juan with a faraway look answered, "Cristóbal would have become an adelantado. Now it is you who have a right to that title when I die."

"I would rather have you home, Abuelo, than inherit a title."

"Thank you, my son, but as I said this is also for your father, Cristóbal. I can't let his memory end with me."

"Then why don't you take me with you?"

"You are better off here. The family needs looking after."

"We would be coming back soon, wouldn't we?" insisted Juanito.

A deep sadness dimmed don Juan's eyes. "I failed Cristóbal and I alone must make amends. When the task is completed I shall send for you or come back to you," he concluded, weakly averting his grandson's eyes.

Juanito smiled through his sadness and he too looked away from his grandfather to hide his tears.

"But I have to do it," he muttered later to himself. "There is no other way."

"It is not just my honor," he told Vicente the next time they met, "it is the whole family's honor—yours and Juanito's. It is a vindication of my whole life and a large part of yours."

He had made arrangements to sail with the fleet that was leaving for Seville in September by way of Cuba. He would be sailing on one of the larger galleons, which would be carrying a shipment of silver from his mines.

Vicente went with him to Veracruz at don Juan's request. He had asked his nephew to go with him alone because he did not want to say what might be his last good-bye to Juanito, Maria, and her children in a strange place. He wanted them fixed in his memory in a secure family setting. When the time came he had to steel himself in order not to break down in his grandson's presence. The hollow look of desolation on his wrinkled face belied the smile he had on his lips as he embraced Juanito and Maria.

He and Vicente, along with a small retinue, left Zacatecas in early August for Mexico City where there was some business to put in order. After a week in the capital, the party proceeded to Veracruz arriving there in early September. On the tenth he boarded the galleon. Vicente accompanied him to his comfortable stateroom next to the captain's quarters.

"The fleet is sailing in one hour, Vicente. Why don't we go out on the deck?"

There on the railing overlooking the great harbor and the teeming city of Veracruz they said their good-byes. There was not much that needed saying between these two men. They had shared too many experiences, had experienced the rigors of battle together, and had borne the same grief and frustration. They had not had many triumphs, but the camaraderie of adversity is often the strongest kind. They stared out at the distant horizon, each with his thoughts in the silent communication of two men who loved each other, but could not verbalize it.

From the shore, Vicente watched until the fleet was but a blur. A cloud of pain crossed his eyes, but his jaw tightened. He whispered to himself, "Adios, tío," and turned his gaze inland.

Don Juan had never before been on an ocean voyage. As an old campaigner, his courage, in the manner of most courageous acts, consisted mainly of making the decision to undertake it in the first place. Fear of danger comes mainly from contemplating it. Once the action starts, one either settles down to the job at hand or is too busy to dwell on the consequences. Besides, unlike his first expedition northward, he knew all the possible dangers, ranging from shipwreck to English corsairs. Women and children had taken these risks over and over again. His main worry was that he would get seasick, which somehow seemed unworthy of an *adelantado*.

Aside from some rough seas, the trip was uneventful. He was treated with the great deference shown the very wealthy whose treasure one is carrying. He made friends with the captain, who was a man only slightly younger than he, who had been virtually everywhere in the Spanish Empire from Florida to the Tierra del Fuego to the Philippines. Don Juan was reluctant to tell him about his one long excursion, which seemed to him small by comparison.

He spent long stretches of time looking out at the endless ocean, both westward in a nostalgia that was becoming mellower by the day, and eastward with a youthful enthusiasm that surprised him. He could hardly wait to see the Spanish coastline his father had left ages ago.

When the coastline did appear, he experienced an exhilaration he had not felt since taking possession of New Mexico for Spain. Oñate's first glimpse of the mother country was at Sanlucar de Barrameda at the mouth of the mighty river that, since the discovery of the New World, had become the most traveled in the world—the Guadalquivir. The convoy slowed almost to a stop as it approached the small bay to allow each galleon to enter the river. Don Juan's ship was the second to enter. He remained on deck admiring the countryside dotted with vineyards. As he sailed peacefully upstream, he thought how different this río grande was from the other Río Grande in his life. The Guadalquivir, which means "large river" in Arabic, was serene, running through a reassuring green countryside, while the other had been, though life-sustaining, harsh and at times threatening.

Don Juan was feeling at peace with his world. There was so much to think about. He reflected upon the fullness of his life as he watched a peasant who had probably never ventured more than a few leagues from his home riding a mule. The serenity and the warmth of the autumn sun joined in lulling him to sleep on his canvas chair. The sun was setting when he awakened as the captain walked up to him saying, "I see you have been enjoying the river trip, don Juan."

"Yes, it's lovely," replied the old man, stretching slightly.

"This is my favorite part of the crossing," remarked the captain.

"You must be anxious to see your family, captain," don Juan answered, thinking of his own family, so vivid in his mind, yet so out of reach.

The convoy would not reach Seville until morning, but don Juan could not sleep. He kept looking out his cabin window for life along the riverbank, but except for a few dim lights from time to time there was nothing but darkness. He awakened at first light, and after a quick breakfast went out to the deck. The sailor on watch yelled at him, "Sevilla!" pointing up river. Don Juan could make out the Tower of

Gold that had been guarding the entry to the port since the Almohade Moslems had built the twelve-sided polygon at the beginning of the twelfth century.

A short while later the Giralda came into view. This ninety-seven and a half meter structure, which dominates the entire city, was also built by the Almohade Moors who, under the leadership of the fanatic Aben Tumart, had defeated the more moderate Almoravides in the early twelfth century. With this aggressive spirit they not only rekindled the holy war, but recovered some of the territory that was slowly being lost to the Christians. The tower, a minaret attached to a mosque, was built in 1176 by two Almohade architects. The belfry crowning the minaret, however, is a Renaissance addition. The name Giralda comes from a huge weather vane in the form of a statue representing Faith which the Spanish added. The Giralda is now attached to the cathedral, which was built during the course of the fifteenth century and remains the third largest in all Christendom.

It was midmorning when the ship docked. Fernando, who had been waiting all morning, broke into a smile as he ran up the gangplank. "Bienvenido a la madre patria, tío. [Welcome to the motherland.]"

"Gracias, Fernando," don Juan said as he embraced his nephew.

Don Juan was anxious to disembark after what seemed an eternity on board. He and his nephew, followed by don Juan's servant, walked slowly along the broad wharf turning up la calle de Carbón. Don Juan was having the usual trouble with the solid steadiness of the cobblestone streets after many weeks at sea. They continued past the Hospital de la Caridad onto a large plaza, from which they had a full view of the cathedral. Don Juan was dumbfounded at the sheer size and beauty of the imposing structure with its magnificent tower. They walked slowly around the north side of the cathedral where don Juan got a better look at the Giralda, and on to the Plaza de la Virgen de loy Reyes to the *posada* that was to be their home for the next two weeks.

During the next few days the New World visitor spent his time between sightseeing, promenades, and the business he had to take care of at the Casa de Contratación within the walls of the Alcázar, which was just a short walk from the inn. His business dealings had to do with the large transfer of silver from New Spain, which included paying the royal fifth.

Don Juan, who was anxious to see his mother's estate and having concluded the business end of his visit to the great city, boarded Fernando's carriage for the four-day trip to Granada across the hilly roads north of the coastal mountains.

Granada, dating back to pre-Iberian times, was given the name Iliberri by the Romans. Under Visigothic domination it bore the name Garnata. The Omeya Moors renamed it Medina Elvira in 711. The Almoravides made it one of their principal fortified cities, but it was not until the fierce Almohades had ousted their more moderate coreligionists that it began to take on the great magnificence that was to be completed by the Nazaries, who conceived the Alhambra, the great mosque, and other extraordinary structural wonders of this rare city. In 1492 Queen Isabel, establishing her headquarters in the nearby town of Santa Fe, finally expelled the last of the Moorish monarchs, Boabdil the minor.

Don Juan had, during his childhood, heard many tales from his mother about the dreamlike city that she had abandoned to pursue a dream of her own in the New World. Now he could see for himself. He was enchanted more by the memory of what his mother had told her children than by the city itself, which was to a great extent in a decrepit state and half-moribund since the dispersion of the *moriscos*, descendants of the Moors who had stayed in Spain after the reconquest. Soon after 1492 popular pressure began to build up against these people whose status was little better than that of slaves. In 1568 they were expelled from Granada to other parts of Spain and between 1609 and 1614 they were banished from the entire country.

## CHAPTER FORTY-FOUR

DON JUAN WAS anxious to get to Madrid. Since King Phillip III had moved the capital back from Valladolid, it was once again the nerve center of the Spanish empire. The origins of this city are shrouded in legend and myth. The first historical mention of it dates from the tenth century, when it was destroyed by King Ramiro II in one of his forays into Muslim territory. Several monarchs, including Fernando and Isabel, held court there, but it wasn't until Felipe II moved his court from Toledo that it became a capital.

King Phillip IV was only sixteen when he ascended the throne upon the death of his father in 1621, while Oñate was enroute to Spain. Don

Juan hoped that he would have better luck with the young king than he had with his father, Phillip III, who had been more interested in hunting and other amusements than in the affairs of state. Word had come from the palace that the young king was a very spoiled and rather frivolous young man who had come under the influence of his mentor, the Duke Olivares who, when Phillip III was on his death bed had reportedly said, "Now, it is all mine." Olivares proved to be a vindictive de facto ruler who was very jealous of his prerogatives.

When the New World traveler arrived in late November, he found a new city of some 50,000 inhabitants still largely under construction. He took up residence in the house his brother had bought during the time that he lived in the capital while he was pleading don Juan's case.

Gaspar de Villagrá, his faithful comrade from New Mexico days, was there to meet him. Villagrá had acted as intermediary between don Juan and the poet, Francisco Murcia de la Llana, who was to write an epic poem about Cristóbal. The meeting between the two New World conquistadors who had not seen each other in twenty years was inwardly emotional but, since it was between two men who had known each other only under harsh conditions, outwardly subdued.

"How long it has been, my dear friend," don Juan said softly, as he looked into Villagrá's eyes.

"It seems like centuries, your excellency," he answered, as they embraced.

That evening they mainly reminisced. Villagrá apologized for not having gone back with the reinforcements in 1601. Don Juan shrugged it off saying, "You at least showed some courage, unlike some of the others. Besides, here we are both of us banned from New Mexico."

"Do you think anything will come of that enterprise?" asked Villagrá indifferently.

"Nothing of great importance," answered don Juan as if wishing to change the subject.

During the next few days their discussions centered on the epic poem. Villagrá informed don Juan that the young Francisco Murcia de la Llana had started to recruit the writers who would contribute individual *cantos* to the poem. Murcia's father, who was a *corrector de libros* for the Council of the Indies, had contact with all the writers in the country.

"I appreciate very much what the Murcias have done," remarked don Juan.

"And they are very grateful for the help you extended to the elder Murcia," answered Villagrá.

"Well, let us hope it all turns out well," sighed don Juan.

Later in the week Oñate received a letter from the younger Murcia advising him that the poem would be completed shortly. He himself would contribute three stanzas, and Villagrá one. The rest would be written by well-known humanists and classicists.

With this part of his mission accomplished, the old conquistador turned his attention to the restoration of his titles. Knowing that the king was very young and that he would undoubtedly be influenced by his advisors, he did not know exactly how to proceed. Villagrá had told him that the Count Duke Olivares would probably exercise great influence over the boy king. Some of the members of the Council of the Indies knew his case very well. During the time that ex-viceroy Velasco, now deceased, had served as president of the council, he had often talked to his fellow members about the founder of New Mexico, who had not been treated fairly.

It was not all business with the New World visitor, however. Vicente had awakened in him an interest in the theater. He had been looking forward to seeing the works of the dramatist whose renown had reached to New Spain. Lope de Vega had recently finished his great work, *El Caballero de Olmedo,* which had been received with raves in Madrid. With the coming of spring don Juan started going to the theater. At the Corral de la Cruz he saw this masterpiece, which was perhaps Lope's greatest dramatic triumph for its brilliant expression of the ideals of medieval Spanish character through the medium of tragic comedy. This great work is about the love of the beautiful Inez from Medina and the aristocratic and honorable don Alonso from neighboring Olmedo, who dies a fateful but brave death provoked by the inexorable jealousy of a rejected suitor exacerbated by small town resentment of an illustrious intruder.

Another contemporary author who excited his imagination was Miguel de Cervantes Saavedra, whose second part of *Don Quijote* had been published a few years earlier. Since he was not an avid reader, he had not read either the first nor the second part of the famous novel, but was impressed by Villagrá's recounting of its highlights. He was even more impressed by the story of Cervantes's heroic, but frustrating life, as told by his old friend. He saw a certain parallel in Cervantes's failure to gain public or official acclaim and his own struggle. Both were combat veterans—Cervantes of the famous Battle of Lepanto, in which he was wounded; Don Juan of several battles of the Chichimecas and the Kansas Indians of Quivira. Finally Cervantes was accused and found guilty—unjustly, he felt—as was Don Juan.

The one other play he went to see later in the year was Cervantes's *La Numancia.* Villagrá had years earlier compared the Battle of Acoma to the battle between the forces of the Roman conqueror, Scipio Africanus, and the people of the walled city of Numancia in 133 B.C. Oñate was very moved as he saw the Numantinos die to the last person rather than surrender. He could not help but think of Cristóbal when the last survivor, a mere boy, threw himself from the wall rather than become a prisoner to be displayed in a victory parade in Rome. He thought, "I must make sure that the epic poem which is being written does Cristóbal justice."

It was early 1622 that he started writing his petition to the boy king. He felt that he had to express himself carefully because his letter might be read not only by a very young man but by the scheming Olivares. On the advice of don Juan de Villela, the president of the council who had served in that august body under Luis de Velasco, he abandoned his plans for a direct appeal in favor of working through the council.

In his petition to the council he asked that his punishment be revoked and that he be restored the title of *adelantado* in perpetuity. The council, impressed by don Juan's service to the crown and the fact that he had paid his six thousand ducat fine promptly, recommended to the king that "your majesty could favor him by lifting the said banishment and suspension of his offices so that he might exercise them later in those provinces."

The message to the king was dated 6 April 1622. The answer was as prompt as it was brief, stating that it would be well for the council to state the nature of the charges. The council was just as prompt in answering the king's letter, stating that although it had not been the practice, in order not to take up the king's time, to send the reports of charges in similar cases, they were enclosing one now since the king commanded it. The king evidently did not want to be bothered because within a week his reply was received at the council in the following brief form: "Postpone this for the time being."

The president of the council had by now become a convinced advocate in don Juan's case. He told the relentless Oñate that he would send another recommendation, but that he would wait a while to avoid giving the impression of importuning the king. He also advised the petitioner to write down a statement of his services for future use.

Once again don Juan had to bide his time. He whiled away the days composing his statement of services, going occasionally to the theater, or merely strolling about the busy city.

One day as he ambled about the Plaza Mayor, he wandered out the exit that led to the Calle de Toldeo. As he walked toward the Puerta de Toledo he came across an imposing group of buildings adjacent to a small church. He noticed an empty lot where a foundation for a large building had been laid. Walking past that, he turned down the Calle del Duque de Alba looking for an entrance to the grounds. He said to himself, "This must be the Colegio Imperial which Farther Martin told me about." It was a Jesuit institution for the training of friar-teachers for service in and out of Spain mentioned by the rector of the Colegio Real in Zacatecas. He was pleasantly surprised by his discovery because he held the militant order in high esteem.

As he stopped to look at the buildings, a young priest entering the grounds stopped to ask if he could assist him.

"Gracias," answered don Juan politely. "I was just taking a stroll."

"Would you like to have a look around?"

"Yes, thank you, if it isn't an intrusion."

Sensing that the old man was a stranger, the young man asked politely, "Where are you from, your grace?"

"Oh, from very far away—Zacatecas in New Spain."

The young Jesuit's face brightened considerably revealing a boyish enthusiasm. "I have been trying to get posted to the colonies, preferably to New Spain."

Don Juan smiled benignly. "Well, if you succeed, let me know. I can perhaps be of some assistance."

The chance visitor ended up meeting the director of the school, which in the tradition of the Jesuits was more than a seminary. The director, a short, strong-looking man with lively, curious eyes, was glad to entertain a traveler from the New World, particularly one about his own age. Over a *merienda,* which don Juan found a bit sumptuous with its meats, melons, crullers, wine, and to please his guest, chocolate, they discovered much about each other. The rich creole from the other side of the vast ocean told the distinguished Jesuit of his experiences and the friar-educator talked of his work in North Africa and within Spain educating young men not only to spread the faith, but also enlightenment in more worldly matters.

Don Juan had not given the Jesuits much thought until he returned from New Mexico, as their presence in New Spain had not been an imposing one. His experience, not always happy, had been with the long-suffering but not overly intellectual Franciscans. Not that he fancied himself an erudite person, but he had always heard two things about the Jesuits: that they were well educated and highly disciplined. In Zacatecas during his later years he had made some friendships at the newly established Jesuit school. In any case, the two men found something to admire in each other—qualities or experiences missing in their own lives.

The sun was setting across the ocean as it always did in the old exile's mind when he took leave of the curate.

Every evening, particularly in those rare instances when the European sunsets approximated those of the deserts in the New World in their blazing magnificence, his thoughts would return to Zacatecas and to New Mexico in a mixture of rekindled excitement and enduring sadness. This day he walked home with a glow, thinking what a good fortune this chance meeting had been. He felt that he finally had not just a friend in Madrid, but a crony whose company he was sure to enjoy. He muttered to himself, "don Pablo Alvarado."

## CHAPTER FORTY-FIVE

When he got home his manservant handed him a message. Don Juan smiled perceptibly as he read it, then sighed deeply as he placed the note on a small table in the vestibule.

The next day he arose early in anticipation. Gaspar de Villagrá, who was the author of the note, was coming to deliver some copies of the poem he had commissioned. When Villagrá arrived, he greeted his old commander with, "Enhorabuena your grace, here is the poem, 'Canciones lugubres'."

Don Juan embraced his loyal captain, then with a tender look and said hoarsely, "How can I thank you my dear, dear friend? Will you read a part of it for me?"

The captain knew that it was not a great or even good poem since it was the product of a strained attempt to write about a very young man who had not accomplished much and who had died of a mysterious illness. It turned out to be a paean to Cristóbal through an invocation of Greek gods and goddesses.

Having read it beforehand, Villagrá selected the best of the individual poems, written by Francisco Cascales, historian of the city of Murcia, which started out by apostrophising Melpomene, the muse of tragedy.

Where, sacred Melpomene, do you take me?
Do you wish me proudly to praise
of the third Felipe his well known greatness?

He then goes on to sing the praises of Juan de Oñate and his son Cristóbal:

The great India he conquered for Felipe,
(Melpomene has informed me)
don Juan intrepid, Cantabrian of Oñate,
and wanted in this his glory him to share
his only and dear son heroic and strong
now in this, now in that hard and ferocious combat,
I should not now take up your time
with my sad and painful thoughts, poet of mine,
don Cristóbal, his dear son,
for whom bathed in these tears I am afflicted,
died, and with him died the gallantry and elegance,
the skill of Mars
ingenuity, industry, cleverness, and art.

Don Juan brushed tears from his eyes, but he was smiling as he again thanked his friend. "And your part, Gaspar, why didn't you read that?"

"Oh, you can read it at your leisure, don Juan."

When Villagrá took his leave, he left the old adventurer still with tears in his eyes and still smiling. It was clear to him that his comrade was not only happy with this bittersweet occurrence, but also relieved that after all the years of waiting, one of his heartfelt objectives had been reached.

## CHAPTER FORTY-SIX

FOR DON JUAN the summer of 1622 seemed to pass quickly—especially after his trip to Toledo with don Pablo, who was a native of that venerable city, which had until fairly recently been the capital. Its history could well be the essential history of Spain. The Visigothic king, Leovigildo, established his capital there toward the end of the sixth century, and King Alfonso VI, his in 1085 when he wrested the city from the Moors. It remained the capital until Phillip II transferred his court to Madrid.

It was the home of Spain's most famous immigrant, Domenico Theotocopulis, born on the island of Crete and known in Venice during his stay there as El Greco. He kept the name when he went to Spain to become one of its most illustrious artists.

Don Juan and don Pablo saw each other at least three times a week. When the Jesuit found out that don Juan had lost a son and had an orphan grandson whom he had left along with his daughter in Zacatecas, talk turned to the conquistador's plans to leave a monument of some sort to Cristóbal's memory. Although don Juan had not been particularly religious, now in the twilight of his life he began thinking in terms of the eternity of the church. Why not a religious monument, not only in Cristóbal's memory, but in his name and that of his entire family? Don Pablo listened in sympathy to the ideas put forward by his newfound friend, agreeing that nothing could be more enduring and appropriate. He suggested doing something for orphan children whose opportunities for an education were limited or nonexistent. Don Juan thought of his orphaned grandson who had everything and who would inherit a fortune and even titles, if he were successful in getting them reinstated. Then his thoughts turned involuntarily to Acoma and the hundreds of orphans who had been left on that forbidding mesa that terribly cold day in 1599. A pained look crossed his face that startled don Pablo.

"Qué tienes, Juan?" he asked in a soft voice.

Don Juan shook his head and answered, "Yes, we need to do something for the orphaned children."

In November of the same year the Council of the Indies, citing don Juan's age and urging the king not to let him die "unjustly and grief-stricken," once again dared to broach the subject of Oñate's petition to the king. They argued that his services entitled him to be forgiven, "in order that he and his descendants may be free from this blot, for they are distinguished people who wish to continue in the service of your majesty."

To this petition the king answered promptly and rather cryptically, "I am amazed that in such ugly cases the council annoys me regarding a decision which I have already taken."

There appeared to be a tone of finality about this latest rebuff by the king, but Licentiate Villela, who throughout his long service on the council—six years as member and now president since 1622—had seen kings change their minds, advised the persistent old New Mexican to send a statement of his service directly to the king. There was a hint of assurance that it would be brought up to the king's attention promptly and as forcefully as those affairs could be to a volatile and indecisive young monarch. It appeared that the case was being handled by the king and his secretaries rather than his chief counsellors. Villela, through his secretary, Juan Ruiz de Contreras, could exercise a certain amount of influence on them. Favors had been granted back and forth on many occasions.

Don Juan dusted off the statement of service he had started over a year before and began working on it again. He showed it to his friend, don Pablo, who was very impressed by his friend's distinguished record. He promised to put in a good word through an acquaintance he had in the court.

Within weeks the statement of services was dispatched to the palace. The report did not have much that had not been said before. Oñate was careful to point out that between his return from New Mexico and the present, he had mined 137,510 marks of silver from his Zacatecas mines, which amounted to over three thousand pounds. The royal fifth from this bonanza came to 129,454 pesos or *ocho reales,* which were known by the English as "pieces of eight." From Real de Pánuco he had extracted 257,800 marks or over five thousand pounds, one-fifth of which was paid to the royal treasury. He pointed out that "most all of the silver and gold that come from the mines of New Spain have been conquered and won by don Juan de Oñate's father, his father-in-law, and his son-in-law."

The direct appeal had its effect. Within two months, in a message signed by Juan Ruiz de Contreras, the council was advised that the king had restored Oñate's title of *adelantado* on 14 July 1623.

When don Juan was apprised by Villela of the king's decision, he clenched his fist momentarily, then he smiled and embraced the president of the council and thanked him profusely.

Don Juan was still elated, but felt frustrated and terribly homesick as he started to write a letter to his nephew, Vicente, but intended for the whole family.

> My dear Vicente, when we were in New Mexico, whenever we had good news which, God forgive my ingratitude, was not very often, you either brought it to me or shared it with me. Knowing how Cristóbal loved you and the feelings you had for him, I consider you guardian of Juanito. Although he is only seven years younger than his father was when he left us, I can't seem to think of him in any other way than the infant son of my own dear Cristóbal.
>
> The news that I have for you is that I am once again *adelantado*. We have triumphed, Vicente, and the victory is partly yours. Moreover, the first monument to my son has been completed and here it is for you and for María and Juanito to read. As you will see, our dear loyal Villagrá has penned one of the *cantos*, an act of loyalty and love that adds immeasurably to the poem's worth.
>
> New Mexico is ever on my mind, although now not with bitterness nor the resentment I once had for a forbidding land that has entombed my only son. My only regret is that I am not young enough to return to it if only for a visit; not only to visit Cristóbal's grave, but to see our dear friends Gerónimo, Cristóbal Vaca, Jorge, and others, who, although I hear they are suffering from the strife between the governor and friars, still manage to prevail.
>
> As you can see, my dear comrade, I am slowly making my peace with that land which we considered so harsh and hostile at times, but which was home for so long to all of us, the birthplace of my grandson so beloved by my son. I dearly hope I shall see all of you soon.

It appeared as if the struggle was over, but the combative Oñate just a few days later dispatched another petition asking for the title in perpetuity. This second petition was sent back to the council for study on 17 July. By 1 September, the council sent back its recommendation that there was no reason to grant him the title for more than two generations.

In early 1624, he once again made the same request and in addition asked for the title of marquis, citing chapter 93 of the royal ordinances pertaining to the matter. The king once again forwarded the petitïon to the council for study. The council stated that no new reasons had been found to justify favors beyond those already granted. The king once again instructed the council to study Oñate's petition "in all its details."

The council meanwhile received a report from the Audiencia in New Spain recommending that the old New Mexican be "favored with the habit of one of the military orders "for himself, his nephew and his grandson." The council forwarded the recommendation to the king without making a recommendation of its own.

The king accepted the advice of the Audiencia and made the nomination, contingent on Oñate's meeting the requirements of the *limpieza de sangre* (purity of blood), which meant that the candidate be proved free of Jewish forebears. At the same time that the king tendered the prestigious appointment, he decided to avail himself of the old miner's experience and named him inspector of mines—*visitador general de minas y escoriales de Espana.*

Oñate could hardly believe his good fortune. He told his ailing friend Gaspar de Villagrá that it was the first stroke of luck he had had since 1598.

"You deserve it, your grace. I wish I had had your courage," smiled Villagrá from his sickbed.

Don Juan looked sad and pensive, no doubt agreeing with his friend that it had taken a mighty effort. He sat down beside the captain's bed as if a great burden had been lifted from his shoulders.

The next day he went to tell his friend the Jesuit of his appointment. Remarking that his faith had borne fruit, Don Pablo rejoiced with him.

"Sí," answered don Juan laconically.

The tired, old conquistador rested for a few days. He took long walks about town, visited with Pablo, and sat in late afternoon, looking from his balcony at the sunsets in the west. He muttered as if communicating with someone across the ocean. His countenance became softer as each day passed. He visited the chapel of the Colegio Imperial, where he sat quietly. He had never been overtly religious, and he had seldom invoked divine help in his prayers. Now he seemed merely to be expressing simple gratitude.

His newfound tranquillity was once more shaken by the news of Villagrá's death. His old friend had recovered from his illness and had left for a post in Nicaragua as *alcalde mayor.* Don Juan had helped him obtain it through his contacts in the Council of the Indies. The news was late in getting to don Juan because Gaspar was stricken on the high seas where he was buried. He found out from the secretary of the council, who had heard about the adventurous poet's death from a captain who had sailed to Spain from the Azores. It was something that made him start to consider seriously his own mortality. Gaspar was, after all, at least a decade younger than he.

It was during this period of reflection that he slowly, but deliberately, started writing his will. Little Juan, now fifteen years old, was to receive the bulk of his estate. The Colegio Imperial would receive a full fifth of his entire fortune. He had already decided that he would pay for a chapel in the college's Church of San Isidro, which would soon go under construction.

He did not finish the will before the start of his inspection trip. The rich *Indiano,* anxious to start working, set out in early 1625, stopping first at Burgos, where his maternal grandmother had lived. He availed himself of the occasion to visit nearby Oñate, his father's home town before he had left for the New World.

*Oñate,* meaning "mountain pass" in the Basque language, reminded him of Zacatecas, which also lay at the foot of a mountain. When he first caught sight of it he remarked to his former servant, Gonzalo Rodríguez Morán y Talavera, now a colleague with the inspection party, "There were two mountains in my father's life, and he was a mountain of a man."

"And so is his son," answered Morán.

"No, Gonzalo," objected don Juan gently. "I am but a hill compared to him, but I hope he knows that I have tried to uphold the family honor."

The old dynamo did not spend much time visiting the village and the cousins, who could not believe that this important and wealthy man from the New World would come to their humble town. The new inspector was in a hurry to get on with his official responsibility. Cartagena, a mining town where he had extensive interests of great value, was his next stop.

His visits were not perfunctory. Mining in Spain had for decades suffered from neglect because of the relative plethora of precious metals coming from the New World. The silver tycoon from the Indies knew what it took to revitalize mines. At Pánuco he had designed new machinery for a more efficient operation. It was probably his mining success, after returning in disgrace from New Mexico, which impressed the young king the most. Now don Juan was determined not to disappoint royal opinion while it was high.

The mining industry in Granada had been deteriorating ever since the decline of the Nazaríes, who had raised the city to its ultimate splendor with the construction under twenty monarchs of the Alhambra, the Great Mosque, and other magnificent architectural monuments. Don Juan had a special interest in this city because of his mother's ties to it. While he was there, in addition to making numerous notes concerning the mines in the area, he took some time for personal visits with his relatives. He stayed at the Hacienda Belicena, a short distance from the city, with his nephew and his family. Together they heard Mass at the convent of San Francisco, which was built on the foundation of an Arab palace. It was the first convent built in the city after the conquest. The convent church, built in 1495, had held the remains of Ferdinand and Isabel until they were transferred to the Royal Chapel in Granada, which was built in 1504, years before the cathedral that adjoins it. In this renowned church don Juan gazed upon the Oñate family chapel, adorned with the coat of arms of the family that had achieved renown not only in the Indies, but in this region through his mother's family as well.

## CHAPTER FORTY-SEVEN

IN THE SUMMER of 1625 the inspection took him to Guadalcanal, not far from Seville, where he bought a home and established his headquarters. In this ancient town where the Romans had developed the first silver mines, he wrote out an extensive report to the king. The report created a very favorable impression at the court and resulted in the publication of a new set of laws and ordinances in September 1625 titled *Neuvas leyes y ordenanzas.*

The *adelantado* was overwhelmed by the honors so belatedly being showered upon him. Francisco Murcia de Llana, corrector for the Council of the Indies, signed the document and mentioned the short epic poem written a few years before. The introduction written by Oñate's secretary, Andres de Carrasquilla, outlined the New Mexico *adelantado*'s background. He pointed out that at more than seventy years of age, and although one of the wealthiest men in the New World, he had left his beloved daughter and grandson to come to Spain without, as the secretary said, knowing exactly for what purpose.

The newly published book earned him a personal audience with the king. Upon his arrival in Madrid before anything else he went to visit his friend at the Colegio Imperial. He told him of his good fortune. Don Pablo laughed and cried to see the exhilaration in the old man's demeanor. Don Juan revealed to him his plans for the Colegio Imperial. Don Pablo answered, "God bless you. Padre Luis will be so grateful, as we all are."

Don Juan was elated at the thought that after all these years of struggle and frustration, he, the much maligned founder of New Mexico, was to be received by the king. Dressed in his captain general's uniform, he presented himself at the palace.

The contrast in ages was striking. The young king received the distinguished, if slightly bent, *adelantado* and soon to be gentleman of the order of Santiago, very graciously. Taking his hand, he barely allowed his elderly visitor time to make his full obeisance.

This was a period in Spain when great deeds and important conquests were becoming very rare. While the king (and his advisors) had earlier deprecated, if not scorned, don Juan's modest deeds, he was nonetheless very interested in hearing a personal account from one of his captains who had penetrated beyond the frontiers of his established empire in recent times.

"According to one of your captains, Villalba, I believe, the Battle of Acoma was particularly fierce. Did you personally fight there?"

"No, no your majesty. I was advised not to for fear of jeopardizing the entire colony should something have happened to me."

"But you did fight the Kansas, I believe. What are they like?"

"They were quite fierce, your majesty."

"Well, we are glad you survived and are here to tell us about it."

After answering the king's youthful and imaginative questions, the honored guest managed to make some observations about the mining industry in Spain. He emphasized the fact that the Spanish mines, some of which dated back to Phoenician, Carthaginian, and Roman times, should be restored and revitalized because the mines throughout the empire were being depleted.

The king asked him what he needed to do in particular. Don Juan answered that a thorough evaluation needed to be accomplished, which included assaying and grading the metals. He also said that he needed to bring six Indians from New Spain to demonstrate New World expertise in smelting and refining.

"By all means, by all means. I should like to meet them. Please keep me informed," answered the king excitedly.

Oñate came away from that meeting wondering if he should not have come to Spain earlier. There seemed to be a bright future ahead for him except for one thing—his age. He got everything from the king he had requested, and more.

Phillip IV would probably never forget the first flesh and bones *adelantado* he had ever seen. The indefatigable septuagenarian, although elated by the sudden attention and recognition, felt a compulsion to get on with his work. Time was getting short for him, he knew, but he did not allow his age to influence his resolve. He started to feel a certain fatigue he had never felt before, but he set out without hesitation on a new round of visits to the ancient mines of Spain.

Before departing, however, he executed a codicil to his will. Although he felt confident that he could complete this excursion, he was conscious of his seventy-five years and of the kind of fatigue new to him, which he started to feel after the euphoria of his audience with the king. Thus, he made provisions in the event of his death. Vicente was to assume his position as *visitador de minas* and his advisors were to continue on this particular inspection to its conclusion.

At Cartagena, feeling ill, he made yet another modification to his will, but completed the inspection. While there he heard Mass at the Church of Our Lady, which was to be the beneficiary of a substantial part of the considerable wealth he held in that city. He also made a donation to the Convent of San Isidro and to the Church of San Sebastián.

The inspection over, he and his advisors resumed their itinerary by embarking on the twelve-day trip to Guadalcanal. The tired feeling that had been tormenting him was now aggravated by dizzy spells. At his insistence, after two days in a country inn, the trip was resumed. Great care was taken to provide for his comfort with frequent stops at the best inns available until they reached Guadalcanal where the tired old veteran had a comfortable home. Here, with servants to care for him, he felt better. Able to dictate and very lucid, he made his final will and testament to which he incorporated all previous wills and documents pertaining to his estate. The entire portfolio was turned over to the notary of Guadalcanal late in the year.

Soon after his arrival he began to feel much better. One cold day in January he announced to his aide and friend, Gonzalo, "I think today I will go to the mine to see how the modernization is coming along."

The kindly, rough-hewn Gonzalo smiled at him. "It will do you good, don Juan. I shall accompany you."

The old magnate's illness had left him very conscious of the fragility of life and with a premonition that there would be no time for a visit from across the sea. He had no regret, but only a haunting sadness at the thought of dying alone. He felt a comforting satisfaction that he had accomplished a mission that by its very nature was a solitary one. He was the patriarch performing a task only he could achieve. Conscious of the futility, he tried to dismiss his desperate longing for the land and the family that were intrinsic to his being.

In his worst moments of delirium he would hold conversations with them and with Vicente, who had helped him out of many an unpleasant situation. When he spoke to Cristóbal, he mainly sought to allay his fears, and when he caressed María he tried to comfort the bewildered child he was leaving behind in 1598. Juan, and that bitter December day of the sad tidings, were frequently in his dreams.

Padre Pablo, hearing of his friend's illness, made the trip to Guadalcanal to see don Juan. This visit by the robust Jesuit priest cheered up the patient.

"You look the same as ever, my friend," remarked Father Alvarado, "perhaps a bit thinner."

Don Juan answered with a trace of sadness, "I know that my days on this earth are coming to an end. I don't feel particularly ill, just tired, very tired." Then he smiled. "And you, Pablo, you look like a young bull."

Padre Pablo stayed a week—one that seemed too short to don Juan. "My duties call me back to Madrid, but I trust you will get better and come to see me and the progress that is being made on our church."

Don Juan shook his head slowly with a faint smile on his wan face. "Adiós, Pablo, pray for me and my son."

The burly priest held don Juan in a long *abrazo,* then turned and walked to his carriage, taking with him the sad thought that his friend would not survive the coming spring. There was a certain comfort knowing that don Juan would ever be remembered by his order, and particularly by his own Colegio Imperial to which the miraculous benefactor from an exotic land was leaving one-fifth of his enormous fortune. He approved tenderly of the stipulations made by the old philanthropic explorer, which made provisions for dormitories and scholarships for the benefit of orphans and others who could not afford to pay for their schooling. All he asked in return was that they pray for him and his family.

Meanwhile, the process to determine don Juan's *limpieza de sangre* (purity of blood) was proceeding in several parts of Spain in total oblivion of the fact that its outcome might not matter much to the *criollo* from across the sea.

The indomitable New Mexican not only survived the spring, but remained intermittently active. Each day he would ask to see the western horizon. On the days when the clouds formations were just right, the flaming sunsets would set his imagination astir. He could feel the hot New Mexico sun shining on his forehead, and he could see the ponderous mesas dominating the arid plains like brooding medieval fortresses. The clamor of battle rang in his ears! Above it he could hear the shrill young voice of Cristóbal shouting with excitement. After those episodes of liveliness, his condition would once more envelop him and drag him back into the long, dark night.

The eighteenth of June dawned to a sky cleaned to a pure blue by a rainstorm during the night. Don Juan woke up bristling with energy. "I want to go to the mine," he announced at breakfast.

During a short ride in a cabriolet he was close to exhilaration and talked about another round of inspections. When they arrived at the worksite they found that there had been minor flooding during the night. The water that had accumulated at the entrance was being bailed out by the miners who had formed a bucket brigade. Don Juan watched for a while, then took his place in the line.

"Por favor, don Juan," exclaimed Gonzalo in an anxious voice.

Don Juan merely chuckled, but as he handed his third or fourth bucket it dropped from his hands and he began to stagger. The miners next to him caught him before he fell, but he was near unconsciousness.

Don Gonzalo excitedly directed them to the carriage. On the way back home, don Juan uttered only a grunt when his aide and friend asked him how he felt.

The doctor, who had not agreed to the visit by don Juan to the mine, was waiting apprehensively. He put him to bed then listened to his heart, which was beating at a rapid rate. Hoping it would have a calming effect, he gave him vervain to drink.

On the second day don Juan awoke with remarkable lucidity. He called his close colleagues and counselors to his bedchamber, where he reiterated some important instructions. After a light lunch he took a short nap. When he awakened about four in the afternoon, he asked to be carried out to the terrace. He requested that his long chair be oriented toward the west. He lay there for a long time, apparently napping. His friends and servants were cheered that he felt well enough to want to bask in the warm Andalusian sun.

As sunset approached he raised his head slightly and began to mutter, "Cristóbal mira, look, the whole horizon is on fire. Our New Mexico is being consumed by majestic flames. But I am here with you my gentle son. Cristobalillo . . . I got everything back . . . everything . . . for you . . . for both of us . . . for two lives only . . . for two lives . . . yours and mine."

The tenacious old frontiersman dropped his head to his chest as if asleep. As the sun sank in the west and the sky started to turn purple, he opened his eyes. "You were right about many things . . . about that Indian boy—about Chai."

ACKNOWLEDGMENTS

I started this novel many years ago. During all that time, besides doing seemingly endless research, I consulted with several people who were a great help to me. I wish to give a special thanks to Herman Agoyo, who at that time was chairman of the All Indian Pueblo Council and is a Tegua speaker, and to Donna Pino, educator, colleague, and friend, who speaks Keres. A special thanks also to Joe Sando, Native American historian and archivist, for his pointed and singular perspectives. Many other kind souls read the manuscript and gave me their reactions. I thank them also.